Hassie Calhoun

"Creating a protagonist who makes such self-destructive choices that you want to just get inside the book and slap some sense into her, yet at the same time making the reader love this character and want to keep reading to find out what she'll do next, always fervently hoping that she'll get it right, is one of the most difficult tasks a novelist can undertake. Pamela Cory has succeeded brilliantly in doing just that with her simultaneously maddening and you-just-can't-help-but-like-her character, Hassie Calhoun. Read this book and be transported to Las Vegas, circa 1959, along with one of the more engaging characters I've encountered in fiction."

Karl Marlantes, author of *Matterhorn*

•

"Like its eponymous heroine, *Hassie Calhoun* proves to be deceptively plucky and resourceful. What could have easily devolved into an all-too-familiar cautionary tale of Las Vegas instead becomes a redemptive portrait of an era ..."

Adam Langer, author of *The Thieves of Manhattan*

•

"Forget the glass slipper and Prince Charming! Hassie Calhoun is a small-town Cinderella fueled by vodka and Lucky Strikes. Determined to trade her Texas roots for Vegas neon, young Hassie endures plenty of hard knocks, hard men, broken dreams, and a broken heart in search of fame and fortune."

Susan McBride, author of *The Cougar Club* and *Little Black Dress*

•

"From the book's opening pages, I felt worried for Hassie Calhoun. Her story, though individual in era and tone, is recognizable. She does things in her youthful naiveté that many of us have done – and regret. This page-turning, in-your-face story explores how a good woman must reach depths before she can understand herself."

Masha Hamilton, author of *31 Hours*

•

"Nostalgia takes it on the chin in Cory's overdramatic but atmospherically pleasing debut ... Cory's alternately gritty and sudsy depiction of early '60s Sin City transports the reader back to a time when the Rat Pack ethos ruled."

Publisher's Weekly

HASSIE CALHOUN

a las vegas novel of innocence

PAMELA CORY

This book is a work of fiction. Names, characters, businesses, organizations, places, events, and incidents are either the product of the author's imagination or, in the case of historical events or persons, used fictitiously. Any resemblance to actual events or persons, living or dead, is likewise intended fictitiously.

For information, write to Scarletta Press, 10 South Fifth Street, Suite 1105, Minneapolis, MN 55402, U.S.A, www.scarlettapress.com.

Library of Congress Cataloging-in-Publication Data

Cory, Pamela
Hassie Calhoun : a Las Vegas novel of innocence / Pamela Cory. – 1st ed

p. cm.

ISBN-13: 978-0-9824584-7-1 (pbk. : alk. paper)
ISBN-10: 0-9824584-7-9 (pbk. : alk. paper
ISBN-13: 978-0-9824584-8-8 (ebk.)
ISBN-10: 0-9824584-8-7 (ebk.)

1. Women entertainers – Fiction. 2. Young women – United States – Fiction. 3. Self-actualization (psychology) – Fiction. 4. Las Vegas (Nev.) – Fiction. I. Title.

PS3603.O798H37 2011
813'.6--dc22

2011006341

Cover Design: Anders Hanson
Interior Design and Composition: Chris Long
Production Management: Mighty Media

Distributed by Publishers Group West

First Edition

10 9 8 7 6 5 4 3 2 1

Printed in Canada

Dedicated to Steven Miller

"Do one thing every day that scares you."

ELEANOR ROOSEVELT

part one

las vegas 1959

chapter one

THE FAMOUS HOTEL looked nothing like she had imagined. It wasn't tall or grand or impressive in any way except for the giant "S" that appeared to rise out of the desert in hot, white neon that glimmered through bold free script, spelling out *Sands* against a mysterious red shadow. Her heart pounded and her emotions grabbed at her throat while a brisk autumn wind blew desert grit around her shiny black heels. A big, blue car rushed past her, its paintwork catching the frenzied glitter of the light. She walked along on her tiptoes, careful not to sink into the soft grass, until she stood directly in front of the sign – "A Place in the Sun" – and remembered where she had come from and why she was there.

She clutched her suitcase and moved quickly, dodging the arrival of a black Cadillac along the wide covered driveway of the pinkish building, then pushed through the solid glass door and into a blast of sound and cigarette smoke, where men in tuxedos and women looking like movie stars packed the lobby. She immediately recognized the strong, jazzy beat of the Latin music made famous by the great Tito Puente – the "Mambo King" that her father adored.

A few steps inside the door, a man's voice said, "Just a moment, miss," and she felt herself held at the elbow. She turned and looked into the face of a tall doorman. He wore a dark green uniform with gold trim, but no cap. He was wide and imposing, intimidating but gently so. She watched him move his balding head as he looked from her face to her feet and back to her face again, then swallowed her anxiety and said, "Hi."

"Hi, yourself," the doorman said. His big smile revealed teeth that had suffered years of smoking cigarettes. "Welcome to the Sands. How can I help you?" Before she could answer, another man stepped up, shorter than the doorman but with a head full of blue-black hair, dressed in a shiny suit with broad shoulders. "Who you got here, Jimmy? Pocahontas?"

The doorman laughed and looked at her. "Is this what Pocahontas looked like, Boss?"

"I can't swear that she was as beautiful as this young lady," he said as he looked directly into her eyes. "And I sure don't know if she was as tall."

She smiled and felt her cheeks warm. "It's the shoes," she said and looked down at her feet and then back into the face of the man who, although smaller than the doorman, seemed larger and stronger and there was no doubt as to which man was the boss.

The man pulled her back from the doorway so that she stood between him and the doorman. A uniformed man walked up to them and focused a big, proud grin on her like she was getting ready to meet someone very important. "Officer Donald McGinley reporting for duty," he said and tucked his policeman's cap under his arm. "Does this pretty lady need help with something?"

"No thanks, Donnie," the man in the suit said. "Everything's under control." He looked back at her and stuck out his hand. "Welcome to the Sands, Miss ...?

"Calhoun," she said. "Hassie Calhoun." She shook his hand, which was rough and hard in places, as if he worked on a farm or in an oil field, like her father. But somehow his touch was soft, his eyes kind and endearing.

"Great name – Hassie Calhoun. Right, guys?"

She smiled.

"I'm Jake Contrata. I'm the general manager of this place. If there's anything I can do to make your stay more comfortable, you just let my right-hand man Jimmy, here, know."

Donnie stood by and nodded until Jake looked at him and said, "Don't you have some bank robbers to catch or something? Jimmy, help the young lady with her bag."

Donnie smiled and shrugged like he was saying, "I get the message," and waved before walking away. Jimmy picked up the bag and said, "Checkin' in?"

She shook her head quickly and said, "That's okay."

Jimmy stopped and frowned behind his smile.

"I mean, I'm not staying here."

Jake crossed his arms over his chest. "You're not? Then why are you here?"

"I came to meet Mr. Berman. Do you know him?"

"Jimmy, do we know a Mr. Berman?"

"I know a Henry Berman. Would he be the one?"

"Yes," she said. Her shoulders relaxed. "That's him."

"Well, well. Henry's doing quite well for himself, wouldn't you say, Jimmy?"

"Yes, sir. He's a lucky man."

"Although, I have to admit." Jake leaned into Jimmy. "I didn't take her for his type. You know what I mean?" Jake laughed out loud.

Jimmy nodded. "Yes, sir. I know exactly what you mean."

"Anyway, Hassie." Jake put his hand on her shoulder. "Do you mind if I call you Hassie?"

"No, sir."

"Good. Henry must be expecting you."

"Not exactly," she said. "I mean, he told me to come and see him if I was ever in Vegas. But he doesn't know I'm here yet."

"Wait a minute," Jake said, dropping his hand. "Henry told you to come see him here, at the Sands?"

"Yes, sir," she said. "I met him in Dallas a few months ago. He heard me sing and gave me his card and –"

"He gave you his card?" Jake said, and then looked at Jimmy. "Did you know that Henry has a card?"

Jimmy chuckled and shook his head.

"Seriously," Jake said, and put his arm around Hassie's shoulders. "Take your coat off and get comfortable." He helped her with her coat, then handed it to Jimmy and said, "Ask the bellman to hold onto Miss Calhoun's things and then go get Berman."

Jake led her to a small seating area away from the crowd and pointed to a simple sofa, a chair and a table barely big enough to hold the oversized ashtray, which contained a stubbed out cigarette with red lipstick on the filter. Hassie turned to see where Jimmy was taking her suitcase, then sat down on the sofa.

"Okay," Jake said. He unbuttoned his coat, sat down and took a cigarette out of a new pack. "So you met Henry Berman in Dallas and you're a singer."

"That's right. I sang in a talent show in Dallas and Henry saw me there. He –"

"Sorry ... but, what kind of talent show?" Jake asked. "I'm trying to understand why Henry would have been there."

"It was a showcase to find new contestants for the Miss Texas pageant."

Jake nodded. "I remember that. My boss sent Henry to look for new show girls," he said, shaking another cigarette loose and offering it to Hassie.

As she pulled it from the pack, she said, "He told me that his boss was looking for a new singer in the Copa Room."

"He told you that?" Jake laughed, throwing his head back. He lit her cigarette before lighting his own and then snapped the lighter shut. "He told you that *his boss* was looking for a new singer ... that all you had to do was show up?"

Hassie smiled at his big laugh and giggled when he snorted, then put the cigarette to her lips and carefully drew in the smoke.

"Sorry, Hassie," he finally said. "I'm sure you're a great singer but you must have misunderstood Henry. Are you okay with that cigarette?"

She let it rest on the ashtray and said, "I know what Henry told me. He said that I had a special talent and that the Copa Room needs singers like me."

"Okay, sweetheart," he said, and ground out her cigarette for her and rested his elbows on his knees. "We don't hire singers without a name in the business – or at least a recording contract." He sat back in the chair, took a deep drag from his cigarette and grinned at her. "I don't know why Henry would talk to you about singing in the Copa Room, but I can see why he would have thought you could be a showgirl. You've got all the right looks for that role."

She crossed her legs, heeding her friend Barbara Crumpler's advice: if you can't say something smart, don't say anything.

"So you come from Dallas."

"Actually, I live in a town called Corsicana. It's about sixty miles from Dallas."

Jake frowned, his head tilted slightly to the right. "You don't sound like the small town Texas girls around here. Where's that charmin' *draaawl* you gals are known for?"

Hassie giggled at his attempt at a Texas accent; how pleased Barbara would be to know that all the years of pounding "proper" speech into her had paid off. "I had a very good teacher growing up."

"I can see that," he said and exhaled smoke. "Sounds like you might be over-qualified for work around here."

She uncrossed her legs and straightened her back.

"You live with your parents?" His tone was cool; his eyes still focused on hers.

She hesitated, and then nodded.

"Your mother *and* your father?"

"Daddy died when I was young. He was an oilman and he – died."

"Sorry about that. Did Mom remarry?"

She nodded.

"Do you like your new dad?" Jake said.

"He's not my dad. He'll never be my dad. He's just a man my mother married because –" She cleared her throat. "She puts up with him so she's got somebody to take her dancing."

"I see," Jake said and then slowly and methodically stubbed out his cigarette. He studied her a while longer before saying, "Hassie, did you run away from home?"

"Of course not," she said, shifting her weight on the sofa.

"So your mom and stepdad know where you are right now, sitting in a hotel in Vegas about twenty yards from a casino?"

She stared at her hands.

"How old are you? Sixteen?"

"Eighteen in a few weeks," she said. "You don't understand."

"Sure I do. And I've met a lot of Hassie Calhouns."

What was he talking about, she thought. He didn't know her.

"You don't belong here, honey."

He held her in his gaze and she noticed that his eyes were an interesting mixture of green and brown with tiny flecks of gold that caused them to glint like mirrors when they caught the light.

"You think this is the answer to all your problems. Well, it ain't."

Her throat tightened and her eyeballs ached but she would not cry in front of this man.

Jake stood up, buttoned his coat and said, "Wait here. There's something I need to do. You'll be fine."

Jake walked away from her, then down the three wide stairs into the casino. She looked around the lobby, which was basically a big, rectangular box with an unimpressive reception desk in the far right corner. A jumble of gambling tables with luscious green tops occupied the middle of the space where people laughed and drank. A marble bounced around a giant spinning wheel and stacks of colorful chips changed hands.

Dozens of elegant couples gathered around the lobby lounge – a brightly lit bar opposite the reception where a trio of musicians pounded out the lively Latin music. The crowd danced and swayed to the strong beat; a small, blonde woman in a silky red dress spilled her drink as she demonstrated the cha-cha for her party of friends. Jewels sparkled, furs fell to the floor; Hassie felt inadequate and plain in her simple shirtwaist dress. She looked around for Jake, certain that he had not come back out of the casino. A long-legged beauty stooped to empty the dirty ashtray. She eyed Hassie and smiled like she and everyone in the lobby not only knew what Jake had said to her, but also believed it to be true. She didn't belong. She *had* run away from Corsicana, but no way was she going back. She studied the fancy decoration on the ceiling; it felt lower than when she arrived. And where did that Jimmy take her bag?

The sight of an attractive older woman made Hassie think of Barbara Crumpler and her years of study at Barbara's *Acadamie des Arts* where she had learned to play the piano, sing and dance and, eventually, to develop her talent for musical composition. Barbara was born in England and was the smartest, most exotic person Hassie had ever known. As a child of an Army officer, she'd lived all over the world and eventually married a Texan she'd met while living in California. Willis Crumpler swept Barbara off her feet at a dinner party shortly after the end of World War II. He had died not long before Bonita Calhoun took Hassie to her first music lesson, but Barbara spoke of him often, remembering how handsome he was – his strong yet genteel features. Willis was the love of her life and she had basically dismissed the life that she'd lived before she met him.

Hassie's first day with Barbara was still vivid – the willowy, middle-aged woman, her graying hair pulled tightly away from her face and anchored by a fire engine red scarf with an unidentifiable design in bright purple and yellow. An ankle-length skirt of soft black cotton hung off her slim hips and fitted over a black sleeveless shirt that resembled a leotard. Her long, red fingernails matched her lips perfectly. She was everything Hassie believed a woman should be and she never grew tired of Barbara's lessons.

Raucous cheers from one of the gambling tables pulled Hassie away from her thoughts. How long had Jake been gone? She didn't exactly know what his job at the Sands entailed, but if it was anything like that of Mr. Silas, her best friend Carol's father, who was the general manager of the Wolf Brand Chili plant in Corsicana, it could be hours before she would see him again.

She sat not far from the wide glass entrance where a reddish glow from the hotel's imposing sign spilled down into the driveway. Clusters of desert foliage sat on either side of the entry doors, which reminded Hassie of the beautiful garden that Barbara's husband had planted when they moved from southern California to the little town near Corsicana called Angus, the home of the great Crumpler family. The garden was leafy and green the whole year round with long-needled pines and prickly holly bushes full of bright colored berries. A special flowering plant called columbine covered the ground and produced rich yellow flowers while deep green shrubs of white gardenias filled the air with a heavenly, honeyed scent. But it was the special trees that came to mind in the red light. The ones that had been brought over to California from a foreign land that bore glossy green leaves and a hard, round red fruit called pomegranate.

After Willis died, Barbara cared for these small trees like they were her children, ensuring that every season they bore rich red fruit. She made a ritual of cutting open the first one of the season, tasting the seeds before sharing them with Hassie along with the story that eating them would ensure happiness in marriage, fertility and abundance. As a young girl, Hassie loved this ritual and listened breathlessly to Barbara's tales about beautiful ancient women and their extraordinary exploits.

These were just some of the many things that Barbara had taught her and she felt real shame at the thought that she had left Corsicana against Barbara's advice and without even saying good-bye. Barbara pushed her to fulfill her father's dream for her to go away to one of the great Texas universities and develop her mind and talents to their fullest; to do everything she could to rise above the life that her mother had chosen. But Bonita believed that going to college was a foolish notion for a young girl – what was good enough for Bonita was good enough for Hassie.

If she stayed under the influence of her mother and stepfather, Bobby, she would never do anything with her life. And living at home in the summer months following her high school graduation, where she avoided being alone with Bobby, had made it impossible for her to comfortably stay in Corsicana. She had tried to tell her mother about Bobby's bad behavior, but Bonita would dismiss her concerns as misinterpretations of Bobby's affection for her or accuse her of teasing him and threaten to punish her if she didn't keep quiet. Hassie would never understand how her mother could take Bobby's word over hers and, whether she'd really ever admit it or not, this lack of concern for her daughter's well-being ultimately drove Hassie away from her own home.

Hassie wanted the life that she'd learned about from Henry Berman. Now she had to convince Mr. Contrata that she wasn't a silly girl having run away from a boring life in a small town. He would change his mind about her after he talked to Henry and really understood that she could sing. In Dallas, Henry had told her that she was the best singer in the contest. He had no reason to say that if he didn't mean it.

She heard bells ring up and down the long row of slot machines on the rear wall of the lobby. Someone called her name; she turned around to see Henry and ran over to meet him. He looked the same as he had in Dallas – dark gray suit and neatly trimmed brown hair. Barbara had joked that he looked like a banker, but Hassie thought he looked more like a Presbyterian minister.

"Hassie?" Henry said. "I heard that you were in the hotel. What are you doing here?"

"Hi, Henry. Are you really surprised to see me?" She smiled and reached out to hug him.

He took hold of her arm and walked toward the lobby bar. "Sort of. I hear you met Jake Contrata."

"Yeah, I met him, and I don't think you've told him anything about our meeting in Dallas. You didn't forget me, did you?"

"No, I didn't forget you," he said. "Things just changed around here after I got back and –"

"And what?"

Henry stopped to survey the area around the bar and then pushed her in the direction of an empty bar stool. "I really didn't think I'd ever see you again."

"So you said the things you said just to have something to say to me?"

A blast of horns drowned out his reply; he shook his head and shouted, "I meant what I said. I just –"

They reached the bar stool and Hassie sat down before saying, "Mr. Contrata said that I misunderstood you and that there's no way you could have offered me a job singing in the Copa Room, but that I look good enough to be a *showgirl*. Is that what you meant, Henry? Did I come all the way to Vegas on that bus so I could wear a skimpy outfit with a big feather hat and dance? I'm a singer, Henry. You know that."

"Hassie, I'm sorry." He stood beside her and motioned to the bartender. "Maybe I was sent to Dallas to find new showgirls, but after I heard you sing, I thought you'd be great in the Copa Room – one day. And I didn't exactly offer you a job."

"That's not the way it sounded to me," she said. "Maybe you were just trying to be a big shot." She thought about Jake's comment about Henry having a business card. "Maybe you were just trying to impress me or something."

Henry pursed his lips and seemed very annoyed with her. "Like I said, things changed. Not long after I got back from Dallas, the Copa Girls were disbanded because Mr. Sinatra was taking over the Copa Room and bringing in a whole new act with Dean Martin and Sammy Davis Jr. The showgirls – the ones that stuck around – are waitresses now. It's not the same place, and Jake's probably right – you don't belong here."

Hassie saw Jimmy coming toward them and smiled as he reached the bar.

"Boss is lookin' for you, Berman," Jimmy said. "Says for you to bring Miss Calhoun back to the Copa Room. And do it now."

"Okay, okay," Henry said and helped Hassie off the stool while waving the bartender away.

They walked away from the lobby down a corridor that narrowed beyond the entrance to the casino. Hassie ran behind Henry and said, "So Mr. Contrata's your boss?"

Henry ignored her and she heard him utter something that sounded like, "Humph."

"Henry," she said. "I really believed you when you told me that I had a special talent and that I should look you up when I was in Vegas."

"That's my point," he said and stopped just short of the entrance to the Copa Room. "I said that you should look me up when you were *in* Vegas – not to come to Vegas especially to see me."

Hassie felt stupid and insulted but stopped when she saw the poster of Frank Sinatra on an easel next to the heavy curtain in front of the Copa Room door. She'd been so caught up in her own thoughts, she'd forgotten that this was where the great man performed.

Henry stood beside her and said, "By the way, didn't you qualify for the Miss Texas pageant?"

She looked up from the poster and shrugged as she said, "It didn't work out."

"Why not?"

"My mother wasn't so keen on the idea and – well, everything changed after I met you in Dallas, and I didn't want to stay in Texas."

Henry frowned. "Hell, you should've at least taken part in the pageant. Maybe you'd have won, and then you could have gone on to college."

"I don't want to go to college," she said and gazed at the entrance to the Copa Room. "I want to work in the Copa Room. Just like you said."

She remained still until Henry took her by the hand and said, "Jake's waiting for us. Just let him sort this out."

They stood inside the entrance, which was dark and a little too warm. Thick, stale smoke hung in the low-ceilinged room, making it feel small and airless. The rows of tables felt cramped and pushed in on top of each other like one should not be able to see the floor between them. The walls and ceiling were the shade of green that her mother had once painted their kitchen because it reminded her of the fields of clover she knew as a child in Oklahoma; the chairs were covered in a deep cherry red fabric. As Hassie surveyed the entire room, she felt a twinge of disappointment at the lack of glamour that she had expected to surround the stars that performed there. With the lights up it was no better than home, just a plain old room.

From a distance, the stage looked small and insignificant. Maybe it was the absence of musicians or a star performer that made it feel like it was just another room. She could hear voices behind the stage and started to move closer just as Henry took hold of her arm, forcing her to take a step back. She looked at him in an effort to protest and heard him say, "Good night, Mr. Sinatra."

Hassie turned to see a man flanked by two men in dark suits moving toward her, his jacket flung over his right shoulder, smoke swirling around his face. She couldn't move and forgot to breathe; Henry's grip tightened around her arm.

As he approached the back entrance, Sinatra nodded at Henry, and then stopped just before he reached the door. In a move that made Hassie tingle, he looked over his left shoulder, taking in her whole body. She smiled at him but he didn't smile back, said nothing and walked out ahead of his small entourage.

After the door closed behind the men, Henry said, "There's no need to be afraid of him, Hassie."

"I'm not afraid of him," she said. "Anyway, he didn't even notice me."

"Oh, he noticed you, honey. You better believe he noticed you."

chapter two

It wasn't that Hassie hadn't expected to see Sinatra; surely he was one of the reasons she had come to the Sands. But the effect he had on her in that fleeting moment was more than just the reaction of a star-struck teenager, like the way her friend Carol squeaked whenever she talked about seeing the new teen idol Fabian at the Dallas Memorial Auditorium. It was the certain recognition that she was in a completely new arena where she could stand next to people like Frank Sinatra and he could look at her and maybe even change her life.

Hassie followed Henry through the swinging door to the empty dressing room over to where the two long, mirrored tables faced each other and round, white light bulbs defined the individual spaces. She sat on a small stool covered in deep blue velvet and swiveled around to look into the mirror. Her cheeks felt warm and her heartbeat was uneven as though any minute she could burst. "Henry, do you really think that Mr. Sinatra noticed me?"

"Why wouldn't he?" Henry replied. "You're beautiful. You have long legs, a nice figure – pretty much the package that guys like Sinatra go for."

"You make me sound like some sort of doll. Ya know, pull my string and I'll sing and talk and even bat my eyelashes."

Henry laughed and walked over to stand behind her, then lowered his head beside hers, looked at her in the mirror and said, "You better get used to it. Gals like you get special attention around here. You can have all the charm and talent in the world but the first thing the men look at is your legs and your ass – and, of course, your tits, if you've got any. You may not like it, but that's the way it is."

Before Henry stood up, Jake Contrata walked up behind them, his expression, as Hassie saw it in the mirror, left no doubt about his mood. Henry stood and turned to face him; Jake perched himself on the edge of the dressing table behind them, his head cocked to one side, a cigarette between his lips. His presence was much more imposing than when she'd seen him in the lobby. And with the shadow of a heavy beard, there was an air of mystery about him that both intrigued and unnerved her. Jake dragged deeply on the cigarette, studied Henry for a few seconds, then exhaled the smoke and said, "What's your job in this hotel?"

"You know what my job is, Jake," Henry said, crossing his arms over his chest. Hassie watched them in the mirror. "I'm the manager of the Copa Room."

"Really? Then why are you never here?" He paused and looked at Hassie in the mirror, then back at Henry. "You're not in your office. You're not backstage. By the way, can I have one of your business cards?"

Henry shot a quick glance at Hassie, then released an exhausted sigh with a look that told Jake to go to hell before he said, "The show's over, Jake. Anyway, Jimmy told me you wanted to see me."

"Give me your version of this thing in Dallas where you heard Hassie sing and filled her head –" He walked up behind Hassie and gently took hold of her shoulders, which sent a slight chill along her arms. "Ya know, I don't really give a rat's ass about that now. I wanna know what you're gonna do with her now that she's here." He stopped like he expected a response, then casually walked to the other end of the dressing table and picked up the phone.

Henry glared at Jake, making the strong line of his jaw more prominent on his otherwise slender face. Hassie whirled around on the stool wondering if the phone call was anything to do with her; the bit of Jake's conversation that she could hear was lost when two women noisily entered the room. One was tall and skinny and dressed like the cocktail waitresses that worked in the lobby, with dark auburn hair worn in a style that was unflattering to her long, thin neck. The other wore a long, yellow dress that Hassie assumed fit her better when she was younger with slightly smaller hips.

"Well, well," the woman in the yellow dress said. "Henry, is there some kind of meetin' goin' on that you forgot to tell us about?"

"There's no meeting, Dotty," Henry said. "What are you two doing here now?"

Before Dotty answered, Jake walked toward them, looked at his watch and said, "I thought you ladies were gone for the night."

"Hi, Jake," the other woman said. "I just came in to change." She went directly to her dressing table and started to undress, then looked at Jake like she expected him to come closer to her.

Jake watched her remove her blouse, then looked at Dotty and said, "Isn't Jimmy off duty now?"

"Yeah, I guess," she said, putting a cigarette to her lips. "Who's the new girl?" She motioned to Henry for a light.

Jake walked back over to Hassie and nudged her to stand. "This is Hassie Calhoun."

Hassie stood up as Jake pointed in the general direction of the two women. "Hassie, meet Dotty and Natalie, two of the Copa Room's finest."

Dotty exhaled smoke and whistled, and then motioned to Natalie, who was mostly naked, wriggling into a white sequined dress.

"Lookie here, Nat. She's a real beauty," Dotty said, then leaned toward Natalie, "And sooooo *yoouunng*."

Hassie saw this woman as a cross between the Mae West doll she'd had as a kid and the women her mother referred to as trailer trash. Her accent was similar yet quite different than the ones she was used to in Texas. What exactly did people from Las Vegas sound like?

Jake clapped his hands and said, "Miss Calhoun – Hassie – is just visiting Henry for a couple of days. Then she'll be going back to Texas."

Hassie expected Henry to say something to Jake; the two women started laughing.

"*She's* visiting Henry?" Natalie said. "What's he gonna do with her? Stick her on a trophy shelf?"

Jake glanced at Hassie and then walked over to stand between Dotty and Natalie. "Tell you what, Dotty," he said. "You're the queen of the Copa Girls, or whatever they're called now. Why don't you be a good hostess and take Hassie around the lounges and casino."

"You're kiddin' me," Dotty said, taking a deep drag on her cigarette.

"I have an even better idea," he said to Natalie. "Take off your dress."

Natalie put her hands on her hips and said, "What? I just put it on."

"I said, take your dress off." He moved closer to her. "I wanna see how it looks on Hassie."

"Fuck off, Jake," she said. "I'm not givin' her my dress." She pushed her right foot into her shoe.

Jake grabbed her arm and said, "That wasn't a request. Now, do it."

Natalie scowled, then pulled her arm out of his grip. Dotty stared at Hassie; Natalie slid the dress to the floor and stepped out of it. She faced him in her single shoe and panties and said, "You'll regret this, Jake," then grabbed her clothes and limped over to the other end of the room.

Dotty picked up the left shoe, waved it and said, "Don't ya think you'll need this?" She lobbed the shoe in Natalie's direction.

Jake picked up the dress and handed it to Dotty. "Help Hassie get into this – thing."

Hassie had never seen a woman take her clothes off in front of men. She looked around for Henry who stood near the door grimacing like the boys at her high school when Coach Hayes called them good for nothin' lowlifes and knocked them down a few notches.

Jake walked over to Hassie with the dress. "Put this on." He eyed her for a moment then walked past Henry and said, "Come on, Berman. The ladies need some privacy and I need you to do something for me."

Natalie reappeared, having re-dressed in her waitress uniform and carrying her shoes. "Hope you enjoy dressing up the cowgirl in my best gown," she said to Dotty. "Now I've gotta go all the way back to my room."

The door swung closed behind Natalie as Dotty shouted, "Poor you!"

Hassie took a big breath and held Natalie's dress an arm's length away. Dotty walked up to her and said, "Okay, Cassie is it?"

"Hassie."

"Hassie, I don't know you. I don't know why you're here. But I do know you're way outta your league." She stared at Hassie for a few seconds before saying, "Well? That dress ain't gonna get on your body by itself. You're a bit taller than Natalie. Get your clothes off and see how it fits."

Hassie carefully kicked off her shoes and removed her belt, then unbuttoned the dress and turned away from Dotty to contemplate how she would exchange her old dress for the sparkly one.

"Don't tell me you're shy," Dotty sniggered. "You're damn sure in the wrong place if you can't even take your clothes off in front of me."

Shy or overwhelmed, Hassie took off the dress and her silky slip and laid them neatly on the stool, then turned to face Dotty in her underwear. Dotty handed her Natalie's dress, then moved back to draw on her cigarette.

"You'll wanna get rid of those stockings," Dotty said. "The garters tend to show through these tight, slinky numbers."

Hassie unfastened her garter belt and rolled the stockings down her legs and off her feet while still attached to the garters.

"That's a nice trick," Dotty said.

Hassie dropped them on her pile of clothes, then stepped into the dress and pulled it up her legs, tugged it over her hips and struggled to get it up to her shoulders. The scent of Natalie's perfume, mixed with the faint smells of her body, was slightly stale and unpleasant. Nevertheless, she pulled the front up over her bra and smoothed the clingy fabric over her body.

Dotty waited for her to fix the straps before saying, "Have a look in the mirror."

Hassie turned back to the dressing table and squatted down to see the top of her body. She looked back at Dotty.

"Does that look good to you?" Dotty asked and stubbed out her cigarette.

Hassie studied her image again and said, "Not really. Something's wrong."

"Try takin' off your bra."

Hassie looked in the mirror and giggled. Dotty chuckled and sat down on the nearest stool. They laughed and Hassie relaxed until she noticed that Jake had come back into the room and stood against the back wall staring at them.

"Having fun?" he said; his tone implied anything but fun.

Hassie stood up straight and put her arms across her chest.

"Not bad," he said, focused on her hips. "Got a problem up top?"

Dotty walked over to Hassie, stood in front of her and removed her bra from underneath the dress like it was a magic trick. Hassie pushed her breasts around the top of the dress until she was sure everything was in place, and then looked at Jake. His silence made her blush; she fidgeted again with the top.

"Don't move," he said.

She dropped her hands to her sides and froze. When she looked at his face, his eyes locked onto hers. An electric spark shot through her body; she felt her nipples harden.

"Dotty," Jake finally said. "There's been a change of plans. Help Hassie fix her hair and makeup. I'm gonna take her to the lounge."

"Ooooh kaaay," Dotty said, motioning for Hassie to sit down at the dressing table.

"Where's Henry?" Hassie asked.

"Hiding from me, is my guess," Jake replied and sat on the sofa.

"Did I get him into trouble?"

"Nah, I just like to bust his balls every now and then." Jake laughed and lit a cigarette.

Hassie tensed at the thought that she really had caused a problem for Henry. Dotty caught her eye in the mirror and raised her eyebrows, then rolled her eyes, which made Hassie smile.

Dotty finished off Hassie's makeup with a light layer of lipstick that reminded her of Revlon's "Cherries in the Snow" that she borrowed from her mother's cosmetic case from time to time. Dotty pulled a brush through her thick, dark hair, then tapped her on her shoulder and motioned for her to stand.

Hassie stood up from the dressing table and walked toward Jake, who'd been sitting quietly, puffing on his cigarette. He didn't stand or move but studied her calmly and deliberately. Before she reached where he was sitting, Jimmy, the doorman, entered the room. He had changed out of his uniform and wore a plain dark suit, white shirt and tie. He stopped when he saw Jake and gave some sort of sign to Dotty, who was busy swapping her high heels for comfortable flats.

"Just the man I want to see," Jake said and stood up.

"What can I do for you, sir?"

"Take your bride out for a nice drink on me. She's been a big help tonight and I'd like to express my thanks."

"That's okay, Jake," Dotty said, checking her own makeup. "You two go and enjoy yourselves."

"No, I insist. Just sign my name – Jimmy, you know what to do."

"That's very nice, Jake. Come on, ole girl." Jimmy gestured with both hands. "Do as the boss says."

"Keep your pants on, Myers," Dotty said and headed for the door. She handed her rhinestone heels to Hassie and kept walking.

Jimmy followed behind her and said, "Your roots need touchin' up."

"Yeah, well, your ass needs liftin'."

Jake laughed as the door closed behind them. Hassie stood beside him, stared after them and said, "Do they hate each other or something?"

"That's them being *nice* to each other." He looked at her, hesitated and then said, "Shall we go?"

She put on Dotty's shoes, which fit well enough but made Natalie's dress a little too short, she thought, and tugged it down her body as she followed Jake out of the room.

Jake guided her along the corridor with his hand firmly pressed against the small of her back. He acknowledged the occasional patron. She felt uncomfortable and, despite the dress and shoes, out of step with the stylish women buzzing around her.

As they walked past the lobby, Jake looked at her and said, "Have you been inside the casino yet?"

She shook her head. "I haven't had a chance."

"Well, technically you're not old enough to go in, but we're gonna walk through now on our way to the lounge – which you're also not old enough to go in. Good thing you know the boss. But take my advice and keep your distance from the casino while you're here. It can be a pretty wicked place."

They walked down the steps into the casino and along a winding path through the slot machines and game tables. About halfway through the big space, a thin, dark-haired man with large-rimmed glasses walked toward them and raised his hand in recognition of Jake. When they met the man, Jake stopped and said, "How ya doing, Eddie? Everything okay tonight?"

"Yes, sir," the man said while he looked at Hassie. "Busy as always, but pretty calm."

Jake touched her arm and said, "Hassie, meet Eddie Munroe. He's the casino's pit boss and was born with about six pairs of eyes."

Eddie grinned and said, "And they're all lookin' at this pretty lady."

"Meet Hassie Calhoun," Jake said. "Hassie's visiting from Texas. We're just headed to the lounge."

Eddie made a motion like he was tipping his hat and said, "Have a good time and tell Sheila I said hello."

"Will do," Jake said and led Hassie along the carpeted path until they stood in front of the door marked "Regency Lounge". Jake opened the door and led her into the dark space.

A pretty blonde waitress with very large breasts seated them in the far corner. When the waitress leaned over to light the candle on the table, Hassie was sure her breasts would fall out of her low-cut blouse. She held her breath until the woman stood up – she could see a tag with the name "Sheila" pinned to her collar – and spoke softly to Jake, nodding and smiling before walking away. The vague light and the cigarette smoke that floated in the room made it difficult to see anything beyond the edge of their table. Conversation stayed at such low volume it sounded like the hum of bees or some other insect that she'd often heard but never seen. In a corner awash with sapphire light, a trio played music that could have come from Willis Crumpler's collection of jazz greats like Thelonius Monk and Miles Davis.

Jake stood to greet two men that Hassie had seen in the lobby earlier, but he kept his hand on her shoulder, gently patting her between comments and polite laughter. She felt safe and grown up and pushed her breasts together with her forearms to deepen the line of cleavage. As her eyes adjusted to the low light, she spotted Natalie sitting close by with a table of men. It was still too dark to see what Natalie wore, but Hassie didn't want another scene over the dress and instinctively lowered her head when she thought Natalie might look her way.

The waitress returned with a bottle snuggled in a large bucket of ice. She looked at Jake for permission to open it and peeled off the gold foil wrapper. Jake set a glass in front of Hassie and said, "I assume you like champagne."

"Uh-huh," she said, wondering if it would taste anything like the bourbon that her stepfather had once forced on her when her mother was out playing bridge.

The light liquid bubbled in her glass while the waitress filled one for Jake. He held it up to her, then touched her glass with his and said, "To Hassie Calhoun, the most beautiful lady from Texas that I've ever met."

She swallowed the fizzy drink, which, thankfully, tasted nothing like bourbon. She smiled and took another sip. The first glass of champagne left her a little dizzy and she liked the intensity of Jake's eyes as he watched her. Even in the low light, she had a close-up view of him and watched the skin wrinkle around his eyes when he laughed. He wasn't a devastatingly handsome man, but something about the way he moved and spoke with such confidence gave her the courage to occasionally touch his arm when she talked to him.

People came and went from Jake's table; Hassie lost count of the number of bottles that were opened and consumed. She accepted a cigarette every time one was offered to her but, having mastered the look from the women around her, spent more time holding it than smoking. Jake introduced her as his "friend" from Texas, which prompted the many Texans in the room to snuggle up close to her and pretend like they knew each other back home and say things like, "Little darlin', you could make a bulldog break his chain." What could have made her homesick just made her glad that she had left it all behind. The sophistication and merriment around her warmed her heart and she didn't care what Jake and Henry said: she had come to Vegas for a reason and she would not easily be pushed out the door.

When Hassie reached the point that she could barely keep her eyes open, she whispered to Jake that she needed to get some sleep. He winked at her, stubbed out his cigarette and said, "Okay, folks. Let's call it a night." He helped her up from her chair. "Let's get you to bed."

As they stepped into lighter, clearer air, Hassie stopped and grabbed Jake's arm. "I don't have anywhere to stay," she said and pulled off Dotty's shoes, which now felt like vise clamps on her feet.

"Just come with me."

He guided her back through the casino, past the Garden Room and lobby toward the second corridor of guestrooms, and then veered left into what felt like a separate building. A plaque at the corridor entrance said "Churchill Downs"; Jake stopped in front of one of the rooms. Hassie's body slightly swayed while she waited for him to open the door. He turned to face her and placed his hands on her hips. She rested her head on his shoulder for a few seconds, then looked back into his face and slurred, "Why you are so ... I mean, why so are you nice?"

Jake laughed softly, took her face in his hand and said, "This is your room for the night. You'll find your bag inside. Just make yourself comfortable and get some sleep." He kissed her on her forehead.

She looked at him with eyes that were barely open and parted her lips with the intention of telling him that she didn't have money to pay for a room. Before she could get the words out, he pulled her close to his body, his lips touching her left ear and whispered, "Do you know how beautiful you are?"

She pushed herself back from his chest and frowned. She felt Bobby's tight grip around her body as he tried to kiss her or put his hand inside her sweater. "Stop!" she shouted and pushed Jake away.

"Hey!" he said and raised his hands in the air. "Just relax. I'm not gonna hurt you or do anything that you don't want to do."

She stood still and looked at him. The strong, masculine lines of his face reminded her of everything that she had loved about her father – the warm, caring way he had of making her feel safe and secure. She believed that he wasn't trying to hurt her and put her arms around his neck, pulling herself close to his body. She picked up the light spicy fragrance of his cologne, now mixed with his body's own scent and a layer of cigarette smoke. He slowly tightened his embrace around her and her face brushed against his abrasive cheek. When she didn't move for a few seconds, Jake took a step back and rubbed his hands up and down her bare arms. The spark of electricity coursed through her body again. He opened the door and walked her inside the dark room.

He switched on the lamp beside the sofa. Hassie sat down on the satin bedcover. She felt light-headed, giddy and nauseated. Jake put his hand on her shoulder and said, "You gonna be okay?" She nodded and forced out a sound meant to say thanks. He laughed, patted her shoulder and said, "Of course you will." He walked to the door and quietly closed it behind him. She fell backwards, arms flung across the bed. "I'm gonna be sick," she mumbled. The ceiling blurred as the room spun around her.

She carefully stood up and stumbled into the dark bathroom, lifted the toilet seat and heaved her entire evening into the cold, white bowl. Her arms wobbled as she pushed herself up from the floor. The tile was cool against her legs. Natalie would love her for ruining her dress. She crawled out of the bathroom, her hands and knees sinking into the warm carpet. The buttery soft light from the lamp by the sofa cast a shadow on a framed print of horses running through a desert. The glow of daylight seeped from the edges at the curtain that covered the entire wall across from the bed. There was no place in Corsicana that could compare to the beautiful style of this room.

Her head throbbed as she stood and moved toward the bed. She pushed the tight dress down her body onto the floor and sat on the bed's edge, remembering that her nightgown was in her bag on the other side of the room. She cocooned herself between the soft, cool sheets and pulled the thick bedcover around her almost naked body. As she burrowed her face into the pillow, she remembered the light fresh scent of the linen at Barbara's house. She smiled at the memory, then breathed deeply and relaxed. Maybe she hadn't been prepared for her first night in Vegas – and maybe she had no idea what she was getting herself into – but as she descended into sleep, she saw a mélange of Jake's smile, Frank Sinatra's chilling gaze, and herself, standing under the lights on a smoky stage.

chapter three

The wind whistled through the empty streets, just like it did on Saturday mornings when she could sleep until her daddy woke her and just the two of them would go to the local diner for pigs in a blanket drenched in warm maple syrup. The drive along Main Street was always quiet and deserted until they reached Seventh Avenue where Charlie Sumter's pickup truck sat in front of the diner like a trusty guard dog. Sometimes the wind would kick up and blow dust and stray bits of trash around. In the wintertime, the cold winds blowing in from the plains would rock the lone traffic light at the intersection, interrupting its slow, amber blink.

Jackson Calhoun had been a field supervisor for the largest oil company in Texas and worked long hours – most nights arriving home well past suppertime. Hassie's mother would practically ignore him when he came home dirty and tired and in need of a good meal. Hassie would run to hug and kiss him. She didn't care that his clothes were black with oil stains, and on those Saturday mornings, she felt lucky to sit with him in the diner.

Once they'd ordered the food and Jackson's coffee arrived, he would ask her about her week at school. When she was in the fourth grade, she got good marks, was well behaved, and Jackson had no real reason to worry about her; nevertheless, he worried about the amount of time that she spent alone in her room – she wasn't interested in joining Girl Scouts or playing after school with the other girls. When Jackson questioned her about these things, she would tell him that the other girls didn't like her; that she was too tall and too skinny and had the wrong kind of hair and wasn't pretty enough to be their friend. Her daddy would shake his head, take hold of her hands and tell her that she was prettier than all those girls put together and that one day she'd leave them all in the dust – that one day she'd be a real heartbreaker.

Jackson was Hassie's whole world until he left Corsicana to fight in Korea. Her mother dealt with his absence by spending more time in the beauty parlor and going to fancy dinner parties with people Hassie didn't know, or playing bridge or canasta at the country club. She'd often leave Hassie with Barbara, who had become a close family friend and who thought it important that, alongside Hassie's music lessons, she be exposed to the arts. Whenever possible, Barbara took her to symphonies or dance performances in Dallas, and she sometimes stayed with Barbara for the entire weekend. Despite Barbara's influence, Hassie longed for her father and the gap between her and her mother grew wider and deeper. She wrote letters to her father begging him to come home and make everything right, but it would be two years before he returned and, by that time, she knew that nothing would ever be right again.

Hassie heard a knock on the door and a woman's voice faintly call out, "Housekeeping." She opened her eyes but didn't move. She waited to hear the knock or voice again but there came no sound. Her mouth tasted about as bad as anything she could remember; her stomach felt concave from lack of food. She didn't know how long she'd been asleep but felt exhausted and weak and made no attempt to fight the heavy eyelids forcing her back into a dreamy state where she was in the lounge with the beautiful people, the cold champagne, the sweet attention from Jake. Frank Sinatra asked her to sing a song that he'd heard she had written. She stood at the microphone and waited for the band, which never started to play because she couldn't remember the song or the lyrics.

She forced herself to wake up and pushed up on her elbows. The melody that she had once picked out on the piano ran through her head; she flopped back down on the pillow, relieved that she'd only been dreaming. She tried to hum the melody but her throat was dry and sore and she almost gagged at the stench of her own smoke- and vomit-infused hair.

She crept into the bathroom where the fluorescent light nearly blinded her and, thinking of Bobby's habit of *accidentally* walking in on her, locked the door. She removed her underwear and stepped into the tub, then stood under the warm shower until she felt the disgusting remnants of her big night in the lounge go down the drain. She poured a handful of shampoo on her hair, massaged it through and then let the soapy water wash over her body. She heard the music in her head again and stood still under the shower's flow while she thought about the words that she had written after her father died – first as an exercise in English class and later as the lyrics to her melody. It was her favorite way to remember her father. She recalled the day she showed the first verse to Barbara and began to softly sing:

How can I remember the days so long ago?
Your arms kept me safe and warm
You made our home a haven, the life I came to know
'Twas never a fear of harm
But days and nights have passed, I know
You rest with God above
You left me broken hearted though
I'll always have your love

Barbara praised her for her efforts and encouraged her to write another verse or two. She had made a few attempts, but it brought the pain of missing her father too close to her heart, especially when she found out that her mother was going to marry Bobby Suskind and that he would move into their house with her and her little brother, Travis.

She tilted her face up into the warm spray of water, hoping to cleanse away thoughts of how much her world changed after her father died. She stood for a long minute and relaxed with the knowledge that she was free of that life in Corsicana; that she had a chance to do something better and that she had to make sure that Jake Contrata gave her that chance.

As she closed her eyes to rinse her hair again, she recalled Jake's face when he looked into her eyes and then gently kissed her forehead. But she knew that he really wanted to kiss her on the mouth and touch her the same way Bobby had wanted. Maybe she wouldn't mind if Jake did that to her. She remembered how he held her arm and ran his fingers along her face and how it made her feel. She could smell his cologne and see his warm, interesting eyes; something strange and exciting stirred inside her.

She stepped out of the tub, grabbed one of the thick towels, dried herself and wiped steam off the vanity mirror. As she leaned over and gently rubbed the towel over her wet, throbbing head she heard a noise at the door. Someone was trying to come into her room. She wrapped the towel around her body, unlocked the bathroom door and called out, "Who's there?"

A key turned in the lock. She opened the door wider and shouted, "Who's there? What do you want?"

"It's me, Hassie," Henry said as he walked in waving the passkey in the air.

"God, Henry." She tightened the towel around her, gripping it at her breasts. "You scared me to death."

He pulled a room service trolley in from the corridor and said, "Sorry. Housekeeping's been knocking on your door for over an hour and when you didn't answer, they were afraid you were in here sick or something." He parked the trolley, walked over to the wardrobe and took a plush terrycloth bathrobe off a coat hanger. "You should put the 'do not disturb' sign on the door if you're gonna stay in bed all day." He gave her a disapproving look and said, "I hear you had a pretty big night."

"Who told you that?" She sheepishly took the robe from him and walked over to the bed.

"Who do you think?" Henry said.

"What did Jake say?" She put the bathrobe on over the towel, and then let the towel drop to the floor.

"Hassie, did something die in this room? It really stinks." He went to the window and opened the thick outer drape; a silky, sheer curtain barely shielded them from the bright daylight. He opened the window before turning back to look at her just as she spotted Natalie's dress piled on the floor next to the dirty towel. He walked over to where she stood and said, "Is that Natalie's dress?" He picked the dress up from the floor and shook the wrinkles out of it.

Hassie took a step back, shamefaced and slightly embarrassed that she'd completely forgotten about the dress after she made such a mess of it during her escapade with the toilet. Henry fussed around with such discerning care, she was sure he was checking out each and every sequin. "Is it ruined?" she finally said.

"I'm not an expert, but these dresses are not meant to serve as battle armor when you're drunk." Hassie giggled nervously while he walked over to the wardrobe and placed the dress on one of the hangers. "Just leave it in here and I'll send someone to take care of it." He closed the wardrobe door, walked over to the room service trolley and lifted the cover from one of the silver dishes. "Now, doesn't this bacon smell good? You must be starving."

"I'm not sure," she said, running her fingers through her wet hair. "My stomach is kinda sensitive. What else you got besides bacon?"

"Believe me, I know how to deal with *sensitive* mornings after. Come here and check it out."

She slinked over to the table of food; a whiff of coffee made her stomach turn. "Ick. No coffee."

"Look. You need some real food. These eggs are the chef's specialty. They're light and fluffy and just what the doctor ordered." He loaded up a fork full and offered it to her.

She wrinkled her nose and walked away. Henry stuffed the eggs in his mouth and poured a glass of orange juice.

"Come on, Hassie. At least have some juice or eat some toast – with strawberry jam. I know you want some sugar."

She walked back to the trolley and eyed the eggs, then picked up a fork and pushed them around on the plate. "Any chance of getting something else?" she said before laying the fork down and walking away.

"Probably," he said while chewing on a piece of bacon. "What do you want?"

She disappeared into the bathroom and shouted through the half-open door, "Chocolate milk."

"Excuse me?"

"I want some chocolate milk." She paused for response. "And a jelly doughnut."

Henry laughed and said, "Do you think you're Elvis Presley or something?"

"What did you say about Elvis Presley?"

"I said – I'll see what I can sort out. Now come out here so I can talk to you."

A couple of minutes later, Hassie came out of the bathroom, now fully dressed in black cotton capri pants and a white short-sleeved blouse. She tucked the shirt into the pants as she said, "So what do you want to talk about?"

"What do you think is going to happen today?" Henry asked. "Do you think you can just stay here in this expensive room for the rest of your life?" He poured coffee into one of the cups and stirred in some cream.

Hassie raised her eyebrows, cocked her head and fell into the closest chair, folding her legs underneath her and sitting Indian style.

"Have you even thought about it?" he said and sipped the coffee.

She didn't look at him.

"Okay, let me give you some clues," he said, put the coffee cup on the trolley and sat down across from her. "First, you gotta talk to Jake. You know he's hell-bent on sending you back to Texas."

She put both feet on the floor and forced on her ballet flats. "Do you really think he'll send me back?" After her evening with him in the lounge, she'd pretty well dismissed that thought.

"Like I said, you're gonna have to talk to him and maybe apologize if you think you've done something that needs apologizing for. That's gotta be your call."

Hassie quickly went over the events of the night before – at least the ones she could remember – smiles and chatter and champagne – lots of champagne, but nothing too bad, she thought. "So what do I do now? Should I call him?"

"No, you just wait," Henry said. "He'll call you or send someone for you when he's ready to see you. I've already called room service. So just stay here and wait." He stood up and straightened his tie before walking to the door.

"Henry?" She jumped up and followed him. "I gotta ask you something."

He stuffed his hands in his pocket and looked at her like he was saying, "What?"

"Did you mean what you said to me last night in the dressing room?"

"I usually mean everything I say, Hassie. What are you talking about?"

She stared down at her feet for a few seconds and then looked at him and said, "That girls like me get special attention from men. That they'll like the way I look and – what did you say – *go for* girls like me?"

Henry lifted her hand, sighed deeply and said, "Look. I told you in Dallas and I'm telling you now. You're a very special young lady. People do double takes when they see you, and that's not just because you're beautiful to look at. You have a certain quality that can't be bought or learned and it comes through in everything you do."

"Is that why you told me to come to Vegas and that I belong in the Copa Room?"

He dropped her hand and crossed his arms over his chest. "You're a good singer, Hassie. You proved that in Dallas and I'm a real fan of yours, but you're not ready for the Copa Room. You shouldn't have come here like this and I don't think you have a chance in hell of staying. Jake likes what he sees when he looks at you, but you're *seventeen* years old. He's never gonna let you stay."

"But you said –"

"What I'm trying to tell you in the nicest way possible is that you are way outta your league here and Jake knows it." He took another step toward the door while saying, "Just wait for him to call you. You'll see."

"Why don't you stay here and wait with me?" she said.

"No can do," he said, opening the door. "You're on your own and you better stay put. Your *breakfast* will be here any minute." He walked out without looking back.

She ambled over to the dressing table and stared at her face in the mirror. Although she liked the way her skin looked in the afterglow of the warm shower, she leaned closer in to look at the red rims of her eyes, which made her think of the old town drunk who always hung around the Collin Street Bakery. Her father would give him a quarter when they stopped by on Saturday morning to buy a fruitcake for her mother. She worked her fingers through her damp hair, which was at least clean now and drying into its naturally wavy style. She pressed her lips together to force color into them and thought about all the times her father – and Barbara – had told her something like what Henry had said. That she was gifted in a way that was difficult to pin down or describe, but she'd never really had a clue about such talk until Bobby started cornering her and telling her that she drove him crazy and that it was her fault that he felt the way he did about her.

She took a deep breath and checked the time; well after noon. No wonder she was ravenous. She went back to the trolley and stared into empty dishes, then walked over to the window and peered out from behind the sheer curtain. She'd not seen this view of the desert, which was flat and desolate and reminded her of the long stretches of Texas plains. She glanced at the small sofa, then crossed her arms and paced around the room. She thought she heard a knock at the door and checked the peephole but no one was there. She'd never stayed in a hotel with room service, but how long did it take to whip up some chocolate milk and deliver a doughnut? She was about to sit in the armchair when the steward arrived at the door. He traded the trolley of dirty dishes for a simple tray that he placed on the coffee table. She signed the slip of paper and thanked him, then uncovered the two biggest doughnuts she'd ever seen, the sight of which made her flinch. She took a sip of the chocolate milk, and then eyed the doughnuts again before picking one up and taking a big bite. The phone rang.

"Jake wants to see you in the Copa Room," Henry said.

"Now?" she said, swallowing the bite of doughnut.

"Of course, now. Do you remember how to get there from where you are?"

"I'm not too sure where I am," she said, realizing that she had no recollection of the walk from the lounge to this room. "I'll find it."

"Well, make it snappy. Today's not a good day to make Jake wait," he said and hung up.

He doesn't mind making me wait, she thought. She grabbed one of the doughnuts, picked up her pink cashmere sweater and hurried out the door. As she moved through the corridor, the vague memory of the night before terrified her. Jake must think her a real floozy – drinking and smoking and flirting with the men at their table. He had every right to send her home; her father would certainly have disapproved of her behavior. She was still going to beg Jake to let her stay. She liked it there and already felt that Henry was a better friend than any of the kids in Corsicana. But what if she had no choice?

What if she had to go home? She thought about her mother and Bobby and the fact that Barbara would push her to go to college. Henry was wrong. She would simply explain to Jake that she belonged in Vegas and, come hell or high water, she was not going back.

She followed the corridor back toward the casino; the Copa Room should be down from the casino entrance. The lobby was calm and quiet; the air had the scent of something sweet trying to cover the stale smell of cigarettes. She walked past the casino and spotted Eddie, the pit boss, at one of the card tables. He waved and she smiled but kept walking as she swallowed the last bit of the doughnut. She reached the Copa Room, opened the door to an almost dark room and waited for signs that someone else was there. She tied the sweater around her shoulders and paced the area near the door until she heard a noise in the front of the room.

"Is that you, Jake?" she called out, still unable to see him.

"Come down front, please," he said. "The room is closed now so we'll sit down here."

Hassie walked toward the stage until she could see Jake's silhouette, his cigarette smoke caught in a single beam of light at the foot of the stage. As she got closer to him, she imagined a look of disgust or pity on his face, but when she could finally see his eyes, he looked just the way she remembered him the night before.

"Am I late?" she asked.

"How are you feeling today?"

"Fine," she said, sitting down in the chair beside Jake.

"Did you enjoy yourself last night?"

"Uh-huh." She waited for his next question for what felt like ten minutes. When she looked over at him, his eyes were fixed on her; he lightly puffed on his cigarette. "Did I do something wrong?"

She waited again. Why was he staring at her?

"Remember yesterday when I told you that you don't belong here and that you shouldn't have left home?"

"Yeah," she said. "But that was before –"

"I'll talk now, please." His face was stern but his eyes were warm and he stared at her until she blushed and cleared her throat. "I know you came to Vegas because Berman told you he could get you a job singing in the Copa Room. Now that you know he lied, what do you think you're gonna do? That is, if you were to stay here."

"I don't know, Jake. I just don't wanna go back to Texas. I wanna stay here and I'll do anything – you know, I worked at the diner in Corsicana last summer and waited tables when Miss Josephine was on vacation. I did a good job and got good tips."

"I'm sure you did," Jake said, leaning back in his chair. "So you're telling me that you came all the way to Vegas to be a waitress?"

"Well, that's not what I came here to do but –"

"Hassie, I'll say it again. Las Vegas is no place for a young girl like you. Look at yourself. In less than twenty-four hours you managed to get totally smashed, practically made a fool – in fact, do you even remember what happened when we left the lounge last night? I mean, before you got to your room and passed out."

"Not really," she said, wondering how much he really knew about her eventful night after he left her.

"That's what I thought. And so you know, I, and just about every man in that lounge, could have taken you to a room in this hotel and done anything we wanted with you. Is that what you came to Vegas for? Because it looks like you'd be pretty good at it."

Hassie's face reddened; she dug her fingernails into her thighs as she recalled the time her stepfather told her that the way she smiled and touched and befriended people would either make her the best nurse in the world or the best whore.

"Look, sweetheart. Do us all a favor and make your plans to go back to Nowhere-cana, Texas. I'll give you money for a plane ticket."

The bitter taste of chocolate caused saliva to pool in her mouth and for a few seconds, she thought that she would be sick. So Jake *was* going to try to make her leave. She put her hand over her mouth and stared at the floor until she regained her composure and could speak to him. "You took me into that lounge last night and gave me all those cigarettes and champagne and if the truth be known, you probably *paid* all those guys to say nice things to me and to practically kiss my feet. So why didn't you just take me to your room and do whatever it is you wanted to do to me?" She stood up and glared at him. "You win, Mr. Contrata. I'll go back to Texas tomorrow." She started toward the back entrance, then turned to say, "And I don't need your money."

Jake jumped up and grabbed her arm, looked her dead in the eye and said, "Hassie, I'm not trying to upset you. I'd just like for you to really think about what you'd be getting into if you stay in Vegas. It's not a fun fair for kids."

"I know that, Jake." She pulled her arm from his grip. "I'm not totally stupid. But you've already made up your mind and won't even give me a chance."

He took his handkerchief from his pocket and gave it to her, then scratched his head and muttered something under his breath. She wiped her nose but didn't move until he looked at her and said, "Henry told me yesterday that one of the girls here in the Copa Room quit and he's looking for a replacement."

"Are you saying that you'd give me her job?"

He put his hands on his waist and sighed heavily. "I'm talking about being a cocktail waitress – not a flapjack flipper in a small town diner. And most of the waitresses here used to be showgirls so they have a certain – style."

"I can do it, Jake. I promise," she said. "I'll work hard and you'll never regret it if you give me this chance."

He stood still staring at her, his chin toward his chest and his eyes deep with concern. "Something tells me that I *will* regret it, but we'll give it a couple of weeks and see how it goes. Now, go find Henry and tell him the good news. He'll tell you everything you need to know about the job."

"Thank you, thank you, Jake." She shook his hand with a masculine force like she'd seen the guys do in the pool hall. He laughed and held her hand still, then pulled her close enough to kiss her cheek, which sent a chill through her body. "I hope you'll still be thanking me in a few weeks." He looked up as Henry entered the room. "Speak of the devil."

Hassie turned and ran toward him. "Henry, you'll never guess what Jake just did." She took his hand and dragged him towards Jake, who had sat down at the small table and lit a cigarette.

"What's this all about, Jake?" Henry asked, squirming out of Hassie's grip.

"Berman, you wanted to give Hassie a job in the Copa Room?" Jake chuckled at the thought and said, "Well, you just did. You just hired her to fill – who'd you say quit?"

"Ginger," Henry said.

"You just hired Hassie to fill Ginger's space on the floor."

"You mean as a cocktail waitress?"

Jake cocked his forefinger and thumb like a gun in Henry's direction and said, "You got it."

"But, Jake," Henry said, lowering his voice. "You know what it's like to work here as a cocktail waitress. I don't think Hassie has that kind of experience."

Jake looked at Hassie and said, "Tell Henry about your experience."

"I was a waitress at the diner in Corsicana last summer for two whole weeks."

Henry rolled his eyes at Jake and said, "Oh, Lord."

"She'll be fine, Berman," Jake said, stubbing out his cigarette. "Has Ginger left yet?

"No, not yet," Henry said.

"Then get rid of her and give Hassie her bed in the girls' quarters."

Hassie smiled at Jake and said, "I think I should go back to the room and get my stuff together. I left it in sort of a mess."

"That would be an understatement," Henry said and walked toward the door.

"Henry, help her get settled and then I want to see you," Jake said.

Henry kept walking and showed Hassie through the door. She moved quickly ahead of him and then turned back and said, "See, Henry. You were wrong. Isn't it exciting?"

He was still shaking his head and caught up to her. "I hope you still have that little bounce in your step in a couple of weeks."

"You can say whatever you like but you heard what Jake said. I have a job and a room and you know what else? Jake likes me. He likes me and he wants me to do well."

"Man, do you have a lot to learn," Henry said and took hold of her arm. "But it looks like I'm stuck with you and I'm gonna give you your first piece of advice." They stopped at the end of the corridor. "You better rehearse what you're gonna say to Natalie about the condition of her dress."

Hassie looked at him and said, "Why would I want to do that?"

"Because Natalie's one of your new roommates."

chapter four

HASSIE HAD no idea what "getting rid of Ginger" involved but took advantage of the time that Henry needed to organize her new living quarters by making sure that all of her belongings were packed neatly into the suitcase that she had *borrowed* from Barbara's attic. The sight of the hard powder blue bag displaying the letters "B" and "C" next to the metal fasteners made Hassie wince with guilt. It was only a few days ago that she had convinced a boy she knew to drive her to the bus station in Dallas while Barbara attended a family dinner in a nearby town.

In the autumn following Hassie's high school graduation and her summer of working at Charlie Sumter's diner, she became Barbara's assistant in the classes for the little girls who began their lessons at the start of the new school year. Barbara had tried to convince her that she should give college a chance, but Bonita insisted that the money that Jackson had left her wouldn't afford Hassie such a luxury and that she would do best to get a job while she looked for a nice man to marry. Hassie believed that her father's hard-earned money had afforded Bobby a new Ford pickup and a membership at the country club, but when Barbara offered her a job at her school, she gladly accepted and knew that her father's dream for her to go to college was gone.

Although the distance between Corsicana and Angus was only about ten miles, the stretches of time that Hassie stayed at Barbara's house increased to the point that she had essentially moved in, which helped ease the pain of her mother's determination to replace her with Bobby and Travis. Barbara became more like a mother to Hassie, and she chose not to think about what Barbara thought or how she felt when she discovered that Hassie had left. She had to focus on her new life. If she didn't do a good job for Jake, all of her efforts would have been for nothing.

Hassie finished packing the suitcase and took one last look around the room. Henry had instructed her to stay there until he came back to get her. She opened the door to the wardrobe and was greeted by the familiar scent of Natalie's dress, now tainted with the unpleasant odor of the champagne vomit. She took the hanger from the wardrobe and laid the dress on the bed. Henry had promised to get it cleaned and she didn't want him to forget. If she was really going to share a room with Natalie, she was certain to have a confrontation concerning the unhappy scene in the dressing room that first night. If the dress was truly ruined – well, she didn't want to think about the unpleasant consequences.

Henry finally came back to get her and they made a winding journey through the hotel to the back of the property and the building that housed the employees' quarters. He led her into a small suite that would have been nice if she lived in it by herself and left her to settle in. The bedroom was longer than it was wide. Two of the three beds had white linens, one with a pink chenille bedspread, the other loosely covered by a worn out quilt. Both beds looked like someone had just gotten out of them; she was sure they had never been properly made up. The third bed pressed up against the far wall under a nice-sized window, which let in the afternoon sun when she opened the Venetian blind behind the faded floral curtains. A neatly folded set of sheets had been placed in the center of the mattress. She imagined the thick quilted bedspread that she'd left behind in her room at Barbara's house; the soft feel of the rich red satin fabric against her skin as she snuggled deep into the bed's warmth. Where would she ever find such comfort in the midst of this basic room?

Built into the long wall opposite the two other beds was a wardrobe with four doors. She opened the first door to a space full of long dresses and a strong odor dominated by stale smoke. Racks and shelves of clothing and shoes were behind each door; the last one housed a single full-length mink coat and a few ratty looking fur stoles amid the smell of mothballs soaked in cheap perfume. Even if she owned her own glitzy wardrobe, there would be nowhere to hang anything.

She closed the doors and surveyed the room for another place to store her things. A rickety wooden chest of drawers sat at the end of one of the beds. She struggled to open a drawer that was crooked in its slot in the chest to find several pieces of odd clothing including something that looked like a black leather corset with red satin garters dangling from the lace trim, some black fishnet stockings and a small rhinestone purse. She carefully removed them from the drawer and tucked them neatly onto one of the closet shelves, then sat down in the floor to transfer her things out of her suitcase into the empty drawers.

Although it had caused a problem between her parents that Bonita spent so much money shopping, Hassie loved her mother's keen eye for fashion and her need to change out her wardrobe every few months. That and the fact that she and her mother were about the same size meant that she had managed to accumulate half a dozen light cashmere sweaters in the popular pastel colors that she alternated with her dungarees or capri pants and a couple of skirts. She shook the wrinkles out of a solid navy blue sheath dress, which reminded her that she'd had to leave her best dress and underclothes in the dressing room in the Copa Room. She laid the dress on the bed until she could find a place to hang it and placed the neatly folded clothes in the drawer, scrunching them together to make room for her bras, cotton underpants and lemon yellow nylon pajamas.

Tucked safely in the side pocket of the suitcase was a small chiffon scarf that her father had given her. It was soft and light, covered in a pattern of fuchsia and red flowers with shades of green leaves and a royal blue border. She held the scarf next to her cheek, remembering the day that he'd come home from work before dinnertime. Since he'd returned from Korea that summer, he worked fewer hours and, although this should have made her mother happy, she was in a terrible state most of the time. She didn't go to the beauty parlor or care how she looked. She'd gained weight and spent most of her day crying and laying on the sofa, sipping Coca-Cola and eating saltine crackers. The kids at school were talking about Hassie behind her back more than usual and, despite her mother's argument to the contrary, Hassie knew something was wrong.

When Jackson gave Hassie the scarf, she told him that Carol had said that her mother was going to have a baby. Hassie wanted to know if this was why her mother was sick and miserable, because wasn't having a new baby what she'd always wanted? Jackson told her not to worry about her mother, and that, yes, it was true, sometime after Christmas she would get a new baby brother or sister. In February the following year, Travis Calhoun was born – a tiny baby with light, almost white wisps of hair and bright pink skin.

It wasn't until Hassie's father died and Bobby Suskind started hanging around their house and spending time with Travis that she started to understand why her father had been so sad when Travis was born – why he rarely held him or comforted him when he cried. She would always believe that Jackson's heart attack had actually been a broken heart, and that her mother and Bobby were totally to blame and another reason that she could not remain at home in Corsicana. She wiped the tears from her eyes with the scarf, then folded it into a neat little square and laid it in the top of the drawer.

"Can I help you with something?"

Hassie jumped at the strange voice and turned around to see a tall attractive woman with strawberry blond hair. "Sorry. I just moved into this room." She picked up the navy blue dress and carefully folded it in half.

"You must be Cassie," the woman said and sat down on one of the beds.

"It's Hassie. Hassie Calhoun." She placed the folded dress on top of her other clothes in the drawer and closed it.

"I'm Stella – the other roommate."

Hassie nodded. "I met Natalie last night."

"She told me." Stella smiled and stared at her. "Are you still in high school, honey?"

Hassie picked up her purse and walked to the door. "It's nice to meet you, Stella. I've gotta go see Henry now."

"Bye-bye," Stella said without expression.

Hassie slipped inside the entrance to the Copa Room, which always seemed to be dark, as if someone was trying to hide something. Henry's broom closet of an office was on the side opposite the dressing room. Light seeped under the door; she lightly knocked before walking into a room where the walls were covered with photographs of showgirls in huge feathered headdresses with long slender legs and tiny waists. There was also a picture of Sinatra, dressed like a character from the story of Aladdin, surrounded by beautiful girls in similar outfits like he was the king and they were his harem of princesses.

"Afternoon," Henry said as he opened the door. "Sorry I wasn't here. I just stepped out for a routine check of things. You been here long?"

"Just a few minutes." She stared at the photo of Sinatra and imagined herself in one of the soft, flowing outfits, sitting at his feet and waiting for him to notice her.

"All settled into your room now?" He laid a pair of glasses on his desk, then shed his jacket and rolled up his sleeves.

"I suppose so," she said.

"I know you've met Natalie, but your other roommate is a woman named Stella. I'll introduce you to her when I see her."

"We've met."

"She's a pretty good egg," Henry said. "And probably glad to see a new roommate. She didn't get on with Ginger particularly well, but Natalie and Ginger – they were best friends. Two peas in a pod, if you ask me –"

"Henry, can we not talk about Natalie and get on with my training?"

"Okay, okay. By the way, I don't think you should work the floor tonight so just relax. I'll take you through everything you need to know, fit you for a uniform and then I think you should just observe the other girls."

"Is Mr. Sinatra singing tonight?" she asked.

"He sure is," Henry said. "The musicians will be coming in to run through tonight's repertoire in a little while. I'll introduce you to everybody later."

"So Mr. Sinatra does a show every night?"

"He usually does at least one show and sometimes two. But he's gotta take a night off here and there and sometimes he pops off to LA or Palm Springs for a few days. And then there's the occasional night that there's not a big enough audience to warrant opening up the room."

"That really happens?"

"Not often, but it's happened a few times. Anyway, for now, we're expecting packed houses, so come with me. I'll show you the service areas. Do you know the difference between a Gibson and a Gimlet?"

"Of course, I do. One has a sort of – One has – Oh, you know." She practically ran to keep up with him.

Henry smiled and barked some orders about the house lights to a couple of guys hanging around the stage. Within a few minutes, the room brightened with the light from four large chandeliers that looked like giant wagon wheels pressed into the rich green ceiling; Henry rearranged some of the tables and chairs. Hassie followed him around the room while he explained the bar and food service areas and then into the dressing room where her evening with Jake had begun. She could identify where each of the other girls sat by the bits of their own lives that were either taped or pinned to the frames of their mirrors. Several had photographs of young children or primitive crayon drawings. Others displayed signed photos of famous people who had probably worked in the Copa Room. She was glad when Henry assigned her an empty spot at the end of one of the rows. The absence of photos or other memorabilia from home would be less noticeable until she had a chance to meet somebody famous. Her shirtwaist dress and other things, piled neatly on the table, reminded her of the look on Natalie's face when Jake forced her to take off her dress and give it to Hassie. She was caught for a moment in the dreaded repeat of that scene when she heard the sharp tone of Henry's voice.

"Are you listening to me?" he said. She nodded as he continued, "You'll need to get your own makeup. If you need help, ask Dotty. She can be a bit of a bossy cow but she knows her way around Vegas better than anyone."

"So where are these uniforms you were talking about?"

He motioned for her to follow him to a wide, deep closet at the far end of the room. "If you ask me, these girls all came out of the same rubber mold." He shuffled through the few pieces and pulled out a short, black, satin skirt with layers of net crinoline attached. "Try this one."

Hassie unzipped her pants and started to push them down her hips when she realized that Henry was staring at her legs. She held the unzipped opening closed with one hand and said, "Do you have to stand there and gawk?"

Henry laughed and said, "Honey, I've seen every woman that's ever worked in this place stark naked a hundred times and never once got a hard-on."

With her face burning, she let the pants drop to the floor, then stepped into the skirt, pulled it up to her waist and buttoned it easily. "It fits just fine."

"Good." He placed his hands on Hassie's sweater over her breasts like the cups of a bra. "I think you're about the same size as Dixie," he said, then motioned for her to remove her sweater and handed her a blouse off a coat hanger. "Try this on."

She could tell by the way Henry held her breasts that he didn't care a thing about her body as a woman. And it appeared that taking your clothes off in front of men was pretty normal around there. She buttoned Dixie's blouse while looking in the mirror. "Are you sure this is the right size? There's an awful lot showing," she said and tugged the scooped neck higher on her chest as she thought of big-bosomed Sheila in the Regency Lounge.

"Come on," he said, removing her hands and adjusting the fit. "This is the way it's supposed to be. You gotta show a little tit."

"A little would be okay," she said. "This is showing a lot."

"I hate to tell you but you ain't got that much to show," he said and closed the closet door. "Now, talk to Dotty about tights and shoes. You'll need to get your own."

Hassie dismissed Henry's comment about the blouse and changed back into her own shirt and pants before asking, "Where do I keep my uniform?"

"Find your own space," he said, walking toward the dressing room door. "You're gonna have to figure out some things for yourself."

They walked back out into the main room; a few guys clustered around the piano on the stage. A tall, lanky black man with a wide, white smile faced their direction. His toasty, brown face reminded her of home; a 'good ole soul', her father would have said.

"Hey, guys," Henry shouted. "We've got a new girl. Come say hello."

Two of the three men moved away from the piano while Henry pulled Hassie up to join them.

"This is Hassie Calhoun," Henry said. "I met Hassie in Texas and she's going to work with us for a while."

The black man stood up and reached out to her. "Hi, Hassie. My name's William Tooting, but everybody calls me Toots. It's real nice to meet you."

Hassie shook his hand and said, "You, too."

"Toots plays a mean saxophone," Henry added. "And a couple other horns every now and then. Right, Toots?"

"That's right, Henry," he said with a light chuckle.

"Hey, Chad," Henry shouted to a stocky, bearded man walking to the back of the stage. Chad sat down behind a double bass, waved and then began plucking softly on the strings like nobody else was in the room.

Henry waved and led Hassie toward the piano. "Bass player," he whispered. "Kinda moody."

When they reached the piano, a strikingly handsome man with piercing, dark eyes and a head of curly, black hair was sifting through sheets of music and humming. Henry waited to make eye contact before speaking like he was interrupting Liberace.

The man at the keyboard finally looked up.

"This is Julio," Henry said. "Julio's Mr. Sinatra's right arm in the Copa Room."

Julio stuck out his hand and said, "Nice to meet you. Henry tells me that you're a singer."

Hassie smiled and took his hand, which was soft, his handshake tentative like he was protecting his fingers. She nodded and stood next to the piano as if someone else was supposed to tell her what to say.

Julio appeared to ignore her and played the introduction to something she was sure was part of Sinatra's show, then said, "What do you like to sing?"

"Now's probably not the best time to get into the music," Henry said and reached for Hassie's arm.

"Why?" Julio said. "If she has such a great talent, we should hear it. Don't you guys agree?"

Hassie looked at Henry and knew that she should walk away. Chad drummed his fingers on his double bass and Julio stared at her. Toots startled her with a riff on his saxophone; the only song that came to her mind at that moment was "God Bless America". She began the first line, and then looked at Julio for support. He started to play with her on the second line; Chad eventually joined them with a simple bass line. She got through the whole song, but her hands were cold and shaky and she wished she could go out and come back in again.

"Not bad," Toots said, applauding lightly. "That's a tough song to sing."

"Okay, so you can sing. Why don't you come back up when you've learned some real songs," Julio said. "I'm sure you can do better than 'God Bless America'."

Hassie felt her face redden and looked at Henry. "I do know some other songs and I like to write –"

"By the way," Julio interrupted. "Henry talks like we're the only musicians in this gig but there's quite a few more of us."

"Yeah, but we're the only ones that matter," Toots said.

The guys laughed; Hassie noticed that Henry wasn't smiling. He had taken a step backwards from the piano and had the unhappy look of a child who had been scolded for something he didn't do. He stood back while she chatted with Julio and Toots for a few minutes, then grabbed her arm and said, "That's it for now. Let's go."

He pulled her along like she was two years old. She tripped over one of the chairs and glared after him as she broke free of his grip and stopped while he charged through the door of his office and slammed it shut. Within seconds, the door opened with a jerk and he shouted, "Get in here!"

She walked into the cramped space and stood in front of the door, leaving it ajar.

"I've changed my mind," he said. He leaned on the edge of his desk over a pile of papers. "You're gonna work tonight. We've got a full house and the other girls moan their tits off when they have to cover an extra section."

She stood still until he looked at her and said, "So what are you standing there for? Go get yourself sorted and be back here at six o'clock."

She wanted to ask a question and then thought better of it and headed for the back entrance. Hassie had promised Jake that he'd never regret hiring her. Fat chance of that happening unless she found Dotty or somebody to help her. She pulled the entry door open and walked right into Jake, and then stepped aside for him to enter.

"Where are you going in such a hurry?" He walked deeper into the room, put his hands on his hips and gave a sweeping look around, his eyes resting back on Hassie.

"I need to find Dotty," Hassie said. She thought he looked very handsome, dressed casually in a light blue shirt without a jacket or tie, and noticed, for the first time, that his nose was a little bit crooked like it might have been broken and didn't quite heal properly.

"What for?"

"I need her to help me get some makeup and other stuff for work."

Jake walked closer to her and said, "For work where?"

"Here, Jake," she said. "You know. You gave me a job here?"

"Berman!" Jake shouted and took off in huge strides that left her scurrying to catch him. He pounded his fist on Henry's door and then walked in and closed it behind him. Hassie need not be inside the office to hear them.

"What the fuck is going on?" Jake asked and didn't wait for an answer. "She says you told her to work the floor tonight."

"We need extra help, Jake. Ginger's gone and –"

"I told you that your only job is to teach her the ropes. What about that statement do you not understand?"

"She knows the ropes, Jake. She's smart and quick and, anyway, it doesn't take a genius to do this job."

"Forget about it. She's not working in this room until I say so. You got that?"

Jake exited the office the same way he went in. He glanced at Hassie but kept walking. She felt weak and unsteady, sat down at the nearest table and waited for Henry to come back out, which he did a minute later. His face was splotchy like he'd had some kind of allergic reaction and his armpits were soaked. The sight of him in that state frightened her, but she waited for him to make a move.

"You heard the man," he said. He wouldn't look at her.

She stood up but didn't speak.

"Get outta here and wait for his highness to tell you when to show up for work."

Henry went back into his office and closed the door. She surveyed the room again and noticed the arrival of a few more musicians before realizing that she was only a few yards away from the stage that Frank Sinatra stood on every night. The brief moment with the musicians was enough to encourage her to convince Jake that, one way or another, she belonged in the Copa Room. She would work as a waitress and she would work hard. But she would also sing on that stage. Of that, she had absolutely no doubt.

chapter five

HASSIE OPENED the window over her bed, allowing in the cool desert breeze, which helped to eliminate an underlying odor of stale perfume and musty dirt that reminded her of an old storage space in their attic at home. The open window was never a problem for her roommates since Stella came in well after she did and Natalie usually came in to sleep after Hassie had gone out for breakfast. Her main contact with the girls was in the Copa Room where she continued to hang out and observe. But, despite her eagerness to go to work, she dared not push Henry after the scene with Jake a few days earlier and she patiently stayed out of everyone's way.

She undressed and smoothed the wrinkles out of the soft woolen skirt before hanging it in the wardrobe. When she opened the door at the end that she had successfully occupied without antagonizing the other girls, she found Natalie's dress, clean and fresh with no evidence of the abuse that Hassie had recently inflicted. Evidently, Henry's careful attention to the dress had paid off and she placed it back in the section of the wardrobe that held all of the other evening clothes. She closed the door with relief that the entire incident was behind her, but she didn't kid herself by thinking that this would make everything peachy with Natalie, who had already let it be known that she wasn't interested in a word Hassie had to say. Stella had also warned her that Natalie held some sort of claim on Jake and that Hassie would be wise to stay away from him.

As she readied herself for bed, she wondered how long Henry –

or Jake – would make her observe the other girls before she could go to work. Although the room and meals were part of the job, she had yet to do anything to earn the money that she needed to buy her own stockings and makeup and would have to make do with the secondhand things she found in the dressing room. All she really cared about was spending time in the Copa Room while Julio or any of the musicians were there. Sometimes she hovered in Henry's office until he grew tired of her and would send her on some useless errand where she'd end up back in the Copa Room, sit quietly and listen to their rehearsal sessions, fantasizing about the day that Julio would call her up on the stage to sing with them. She'd taken his advice and would be ready to sing one of the *real* songs that she knew – something like "I Get a Kick Out of You" or "I'll be Lovin' You, Always," which was one of her daddy's favorites and the one to which he'd taught her to waltz. All she needed was a chance. A chance to work and show Jake how good a job she could do, and a chance to sing somewhere besides the shower.

Toward the end of her first week at the Sands, Henry called her into his office and told her that they needed her on the floor that night and that she should ask Dotty to take her to have her hair and nails done. She was surprised at how little Henry actually said and sensed that he was still opposed to the idea. But she hadn't seen Jake for days and decided to take Stella's advice to just do the job as she'd been instructed and keep her thoughts and opinions to herself, including her not-so-subtle hints that she wanted to meet Sinatra.

The Copa Room was closed to outsiders during Frank's rehearsals with the band and he rarely hung around after the shows. But she'd heard some of the girls talk about him and more or less brag about the time they'd spent with him in his grand suite, which had its own swimming pool. Some of the conversations made her uneasy, like she was finding out that Jesus kept a bunch of women in a cave. But, mostly, she wondered what she would say when she met him; what it would be like to touch him or kiss him. She felt her face get warm and rushed out to meet Dotty.

The job proved harder than expected; most nights it seemed that every man in the room felt at liberty to put his hands on her. But her naturally friendly nature made it easy for her to smile and chat amiably with her customers, which soon started to pay off in the way of big tips. She also noticed that Jake usually came in at some point during her shift and parked himself at his table in the back of the room. Then one night a few weeks later, he had already occupied his table when the band started their trademark rendition of "Old Black Magic," announcing Frank's arrival on stage.

The first time she heard Julio's introduction of the man, she got goose bumps up and down her arms and thought it was really classy. Now, it just sounded corny, but the audience loved his big entrance and cheered like they'd arrived in heaven and he was the good Lord Almighty. However, Hassie loved to watch him perform, croon through his old standards and make the women in the room squeal during the applause. One night a woman gave him her panties at the end of the show, which he put to his lips and then stuffed in his pocket.

After she came on shift one night, she noticed that Jake sat at his usual table with two men she'd never seen. One was big like Jimmy the doorman, and wore a hat despite the fact that they were indoors. The other man was even bigger, almost completely bald and had the look of someone with a lot of authority, like the oil and cattle men she'd met during her stint in Charlie's diner. Stella worked Jake's table. The big, bald guy seemed to know her very well and kept his hand firmly attached to her butt. A bottle of Jim Beam sat in the middle of the table and they all smoked cigars.

There was a convention of tool salesmen in town that week, and it felt like every one of the attendees was in the Copa Room that night. Sinatra wowed them and they got drunk and sloppy until the lights came up and Hassie could close out their tabs and send them on their way. She was headed to the dressing room when Jake shouted for her to come over to his table. She pretended that she didn't hear him but when he shouted louder, she took a big breath and walked to the back of the room.

Jake stood up, put his arm around her shoulder, pointed her toward the big man and said, "Hassie Calhoun, I'd like for you to meet my boss and good friend, Sid Casper." Jake kissed her on the cheek and pulled her down into his lap. "Sid's visiting from New York."

Hassie forced a smile for the man and then tried to stand up, but Jake gripped her thigh until it was almost painful.

"Well, Cassie." Sid said. "Aren't you a little beauty."

Jake patted her thigh and said, "Hassie came to Vegas from Texas a few weeks ago with stars in her eyes. She wants to sing with Sinatra."

Sid reared back to laugh and then blew a mouthful of cigar smoke in Hassie's face. "You don't say." He laughed again. "Whatever gave her that idea?"

"Henry gave her the idea," Jake said.

"Henry who?"

"Henry Berman."

"You mean Freidman's queer nephew?" Sid blew smoke in Hassie's face again. "That's the funniest thing I ever heard. Ain't it, Benny?"

The man with the hat nodded and gave Sid a sign that said he agreed.

"What does Frank say?" Sid asked, his eyes fixed on Hassie.

"Nothing," Jake said.

After a moment of silence, all three men laughed. Hassie's face grew hot with humiliation. She forced herself out of Jake's lap, then looked at him and said, "Can I go now?"

Sid took hold of her arm at her wrist, gazed up at her and said, "You know, Jake, this little lady looks like trouble to me."

"Everybody's trouble for you, Sid," Jake replied.

"No, I'm serious. This one's definitely trouble." He stared at her a bit longer, and then looked at Jake and said, "By the way, what's her goin' rate? She's a little skinny but the face is –"

Jake stood up, pushed Hassie aside and grabbed Sid's tie at his throat. "She's just a kid who ran away from home, you fucking ape."

Hassie took a step back just as Sid grabbed hold of Jake's forearm and pulled it away from his tie. No one said a word while he stared at Jake with a tightly clenched jaw. He finally let go of Jake's arm, straightened his tie and said, "Like I was sayin', she looks like delicious trouble. What's her goin' rate?"

Hassie ran from the table and almost fell over her own feet trying to get to the dressing room. She kicked off her shoes and wiped the residue of lipstick off with a tissue, then looked into her mirror and saw Jake walking up behind her. She grabbed the edge of the table and let her head drop; tears fell onto the surface and she wiped her nose with the dirty tissue.

"Hassie, listen to me," Jake said. "Sid's a disgusting animal with shit for brains sometimes."

She didn't look at him and started to cry.

"But he's my boss. Hell, he's everybody's boss. And he's not called 'The T-Rex' for nothing."

Hassie turned around to face him but her chin fell to her chest as she leaned back on the table. "He thinks I'm a prostitute."

Jake took a few steps closer to her, lifted her chin and said, "I warned you that you didn't know what you're getting into, didn't I?"

She picked up another tissue and blew her nose. "Everything's been going just fine, Jake."

He took hold of her arm. "Look, we need to talk. Will you come with me to some place quiet, away from drunks and assholes?"

He seemed sober, but she didn't trust being alone with him. "Can't you just say what you need to say here?"

"I'd rather not. These walls have eyes and ears. Come with me to my suite. I'll order some coffee and I swear on my father's grave, I won't touch you."

His eyes told her that he was sorry; that he would just talk to her. "Okay," she said softly and turned away from him. "I'll change and be there in a few minutes."

She sat down on the stool, looked in the mirror and blew her nose again. Thick black streaks ran down her face and she'd smeared her lipstick on her chin. Her eyes welled full of tears; she put her head in her hands and sobbed. For the first time since she'd arrived at the Sands, she understood how Barbara must feel about her disappearance from Corsicana and was glad that Barbara had no idea of her whereabouts.

Jake's suite was a large, sprawling space with a scattering of low lamp light and a wall of deep gold draperies that made the room feel dark and mysterious. The décor was plush and masculine with rich, dark furniture and fabrics of deep red with black and gold accents – nothing like the sky blue and pale yellow room she'd stayed in that first night, or anything else she'd seen in the hotel for that matter.

Jake poured coffee into one of the cups followed by a dollop of cream from the silver pitcher. "Are you sure you don't want anything?" he asked. "There's some soda and juice in the fridge. Or something stronger, if you want."

"I'm fine right now," she said. "What happened to Sid?"

"He's a big boy and can take care of himself." Jake sat in the armchair and put his cup on the coffee table, whirled his spoon around the coffee for a few seconds, and then looked at her, saying, "Sit down."

She hadn't really talked to him since she started working in the Copa Room and sensed something different in his attitude toward her. She sat on the sofa and waited for him to speak.

"I don't know what's happened," he finally said.

"What do you mean?"

"I'm a belligerent bastard by nature. I run hard and fast and usually don't give a crap about anybody or anything as long as I get my way. I use people and God knows I use women – like all men use women. For pleasure. And I don't let emotion figure into it."

"Jake, why are you telling me this?"

He leaned over to rest his elbows on his knees, stared at the floor and then looked up. "The Jake Contrata I know would have had you in bed that first night and every night after that until he got tired of you or put you on that bus back to Texas. *That* Jake wouldn't care that you were seventeen years old and that he was taking advantage of your youth." He sipped the coffee, then stood up and walked away from her. "The Copa Girls who turned cocktail waitresses are hookers and make way more money for the hotel selling their bodies than they ever make serving drinks. By letting you work in the Copa Room, I was making you one of those girls. Big deal, huh." He turned to face her. "You are so young and so stupid to think that you can play in this arena. I let you think that you could work here like you worked in a two-bit diner and – worse than that – I decided that I would protect you."

He sat back down in the chair and lit a cigarette. "Look. It's not easy for me to say I'm wrong. I'm not sure what's going on here but I really don't want you to get hurt and I'm gonna do both of us a favor and put you on the first plane out to Dallas tomorrow. We'll get you home from there. You can tell you mother whatever you want and I'll back your story."

"I'm not going home," she said and walked over to the fridge, pulled out bottles of Coca-Cola and orange juice, studied both of them, put the cola back and closed the door. She opened the orange juice, poured it into a glass and walked back to the sofa. "I want to stay and work in the Copa Room and if I have to be a hooker, so be it." She sat down beside him and crossed her legs while sipping the juice without looking at him.

"Hassie, I –"

"Remember after that first night in the lounge when you told me that you thought I'd be quite good at going off with the men – letting them do whatever they wanted? Why don't I give it a try?" She looked over at Jake who was staring at her like she'd accused him of rape, then smiled and said, "Would that make you or Henry my pimp?"

He stifled a smile and said, "What do you know about pimps?"

"Is there a sign above my head that says 'Ignorant Hick from Texas'?"

"Not exactly," he said and exhaled smoke. "But I don't think you know as much as you think you do, and I'm not going to let you make a mistake that you'll regret for the rest of your life."

"Is there a rule that says if you work in the Copa Room you have to be a hooker?" she asked and sat down.

"It's an unwritten rule, Hassie. Part of the wicked world of Vegas and life at the Sands."

"So I can work there and just serve drinks?"

"Yeeees, in theory."

"Then that's what I'm gonna do, but I don't want you to watch over me like a German shepherd," she said. "I can take care of myself, and I don't have any problem saying no to the likes of Sid Casper."

"I'm already breaking every law in the state of Nevada by even letting you in this place. What if some drunk guy goes for you and gets pissed off when you turn him down and then suspects that you're underage and decides he wants to make trouble. You know, it's bound to happen one day, and I could be in deep shit. Do you think I should take that risk?"

She finished her juice and reached for the pack of cigarettes, which he took from her and said, "You know you don't want that so stop pretending that you do."

She had a way of smiling with just one side of her mouth. She used this when she looked at him, and then sat back in the seat. "I'll be eighteen in a couple of weeks."

"Legally, you need to be twenty-one." He ground out his cigarette and assumed the position where his elbows rested on his knees and he looked at the floor.

"I happen to know that there's more than one girl here who's not twenty-one."

He reacted like he'd been shot, then leaned back in the chair and just looked at her. "So what do want me to say?"

"That I can carry on working in the Copa Room as a cocktail waitress and that you'll let me prove to you that I can handle myself in this *wicked* world."

"I don't think you know what you're talking about, but if you want to take the job on an equal playing field with the other girls – it might be fine but it also might be a tough lesson to learn." He shook his head and stood up. "Okay. You're on your own."

She stood up from the sofa. "I've got Henry."

"Henry's help and a nickel will get you a bad cup of coffee." He reached out to her and said, "Come here."

She hesitated a few seconds, then moved closer to him until he grabbed her and pulled her tight against his chest where his spicy scent was tainted ever so slightly by the smell of Sid's cigars. His breathing was shallow and she could feel his heartbeat. In a sudden move, he kissed her, but their mouths didn't hit just right. She pictured Natalie standing there in his arms and took his face in her hands and guided his lips to hers. He held her tight and kissed her slowly and luxuriously, parting her lips and teeth with his tongue. He kissed her again and again until she became restless and pulled out of his arms.

"I better be going now," she said; she could feel that her face was flushed. His penis was hard against her stomach like those times when Bobby would corner her and rub up against her while he tried to kiss her or stick his tongue in her ear, then tell her that he was just "joshing" with her and slap her on her butt.

Jake loosened the embrace and pushed a tendril of hair away from her eyes. "I've kept you out very late," he said. "Are you gonna be okay?"

"You don't have to worry about me, Jake. I'll be just fine."

They walked to the door. He opened it and put his hand on her shoulder; she turned to him and said, "See ya tomorrow?"

"That you will," he said and backed away. "And, by the way, Sid's not really a bad guy. That was mostly the booze talking tonight."

"Oh, yeah?" she said. "I still think I'll keep my distance, if you don't mind."

"If I were you, I'd get to know him – in broad daylight. He's very important in our company." He nodded his head slowly and repeated, "Very important. I'm sure he knows he upset you so if he tries to apologize, let him. It's much wiser to have him as a friend than an enemy."

She nodded and smiled and walked out the door, her lips still feeling the warmth of Jake's mouth. Had she been silly to pull away from him just because his closeness brought back her disgusting feelings about Bobby, who had no right to touch her or kiss her? Jake wasn't trying to hurt her. She believed that he was just trying to protect her and had all but admitted that he had put his own selfish motives on hold for her sake. At least he'd agreed to let her stay at the Sands.

She strolled through the corridor back towards her room, past the Copa Room and casino. Julio sat behind the piano in the lobby bar, tinkling through requests from a group of women who had apparently been deserted by their men. Hassie stopped for a minute and listened to Julio's sultry rendition of "The Shadow of Your Smile" with one of the women slurring through an off-key attempt at the vocal.

Watching Julio play made her think of her own piano, though just a basic upright – nothing like the baby grand he was playing. She missed the afternoons when she was home after school, supposedly practicing her lessons, and would play her favorite songs and work on her own melodies. She wasn't as good as Julio, but if she ever got the chance to sit with him, she'd tell him about the songs she'd written – maybe even get some advice from him.

She started to walk away just as Julio spotted her and motioned with his head for her to join them. She walked over and stood at the end of the piano as he started to play "I've Got You Under My Skin." He smiled and mouthed for her to sing along, which turned out to be a solo when none of the tipsy women could recall the lyrics. She moved closer to the keyboard and sang like she was performing on the big stage while Julio embellished the accompaniment to match her jazzy style. When they reached the end of the song, the small group of onlookers applauded and cheered while Julio offered her a mock salute. She smiled good night to Julio; the thrill of singing with him boosted her energy and she carried on to her room.

Her legs ached. She walked down the long corridor that emptied into the back of the property and the building that housed the employees' quarters. Despite Sid's crass treatment of her, the night had been one of interesting surprises. As she walked into her empty room, she was glad for the space on her own and cracked open the window.

She shed her clothes and put on her pajamas, then sat on her bed with her purse. She yawned and considered going straight to sleep but forced herself to focus on her nightly ritual of counting her earnings, flicking the crisp new bills that would have come from the casino and then stowing them safely in her father's sock. If Jake was right and she was so stupid, then how did she end up with a job in less than a week of stepping off that bus, making more money than she'd ever dreamed of? She had grown up in a fairly well protected environment, where between her home, school and her classes with Barbara, someone was always telling her what to do. Now, where nothing seemed to be weighing her down, she was discovering that she had a strong instinct for survival – something that her mother would never appreciate and her father would never see. Most of all, Jake had treated her like a grown woman and had admitted and even shown her that he had feelings for her. When would she admit that she had feelings for him? And when would she show him?

chapter SIX

THE COFFEE SHOP at the Sands reminded Hassie of Charlie Sumter's diner in Corsicana except that the colorful, upholstered chairs in the coffee shop were a lot nicer than the well-worn chrome and dull red vinyl ones at Charlie's. And the coffee cups were elegant ivory china, not the hard pale green plastic mugs with coffee stained bottoms. She loved to sit there in the morning with her coffee and breakfast of toast and strawberry jam; sometimes a jelly doughnut, but she'd mostly given them up when her Copa Room skirt started to pinch at her waist.

Henry usually came in for his mid-morning coffee break while she was finishing her breakfast and they'd mull over the latest gossip or news of a new act coming to Vegas. After Sid Casper's crude reference to Henry being somebody's "queer nephew," she'd been looking for an opportunity to ask Stella, what Sid thought was queer about Henry. As she dug around her purse for a tip to leave the waitress, Stella walked through the coffee shop entrance. Hassie raised her hand and waved her over to the table.

"Want some coffee?" she asked as Stella slid into the booth. She'd always thought that Stella had the most amazing eyes. They were big and bright and a beautiful shade of brown that perfectly complemented her strawberry blonde hair.

"Yeah, but I only have a few minutes."

Hassie caught the attention of the waitress behind the counter and lifted her cup. The waitress smiled and nodded. She turned back to Stella and said, "Whatcha been up to? We haven't really had a chance to talk for days."

"Yeah. Been pretty busy."

The waitress set a cup and saucer in front of Stella and filled both cups.

Hassie slowly stirred two spoonfuls of sugar into her coffee and said, "Can I ask you something? And promise you won't laugh at me."

Stella nodded and sipped her coffee.

"Why would anyone refer to Henry as someone's queer nephew?"

Stella's coffee went down wrong and she sputtered and coughed into her white paper napkin.

"Are you okay?"

Stella nodded. "Are you asking me what a queer is?"

"I guess so."

"Haven't you ever heard of two men being queer? Homosexuals? Fruits? Dandy Andys?"

Hassie giggled nervously and shook her head.

Stella sat back in her seat and chuckled. "You really are from the sticks aren't you, Pocahontas?"

"Come on, Stella. You said you wouldn't laugh. What does it mean?"

"A queer – homosexual – is a man who prefers sex with another man than with a woman."

Hassie's face got warm as she considered what Stella was saying. She sipped her coffee, then looked at Stella and said, "How? I mean, how do they do that?"

"You mean have sex? How do you think? They've got mouths and hands and asses –"

"Stella!" Hassie whispered a shriek as the picture became clear. "You mean they actually do it there?" She felt her sphincter tighten and was annoyed that Stella was so amused.

"I don't buy this innocent act of yours," Stella said and laughed again. "Anyway, who said that Henry is queer?"

"Sid Casper," Hassie replied. "By the way, how well do you know Sid?"

"Why do you ask?"

"I met him with Jake a few days ago and let's just say that our first meeting was something I'd like to forget."

"You know who he is, right?" Stella asked.

"Jake told me that he's one of the big bosses from New York

and is very important in their company. But he seemed to be very friendly with you that first night. Is he one of your –" She paused in search of the right word. "Customers?"

"What do you mean is Sid one of my customers?"

"I just wondered if Sid was one of your regular guys when he's in Vegas."

Stella swallowed a sip of coffee and said, "I don't know Sid in – that way. He likes the French girls at the Tropicana." She studied Hassie for a few seconds. "What do you really want to know?"

"Somebody told me that the cocktail waitresses in the Copa Room now used to be Copa Girls."

"Yeah, so what?"

"And that the Copa Girls were also house prostitutes."

Stella moved uncomfortably in the seat and placed both hands around her coffee cup. "So you're saying that the girls working in the Copa Room as cocktail waitresses – except you, of course – are hookers."

"It's no big deal, Stella. I just wanted you to know that I know all this stuff – that I know where you are every night until the wee hours and that you don't have to treat me like an innocent child."

"Hassie, nobody thinks you're an innocent child," Stella said. "How can you be sleeping with Jake and be an innocent child?"

"Who says I'm sleeping with Jake?" she replied, trying not to look alarmed.

"Why else would you not be working the Copa Room like the rest of us? Sorry to tell you this, but most of the girls know what it's like to be the new girl and number one on Jake's list."

Hassie felt her face flush and pulled her scarf up around her neck.

"Why do you think Natalie despises you so much?" Stella asked. "She thought she had something special with Jake, plus she thinks she's in love with him or something. And then you showed up and he started acting strange and doesn't want anything to do with her now."

"I had no idea," Hassie said. "But, Stella, I'm not sleeping with Jake. We're just friends."

Stella laughed and motioned for the waitress. "He's just guarding your every move because he's such a nice guy?"

"We're just friends," Hassie said as the waitress deposited the check on the table.

"Whatever you say. But, if I believe you, how much you wanna bet that Jake will be in your pants before the end of the month?"

The urge for Jake to touch her tugged at Hassie's groin. She shrugged and said, "I don't know."

"I bet you a hundred dollars." Stella threw a dollar bill on top of the check and stood up. "One. Hundred. Dollars."

Hassie shook her head and watched Stella walk away. She sat alone for a while longer, thinking about her last conversation with Jake, then touched her fingers to her lips at the thought of the softness of his slow, sweet kisses and how he smelled and how he held her. And, suddenly, it was okay that he wanted to do more than just kiss her. After all, he had told her how much he cared about her, just like Bobby did the night after her high school graduation party that she was only allowed to attend if Bobby drove her home. But when he arrived and she told him she didn't want to ride with him because he'd had too many beers, he'd grabbed her arm and pushed her into the front of the pickup truck. About halfway between the party and home, he'd pulled off the road onto a dirt track between two fields of crops. When she'd ask where he was going, he'd told her that he was taking her to Candyland and that she was going to love it there. He'd stopped the truck and turned off the ignition and before she knew what was happening, he'd grabbed her and tugged at the buttons on her dress. When she'd resisted and shouted at him, he took hold of both of her hands and pushed her down in the seat. His weight and strength had been too much for her and his body anchored her legs so that he could hold her down with one hand while he pulled her skirt up and forced her panties down around her knees. She'd continued to fight and scream as he fumbled with his belt buckle and cursed at her to be quiet. But she'd screamed louder and longer and eventually worked one of her legs out from under him. When she'd kicked him in the chest, he fell back from her and she sat up, pulling up her panties as she tried to open the door. He'd grabbed her arm, breathing heavily as he sat behind the wheel, staring out into the night. She'd stayed quiet, waiting for him to speak. After a few minutes, he'd started the engine, looked at her and said, "If you ever tell your mother anything about this, I'll kill you."

She moved uncomfortably in the booth with the dreadful memory and wished that dealing with men didn't have to be so complicated.

But what if Stella was right? What if Jake just wanted to add her to his list of women and he actually didn't care about her? And what was this business about Natalie and Jake? She didn't really understand all of what Stella had said but she was determined to show Jake that she could handle herself as an adult. Maybe she should tell him about the things that Bobby did to her. At least then he would know that she wasn't completely ignorant of things to do with sex, even if she was still a virgin.

On the evening of November 27, Hassie arrived at Henry's door an hour before time to start work. She started to knock but when she heard him on the telephone, she pushed the door open and stuck her head in. He motioned for her to enter with a manic flick of his wrist and finished his call within a few seconds.

"What are you doing here so early?"

"Does anybody know that tomorrow is Thanksgiving?" she asked as she sat down.

"Of course, honey. Don't you know that the Copa Room will be closed tomorrow night?" he asked and leaned back in his chair. "Sinatra's not here this week. Half of the girls have tonight off. It's probably gonna be pretty slow."

Hassie stared into her lap before saying, "I've always been home for Thanksgiving. It was my daddy's favorite time to be there with us. We'd cook and eat all day and he'd drink bourbon until his face got red and my mother would send him to bed."

Henry walked around his desk and perched on the front edge. "Have you talked to your mother yet? Does she even know where you are?"

She shook her head. "She doesn't care where I am."

"Of course, she cares," Henry said. "And she must be worried sick. Why don't you give her a call tomorrow? Just wish her a happy Thanksgiving and let her know that you're okay."

She stood up and walked to the door, hesitated as she turned the knob and looked back at Henry. "Have you seen Jake today?"

"Nope. Do you need something?"

She shook her head and opened the door. "I was just wondering if he's said anything about me. If he thinks I'm doing a good job."

"Sorry, but that's not the way Jake operates. If you're doing a good job, he'll never say. But try screwing up and you'll get his attention in a big hurry."

She smiled softly and said, "Thanks, Henry. See you later."

Hassie heard a couple of guys say that their flight to Chicago had been cancelled because of bad weather; what better place to be stranded than Las Vegas and the Copa Room? So much for a slow night, she thought as she ran from table to table. Without Sinatra, the musicians had a night to jam through their own list of standards. Hassie still had high hopes that Julio would give her an opportunity to sing.

It was close to midnight before she could stop and listen to the band. Despite the heavy cigarette smoke and rambunctious atmosphere in the packed room, they played like no one else was there until Julio bid the audience farewell and the band played its final number. She listened and watched them intently before one of the men at the largest table in her section shouted to her to bring their check.

She nodded at the man and returned to the table with the leather folder containing the check. She smiled, laid it on the table and walked away. When she returned to collect the payment, the man handed the folder to her, grabbed her hand and said, "Wait a minute, sugar."

She felt a big hand push something in her cleavage. She flinched, backed away and pulled out several bills. Before she could speak, the man stood up – his face an inch from her nose – and told her to be in room 720 in the Arlington wing at two a.m.

"Sir, my job is to serve drinks," she said, maintaining her smile, and dropped the money on the table.

"You're kiddin', right?" the man said, smearing his wet mouth across her hand. "Did you hear that, fellas? Her job is to serve drinks." The men at the table laughed and Hassie tried to walk away.

"Where you goin'?" The man took a tighter hold of her arm. "You forgot your money."

"Sir, you've already given me a very nice tip for your drinks." She tugged back from him, but one of the other men was standing behind her now.

"Look, doll. If you want more money, I'll give you more, just –"

"I believe the lady said she's not interested in your money," a voice behind Hassie said. She turned to see Jake push the other man out of the way.

"I ain't talkin' to you, pal," the man at the table said.

"You ain't talkin' to her either," Jake said, leading Hassie away from the table.

Jake had a tight grip on her wrist and didn't stop walking until they were outside the Copa Room doors.

Hassie winced and pulled her hand away in an exaggerated jerk. "What are you doing, Jake?"

"What does it look like?"

"I told you I could take care of myself."

"Oh, yeah," Jake said, dragging her along the corridor by her arm. "That's not the way it looked to me."

"Where did you come from, anyway? You're not my bodyguard."

Jake steered her to the side of the corridor and stopped. "Shut up." He grabbed her and held her so tight that she couldn't move. He fiercely pressed his lips to hers, kissing her again and again. He held her face in his hands and said, "I'm tired of this game, Hassie."

"What game?" she said. Her lips were stinging.

"Do you want to stay in Vegas?"

"Yes," she said softly and pulled his hands away from her face.

"Do you really want to work in a room full of hookers and pretend you're not one?"

She looked into his face, waiting.

"Why don't you just grow up and behave like the woman that you tell me you are and come with me to my suite."

Despite the mighty thump in her chest, Hassie felt calm and steady but speechless. She still couldn't imagine spending her life as a prostitute, and when she looked at Jake, she knew that she didn't want to be without him – that she actually wanted him in the same way he wanted her and she'd known it since the day she arrived.

"So," he said, lifting her hand to his face. "What'll it be? One of Henry's girls or Jake's woman?"

She barely stifled a smile as she said, "Not, *one* of Jake's women?"

He gave her a look that said he was not amused and then took hold of her arm and walked down the corridor to his suite, neither of them attempting small talk. When they reached the door, he stopped and said, "I'm not forcing you to do anything you're not ready for."

"I know," she said. "But I need to ask you something."

He opened the door and followed her inside, then switched on the light and pointed her to a chair. "Okay. Shoot." He sat down and lit a cigarette.

"Are you involved with Natalie? I mean, are you sleeping with her?"

"What makes you ask that question now?"

"Just something that Stella said. And I think Natalie's in love with you."

"Well, that's news to me," he said and stood up. "Look, there's no one else in my life right now. Remember what I said to you the other night about how I'm different with you?"

She didn't make eye contact and said, "But Stella said –"

"Forget what Stella said. Those girls don't know half as much as they think they do." He stubbed out the cigarette before leaving her alone while he went into the bedroom.

She wasn't completely satisfied with his answer about Natalie. She pressed her lips together thinking that she must need lipstick, then jumped at the sound of a loud crash and the distant sound of Jake saying, "Shit."

She felt a nervous giggle erupting from her chest and walked toward the bedroom. "Are you okay?" she asked and stuck her head around the open door. She couldn't see where the low light was coming from and called out again, "Jake? Is everything okay?" There was an invisible something in the air that excited her.

"Everything's fine," he said.

She couldn't see him until he struck a match. He leaned over and lit a candle on the bedside table. He looked up and held out his hand with a motion to join him. She moved further into the room and walked around the end of the bed. He stood in the shadow of the candlelight, his bathrobe closed but not belted.

"This is for you," he said, pointing to another robe lying on the bed. "I'm going to get us a drink while you get comfortable."

She nodded and moved close enough to touch him. They stood perfectly still for several seconds, her hands behind her back to hide her nervousness. He ran his right forefinger down her left cheek and across her mouth, back to the center of her lips. He lingered for a few seconds until she kissed his finger and drew herself closer to him.

"Are you okay?" he said, stroking her hair.

"I'm not sure what I'm doing here."

"I hope you're falling in love," he said and kissed her shoulder as he unhooked her skirt. She let it drop to the floor, and then unfastened her blouse. He helped her with a stubborn button and pushed it off her arms. She froze like she expected him to do the rest, staring into the eyes that she still hadn't learned how to read.

He pulled her into his arms; his bathrobe fell open. Their bare chests were separated by her strapless bra, which he removed and let drop to the floor. She loved the velvety texture of his skin and the way the hair on his chest felt against her breasts – a feeling she'd never known but that felt so good and so right. His erection rested against her soft belly; her groin started to ache. He ran his hands up and down her arms and said, "Are you cold?"

She shook her head. "It's all so ... you're so ... I don't know. I guess I'm a little nervous."

"Don't be," he said and pulled her close. "You know I would never do anything to hurt you."

For a quick moment, she thought of Stella and her challenge of Hassie's knowledge and experience with sex, especially where Jake was concerned. She realized that she was very close to losing that bet and that she may be in for way more than she ever dreamed about. But Jake was so kind to her and she had feelings that she couldn't quite understand. She pulled back from him and looked directly into his eyes. "You really do care about me, don't you?"

"I more than care about you, Hassie. That's what I'm trying to show you." He kissed her, slowly at first, then more aggressively until she responded by opening her mouth and allowing his tongue to touch hers, then encircling his neck with both arms, pulling him closer and taking his tongue deep.

He pulled away from the kiss, removed his robe and pushed her down on to the bed. She landed on cold sheets and pulled his body close. She gazed up at him while he slowly straddled her across her thighs, thrusting his weight on to his arms. He lowered his body over her chest, his lips almost touching hers and said, "Hassie, I want to make love to you like –" He stopped and she sensed a fear that he was upsetting her. "Are you okay? Am I hurting you?"

Hassie took hold of Jake's face with both of her unsteady hands, shook her head and whispered, "I've never done this before."

He kissed her tenderly and moved his hand down her body. "Just relax." He kissed her neck several times while reaching down to remove her panties. "If you want me to stop, just tell me."

He gently parted her legs with his hand; she took in the familiar scent of his spicy cologne. She loved the way he touched her, a soft moan escaping her as his finger moved gently inside her, her grip on his neck nearly desperate.

He moved his body on top of her and kissed her face and neck until his lips found hers and she could feel his sweat roll down her breasts. She tried to relax as the heat from his penis forced her legs farther apart, the apprehension fading with his strong, yet gentle movement inside her; his loving whisper into her ear easing the stabbing pain and creating the feeling that he was giving her something that she had been missing and wanting for a long time.

The slow movement quickened and she began to feel the pleasure that she had only ever imagined. Then without warning, he took hold of her hands, gently pushing them onto the pillow behind her head, and called out her name – once and then again before he lay still on top of her.

A moment later, he rolled over and held her in a loose embrace. When she looked into his face, she saw no real emotion and wondered if he had been disappointed by her lack of experience. But, as if he had read her mind, he kissed her gently on her forehead and said, "Are you okay?"

She nodded and said, "I'm sorry if I –"

"You have nothing to be sorry about. You are gorgeous and sexy and I couldn't be happier." He smiled, chuckled lightly and said, "I'm probably the last thing you need right now – hell, according to most people around here, I'm behaving like a horny, lecherous toad. But you do something to me, Hassie Calhoun. Every inch of your body, every strand of your hair makes me crazy for you. Like no other woman I've ever known. Don't ever forget that."

He wrapped her in his arms, his face resting close to hers. She lay gently against the slow, contented rhythm of his breathing, lovingly wanting to remember that exact moment for the rest of her life. She kissed his chest and snuggled deep within his embrace, then breathed deeply and said, "I know it's late but, before we go to sleep, do you think we could do that again?"

chapter seven

IT MIGHT have been her imagination, but Hassie felt that the entire staff at the Sands knew about her relationship with Jake. They would smile at her in a knowing way, and she wondered if they thought she was a fool for letting herself get involved with him. But no one really discussed it with her except Stella, who also raised the issue of birth control and took her to a gynecologist to be fitted for a diaphragm. Natalie tried to intimidate Hassie with remarks that she still spent time with Jake, but Hassie remained confident and unflappable and was delighted when Jake insisted that she move into his suite. Before the move, Natalie and Jake's previous relationship was often a sore subject between Hassie and Jake. He had yet to convince her which story was the accurate one, but continued to insist that Natalie had never meant anything more to him than an easy lay.

Regardless, nothing was more important to her than being the woman in Jake's life. He immediately took her off the Copa Room floor and gave her the job of assistant manager, which didn't set well with Henry, especially after she assumed a place in his office. She took it upon herself to clear out stacks of old photos and memos but made sure to reorganize them so that she could never be accused of disrupting his *system*. She knew this would test his patience but decided that it might be the best way to force him out of his sulk. She could sense that he wanted to say something to her just about every time she entered the room, but he would merely huff around, ignoring her, and then stalk out as if he had something important to do that didn't involve her.

She was determined to be an important part of the Copa Room

operation, and monitored the nightly reservations list as it was received from the concierge at the end of each day. She walked into the office with the latest list in her hand.

"So I see we're just barging into my office now," Henry said, glaring at her from behind his black-framed reading glasses.

"This is *our* office, Henry," Hassie said. "Remember what Jake told you."

"Oh, don't play the Jake card with me." He stood up and walked away from where she stood. "I've been through this with every bimbo he's had the hots for since the beginning of time."

Hassie didn't move or respond at first, then looked at him and said, "I know you don't mean that, Henry. First of all, Jake's never had the hots for anyone like he's got the hots for me." She smiled and walked toward him. "And, secondly, I think the official age for a bimbo is eighteen and I'm not quite there yet so that make's me a *bimbette*."

They stood facing each other for a few seconds – Henry's dead serious expression finally breaking into a big smile followed by his silly titter. He pulled her into his chest, wrapping both arms around her and said, "You're a little bitch, ya know."

She smiled at him and replied, "Takes one to know one." She hugged him and waited for him to sit down behind his desk before perching on the edge of one of the visitor's chairs.

"So are you still mad at me?" Hassie asked, leaning on the desk in front of him.

"I was never mad at *you*," Henry said. "I just get fed up with Jake running my life."

"He's the boss, Henry. And I thought that you would be pleased to have me working here with you."

He moved some papers around his desk then looked at her and said, "Let's discuss this later. Did you have something to talk to me about?"

"I picked this up from the concierge," Hassie said and handed him a piece of paper. He studied it for a minute and then said, "This is it? This is the reservation list for tonight?"

She nodded and bit her lip. "Not too good, is it?"

"I knew occupancy in the hotel was down this week, but this little list doesn't warrant opening the doors."

"Seriously? Would that mean cancelling Frank's show?" She remembered Henry telling her that this had happened in the past, but the room had been so busy prior to Thanksgiving, she hadn't really noticed that business had slacked off.

"I need to run it by Jake –" He stopped and tapped his finger on his desk. "No, I don't," he said and jumped up. "*We* run the Copa Room now."

He pulled on his jacket and shoved his glasses in his top pocket. "I'll get a message to Frank and you can have the pleasure of telling Jake."

"I don't know, Henry," she said, following him out of the office. "I think we should talk to Jake before you tell Frank." She was speaking to his back as he exited the room.

Hassie surveyed the empty room for a few minutes before going back into Henry's office to locate Jake. The low glow on the stage caught her attention and she immediately fell into her fantasy of singing among the musicians, then remembered what she was supposed to be doing and walked back into the office. She called everyone she knew that might know of Jake's whereabouts and left a message with each of them to have him call her in Henry's office as soon as he got the message.

Henry's desk was piled with papers of all sorts and if there was any order to their placement, she couldn't see it. On the top of one of the piles was a local magazine, its front page dominated by a photograph of five men. She looked closer and recognized Sinatra, then read on to discover that the group was known as the "Rat Pack" and was scheduled to perform in the Copa Room after the New Year. It went on to say that these famous men were going to make a movie in Vegas and that anyone who lived in the area could expect to see them around for a couple of months. She recognized Sammy Davis Jr. and Dean Martin and the caption identified the others as Joey Bishop and Peter Lawford. It all sounded terribly exciting – a bit of Hollywood right there in Vegas.

When she finished reading the entire magazine, she realized that she had been sitting in the office for over forty-five minutes without a word from Jake or Henry. She quickly tidied the desk and gathered her belongings, locking the door as she went back into the Copa Room. She could hear voices behind the stage, but the room was empty with a vague aura of light emanating from the stage and bar area.

She approached the stage to see if she could spot anyone and called out once, but when there was no reply, she turned to exit through the back entrance. As she reached the last group of tables, she sensed that someone was sitting there and picked up a faint whiff of cigarette smoke. She continued through the room, nearing the occupied table, but before she could make out a face, she heard someone say, "Hello, Hassie."

There was no mistaking that voice. She took a tentative step and then stood next to the chair across from where Sinatra sat. She'd met him a couple of times now but had no reason to believe that he would remember her name.

"Have a seat," he said, exhaling a nostril full of smoke. "Hassie. That's a nice name. Where does it come from?"

"My mother," she said, fiddling with her fingers. "She's from a tribe of Choctaw Indians in Oklahoma. Evidently, I was such a chubby baby, my mother named me Nia Hushi, which means 'fat bird' in Choctaw."

"Interesting," Sinatra said. "But where did they get Hassie?"

"My mom wanted to call me Nia but my dad started calling me Hassie – from Hushi, I guess – and the name stuck."

Sinatra chuckled softly and stared in her direction. "How did a sweet young thing like you end up in big, bad Vegas?"

"It's kind of a long story, but it's all worked out pretty well." She wanted to ask him if Henry had spoken with him about the show but assumed by the way he slumped in the chair that he'd been told that it had been cancelled.

Before she could say anything more, he sat up and said, "What does a guy have to do to get a drink around here?"

"Sorry, Mr. Sinatra," she said and jumped up. "What would you like?"

"Relax, kid," he said. "I'll have some JD. And the name's Frank."

She ran around to the bar and located a bottle of Jack Daniels. She poured it over two ice cubes and set the glass on a tray, then softly laughed as she realized that she was behaving like a cocktail waitress instead of a hostess. She poured herself a shot from the bottle and took both glasses back to the table.

"Thanks," he said as he lit another cigarette. "Ya know, it's actually kinda nice to have a night off."

"Oh, good," she said. "I'm glad you feel that way. I was worried." She stopped and smiled. "Listen to me. I'm just rambling along like I sit across the table and talk to you every day."

"That wouldn't be so bad," he said. "I'd sit across the table from you any day of the week."

She caught his kind smile before looking down at her hands. There was something quite magical about this man, and she was careful not to say something stupid. "How long have you known Jake?"

"So we're gonna talk about him, huh?"

"It's just that –"

"Don't worry, doll. Us boys shouldn't tread on each other's territories. And there's no mistaking how he feels about you."

"Really?"

"Sure," he said, sipping the drink. "But I wanna know more about you. If one of my daughters ended up in Vegas at the age of – what – nineteen?"

"I'll be eighteen in two days."

"December twelfth?"

"Uh-huh."

"Well, I'll be damned," he said, drawing deeply on the cigarette. "And your father is okay with this?"

She wanted him to believe that she could make her own decisions. "I came to Vegas to be a singer."

He looked at her like she'd said the most ridiculous thing he'd ever heard, which embarrassed her until he said, "Well, can you sing?"

"Some people think so," she said. "I did well enough at a contest in Dallas to qualify for the Miss Texas pageant."

"I see. A beauty queen that needs a talent." He blew smoke up into the air and stared out into the room.

She felt silly and inadequate and wished she'd kept her mouth shut. Maybe she should just excuse herself and go find Jake. She swallowed the last of her drink and pushed her chair back to stand up.

"Sing something for me," he said, stubbing out the cigarette.

"Now? Right here?"

"Why not? You're in the Copa Room for Chrissake." He stood up and walked toward the stage, shouting out, "Julio? You back there?"

One of the other musicians appeared and said, "Sorry, Mr. Sinatra. Julio's playing in the lobby lounge. You want me to go get him?"

"Nah. It's okay," he said and turned back toward the table where Hassie still sat. "Come here." He motioned her forward.

She moved quicker than she meant to, and then slowed her pace as she got closer to him. They walked up on the stage; he looked at her and said, "I'd offer to play for you but I'm kinda rusty."

She laughed and walked over to the piano. "I can play for myself as long as you don't expect me to be as good as Julio."

He nodded his approval and said, "Sit down and show me whatcha got."

Hassie sat behind the keyboard and played a few chords. The large pile of music beside the piano made her think of the trips with Barbara to the big music store in Dallas where she would buy as many pieces of sheet music as the money her father had given her would allow. She'd practice the songs until she knew them by heart and would play for her father on Sunday afternoons while he sat in the living room and read the newspaper. He loved her jazzy renditions of the Cole Porter and Duke Ellington songs that she learned. Sometimes he would whistle the melody along with her or purposely sing the wrong lyrics until she almost doubled over with laughter. She never got up the nerve to sing for him – something that she deeply regretted after he died. It had been a while since she'd sat at a piano; maybe she should wait for Julio.

"So?" Sinatra said as he walked over to the piano. "What's it gonna be?"

Her heartbeat quickened, which seemed to bolster her nerve as she blurted, "How about 'I Got It Bad And That Ain't Good'?"

"It's one of my favorites," he said and smiled.

She sat still for a minute, then played the sultry intro and eased into the vocal, tentatively at first until she heard Sinatra scat softly underneath the main melody, then relaxed and let herself go. When she finished the first verse, arriving at the saxophone interlude, she heard Toots pick up from behind her. His version sent chills through her entire body; she felt a huge lump in her throat and thought of her father and his love for this music. Moments like this made her miss him terribly. When Toots finished the interlude, Sinatra took over the song and sang directly to her while she played, then finished with Toots's saxophone embellishment. She wanted to applaud or say something but just waited to see what Frank would do next. He said something to Toots that she couldn't quite hear, then turned to her and pointed two fingers containing a newly lit cigarette at her. "You're good, kid."

"Do you really think so?"

"You're good and you're beautiful," he said, walking down off the stage. "A lethal combination."

Hassie could feel the melancholy that Sinatra projected as he made his way back to the table and swallowed the last of his drink. She watched him as he picked up his coat and walked to the door. He never looked back or spoke to her but quietly left the room; Toots had also disappeared.

She sat at the piano for a few minutes, her face warm with emotion and her pulse racing ever so slightly. She walked off the stage and over to the bar, a smile erupting across her face as she recalled Sinatra's words. She leaned down in search of a bottle of vodka, reading the various labels out loud. When she stood up, she spotted Jake sitting at the other end of the bar. She gasped softly, "Jake, what are you doing here?"

His eyes weren't shining and the look on his face was not the one that she had grown to know and love. She stood there, waiting for him to speak. He stared at her for a few seconds more and then finally said, "Did you enjoy your evening with Frank?"

A slight chill shot through her body at the tone of his voice. She poured vodka in a glass and, without looking at him, said, "Would you like a drink?"

He moved down the bar until he was standing in front of her. "No, I would not like a drink. And how many drinks did you have with Frank?"

She took a big sip from her glass, then set it on the bar and said, "He was just on his way out. I'm sure you know that his show was cancelled tonight."

"Yeah, and by whose authority?" Jake picked up her glass and swigged back the rest of her drink.

"Henry's," she said carefully, and then waited a few seconds before saying, "And mine."

He shoved the glass across the bar towards her and laughed. "You and Henry. Looks like I created a monster."

She relaxed her shoulders and reached for the vodka bottle and another glass, poured another shot in each glass and handed one to Jake. "You said that you wanted me to help Henry run this place. There were only a few seats reserved for tonight's show. We rebooked them for tomorrow and gave the guys the night off." She swallowed about half of her drink and said, "What would you have done?"

"I would have done exactly that," he said and reached for her hand. "I just might not have played footsie with Frank while doing it."

Hassie finished her drink and tucked the bottle back in its place under the bar, then walked around to where Jake stood and put her arms around his neck. "Why, Mr. Contrata, I think you're jealous."

He pulled her close to him and said, "Oh, no you don't. I may be a lot of things, but jealous of Frank Sinatra, I ain't."

"Hmm," she said, and then hesitated before saying, "Do you know how happy I am to be with you?"

"No, tell me." He kissed her neck and she felt his arousal as he pulled her close.

Her voice cracked as she recalled the last real memories of her father. "I haven't been this happy since I was about ten years old before my father went off to Korea."

Jake held her tight and said, "I'll take that as your way of saying that you're madly in love with me." She sniffed back the emotion and laughed as he took hold of her hand and said, "Let's get out of here."

Although the demands of Jake's job left her on her own much of the time, Hassie was quite happy to concentrate on working with Henry or just hanging out with the musicians in the Copa Room. For the most part, she kept Jake's hours, which meant that she was late to bed and late to rise, which also meant that she usually didn't appear for duty until well after noon. Everything ticked along very nicely – until the afternoon Dotty returned from a leave of absence to attend to her dying mother in Missouri.

"Jimmy told me that you've taken over the Copa Room, but I had to see it for myself."

Dotty stood inside the entrance to the dressing room. “Hi, Dotty,” Hassie said but didn’t move. “Welcome back. Sorry to hear about your mother.”

“Thanks.” Dotty surveyed the room in silence and then exhaled a cloud of cigarette smoke before sitting down. “Seems I’ve missed out on a lot of excitement around here.”

“If you mean my promotion to assistant manager of the Copa Room, that’s not all that exciting really.”

Dotty laughed and then choked on a chest full of phlegm.

“God, Dotty,” Hassie said, moving closer to the sofa. “You sound terrible. Are you okay?”

“Oh, stop your cluckin’. I’m fine.”

“You don’t sound fine, and I doubt that cigarette is helping you.”

“Look, miss know-it-all. I don’t need you to tell me what to do. And what’s this horseshit about *assistant manager*? That’s the funniest thing I ever heard.”

Hassie pulled one of the dressing table stools over to Dotty and calmly sat down. “You may not know this, Dotty, but Jake and I are ” She stopped to consider her words. “Jake and I are together now, and he gave me this job to help Henry.”

“He gave you the damn job to get you off the prostitute roster,” Dotty said. “And I guess he forgot that takin’ care of the Copa Girls is my job – the job I’ve had since you were a prissy little girl.”

“I’m sorry, Dotty. I didn’t know that you had an official job or anything.” With just enough sarcasm to make her point, Hassie said, “Do you want me to have a talk with Jake about all this and remind him?”

Dotty laughed and ground her cigarette in the nearest ashtray. “Damn, girl. You went and grew some balls while I was gone.”

Hassie waited before responding, then caught the smile on Dotty’s face and softly giggled. “Seriously, Dotty. I didn’t mean to take your job. I’ll talk to Henry and sort out some other duties.”

Dotty ignored her and walked over to the large wardrobe and then said, “I am curious about one thing.”

“What’s that?”

“How the hell did Natalie deal with you after you stole Jake from her?”

“Well, first of all, I didn’t *steal* Jake from her, but mainly, we stay outta each other’s way.”

"You're roommates and you stay outta each other's way?"

"We're not roommates any more," Hassie said. "I live with Jake now."

"Holy shit," Dotty said, looking over her shoulder from the rack of skirts and blouses. "That musta sent Natalie into orbit."

"I wouldn't know. Jake told me to forget about her and he had some sort of talk with her about it all."

Dotty closed the wardrobe door and turned toward Hassie. "A word to the wise." She slowly walked up to where she was directly in Hassie's face and said, "Natalie will *never* be okay about this. Jake can screw around with whoever he likes but he's got a lot of history with Natalie – he's even made her some ridiculous promises, and he's dumber than a box of hair if he thinks he can just waltz off into the sunset with Little Miss Texas. Believe me. I know what I'm talkin' about."

Even if Dotty was right, Jake was the most powerful person at the Sands. He always got his way; she was living proof of that. "Well, Jake and I are in love." She wished she could take the words back as soon as she said them.

Dotty laughed out loud and said, "Well, lah-de-fuckin'-dah." She laughed some more and Hassie felt her face flush. Eventually, Dotty regained her composure and had another coughing fit.

"I've gotta go meet Henry now," Hassie said and turned to leave the dressing room.

"You may not believe it, but I like you. I can see why Jake's into you and I'm sure he means it if he says he loves you. But I remember the day not so long ago when Natalie stood here telling me the exact same thing and she wasn't much older than you are now. It's nothin' to do with you or her – it's Jake. He likes the chase and then gets bored with the catch. It's all new to both of you right now. Just wait for the next young thing to come through the door and you won't look so good any more."

"It's not like that with us."

"I'm an old broad, Hassie. I've been around and seen a lotta shit." Dotty walked over to Hassie and put her arm around her shoulder. "I can see that you really love the ole snake. But I'd hate to see you get hurt."

"You sound like Henry," Hassie said.

"Then you should listen to him. He knows Jake all too well and has been hurt by him too."

"Hurt how?"

"It's best if he tells you," Dotty said. "But ask him after he's had a few drinks."

Hassie left Dotty and walked out into the Copa Room. Jake and Henry were sitting at a table with Donnie McGinley, deep in conversation and giving away nothing in their expressions or tone of voice. As she got closer to them, she saw Henry whisper something to Jake; Jake turned around with a jerk.

"Hello, gorgeous," he said, standing up to greet her. "Where've you been this afternoon?"

"With Dotty," she said. "What are you guys talking about?"

Jake looked over at Donnie and then said to Hassie, "You remember Officer McGinley?"

"Of course."

Hassie nodded as he stood up and said, "Please. Call me Donnie."

She smiled and then looked at Henry. "Dotty just reminded me that the Copa Girls and the dressing room are her territory. She wants to keep her job in the dressing room so I need to let her."

"She doesn't really have a job," Henry said. "She appointed herself in charge of the girls once upon a time and it seemed to work. So we just let her do it, but she doesn't get paid or anything."

Jake stood and put on his jacket, "Henry, handle this. Come on, Hassie," he said, taking her by the hand. "Let's do like real people and have dinner together tonight."

Jake left instructions not to be disturbed and had a lovely, romantic dinner brought to the suite, complete with champagne and the hotel's chocolates imported from Switzerland. Midway through the meal, a package was delivered from one of the hotel shops, which he insisted that she open as soon as the room service was finished. The box was wrapped in shiny silver paper topped with a huge red bow. She removed the lid to uncover the most elegant black negligee that she'd ever seen.

"Jake, this is beautiful," she said as she pulled it from the box. "I've never had anything this sexy."

"It's nowhere near as sexy as it's gonna be after you put it on." He walked around the table and pulled her to her feet, then proceeded to remove her clothes. She stood still while he dressed her in the gown; he finished by tying the satin ribbon just under her breasts. When his hand brushed against her, she took hold of it and began to kiss his fingers, slowly sucking on the tips. They had spent the entire evening engulfed in each other's eyes but had had very little physical contact. When she put his pinkie finger in her mouth, he picked her up and took her to their bed and their first real kiss of the night.

Their lovemaking had become something of a drug for Hassie – and for Jake – something that they both needed to function properly. Hassie grew to understand the depth of Jake's feelings for her, which made it impossible to let Dotty's comments leave any doubt in her mind and heart. How could Jake have ever loved Natalie the way he loved her? She ached and yearned for him with a passion that was beyond anything that she'd ever imagined and believed that he could never do anything to diminish her love for him.

As they lay in each other's arms, her body wrapped around his in every possible way, she remembered that she would be eighteen years old the next day and wondered if she'd feel any different. It hadn't been that long ago that she'd had those girlie conversations with her friend, Carol, when they couldn't imagine being as *old* as eighteen. She'd always imagined that her life would all be worked out by this time and her destiny in the world of adults would be set. After all, her mother had barely turned nineteen when she married her father.

Jake lifted her arms off his body and scooted away from her, then whispered, "Wait right here."

He went into the living room and clattered around for a few minutes, then came back through the door carrying a large tray with a bottle in an ice bucket and glasses. He walked toward her, singing "Happy Birthday" in a deep, low voice and set the tray on the bed in front of her.

"My birthday's not until tomorrow."

"It is tomorrow," he said and kissed her. "I wanted to be the first to wish you a happy eighteenth." He sat on the edge of the bed and poured two glasses of champagne. "To you, my love and my life." He touched her glass with his, took a sip and said, "May we spend the next eighteen and the next eighteen and the next eighteen years together."

She didn't know whether it was the champagne, the intense sex or the reality that she was turning eighteen that made her so emotional. She was consumed with the love she felt from Jake but also saddened by the thought of her father who died the day before her fifteenth birthday, after which she thought she would never celebrate again. But the next year, when she turned sweet sixteen, Barbara came over to cheer her up and convinced her that it was a day to celebrate life – both her own and that of her father.

"Are you okay?" Jake said. "Did I do something wrong?"

"No. God, no. I just –" She reached for his hand and felt a tear drop from her cheek.

"Shhh," he said. "If you think it's sad to turn eighteen, wait till you're my age."

She laughed and wiped her face with her hand. "I love you, Jake."

"And I love you." He downed the champagne and refilled their glasses, then put his hand on her leg. "I need to tell you something else."

"What?" she said. "Is something wrong?"

"I have to go to LA tomorrow – today. To meet Sid," he said without looking at her. "I'm really sorry."

"When will you be back?"

"In a couple of days," he said, pulling her close. "Henry will look after you and you'll have this big suite all to yourself."

"First of all, I don't need looking after." She wriggled away from him and set the glass on the tray. "And, anyway, there are plenty of people around to hang out with."

"Yeah," he laughed. "Like your best friend, Natalie?"

"Very funny." She got up off the bed and walked toward the bathroom. She was disappointed that Jake could put his work ahead of her and, much to her surprise, Sinatra's face shot through her mind with thought of his last comments to her. Her spine tingled, she looked back at Jake, hesitated a few seconds and finally said, "Don't go away. I'm not finished with you yet."

chapter eight

IN THE early morning of her eighteenth birthday, Hassie burrowed deep into the bedcovers, recalling her birthdays as a little girl when she'd help her mother make angel food cake with fluffy white icing. She'd stand on a stool next to Bonita while she moved the Sunbeam electric eggbeater around the big, red bowl until the runny mixture was firm and sweet and could be spread over the freshly baked cake. After her mother finished icing the cake, she would pull the metal beaters from the small appliance and give them to Hassie to lick clean. Even in the kitchen, Bonita was beautifully dressed in a crisp cotton blouse and wearing the small gold locket on a delicate chain that was a wedding present from her father. Hassie thought that her mother was the most beautiful mother in Corsicana and loved all the fuss that Bonita made for her birthday. But after her tenth birthday, her father went off to Korea and her mother never fussed over anything she did again.

Although she had tried to keep Barbara out of her thoughts and, thus, force the guilt of leaving Corsicana aside, she knew that Barbara would be thinking about her today and imagined her sadness over the reminder of Hassie's disappearance without even a note or a clue as to where she was going. She'd been gone for over three months but had convinced herself that Barbara understood that she'd left because she wanted to make a better life for herself – they'd discussed this more than once. But she also knew that Barbara only ever wanted the best for her and would never believe that going off to work in a nightclub in Vegas – even if it was the Copa Room – could in any way be better for her than going to college. Still, it would be nice to hear Barbara's voice, and she was willing to bet that, regardless of how Barbara really felt, she wouldn't want to say anything to upset her on her birthday.

She decided to order some breakfast before calling Barbara. The phone rang just after she spoke with room service. She answered it and heard what sounded like a man coughing while covering the receiver with his hand. She waited a few seconds and then said hello again.

A familiar voice said, "Is that the birthday girl?"

"Good morning, Mr. Sinatra," she said.

"I told you. The name's Frank."

"Good morning, Frank, and how do you know it's my birthday?"

"You told me you'd be eighteen on the twelfth of December. That's today."

"Oh, yeah," she said. "But I didn't expect you to remember."

"Don't feel too flattered. It happens to be my birthday too."

"You're kidding me? I have the same birthday as Frank Sinatra?"

"Well, at least the same month and day," he laughed. "So, listen. If I know the knuckleheads in the Copa Room, they'll be promoting some kind of drunkfest after the show tonight. I just wanted to make sure you'll be there and we'll have a drink to celebrate."

"I'll be there," she said. "And, Frank?"

"Yeah?"

"Thank you. This was really very nice of you to call."

"Don't mention it. See you later."

She hung up the phone and sat down in the closest chair. Had Frank Sinatra really called to wish *her* a happy birthday? And it was his birthday too! All of a sudden, the day without Jake wasn't going to be so bad. She'd promised Henry and Stella that she would have lunch with them, which gave her time to shop for something special to wear that night – something that she could imagine Frank would want her to wear or maybe even buy for her.

Hassie jumped up when the doorbell rang and she ushered the room service steward in and out of the room. She filled a coffee cup, stirred in some sugar and took a big bite out of the buttered toast, then hurried into the bathroom for a quick bath. As she sat on the side of the tub to adjust the water temperature, she remembered her intention to phone Barbara and turned off the faucet. She took her coffee cup from the vanity and walked back into the bedroom and then hesitated. Did she really want to take a chance that Barbara would not be happy to hear from her or even worse, be angry with her? She decided that she'd leave the phone call until after lunch. If she felt that it was the right thing to do, she'd still have plenty of time to speak to Barbara before her evening in the Copa Room began.

Henry and Stella were already seated in the Garden Room when Hassie arrived. She gave her packages to the maitre d' to look after, and ran over to the table.

"Been shopping, I see," Henry said as he stood to greet her with a kiss on the cheek.

She smiled at Henry and hugged Stella.

"Happy birthday, honey," Henry said.

"We ordered some champagne," Stella said. "Where's Jake today?"

"He had to go to LA to meet Sid." Hassie watched Henry's reaction to this news. "Did you know about this meeting, Henry?"

"Believe it or not, Jake doesn't tell me his schedule."

"So this was just some routine meeting that couldn't take place anywhere but LA or any other time but today?" The waiter arrived with the bottle; Henry gave him the nod to open it.

"Hurry up and pour the bubbly," Stella said. "Our birthday girl's a little uptight."

"I'm not uptight," Hassie said. "It just seems to me that this trip could have waited until tomorrow."

"Well, you better get used to it," Henry said while the waiter filled the three glasses and placed the bottle in an ice bucket.

"Used to what?" Hassie asked.

"Everybody around here – including Jake – jumps when Sid roars."

Hassie picked up her glass and said, "You mean, the T-Rex?"

Stella and Henry exchanged looks while Stella said, "So you've been warned?"

Henry lifted his glass, looked at both women and said, "Forget about Sid. To Hassie on her eighteenth birthday." They clinked each other's glasses and took a sip before Henry continued, "I would say that you're a real woman now, but I think Jake took care of that a while ago."

Stella and Henry laughed while Hassie pursed her lips before saying, "You two don't know everything."

Hassie decided not to be annoyed by Jake's absence and relaxed as they enjoyed the chef's special meal of roast beef served with a side dish that looked like a fancy version of the succotash her mother used to cook. The champagne loosened her tongue and she told Henry and Stella about Jake's birthday dinner the night before. "It really was the sweetest thing," she said. "And you should see the incredible nightgown he gave me. Not that I really wore it."

Stella smiled as Hassie giggled. Henry excused himself to the men's room and Hassie waved to the waiter for more champagne.

She waited for the waiter to refill their glasses and then said, "I had a phone call from Frank this morning."

"Frank who?" Stella said.

"Sinatra, silly. How many Franks do you know?"

Stella took a long draw on her cigarette before speaking again. "Why was he calling you?"

"To wish me a happy birthday, and you're never gonna believe this but today is his birthday too. Isn't that cool?"

"Isn't what cool?" Henry said, sitting down at the table.

Hassie swigged back the champagne and said, "Frank and I have the same birthday."

"Oh, yeah," Henry said. "I heard the guys in the band talking about Frank's last week. I just didn't catch the date. How did Frank know it's your birthday?"

"I told him the other night when I talked to him in the Copa Room. You know, that night that his show was cancelled?"

Henry nodded and put his hand over his glass as the waiter offered to refill it. "So he just called to wish you a happy birthday?"

Hassie hesitated; the hairs on her arms tingled. "He asked me to join him for a drink in the Copa Room tonight after his show."

Henry leaned back in his chair while motioning for the check.

"Does Jake know about this?" Stella asked, coolly.

Hassie drained her glass and said, "Jake's not here, is he?" She pushed her chair back from the table and hesitated before standing up and saying, "When Frank Sinatra asks you to join him for a drink, you don't turn him down." She smiled and waved. "Thanks for the lunch. See you in the Copa Room in a little while." She walked toward the maitre d' to collect her packages. When she glanced back at the table, Henry waved to her with a tentative smile like it was an afterthought.

Hassie opened the suite door to find a large spray of flowers on the entrance table. She dropped the packages on the armchair, took the card from the plastic holder and read the message out loud, "Happy birthday, my darling. I miss you and hope you're having a wonderful day. Love, Jake."

She put the card on the table beside the flowers and kicked off her shoes, realizing that she expected that the flowers might be from Frank. She looked back at the big pink roses and white lilies, imagined Jake's careful attention to their selection and suddenly missed him and wished he'd walk through the door and take her to bed. She breathed deeply and decided, with the help of the champagne, that she wanted Barbara to know what a good life she had and how happy she really was.

She held the receiver with both hands as Barbara's phone rang three, then four times and was about to put it down when she heard a click followed by Barbara's voice.

"Hi, Barbara."

"Hassie?" Barbara said almost inaudibly. "Hassie, is that you?"

"Yes, it's me. It's my birthday. I just wanted to talk to you and –"

"Hassie, where are you?" She could hear the sentiment behind Barbara's clipped English accent. "I've been so worried. And your mother – Hassie, you shouldn't have left without telling someone where you were going."

"Don't worry. I'm fine. I'm living a new life and I'm really happy."

There was a long pause, and Hassie could imagine Barbara's softly lined face, her graying hair twisted into a tight bun with a colorful chiffon scarf tied around it. She pictured her sitting in the leather wingback chair in her husband's study; the walls lined with photos from their travels around the world and the magnificent oversized globe on which Barbara pointed out the exotic locations of all her adventures. Barbara cleared her throat and said, "I always thought that you could talk to me, child."

Her sad tone brought a huge lump to Hassie's throat and she pulled the receiver down to her chest while she sniffed and breathed deeply. When she felt in control of her emotions, she lifted the phone to her ear and said, "I just had to get out of there. I'm sorry that I deceived you, but I knew that you'd stop me if you knew I was planning to leave."

"Did you ever consider that I might have helped you? It would have been much easier to know where you were going than to agonize over the speculation that something unthinkable had happened to you."

Hassie suddenly felt immense guilt. "I'm sorry I worried you. But I'm not sorry I left. I met some people who gave me a chance to do something good with my life. I'm even doing a little singing."

"So you went to Las Vegas?" Hassie could tell that Barbara was trying to keep the emotion out of her voice.

"Yes. How did you know?"

"I doubt there's a person alive who knows you as well as I. I know that stubborn, crazed determination of yours when you set your mind to something. I just wanted you to use it to do something great."

A chill ran through Hassie's body as she heard those words. "I *will* do something great. Would you believe me if I told you that I sang for Frank Sinatra and that he thinks I'm really good."

"I'm sure he does, Hassie," she said softly, then paused again, and Hassie knew that Barbara would be thinking about her own life. "Have you spoken with your mother yet?"

"No. Is everything okay at home?"

Barbara sighed and said, "I wouldn't know. Bonita blames me for your running away. She says I put big ideas in your head and that, basically, I'm the root of all your problems."

"That's ridiculous and she knows it."

"May be, but I'm thankful for the distance between Angus and Corsicana. And, anyway, you're the one who really has to answer to her for your actions. At least let her know where you are."

Her stepfather's evil grin flashed in Hassie's mind; she heard her mother scolding her for being ungrateful for Bobby's offer to drive her to work at the diner and knew that she was nowhere near ready to face anything to do with her family again. "I'll think about it, but maybe you could tell her that I'm okay?"

"Just between you and me, where can I reach you if I want to send something to you. I got a special gift for your eighteenth birthday and I'd really like to give it to you."

She hesitated with the thought that anyone – even someone she trusted – would know where to find her. It had been easiest to deal with her life away from Corsicana knowing that no one there knew where she was.

"Hassie, you're eighteen now," Barbara said. "You can do whatever you like – make your own decisions and deal with the consequences the way you like. Just don't turn your back on your past. A lot of people care about you and only want the best for you."

"You can reach me at the Sands Hotel in Vegas. Just address it to me here and I'll get it."

"Take care of yourself, my pet. And it would be lovely to hear from you occasionally."

Hassie hesitated before saying, "Barbara, I'm sorry. I sorta – took – your suitcase. I didn't have any money to buy one and –"

"It's okay. It's how I knew that you'd run away and not been kidnapped by some deranged pervert."

Hassie laughed and paused while Barbara continued, "Just promise me you'll bring it back to me someday."

Hassie hung up the phone and released a deep sigh. It pained her to think that she had caused such heartache for Barbara, and she knew that she would eventually need to make it up to her.

Sinatra's show was already underway when Hassie arrived at the Copa Room. She had fallen asleep after her phone call with Barbara and would probably have slept through until morning if Henry hadn't called and woken her. She did the best she could to freshen up, then put on her new dress and got to the Copa Room in just minutes. As she made her way through the corridors, she realized that she hadn't had a phone call from Jake all day, nor had he told her exactly when he'd be back.

Henry sat at a table near the entrance and motioned to her after the doorman let her in. He helped her with her chair, and then leaned over to whisper, "You look beautiful, honey, but you'd look better with a little lipstick."

She touched her lips and rolled her eyes, then motioned to the waiter for a drink. At the end of Frank's first set, Hassie grabbed her purse and headed for the dressing room and her old dressing table at the far end. As she rounded the first row of tables, she saw Natalie coming toward her from the opposite end. Thanks to Jake, she'd been able to avoid a real confrontation with Natalie thus far and wasn't sure that tonight was a good time to test her luck. Her first instinct was to backtrack and take another route, but she decided to carry on, pretending that she didn't see her. Natalie slowly walked toward her, smiling and slightly shaking her head.

"So, today's your birthday," she said.

"Yeah," Hassie nodded and paused.

Natalie reached out and put her hand on Hassie's shoulder and said, "Well, enjoy it. Too bad Jake's got more important things to do." She patted Hassie's shoulder and then walked away. Hassie could hear Natalie laughing but continued on and took her lipstick out of her purse. She looked into the mirror and realized that, eighteen or not, she really was no longer the young girl from small-town Texas who had arrived in Vegas only a few months before. She pressed her lips against a tissue, then checked her dress in the mirror, returned to the table and asked Henry to order a bottle of champagne. When he glanced at her in protest, she gave him a look that said it wasn't up for discussion; he signalled for the waitress and whispered his request.

Sinatra finished his show with his signature chat with the audience before singing the closing number. When he announced that he would end with "You Make Me Feel So Young," he dedicated it to a friend who was celebrating a special birthday, which prompted the band to launch into "Happy Birthday" and direct it to Frank. The audience was so thrilled to be a part of Sinatra's birthday celebration, they forgot about his attempt to sing to her. She was still touched by the sentiment in his choice of song and waited patiently for the crowds to settle down and his eventual exit from the stage.

Henry stood up, adjusted his coat and tie and said, "I've got some schmoozing to do. You okay right here?"

Hassie nodded, waved him away and observed the excited crowd as they finished their drinks and closed out their tabs. The musicians lingered around the stage, chatting and smoking. She'd seen a dress in a magazine that she pictured herself wearing when she sang on that stage some day, complete with long white gloves and sparkling jewels.

"A penny for your thoughts," a voice behind her said.

She turned toward the voice just as the man sat down. "Hi, Frank," she said. "It was a great show tonight. I mean, it's always a great show. It's just that tonight –"

"Did you catch my dedication to you, kid?"

She nodded and said, "Yeah, thanks."

"The band kinda stepped on it but all the intentions were good. What are you drinking?"

"Henry and I just finished a bottle of champagne."

"Then, champagne it is," he said, motioning to the barman for service. He opened a fresh pack of cigarettes and tapped against the bottom to knock a couple out. "You smoke?"

"Not really," she said, wrinkling her nose. "I used to but I didn't really like it."

Frank laughed and said, "Good for you. It's a nasty habit." He lit the cigarette and took a deep draw and then exhaled as he said, "So how does it feel to be eighteen?"

"Great, I guess." She sat up straighter in the chair and smoothed her dress across her lap. When she looked back in his direction, Frank was staring at her and grinning like he knew something that she needed to know. She wanted to say something clever or maybe even flirt with him a little bit, but before she could think up a complete sentence, the waitress arrived with a bucket containing a bottle of champagne and looked at Sinatra for permission to open it.

He nodded and pointed to Hassie. "That's for the lady. I'll have my usual."

"Yes, sir," the waitress said and set a glass in front of Hassie.

"Where's our friend Jake?" Frank asked.

"He had to go to LA on business."

"On your birthday? Tsk, tsk," he said, shaking his head.

"He said it was important, and we had a little celebration last night."

"That's nice and very generous of you to defend his not being here now. I don't know too many women that would be so understanding."

Hassie had spent most of the day defending Jake's absence and was reminded again that she hadn't spoken with him at all. She took a big swallow of champagne and decided to change the subject. "I saw an article about your – Rat Pack? Is that what it's called?"

"That's it, doll. Bunch of good guys, talented and all. Good friends too. They'll be in Vegas in a few weeks. You'll like 'em and they'll *love* you."

Hassie smiled as Frank's drink was delivered. He raised the glass and said, "To Hassie and all things young and beautiful."

She touched her glass to his then took another big sip. The waitress refilled her glass before she left the table. Hassie felt relaxed and calm and wanted to have a real conversation with Frank. She picked up her glass again, but as she prepared to take another sip, a hand reached from behind her and took the glass away; she heard Jake's voice, "I think you've had enough."

"Hello, Jake," Sinatra said. "Nice of you to join us. I thought you were away on, uh, business."

When Hassie turned around to face Jake, she stared directly at Natalie. She looked at Jake, then at Frank and back at Natalie.

"Frank, you remember Natalie?" Jake said, offering her a chair at the table.

"Sure," Frank said, then looked at Hassie. "Jake, you do know that today is your lady here's birthday?"

Jake motioned to the waitress for more glasses and ignored Frank's question. Hassie couldn't look at anyone and felt her face getting red and hot. She could feel them all staring at her and tried not to show the horror she felt at seeing Natalie there with Jake. The champagne made a sudden rush for her head and she had no choice but to leave the table. She stood up, excused herself and ran out the Copa Room door.

She rushed through the corridor like the place was on fire, each step an effort to stay on her feet. As she rounded the corner by the lobby, she heard Henry call out to her. She ignored him and kept going until she caught her heel and stumbled against the wall.

"What the hell is wrong with you?" Henry said, reaching out to steady her.

Her face was wet with tears and she tried to avoid looking at him. She pulled her arm out of his grip and mumbled for him to leave her alone.

"Come on, honey. What happened?"

"Jake showed up."

"I know," Henry said. "He planned a little party for you."

"What are you talking about?"

"Jake told you he wouldn't be back tonight so that he could surprise you. There's a cake and champagne and the guys are all pitched to sing to you." Hassie looked at Henry like he'd given her the worst news of her life.

"Honey, what's going on?" Henry said, pulling his handkerchief from his pocket.

"Jake came in with Natalie and sat down at the table with me and Frank." She took Henry's handkerchief and wiped her nose and face. "He was mean to me."

"Wait a minute," Henry said and steered her back toward the Copa Room. "Something's wrong here. I saw Jake a little while ago and he was heading for the Copa Room and looked in a great mood. He must have spotted you with Frank and jumped to the wrong conclusion. And, of course, Natalie was standing there waiting to pounce." Henry took hold of her hand and said, "Come on. We're going back."

Henry practically dragged Hassie along the corridor, shouting at her to pull herself together and give Jake a chance to explain. The image of Natalie's smug face made her sick. When they reached the Copa Room entrance, she pulled away from Henry and turned to leave. "I can't do this, Henry. I can't face them now."

"Yes, you can," Henry said and pushed her through the door. "Now go."

As they got closer to the table, she could see the back of Frank's head and Jake and Natalie's faces. She resisted Henry's tug on her like a reluctant dog on a leash and silently begged him to let go of her. When they reached the table, Henry stood her between Sinatra and Jake and said, "Jake, Hassie needs to talk to you."

"There you are," Frank said. "We can't have a party without the birthday girl."

Hassie froze and looked at Jake. He finally stood up, pulled out a chair and pointed for Hassie to sit down. Natalie got up and left.

"Frank, can you give us a little privacy, please," Jake said and sat down.

"Sure," Frank said. "You two love birds have a good evening now."

Henry followed Sinatra away from the table, and Jake sat quiet and still. Hassie waited for him to speak but he just kept flicking his cigarette into the ashtray, his face puckered into a grimace of disgust and contempt. She finally forced the conversation by saying, "Why are you mad at me?"

"I'm not mad at you, Hassie," he said, his stare cold and intent. "I'm disappointed."

"You're the one who left me on my birthday."

"But I came back." He paused and stubbed out his cigarette. "I came back and found you practically in the arms of another man."

She reached for his arm. "Who, Frank? We were just talking."

Jake jerked his arm back and jumped up with such force that his chair fell over. "I know what I saw," he shouted at her. "You were completely in his face. Did you kiss him? Were you planning a sexy night in bed while your fool of a lover was away."

"Jake, that's crazy –"

He grabbed her chin with his right hand and pulled her within an inch of his face. "I'm not crazy. You're behaving like a little whore, and I don't like being made a fool of." He pushed her away and continued, "You go and do whatever you like with Frank – screw his brains out. I don't care. But I'll tell you one thing. He will never really care about you and he will certainly never love you." He straightened up and put his cigarettes in his coat pocket. "No one will ever love you the way I have loved you."

He didn't give her a chance to say a word; he just walked away and spoke to a couple of the musicians. She looked around for Henry, but the room was almost empty now. She'd never seen Jake so angry and had no idea how to handle things with him. She remembered his reaction the night he saw her in the Copa Room with Frank. He'd said that he wasn't jealous of Frank, but why else would he parade Natalie in on the night that he had supposedly planned a party for her? She stood still, hoping that he would finish his conversation and then come back to talk to her again. But when he turned away from the stage, he looked past her and walked straight to the door where Natalie stood wearing a big smile as she reached out to take his arm, and the two of them left the room together.

chapter nine

HASSIE LAY in her old bed in Stella and Natalie's room, propped on one elbow and still in shock over Jake's behavior the night before. Stella drew open the curtain over the bed and said, "You can't give up on him, Hassie. I don't care what you think you saw."

"Stella, he left the Copa Room with Natalie. Do you think they went to feed the goldfish?"

Stella laughed and sat down on the edge of Hassie's bed. "I only know what you've told me, and Lord knows, Natalie doesn't give a shit about you. But Jake loves you. He never cared what Natalie did when he wasn't interested in seeing her. She had to really work at spending time with him."

"Well, she didn't have to work too hard last night. He made sure she was right by his side."

"Uh-huh," Stella said, and walked over to her closet. "And why do you think he did that? He was hurt to see you with Frank. And by the way, Frank's no innocent bystander in all of this. He knew what he was doing."

Hassie sat up as Stella handed her a bathrobe. "What do you mean?"

"Everybody knew that Jake was planning to surprise you. Frank had to know that Jake would show up at any minute and he chose to take over the party and put you in a compromising position."

"Then why didn't Jake get mad at Frank? Why did he treat me like I committed such a sin?"

"You should ask him. Go and talk to him."

"I can't stand the thought of finding Natalie in our suite."

"Then ask Henry to tell him that you want to talk to him on neutral ground – in the Copa Room or somewhere." Stella finished dressing and started to brush her hair. "Hassie, do you love Jake?"

"Of course, I do." Her chest tightened at the thought that she might have lost him.

"Then fight for him. That's all I'm going to say."

Stella left the room and Hassie decided to get out as quickly as she could in case Natalie showed up. When she stepped out of the shower, the phone rang. She hesitated at first and then thought that it might be Henry looking for her. On the fifth ring she picked up the receiver and said a tentative hello.

"Hi."

Her stomach jumped at the sound of his voice. "How'd you know I was here?" she said.

"Because you weren't in bed with me."

She felt that he was trying to confuse her and wasn't sure what she should say.

"Are you there?" Jake asked. He waited a few seconds and then said, "Nobody sleeps in this bed but you and me. I've told you that a hundred times."

"Then where did you go with Nata –"

"Hassie, come back. I want to talk to you and I'd prefer not to have an audience."

She still didn't know what to think of his exit from the Copa Room with Natalie on his arm, but he had made the first move and she thought of Stella's advice to talk it out with him. "Okay," she said. "I'll be there as soon as I finish dressing."

"You don't need any clothes."

"Yeah, well, I don't want to get arrested before I get there." She hung up and thought again about Stella's suggestion that Sinatra was really to blame. Why would he do such a thing? Wasn't Jake a friend of his?

Hassie borrowed a dress from Stella and left her clothes from the night before in the bottom of Stella's wardrobe. She didn't bother with putting on makeup except for the lipstick that she had in her purse. Her eyes were puffy and red – telltale signs of her extreme lack of sleep. She picked up her purse and started out the door just in time to meet Natalie coming in.

"Why did I know you'd be hanging around my room?" Natalie said as she pushed past Hassie. "Afraid to go back to Jake? Of who'd be in *his* bed?"

Hassie hesitated for a few seconds before saying, "Go to hell," and slammed the door behind her. She walked toward Jake's suite, the vision of Natalie in bed with him burning her gut and ripping at her heart. She didn't want to believe that Jake would lie to her and she couldn't give Natalie the satisfaction of thinking that she cared what had actually gone on between them. She'd have to trust Jake until she had a valid reason not to.

When he opened the door, she saw a different man from that of the night before – softer features and loving eyes. She entered the dark room; he closed the door, took hold of her arm and pulled her close. She stood still in his embrace, but neither said a word for several seconds. She wanted to hear him say that he was sorry. That he had overreacted and should not have treated her so badly. That he certainly shouldn't have left with Natalie.

He never said anything of that sort nor did he acknowledge that there had been a moment's problem between them. He kissed her tenderly and told her he loved her, then led her to the bedroom and took off her clothes. Her mind was full of comments and protests, but she couldn't resist his gentle touch and sensuous mouth. He made love to her with a slow, deliberate passion that left her breathless and made her forget the pain and anger that he had caused the night before. Exhaustion finally overtook her and she fell asleep while hearing Jake order coffee and jelly doughnuts.

When she awoke and went to the closet to get her bathrobe, the space where her clothes usually hung was empty. She looked around the room and checked another closet and the bathroom. There was no sign that she had ever been there before, let alone lived there. She put on Jake's robe and walked into the living room. "Jake, where are my things?"

"I asked the housekeeper to take them away," he said without looking at her.

"Why did you do that?"

"Did you have a nice nap?"

"Jake, I asked you a question," she said and moved closer to where he sat. "Why did you have my clothes removed from the room?"

"Because I was angry. I wanted no reminder of you." He sipped his coffee and looked at her. "Don't worry. I'll get it all back."

She stood, staring at him, waiting for him to say something else or at least offer an explanation. He carried on stirring his coffee, lit a cigarette and walked over to the telephone. She felt off balance and wanted to lash out at him until the reality of the situation the night before, coupled with Jake's mood swings, forced her to question for the first time: Was this her fault? She didn't think so. Was it Frank's? No.

Jake hung up the phone and turned to her, saying, "They'll be back with all your things in a few minutes. Relax and have a doughnut."

"I don't want a doughnut." She struggled not to cry and stayed still while he walked back to the armchair and picked up the newspaper. She waited for him to sit down before saying, "You told me you wanted to talk to me when you called me earlier."

"I did talk to you," he said without looking away from the paper. "If I recall correctly, I talked to you several times."

His sarcastic grin made her want to slap him. She walked over to his chair and stood where he had to look at her. "Don't you have anything else to say to me? Like you're sorry for overreacting and for ignoring me and hanging out with Natalie? And how do I know that you didn't sleep with Natalie?"

Jake looked at her like she was speaking gibberish, and then calmly said, "I think you have conveniently forgotten the real issue here. The fact that I found you making bedroom eyes to another man and that you don't even have the sense to recognize that Frank was just lapping up your adoration with not a goddamn care in this world that you and I are together. His motives are obvious and you're playing right into his slimy, little hands. No, sweetheart. I don't owe you any explanation, and I certainly don't owe you an apology. You're lucky I'm speaking to you at all."

"I'm *lucky* you're speaking to me?" She shouted and threw her hands in the air. "After everything you've put me through, I'm the lucky one?" She glared at him; the feeling in the pit of her stomach told her that something had changed between them and she wondered if it would ever be the same again.

He stood up to reach for her, pulling her close to him. "Okay, that's enough. Calm down and stop acting like a spoiled brat."

She pushed away from his chest with both hands and fell backwards onto a side table, knocking the crystal lamp onto the floor. The loud crash startled her, and she ran from the room. She crumbled on the edge of the bed, disgusted with herself for allowing Jake to get to her and cause her to lose control of her emotions. She put her face in the pillow and screamed through her frustration and anger. She wanted to get out of the room – to find Henry or Stella or anyone who could help her make sense out of what was happening – but she needed to calm down and to come to grips with the fact that Jake had control of her life and that she had nothing without his say so and nowhere else to go.

Hassie wished she could just close her eyes and wake up to find that she'd had a bad dream. She drifted in and out of a restless sleep, and when she opened her eyes it was completely dark in the room and she'd been covered with a blanket. She felt disoriented and struggled to remember what had happened earlier until she entered the living room and saw the broken lamp on the floor. Jake had left and the rest of the room was tidy and normal. Then she remembered the issue with her clothes and toiletries and went back to check the closet. When she opened the door, she found her clothes in exactly the same order she remembered and everything was in its place in the bathroom including a small, cut-glass bud vase containing a single red rose. She breathed deeply and took a tissue to blow her nose. Why couldn't Jake just sit down and talk to her – explain his actions and help her understand what she did that angered him so much? Why did he have to rub Natalie in her face and then jerk her emotions around like she meant nothing to him?

She shook her head at the thought that she had so childishly been flattered by Sinatra's attention. *When Frank Sinatra asks you to join him for a drink, you don't turn him down.* How stupid could she be? Surely Jake could see that Frank had basically set her up – some egotistical game among men.

She soaked a washcloth in hot water and spread it over her face. In the warm dark behind the cloth she saw Barbara's face, and Jake's – when he saw her with Sinatra. She burst into a sob, then threw the washcloth in the sink and stared into the mirror. As she left the bathroom to find some clean clothes, she heard the door to the suite open and close and waited to hear Jake's voice. There was movement in the room, but she practically held her breath, hoping that he would go away and just leave her alone.

Another long moment passed before she decided to face Jake. She tightened the sash on her robe and called his name as she entered the living room. A small man in a white jacket leaned over the broken lamp and jumped up when he heard her voice. "Sorry, ma'am. I didn't know anyone was here."

"That's okay," she said, pulling the robe closed around her neck. "Are you here on your own?"

"Yes, ma'am. I'll clean this up and be back with a new lamp shortly."

"Take your time," she said and went back into the bedroom. So Jake hadn't come back after all. It was already mid-afternoon. She drew a bath and poured the turquoise bath crystals under the spigot, forming fragrant clouds in the steaming water. She waited for the man to leave before she stepped in. She slid comfortably down into the bubbles, hiding in their whiteness, the hot, soapy water causing a stinging reminder in her groin of their recent lovemaking.

Hassie knocked on Henry's door while pushing it open and peered in to see if he was there.

"Hi, honey," he said. "I was just deciding whether or not to worry about you."

She sat down across from him and looked around for signs of leftover food. "You got anything to eat? I'm starving."

Henry laughed and picked up the phone. "I'll get you something. Anything in particular?"

She shook her head and smiled. She'd been thinking about how to talk to him about Jake without starting a defensive argument.

He hung up the phone and said, "The chef will send you one of those nice big hamburgers you like."

"And some French fries?"

"Of course." He smiled and nodded and moved a short pile of papers to the side of his desk. "So. Did you patch things up with Jake?"

"Sort of."

"I told you that he had just misread your meeting with Frank," Henry said and winked at her.

"Do you know where Jake is right now?"

"I haven't seen him all day. When I didn't see you either, I assumed you two were making up for yesterday."

She felt him studying her and was careful not to give her feelings away. "I – We spent the morning together but then I fell asleep and I don't know where he went."

"Well, let's get you some food, and I'm sure he'll show up soon."

Hassie stayed in Henry's office for a couple of hours and savored every bite of the thick burger loaded with cheese and all the usual fixings, then munched on the fries while trying to stay out of Henry's way. She finally strolled out into the Copa Room and nervously paced around, hoping Jake would come in and tell her that everything was fine. But there was no sign of him nor had any of the others seen him all day. Where could he have gone? How could he treat her with such loving care that morning and then behave like she didn't exist?

Then there was Sinatra, whom she couldn't seem to get off her mind. He'd been so kind and considerate – his apparent role in her meltdown with Jake just didn't tally. And now, Jake had made up his mind that she was up to no good with Frank, even if he really believed that Frank was playing her for a fool. She wished that Frank would walk into the Copa Room and sit down to one of their comfortable conversations and that everything would go back to the way it was before her birthday. Henry interrupted her thoughts with a message that she had a phone call from Jake. She reluctantly went back to Henry's office, took the receiver from him and said, "Jake? Where are you?"

"Pack your bags," he said. "We're going to New York tonight."

"Do I have a choice in the matter?" Although she hated his tone and assumption that she would do whatever he said, she relaxed with the thought that he wanted her to accompany him to the city where his business was so important, not to mention the place that she had always dreamed of visiting.

"Of course, you have a choice. I have to go to some meetings and thought you would like to go and see the big city. If you don't want to go –"

"I don't know what to pack," she said quickly. "Isn't it very cold there right now?"

"Just take whatever you have and we'll buy anything you need."

She hesitated, and then coyly replied, "Will I need my black negligee?"

"Maybe I'll buy you a new one," he said. "Now, get yourself packed and I'll see you in a couple of hours."

She hung up the phone and stood still behind the desk. Despite his playful response, his tone was cold and tense. Uneasiness settled over her as she realized that something was wrong between them and that the time she spent with Frank was less complicated and more exciting.

Henry poked his head around the door and said, "Everything okay?"

"Yeah. Apparently, we're going to New York tonight."

"Ooh, fancy," Henry said, fanning his face with his hand.

Hassie laughed, walked to the front of his desk and hugged him. "You are my favorite person in the world."

"I doubt that's true," he said, enveloping her in his arms. "But I want a present from New York. Something fabulous and expensive."

She pushed back from his embrace and said, "Henry, sometimes he scares me."

"Who, Jake?" He took her by the hand and walked out into the Copa Room.

"Seriously. Is he a monster?"

Henry motioned to the bartender as they sat at the nearest table. "Jake is Jake. He's a strong, powerful character and I'll tell you one thing, little lady. Since I've known him, he's never remotely cared about a woman the way he cares about you. If I had to bet? I'd say he loves you a lot, and I've never come close to taking that wager with any other woman in his life."

"Including Natalie?" she asked.

"Including Natalie."

They sat across the table from each other, glasses of vodka between them. "Thank you, Henry. I needed to hear all that." A wave of comfort and calm fell over her body as she touched her glass to his and smiled, but his expression said that he had something else to say to her. "Is something wrong?" she asked.

He hesitated and pressed his lips together, then looked at her and said, "Maybe it's none of my business but –" He stopped and took a deep breath.

"But what, Henry? What are you trying to say?"

"You know how much I care about you and probably worry too much. And you know that much of the time I'd like to strangle Jake." He stopped again, and then leaned his elbows on the table to where he was only inches from her face. "I'm having a hard time watching you when you're around Frank."

"What does that mean?"

"If you are so in love with Jake and so worried about what he's doing with Natalie and so determined to be the only woman in his life, you shouldn't be flirting with Frank." Henry leaned back in his chair and put his hands on his waist.

"That's ridiculous, Henry."

He looked at her and said, "Look. I get it. He's Frank Sinatra and he's paying *very* close attention to you, which I understand is very flattering, but have you really thought about how that makes Jake feel?"

She pushed her chair back and stood up. "I need to go pack now. See you in a few days." She walked away from the table and didn't look back. Henry's words stung and her reaction had probably validated them. As she walked back to the suite, she recalled Frank's face when he dedicated a song to her the night before. She *was* flattered by his attention and she honestly didn't want that to change. But if Henry was right, whether she meant to or not, she was nearing the line between harmless flirtation and deliberate betrayal. And she was smart enough to know that crossing that line was dangerous and could have disastrous results.

chapter ten

FROM THEIR ROOM on the tenth floor of the Plaza Hotel, Hassie looked out over a jumble of bare trees and evergreens in Central Park, fenced inside a rectangle of tall buildings and surrounded by lanes of noisy traffic crawling through the busy streets of Manhattan. Come to think of it, from where she stood, the city seemed to operate on a system of right angles: the park, the buildings, the streets, all squarish and compacted into a small space, yet massive and alive with people. She could see the cold air hovering over the city in a fine, gray mist that differed so from the blue sky she'd left behind in the Nevada desert. She shuddered as she watched a carriage driver place a red and black checked blanket over the dark brown horse in the street below. She was yet to understand what held Jake so dear to such an obtrusive place, but was thrilled at the opportunity to share it with him.

"So what do you think about the city so far?" Jake said as he finished tying his necktie.

She walked away from the window, over to where he stood and straightened the tie's knot. "Are there always so many people on the streets? And are they always in such a hurry?"

He smiled and took hold of her shoulders. "Were you expecting to see tumbleweeds rolling along Fifth Avenue?"

She cocked her head and grimaced. "I wasn't expecting it to be quite so cold."

"Is that your way of telling me that I should buy you a fur coat?" He pulled on his jacket and stuffed a pack of cigarettes in the pocket.

She took hold of his lapels and drew her lips close to his. "Well, you did say that you would take me shopping. I noticed a fancy store right next to the hotel when we arrived this morning."

He kissed her and looked at his watch. "I'll be back in a couple of hours and we'll go over to Bloomingdales. Have some breakfast and take it easy. It's gonna be a busy few days."

She relaxed in a deep, hot bubble bath and reflected on their arrival at the sprawling airport where they were immediately flanked by two men dressed in dark suits and then hustled into a long, black limousine. Jake's careful attention to her during the long journey from Vegas was a bit puzzling, but she no longer wanted to question his motives. If it had been his intention to put the incidents with Frank and Natalie on her birthday behind them, she wasn't convinced that plopping her in the middle of a strange and manic city was the best place to do so. But she'd give it a chance. Eventually she dried off with a warm towel from the heated rack beside the tub before wrapping herself in the thick terrycloth robe.

After an hour she grew tired of waiting in the room. She put on a cashmere sweater over a fitted wool skirt that fell to the top of her calves and then flared out into a single kick-pleat in the back and a pair of low-heeled pumps. As she stepped out into the corridor, she draped her lightweight camelhair coat over her arm. A chambermaid walked past her and smiled, and then pointed her in the opposite direction toward the elevators. Downstairs, she drifted through the rambling corridors and lobbies of marble floors and pillars with rich, mahogany doors and ornamented archways. Under the sparkling glow of crystal chandeliers, the luster of burnished gold throughout the space evoked images of enchanting palaces that she'd only seen in the movies. In the midst of such grandeur, the Sands seemed like a tawdry cement box with too much shiny metal that had bypassed elegance altogether.

She entered the main lobby, a virtually ceiling-less space of more marble and partially mirrored walls with three revolving doors shuttling crowds of people in and out of the cold. The young children in tow had bright red cheeks and runny noses and caused her to focus on the life-sized illustration of a strange looking little girl hanging on a long wall across from the reception desk. She wore a black, pleated skirt with suspender-like straps over a white puff-sleeved blouse, white knee socks and black Mary Jane shoes, and had such an irreverent demeanor that Hassie moved closer to see a small brass plate mounted on the base of the frame that simply said, "Eloise." She studied the odd features of the girl for a moment longer and then decided to venture into the square in front of the hotel.

She pushed through one of the heavy doors and gasped as the cold air hit her face, then buttoned her coat and pulled the collar around her neck. She crossed the wide driveway in front of the hotel lined with taxis until she stood in front of a beautiful statue of what looked like a Greek goddess planted in the center of a round cement fountain. Immediately to her right was the side entrance of the great Bergdorf Goodman department store. She crossed 58th Street and landed in front of the *Paris* cinema, then veered left past Bergdorf Goodman's windows, which glistened with fake snow and shiny Christmas decorations amid an array of elegant gifts like she'd seen in the Neiman Marcus in Dallas. She stopped to look at a display from the jewelry department and a pair of diamond and emerald earrings that looked like they'd been borrowed from one of the rich Texas oilmen's wives.

At the corner of Fifth Avenue, she rounded the department store and ran head on into throngs of people bound in heavy wool and fur coats, topped with hats and scarves and earmuffs; their dynamic movements against the frigid atmosphere left her motionless until she realized that she stood at the top of the most famously decorated street in the country, which, as she looked down toward the Empire State Building, seemed endless. The spectacular lights and tinsel bedecked with sprigs of snow-frosted holly and gigantic metallic-glazed balls made the big wire snowflakes covered in white lights along Main Street in Corsicana look like a kindergarten class project. Slightly embarrassed by the simplistic image of her hometown, she took a deep breath and dodged an oncoming barrage of women exiting the department store loaded with packages and wrapped snugly in full-length fur coats. Her simple wool coat was getting thinner by the minute, and when she saw two of the women laugh at the sight of her, she decided that she would wait to visit the many wonders along Fifth Avenue with Jake or at least in the warm comfort of the big black car.

She backtracked to 58th Street and crossed over to the hotel at its side entrance. The sign on the door said "Oyster Bar" but a sudden gust of cold wind kept her moving and she whirled through the dark wood revolving door, landing in a lowly lit room full of cigar smoke and the voices of men. She felt out of place and, although she consciously avoided eye contact, could feel the men watching her as she moved past the u-shaped bar looking for another way out.

When she finally had to admit that she was lost under the low glow of the large Tiffany lights, a man sitting at the end of the bar turned to catch her eye and then stood up to prevent her walking past. She froze and waited for him to speak.

"I think you made a wrong turn," he said and then smiled with a familiarity that made her shiver. He was dressed in a stylish charcoal gray flannel suit like one that Frank sometimes wore in his show. His dark hair and moustache had streaks of whitish-gray and, even in the low light, she could see his light hazel eyes, which stayed focused on her face.

She took a tentative step and then looked at him and said, "I'm on my way back to my room."

In a swift but casual move, he put his hand on her elbow and said, "Do you want some company?"

Hassie looked away from the man and into the faces of three men sitting at a table beside the bar, each more interested than the other in the answer that the man at the bar awaited. She pulled her arm from his grip and headed toward the amber glass paned door that she'd spotted on the other side of the room. When she reached the corridor, she breathed deeply before looking back at the door, which displayed a small plaque that said, "Gentlemen Only". She rushed straight for the bank of elevators and back to the safety of her room.

When she opened the door, Jake was standing at the window, smoking a cigarette and turned to practically pounce on her. "Where've you been? I told you to stay here until I got back."

She unbuttoned her coat and removed it as she said, "It's freezing out there. I've got to get something warmer to wear."

He took her coat from her and threw it on a chair, then took hold of her arm and said, "Hassie, I don't want you roaming around this city on your own. If you have to go out when I'm not here, you let Gino know."

"Who's Gino?" she asked and spotted a bottle of vodka.

"He's the guy who was with the driver that picked us up from LaGuardia. He's here to help us with whatever we need and he's supposed to keep an eye on you. I don't know how you got past him this morning, but I'm damn sure gonna find out."

Despite the fact that her palms were sweaty from the encounter in the Oyster Bar, she rubbed them together and pretended that she was still cold, then took a glass from the console table and said, "I need to warm my blood. Then can we go shopping?"

Jake walked over and took the glass from her, poured some vodka in it and gave it to her. "I want you to listen to me," he said and pointed her to the sofa. "You are a guest in this city and a very important one. There are plenty of people geared to show you around or take you sightseeing. Just speak up and don't go wandering off by yourself again. Now, finish your drink and I'll take you shopping. You're gonna need a couple of nice dresses too."

"I have plenty of dresses, Jake. I need a warmer coat and some gloves and a hat or something."

He sat down and took the last draw on his cigarette before stubbing it out. "For once in your life, just do as you're told. I'm taking you to some fancy clubs and I know what you need to wear."

"If you really want me to look the part, I saw some pretty spectacular earrings at that store – something Goodman." She smiled and sipped her drink, finally relaxing after the confrontation in the bar.

Jake frowned and said, "I'll make the shopping list, if you don't mind. Now, drink up. The car's waiting."

They bought dresses at Bloomingdales and shoes and scarves and a hat at Saks Fifth Avenue before ending up at the fur department at J. Mendel on Madison Avenue. Hassie's opinion about Jake's selections didn't much matter to him, but the reception that they got at the exciting clubs where he had once worked let her know that Jake knew exactly what he was doing. He was in his element and she was obviously "his woman."

The black limousine was waiting for them every time they stepped out to go somewhere, and they spent evenings in the Copacabana Club and a place called Jilly's that Frank had once talked about in a magazine interview. Bobby Darin headlined at the Copacabana and the women screamed through the entire set just like they did when he performed on *The Dick Clark Show* on television. But the numerous photos of Sinatra scattered around the enormous space made her wish deep down that they were watching him perform, or at least that he were somewhere nearby. Jilly's was almost a shrine to Frank, and she started to doubt Jake's claim that he was the bigger player in New York, never mind where Sid Casper figured into all of this.

Hassie loved the attention that they got everywhere they went, but she began to tire of the late nights, especially when Jake would disappear into a back room with other men and leave her sitting alone with Gino the Giant, who made Jimmy, the doorman at the Sands, look like one of the seven dwarfs. But Jake's promise to take her to a Broadway show kept her spirits up, and when she stepped out of the limo at the theater the following night, she stood under the impressive marquee where "The Sound of Music" was spelled out in bright white lights.

As they stood in the crowded lobby during the intermission, Hassie's mind drifted back to the opening scene when Mary Martin had appeared alone on the stage and sung the rapturous title song with glorious orchestral backing. In the midst of her adoration, Jake walked up, handed her a glass of champagne and said, "You look like you've just seen a choir of angels."

"Stop it, Jake," Hassie said and sipped the drink. "Don't you think this is wonderful?"

He shrugged and said, "I guess so. Although I can think of a thousand other places I'd rather be right now. One of which is having dinner next door at Del Campo."

"How can you think about dinner when such great music is being sung? I'd give anything to stand up there and sing to an audience like this every night."

When the bell rang signaling the end of intermission, Jake took the glass from her and left it on the bar, then took hold of her arm and steered her back to their seats. "Don't let all of these big city productions put big ideas into your head."

"What does that mean?" she stopped to wait for an answer, blocking the path of a long line of people behind them. Jake tugged her forward and carried on down the aisle. When they were seated, she looked at him and started to say something further when the lights went down and the orchestra brought the room alive with a medley of songs from the show.

When the show was over, they exited the theater through a side entrance that emptied into a small alley where Gino and another giant whose name Hassie didn't know waited to accompany them to the end of the alley, around the corner and through the entrance of a small Italian restaurant. They were greeted by the strong, pleasant aroma of garlic and other Italian spices and Hassie suddenly realized that she was ravenous.

As Jake helped her remove her mink stole, a small, dark-haired man with a thick moustache came rushing toward them, grabbed and shook Jake's hand as he shrieked, "*Buona sera,* Signor Contrata." He snapped his fingers and shouted something in Italian to the nearest waiter, then looked back at Jake and said, "Ah, the signorina is *bellisima,*" then bowed as he took hold of Hassie's hand and kissed it without his lips touching her.

"Grazie, Paolo," Jake replied. "Please meet Hassie Calhoun."

Hassie nodded, and Paolo's huge smile revealed a gold-capped tooth near the front of his mouth as he said, "Signorina Calhoun. You are a special guest in my restaurant tonight. Whatever you want, we make for you. A nice veal parmigiana, a juicy T-bone steak, you name it, you got it." Before Hassie could respond, he clasped his hands at his waist, looked back at Jake and said, "Signor Casper is waiting for you."

Hassie didn't move while she said, "Sid's here?"

Jake took hold of her hand and pulled her along as he said, "Yes, Sid's here. It's time for you to meet the enchanting Mrs. Casper. Just be nice and try not to look so gorgeous."

They walked through the intimate space that was crowded with tables covered in red and white linen cloths and decorated with candles lodged in wine bottles. Stalks of garlic cloves hung from strategic points around the room while trolleys of meats and cheeses were wheeled around by the friendly waiters, one of which sang along with the voice of an operatic tenor wafting from the sound system. Every table was full of chatty customers and every plate of food looked delicious.

Gino opened the door to a private dining room where they were greeted by Sid's loud bellow of laughter and a cloud of cigar smoke.

Although six people already occupied the table, Hassie only recognized Sid and moved closer to Jake as the other men stood to greet them. The four men nodded and offered their names, which she could only remember as Angelo and Marco with somebody Bertolino and maybe Gamboli. A tall blond woman that reminded Hassie of an older version of Stella remained seated and was eventually introduced to Hassie as Myra Casper. The two women were seated on opposite sides of the table and were mutually excluded from the business conversations among the men.

After the second course was cleared from the table, Myra motioned to Hassie that she was going to the ladies room, which Hassie delightfully accepted as an invitation to join her. When they were clear of the room and the earshot of Gino and friend, Myra turned to Hassie and said, "Is this your first time?"

Hassie nodded tentatively and said, "You mean in New York?"

"Well," Myra hesitated. "All right then. Is it your first time in New York?"

They chatted about the wonderful shopping and the fantastic nightlife, and Hassie was thrilled to learn that Myra was also a fan of the theater. She also seemed to be involved in a lot of things to do with the museums and the opera, and suddenly Hassie understood why Sid spent so much time in Vegas or LA. But judging by the size of the diamonds in the rings on her fingers, she got along just fine wherever Sid stayed.

The evening turned out to be a roaring success as far as Jake was concerned, and Hassie had to admit that it hadn't been so bad, even if she didn't understand a word of what was being discussed. The next morning, the black car picked them up at the hotel and made one last journey through the city on the way to LaGuardia Airport, the enigmatic Empire State Building almost always in sight. Hassie was still annoyed at Jake's suggestion that she should leave the excitement of the big stage behind her, but had already been thinking about her next trip to the city and knew exactly where she would go. The clubs were bigger and more sophisticated than the lounges in Vegas but she'd found the real magic of New York inside the grand Broadway theater.

As they rode along the freeway, she thought about the events of the previous days, snuggled up close to Jake and put her head on his shoulder. "I had a great time," she said. "Thanks for asking me to come with you."

Jake took hold of her hand, kissed the top of her head and said, "It's a pretty great place, isn't it? Now you can say you've been here. Not too many people get the chance."

She sat up straight and looked at him. "I'll be coming back, won't I?"

"Why do you need to come back? You've seen everything that's worth seeing. Believe me, it'll be the same the next time and the next."

"But I'd like to see some more shows – different ones with different stars in them."

He lit a cigarette and rolled the window down just enough to let the smoke escape. "Don't you see enough shows and stars in Vegas? I can't think of a reason why you'd want to come back to New York. It's a long way from home, and you said yourself that it's too cold."

She sighed and pulled her hand from his, then stared out the side window and decided to leave it alone.

"Don't sulk like a child," he said, which she took as an invitation to say what was on her mind. "Why do you always have to shoot the air out of my bubble?" Jake laughed and took hold of her face like he was going to kiss her. She pushed his hand away and said, "I'm serious. And kissing won't help."

He leaned back in the seat and said, "So, what will help? What can I say that will make you understand that it's stupid for you to fantasize about being the next star on the great stages in New York."

"Why do you say that?" she said. "You've never even heard me sing."

He took a big puff of the cigarette and then threw it out the window. "Look. If you're hell-bent on being a big star, go for something you're good at. I hear Hugh Hefner's looking for Playboy Bunnies."

Hassie said very little to Jake on the return to Vegas and slept during most of the flight. She was actually happy to get back to normal life at the Sands and didn't mind at all that a refurbishment project took up more and more of Jake's time, which meant that she had more free time to pursue her desire to do something constructive with her music. Although she had been exposed to some of the greatest singers in the world since her arrival in Vegas, nothing compared to the spectacle of a Broadway show, and she was constantly lulled by the melodies from *The Sound of Music* that stayed in her head. So what if Jake didn't take her seriously. She figured out the pattern of rehearsal time versus down time for the musicians and found several hours a day that the Copa Room was empty and she was free to use Julio's piano.

Once she gained access to the Copa Room on her own, she would play for as long as she could – both the melodies that she never wanted to forget and the ones that she had written during her last few months with Barbara. Some were still coming together on the keyboard and needed to be written down. She still had hopes of working with Julio and camped out in the Copa Room while Jake was in LA. She took a back seat to the Rat Pack rehearsals but patiently waited her turn and one Thursday afternoon ended up on stage with Julio at the end of a session.

"Julio, can I ask a favor?"

"Of course, you can," he said, standing up from the keyboard. "Just give me a minute to go to the cat box."

She smiled and waved for him to go, then sat down at the piano. She played the melody of the song that she had concentrated on the most, aware that the middle section was not quite there yet.

Julio's return startled her as he said, "What's that you're playing?"

"Just a little melody that I wrote."

"Sounds pretty good. Is there more?"

"Yeah, but I'm still working on it."

He sat down beside her on the left side of the piano bench and said, "Let me hear it from the top."

She played the melody through once. "And then it repeats."

"Okay." Julio played a few chords. "Now play it again." He played along with her until they'd finished two verses. Then, as if overly inspired, he nudged her off the bench and carried on with a short bridge before repeating the verse melody in a different key.

"Wow," she said, leaning on the piano. "That sounds like a real song."

"It is a real song, chica," he chuckled. "And a damn good one. Now we need some lyrics."

"I've got some of those as well."

"Let's hear 'em," he said and played a brief introduction.

She sang the lines that she had written to fit with the music until they reached the bridge. "It needs some more work, I guess."

Julio stopped playing, leaned on the piano and said, "This is good, Hassie. What or, I guess I should say, who are you singing about?"

"My father. I wrote a poem after he died and my teacher thought it would be nice lyrics for my song."

Julio hummed the first line of the song and said, "Keep working on the lyrics and think about a few lines for the bridge. Write it all down and let me know when you've finished."

"Do you really think it's good?"

He nodded and said, "I think it's good and you've got some real potential here."

"Thanks, Julio. I'll keep working on it."

"Henry was looking for you earlier," Julio said. "Did you see him?"

She started toward the door, shook her head and said, "No, but I'm meeting Stella for a late lunch now. I'll catch him later." She was grateful for the tedious hours she'd spent all those summers in music theory classes writing out all the keys – the sharps, the flats, majors and minors, whole notes, half notes, triads, common and cut time. She still had the notebooks of musical staves that Barbara had given her during her last year of study. She would transcribe the notes of her melodies into one of the notebooks. With Julio's help to fill out the harmonies, the song that she'd only ever sung in the shower had a chance to be heard by others.

As she entered the Garden Room, Hassie realized that it had been weeks since she'd actually spoken with Stella, whom she spotted sitting at a table near the window. She rushed over and sat down, now almost half an hour late.

"I'm so sorry I'm late," Hassie said, removing her jacket. "Have you been waiting long?"

Stella stubbed out her cigarette and said, "Just long enough to smoke two cigarettes and drink a martini."

Hassie eyed the empty martini glass and said, "That sounds like a great idea. Do you want another one?"

"Why not," Stella said. "But don't think I forgot about your trip to New York." She eyed Hassie's dress and studied her face before saying, "You look like a new woman."

They ordered drinks and the chef's version of a Waldorf salad, which included chunks of chicken on top of the traditional salad of apple, celery and walnuts mixed into lettuce with a light mayonnaise dressing.

Stella buttered one of the sesame seed rolls that the waitress left on the table and took a big bite as she said, "So did you see the big hotel – the Waldorf Astoria?"

"We saw it from the car but didn't go in," Hassie said. "We actually stayed at the Plaza, which was unbelievable, Stella." She recounted the details of the magnificent building, the shopping trips and the bits of sightseeing they'd done. When they'd finished the meal, the waitress cleared the table and Stella asked for another drink. When the waitress looked at Hassie, she shook her head, then hesitated and said, "Oh, all right. Make it two."

Stella lit a cigarette and exhaled the smoke away from the table. "So how was it travelling around New York with Jake? From the way Natalie talks, you'd think he owns the city."

Hassie ignored the reference to Natalie and said, "He knows exactly where to go and a lot of people know him. We went to that big club he used to manage and all the hot spots." She hesitated at the thought of the dinner in the Italian restaurant after the theater.

"So what aren't you telling me?" Stella asked as the waitress set their drinks on the table.

Hassie stirred the olives around in the drink while she considered what to say. "Do you really know anything about Jake's life in New York before he came to the Sands?"

"I know he was the manager of the Copacabana and that when he came to Vegas to run the Sands, the whole town talked like Jesus Christ had arrived."

Hassie nodded and said, "Don't you ever wonder who Jake and Henry and even Sid are talking about when they mention the *big bosses*?"

"You mean to tell me that you just spent almost a week with Jake in New York City and you don't know who the big bosses are?"

Hassie sipped her drink. "I know they like to ride around in long black cars and have guys called Gino shuffle them in and out of the clubs and restaurants." She pulled one of the olives off the toothpick and said, "I guess I was just never around things like that in Texas. It must be part of living in New York."

Stella sighed and said, "I think you should discuss this with Jake. On second thought, maybe you should just keep it to yourself until you go back to New York again."

"Well, according to Jake, I don't need to go back." She swallowed the rest of her drink. "But the trip was a real eye-opener where the world of music is concerned."

Stella motioned to the waitress for the check. "How so?"

"We saw this fantastic show on Broadway. It was the most incredible production – wonderful singers and dancers and costumes – a star named Mary Martin. I've never seen anything like it. And I thought I'd seen a lot of great shows."

"And what does this have to do with you?"

Hassie took a deep breath before she said, "I've been studying music since I was a young kid and I really love to sing. But I also had a great teacher who taught me to play the piano and encouraged me to be creative with what she said was a natural ear for melodies and harmonies and that I could be a really good musician if I worked at it."

"So are you saying that you want to move to New York and become a big Broadway star?"

Hassie wasn't sure that she liked the tone of Stella's voice and decided to keep her thoughts to herself. "All I know is that I want to go back to New York again. And I'm going to do so, with or without Jake."

chapter eleven

Hassie snuggled up to Jake from behind as they lay in bed. "Ya know, you're different when Sid's around."

Turning to face her, he asked, "Is that you're way of saying that you wish he hadn't moved into the Sands?"

"About that," she said. "I thought Sid lived in New York. With his wife."

"It's Sid's business what he does, but between you and me, I don't think that's much of a marriage. Myra pretty much does whatever she wants to and Sid – begrudgingly – pays the bills."

She kissed his cheek and said, "All I know is that you've been away since almost the minute we got back from New York. And now Sid's got you running around like his personal slave."

Jake pulled her close to him and said, "Just because Sid's the big boss doesn't mean that he tells me what to do. I'm my own boss." He was quiet for a few seconds like he was waiting for her to agree with him. "Anyway, how am I different when Sid's around?"

"I don't know. Just different." She ran her fingers up and down his chest.

"Like how you're different when Sinatra's around?"

"That's ridiculous," she said and pushed back from him. "Frank's old enough to be my father. Sid's just a lecherous drunk who, by the way, is a little too friendly sometimes."

Jake laughed and sat up. "Sid knows better than to mess with you, but at least you know where you stand with him. Frank likes to play games, and you fall for his insincere bullshit every time."

Hassie pushed herself up on her arms and glared at Jake. "Why would you say something like that? You say you're not jealous of him, but that's not the way it sounds to me."

Jake stood up from the bed and turned to face her. "You can believe whatever you like, but Frank is after you to get back at me."

"Get back at you for what?"

"That's not important," he said and walked toward the bathroom. "Anyway, I shouldn't have to beg you to stay away from him."

"Jake, I hardly ever even see Frank these days. Between his filming schedule and the Rat Pack shows, he's busier than all the rest of us put together."

He stopped at the bathroom door, turned to look at her and said, "You heard what I said."

It became common knowledge that the filming of *Oceans Eleven* took place during the day, but the actors would drift back to the Sands in the afternoon, hang out in the steam room or grab a little rehearsal time in the Copa Room where the bar never officially closed. On an afternoon that Hassie expected it to be quiet in the Copa Room, the musicians were all there, warming up amid coffee, beer and cigarettes.

She went into Henry's office and interrupted him on the telephone. "What's going on out there?"

Henry put the phone down and removed his glasses. "Nothing that I'm aware of. Did you speak to Julio?"

"Not yet. I didn't want to bother him if something special was happening. Maybe there's an important guest coming in or something."

"Let's go see," Henry said, escorting Hassie through the door.

As they approached the stage, the guys started packing up their instruments; a couple of them quickly disappeared.

Henry rushed forward and called out, "Julio, what's happening?"

"False alarm," Julio said, stubbing out his cigarette.

Henry and Hassie stood beside him at the piano and waited for the rest of the story.

"Evidently the boys had a mild disagreement this morning about one of the routines in the show and Frank decided they should have an impromptu rehearsal."

Henry laughed and said, "I bet that was a colorful debate."

"Ay, ay, ay," Julio responded. "But Frank's the boss and, evidently, he changed his mind."

Hassie focused on the guys clearing the stage and a possible opportunity for some time with Julio. When she turned back to speak to him, Henry sat on the piano bench beside him and they were speaking in low voices with a soft undercurrent of intimacy. She unintentionally stared at them until Henry looked up and then stood and moved away from the bench. Hassie blushed and fidgeted with the notebook in her hand.

"I was wondering," she said, clearing her throat. "I was wondering, Julio, if I could show you my song. I mean, I've written some stuff down and you said you would help me –"

"Let's see it, chica." Julio took the notebook from her and Henry walked away while saying, "Hassie, come see me when you finish with Julio."

"Have a seat," Julio said, propping the music on the piano. "Wow, did you do all this?"

"It's not like I had that much else to do. I hope you can read it."

Julio started to play the notes that Hassie had written, then stopped and looked closer at the manuscript. "Did you mean to change the key from major to minor?

She nodded and said, "I reworked the lyrics and it just sounded better in the minor key."

Julio played the notes as they were written, eventually embellishing the simple chord structure and reading the lyrics along with the melody. He got through the whole song once and then played it again, then stopped and leaned on the top of the piano. He studied Hassie for a few seconds and then said, "Your instincts were right and this is ... really ... great."

"Do you really think so?"

He played a new introduction and said, "Sing it for me."

She heard the intro as if it were being played by a lone saxophone or muted trumpet then took a deep breath, closed her eyes and let the music take over. She sang the song all the way through. Julio played a short reprise of the verse; she sat quiet and still. When he played the last note, he turned to her and put both arms around her, his silence, saying all that she needed to hear.

She stood up and took her notebook from the piano. "Can we work again later?"

"Of course. Don't forget that Henry wants to see you before you leave."

The door to Henry's office was open; she walked in and said, "What's up?"

"Close the door and have a seat," Henry said and set a bottle of vodka and two glasses on the desk.

"What's goin' on, Henry? You don't usually set up a bar in your office."

Henry cleared a space on his desk and removed the cap from the bottle. Without looking at Hassie, he poured the clear liquid into each glass, replaced the cap and pushed a glass in her direction. He moved the other glass closer to him before leaning back.

"Henry? What's going on in that handsome head of yours?" she said.

He took a sharp swig from his glass. "Jake had a little chat with me last night."

"About what?"

"He thinks you spend too much time in the Copa Room and asked me to ... ban you from coming here during the day."

"He what?" She leapt up and grabbed the edge of the desk.

"Calm down. He thinks it would be for your own good. At least for a few weeks while he's still so busy with the hotel."

"Oh, I get it," she said and walked toward the door. "He wants me out of here while he can't watch every move I make." She walked across the back of the room, her jaw clenched tight enough to crack her molars. "I know this is about Frank. He can't stand it when he doesn't have both of us on his radar. This is really sick, Henry. What does he think I do when I'm here? Jump on Frank in front of God and everybody?"

"Hassie, please sit down." Henry stood behind his desk and motioned for her to come closer. "He just wants –"

"Did you agree to this insane idea?" She stared at him and waited for a response. "Huh? Did you?"

"He's my boss. What am I supposed to do?"

Hassie picked up the glass and swallowed the contents. "You must be fuckin' kidding me," she screamed into his face. "I thought you were my friend."

"I am your friend, honey. I just don't have a choice in the matter."

"Well, I have a choice," she said. "I choose to tell both of you to go to hell. *No one* – not you, not Jake Contrata – no one will *ban* me from this room. You got that?" She spun around and left the room, slamming the door behind her. Someone from the stage called out to her, but she had a single mission at that moment and Henry's betrayal stung worse that anything she could remember.

She raced around the hotel in search of Jake and left messages with anyone who was likely to see him. She was too angry to even feign a civil front with the staff and did everything short of threatening them with their jobs if they forgot to give him the message. When she was convinced that she had checked everywhere he might be, she went back to their suite and burst through the door with a certain show of bravado. But when she realized that Jake wasn't there either, she threw herself into the nearest chair and screamed, "I hate yoooou!" She walked over to the bar and poured another drink, downing it in one gulp. She poured another shot into the glass and raised it to her lips just as the door opened and Jake walked in.

"I hear you're looking for me," he said, removing his coat. "Isn't it a little early to be emptying the decanters?"

"Why, Jake?" She stood there ready to leap at him.

"Because you'll get drunk before sundown?" He walked toward her with an air of sarcasm that enraged her. Before he could realize what was happening, she lobbed the glass at him and screamed, "What is wrong with you?"

Jake dodged the glass and grabbed her by the wrist, pulling her with such force a sharp pain pierced her shoulder. For a second, she believed that he would really hurt her and gave in to his forceful grip.

"Now, calm down," he said and poured another drink. "Here. Let's sit down and behave a little less like animals."

Hassie stared at him like he was a stranger, nauseous at the thought that, again, Jake had control of her life. "Why are you doing this to me?"

Jake poured himself a drink, sat across from her and loosened his tie. "What do you think I'm doing to you, darling?"

She cringed at the sound of the word *darling* and stared into her glass.

"I assume Henry told you that I think you should find something else to do with your time while the guys are working in the Copa Room."

"He told me you *banned* me from going there during the day. How could you do such a thing?"

"I think you're being a little overly dramatic here," he said. "Or maybe it's the way Henry relayed my instruction." He stood and walked over to the broken glass lying in the floor. "Anyway, let's work on another hobby for you while Frank and the boys are here."

"How many times do I have to tell you? My music is not a hobby."

In a swift, nearly violent move, he kicked the broken glass across the room and turned back to her, "It's not up for debate." He picked up his coat and headed for the door. "Now, get yourself together and join me for dinner at eight o'clock."

She made no sound and didn't move until he had left the room. Up until then, she had been too outraged to cry, but as the vodka kicked in and the reality of what she had just been through set in, she screamed out in angry sobs.

She had another drink and sat calmly in the armchair until she realized that she was sitting in the dark and had no idea what time it was. Her shoulder ached and her throat was raw from screaming. In an almost robotic move, she went into the bathroom and removed her clothes, avoiding the mirror and leaving all the lights off except for the one in the hallway. As she turned on the water to draw a bath, she heard the phone ring. She quickly set the stopper in place and went to answer it.

"Hassie, please don't hang up," Henry said, his voice desperate and shaky.

She held the receiver for a few seconds; her feet were freezing and she was naked.

"Are you okay?"

"No, Henry. I'm not okay. And I'm trying to have a bath." She hung up the phone and went back to the bathroom where the tub was filling up. She stepped into the hot water, immersing herself in safety and comfort, like she imagined a mother's womb would be. She started to cry again, thinking of her conversation with Barbara and her suggestion that she should call her mother, but she still had no real desire to speak to Bonita. With Hassie out of her sight and mind, she could devote all her time to Bobby and Travis. Hassie had learned when she was very young that Bonita had had a terrible time giving birth to her and almost died in the hospital. She believed that her mother blamed her for causing her problems and her subsequent difficulty with having another child. Hassie knew that her father loved her very much, but she also knew that he wanted a son, which made her cry with delight when her little brother was born. It would be a few years before she would understand why Jackson kept his distance from the child, but she clearly understood that Bobby had given Bonita the child that she had longed for. Jackson was dead and Hassie had only memories of him. What did she have of Bonita?

At one minute past eight, Hassie walked into the Copa Room and stood in the back. The place was full of jolly patrons; the girls rushed around like there was a prize for the fastest service. Between the steamy bath and a brief nap, she'd managed to exorcise most of the alcohol from her system, but the room felt hazy and cold. She wanted to leave.

"Now, isn't that better?" Jake said, taking hold of her elbow from behind.

"Better than what?"

He laughed and moved her to a table in the front of the room with a strong grip of her forearm. "Let's have a nice dinner." He waited for her to sit and helped her move her chair to the table, then motioned to one of the waiters to bring the first course. "Would you like some champagne?"

Hassie hesitated then looked into Jake's eyes. Without smiling, he took her hand and repeated, "Champagne?"

She nodded and took her hand away. Donnie McGinley suddenly appeared by Jake's side, whispering to him, and Jake excused himself from the table. As the main course was served, Hassie focused on the stage and anticipated who would be on first. She loved it when Frank came out on his own, but sometimes Frank, Dean and Sammy would all appear at once and the crowd would go crazy.

Jake sat down just as the table was being cleared. "Sorry 'bout that," he said, grinding out his cigarette. "How's the champagne?"

"Fine," she said without looking at him. She could feel his eyes boring into the side of her face.

"Sid may join us in a little while."

She didn't really care and focused her attention on the stage as the lights dimmed and the band started to play the Rat Pack intro. Frank and Dean came out and shook hands with people sitting at the tables at the foot of the stage while Sammy wheeled out the infamous "rolling bar," then waved to the audience while Dean pretended to push him off the stage with an imaginary broom. Hassie relaxed and was grateful for the lighter atmosphere.

Jake was up and down from the table like a jack-in-the-box. Hassie nonchalantly looked around the room for Henry during the breaks when the band played for however long the guys were off stage. The room seemed airless; the patrons moved around in an almost cartoon-like manner. An overweight man wearing cowboy boots and a bolo tie chatted with every woman within his reach except for the woman that he'd earlier introduced as his wife – a badly bleached blonde who'd been poured into a shiny blue dress and now sat alone at the table. Her face sagged, not only with age, but also with the strain of acceptance that she was no longer important to her husband – that he preferred anyone else in the room to her. Hassie was overtaken by a sense of pity and disgust. What made these people tick? Jewels, fancy clothes, expensive cigars and high-priced booze? Sure, they were thrilled to be in the presence of such greatness as Frank Sinatra and the Rat Pack, but how much of what they were experiencing tonight really meant anything to them? And how much would they remember?

After Frank and Sammy finished clowning through their crowd-pleasing rendition of "Me and My Shadow," Hassie felt that the show seemed to go on longer than she remembered. She was exhausted and wanted to go back to the suite. When Joey Bishop started another monologue, she waved for Jake to come to the table, but he gave her the "I'm busy now" sign so she decided to leave. She pushed her chair back and started to stand up just as Sid reached the table.

"How we doin' here, Hassie?"

"Fine, Sid." She forced a smile and pulled her chair back to the table. "How are you?"

"If I was any better, I'd get arrested," he said, eyeing the untouched piece of prime rib on her plate. "Do I need to have a word with the chef?"

"No, Sid, it's fine. I just wasn't very hungry tonight." She willed him to go away and craned her neck above the crowds in an effort to locate Jake.

"So, where's our boy?" Sid said, relighting his cigar.

"Our boy?" Something about this remark was funny to Hassie and she laughed out loud. "If you mean Jake, he seems to be very busy with Donnie tonight. I'm still trying to figure out why he asked me to join him for dinner. I think he's been in that chair for a total of three minutes."

Sid shook his head and made a tsking sound as he said, "Shame on him. If I had a woman like you on my arm, I'd never leave her alone."

She looked at him like he was the king of morons. The audience laughed and applauded as Joey Bishop waved good night. The band started the intro for the closing number as Sinatra walked to the front of stage.

"Frank's a real charmer, ain't he?"

Hassie ignored Sid's comment and said, "How's your lovely wife?"

"Enjoying spendin' my money," he said, and then focused on Frank's closing remarks. "Ladies and gentlemen," he said, gently flapping his arms to quiet the applause. "You've been a very naughty audience." The roar from the crowd was deafening; Hassie felt that her head would burst. "And that's the best kind. Isn't it, boys?" The crowd cheered as Sinatra turned to acknowledge the guys on either side of him, raising his glass and bowing.

Sid puffed on his cigar and laughed at the guys' encore performance of "Luck Be a Lady." Hassie felt a wave of nausea pass through her and slipped away from the table toward the dressing room. Once inside, she breathed deeply and fanned her face with a flyer she found on the dressing table.

She could feel sweat forming on her forehead, but when she reached up to wipe it away, her hand was cold and shaking and her heart started to race. She made her way to the sofa, which was normally the most uncomfortable piece of furniture she'd ever known. As she slowly sat down, she thought about Jake and how her feelings were changing and how she didn't quite understand why. But she was starting to understand what was behind the sniping, hurtful arguments that her parents used to have. She heard herself with her mother's same tone of voice saying that she was miserable and that Jackson didn't understand her needs and too easily dismissed their conversations as childish and a waste of time. With a sense that something was terribly wrong, she began to experience what she could only relate to as her life flashing before her eyes – images moving uncontrollably through her mind – scenes from her childhood, her first day of school, a dance recital where she wore a daisy costume, running around the back yard with their dog, sitting in her father's lap in the car pretending to drive, performing for him in the living room, and standing beside his casket.

She snapped back to reality as two girls noisily entered the room. She wanted to escape without being seen but the position of the sofa made that nearly impossible. She stood up, rushed over to a mirror and pretended to fix her hair. As the girls walked past, absorbed in their gossip, she reapplied her lipstick and snuck back out into the Copa Room, which had more than half cleared and there was no sign of Sid or Jake. She felt strangely alone and glanced toward Henry's office, wishing she could erase the nasty scene they'd had earlier that day. She walked to the middle of the room to have a last look around.

"Hey, Hassie," Julio called out from the stage. "Come up here, chica."

She waved to him and shook her head. "Not tonight, Julio. I'm really beat."

"Aw, come on. I want Toots to hear your song. His sultry lips belong in it. You said so yourself."

"I'm sorry, Julio. I just can't deal with this tonight."

Sinatra walked out and stood in front of the bandstands. "What's the matter, doll? And what's this I hear about a song?"

She looked back, first at Julio and then over to Frank. "It's nothing."

"Sounds like something to me," he said and lit the cigarette between his lips.

"It's nothing I want to talk about now," she said and took a couple of steps closer to the door.

"Then you should come around tomorrow afternoon," he said. "After we finish filming."

"Probably not a good idea," she said.

"Why not?" He stared at her, dragging on the cigarette.

"It's just not, Frank." She stood still for a moment and then hurried to the back entrance while muttering, "Good night." She left the Copa Room knowing that if she hesitated for another second, she would turn around and go back. Frank wanted to hear her song. Why in God's name would she walk away from Julio's invitation to stand on that stage and do the one thing she'd been desperate to do since the day she arrived at the Sands? She hated Jake for ruining her chances of getting Frank's support for her music. But if she went against Jake now, she wouldn't have a chance in hell of convincing him to change his mind about the time she spent in the Copa Room, or worse – that he would send her away from the Sands for good.

She opened the door to Jake's suite expecting it to be empty and dark with no sign of him for several more hours. But as she turned toward the bedroom, he stood in the doorway, his shirt unbuttoned to his waist, a glass of whiskey in his hand. He took a swig of the drink and, without expression, said, "What happened to you?"

She laid her purse on the console table and removed her jacket. "Nothing happened to me, Jake. While you were running around the hotel with Donnie, I sat at that table with Sid until I thought I would vomit."

"I went back to meet you after the show, but Sid said that you left. Where'd you go?"

Hassie wasn't in the mood for Jake's sick games, walked over to the bar and poured a short drink, then downed it before looking at him and saying, "I went backstage to seduce Frank." She poured another shot and then walked toward Jake. "But guess what? He turned me down flat. So, see. You don't need to worry about me going to the Copa Room when he's there." She walked past him into the bedroom and kicked off her shoes.

Jake followed her, grabbed her arm and pulled her close to his body, then kissed her neck before speaking close to her ear. "I don't believe you."

She pushed back from his chest and said, "What? That I went back to seduce Frank or that he turned me down?"

Before she could take another breath, Jake pulled her in tight and kissed her, his mouth groping for her lips and tongue. She stood still while he unzipped her strapless dress, allowing it to fall to the floor. He picked her up and took her to the edge of the bed, then stepped back and looked at her.

As she folded her arms across her half-naked body, Jake moved closer to her, took her face in both hands and rubbed his thumb across her lips before saying, "I know you are lying. Because Frank would never turn you down."

chapter twelve

WHEN HENRY WAS angry with her, Hassie had learned that she needed to take a closer look at her own actions. And as she did so, she knew that she'd been wrong to blame him for Jake's high-handedness. Actually, she'd been plain rude – a trait that she'd picked up from her mother and one more thing that she'd promised herself to overcome. She owed Henry an apology and smiled with the image of his determined jaw when she would stand in front of his desk and let him know that she'd been wrong.

She skipped breakfast, went over to Henry's office and knocked lightly before opening the door just enough to get a sense of his mood. He studied a piece of paper and looked up at her but didn't speak. She walked in and stood in front of his desk, waiting a few seconds before finally saying, "Henry, I'm so sorry."

He barely acknowledged her presence; she sat down and leaned on his desk. She knew that he knew why she was there, but he wasn't going to help her. When she couldn't stand the silence any longer she stood up and said, "Okay. I'll beg for your forgiveness if I have to. But you know how much I love this place. And I've been making some real progress with my music. It made me crazy to think that I couldn't come in here any time I wanted." She waited again for him to speak. "People say all kinds of things when they're angry. I know it wasn't your fault. Please forgive me."

"You're the one who decided the man was Prince Charming." He looked up at her and removed his glasses before settling back in his chair. "Now do you believe that he's just a royal asshole?"

Hassie sat back down and smiled. "I'll admit that he's on shaky ground right now, but I know I behaved badly. I need to hear you say that you forgive me."

"Okay, I forgive you," he said. "Now get the hell out of here."

"What?"

"You're not supposed to be here."

"Then let's go out for coffee." She stood up and pointed to the door. "I really need to talk to you."

"I don't think there's anything more to say."

She stood in front of him and said, "Please. Just have one cup of coffee with me and I promise I'll behave.

He hesitated, appearing to be preoccupied with something on his desk and then said, "I'll meet you in the coffee shop when I finish here."

She started to argue with him, but he put up his hand and said, "That's the best I can do."

Despite her attempt to lighten the mood, it was obvious that Henry needed a little more time. "Okay, I won't push you, and I swear, I won't do anything to get Jake upset with you."

"Good. I'll see you in a few minutes."

She left the office and walked toward the back entrance, thinking about the confrontation with Jake a few nights before and the disturbingly erotic sex they'd had after her story about seducing Frank. She glanced at the stage, now dark and empty, and pictured herself sitting at the keyboard, playing and singing her song while Frank leaned on the piano and listened – cigarette smoke curling around him while he hummed along. She continued on, wondering if Frank would ever ask her to sing with him in one of their shows, then opened the door to the corridor and came face to face with Natalie.

"Still lookin' for Jake?" Natalie said, her expression smug and full of disdain, the freckles across her nose and cheeks a little more prominent than usual.

Hassie ignored her and walked through the door.

"Aren't you supposed to stay away from the Copa Room now?"

Hassie turned to look at her. "How do you know that?"

"You still don't get it, do you?"

Hassie said nothing but her demeanor said, "Get what?"

"Jake and I are very close. He tells me everything."

"You're a liar," Hassie said and knew that if she didn't get away from the woman, she'd do something extreme. She jerked the door open and went back into the Copa Room. She stood just inside the door while she calmed down. Why did she let Natalie get to her like that? She heard Henry shut his door and looked over just as he walked toward her, shaking his head and grimacing.

When he was in earshot, she said, "Henry, I'm sorry –"

"Hassie, what are you doing here?" He walked up to her, grabbed her arm and frog-marched her back outside. "I said I'd meet you in the coffee shop."

"I tried to leave, but ran into big-mouth Natalie who is such a witch. I had to get away from her –"

Henry stopped and grabbed Hassie by her shoulders. "This is insane. You've gotta get a hold of yourself or find another friend."

"I'm sorry," she said.

"Do you realize how many times you've said you're sorry to me in less than thirty minutes?" He let go of her and started back down the corridor.

She was now at a loss for what to say or do and followed him in the direction of the hotel coffee shop. When Henry reached the entrance, he turned to see her behind him. She ran up to him and bit her lip, another apology on the tip of her tongue. They sat in a booth at the back of the room, and Henry motioned to the waitress who quickly appeared at the table.

"I'll just have coffee," Henry said and looked at Hassie.

"Make that two," she said and then remembered she didn't have breakfast. "Wait. Do you still have any of that pecan coffee cake I had the other day?"

The waitress smiled and said, "I'll check and see."

Henry took a small book from his pocket and thumbed through the pages like Hassie wasn't even there. The woman placed two cups on the table and filled them, then returned with a pitcher of cream and set the coffee cake in front of Hassie. Henry smiled his thanks, put the notebook in his pocket and stirred some cream into the coffee before saying, "Okay, let's start over. You came to see me this morning. Was it just to apologize for being such a bitch to me or is there something else on your mind?"

Hassie stirred sugar into her coffee, then cut off a piece of the cake with the fork and held it up to him as she said, "Want a bite?"

Henry shook his head and said, "No, thanks. That's your kind of food. I swear I don't know how you stay so slim."

She smiled and swallowed the first bite, then laid the fork on the plate and considered her thoughts for a moment. "The basic problem is that Jake always has to be in control," she said very seriously and was surprised when Henry laughed.

"Tell me something I don't know," he said. "And what do you expect – considering the way you arrived on the scene and immediately became dependent on him."

Hassie looked at Henry and shrugged. "I guess. It's just that I thought we had more than that. My life is here with him now. I thought we shared everything."

"Well, that's where you're wrong. Jake doesn't know how to share. Jake takes and then Jake takes some more."

"That's very harsh, Henry." She thought about the trip to New York and her closet full of new clothes and shoes. "He's not that totally selfish."

Henry gulped the last swallow of coffee and motioned to the waitress for more. She refilled their cups; Henry grew more agitated as he stirred in the cream. "So which is it – is Jake determined to control your life or just a nice guy with your best interests at heart?"

Hassie let out a big sigh and picked up the fork.

"Let me tell you a little story." He paused for a few seconds until she looked into his eyes. "When I started working at the Sands almost three years ago now, I'd just graduated from high school, my uncle's protégé and – in his mind – the next great hotel operator in Las Vegas."

She swallowed another bite before saying, "Sorry, but who's your uncle?"

"He was a very wealthy Texan who invested heavily in the development of the Sands. He was instrumental in hiring Jake for the job as general manager."

"Shit," she said softly. "He must have a ton of money." She laid the fork on the table beside the plate and blotted her lips with her napkin.

"He's dead now. Died just about two years ago from complications after surgery. But when I first arrived at the Sands, he was alive and kickin' and damned determined that I would learn from the master – the one and only Jake Contrata. Only problem was, Jake wasn't that interested in having a 'snot-nosed boy' running along behind him and pretty much set out from day one to turn me against the hotel management business and send me packing. And, as we both know, Jake never intends not to get his way."

Henry paused to ask the waitress for water. "Anyway, I took to the job like a duck to water, and my uncle was so proud he started giving Jake orders to give me an office and a secretary and all kinds of shit that drove Jake crazy. But I was basically untouchable and for a few months, I was top of the heap. Coulda had a dozen women a night – you know the scene."

The waitress arrived with two glasses of water. Henry took a big gulp and cleared his throat before continuing, "Trouble was, I didn't want a dozen women. I didn't even want one." He paused and looked at Hassie, who sat very still and said nothing. "I met someone the first week I arrived. Someone that I knew from the beginning was the one for me."

"Julio," Hassie said softly.

Henry nodded and swallowed. "We had four glorious months together before the shit hit the fan."

"What happened when Jake found out?"

"Let me tell the story. Despite the fact that Jake had strict orders about how I should be treated at the Sands, he never got off my back and I swear – even though I can't prove it – he put that sleaze-ball, McGinley, on our ass. Anyway, Julio and I were as careful as two people who worked together could be, and I really don't think he could have found out about us without some help."

"Okay, this is probably gonna sound pretty naïve, but why did it matter that Jake found out about you and Julio? It didn't sound like you were hurting anyone."

"My uncle was a conservative old fart – mind you, he was one of the biggest hypocrites to ever live – and he would have died if he'd known his favorite nephew was a fruit. Jake knew this and saw it as an opportunity to blackmail me and Julio, and basically *banned* us from seeing each other outside of the Copa Room. You see, it turns out that Jake was worried about people finding out that there were *homos* working at the Sands. He demoted me to manager of the Copa Room and dared me to whine to my uncle. Then, he told both of us if we didn't do what he said, he'd tell my uncle, who surely wouldn't want to leave any of his vast fortune to a pathetic little queer."

"God, Henry," Hassie said, covering her mouth with both hands. "I feel sick."

"Yeah, well, here's the best part. A day or so after the last big threat, he came into my office and sat down – which, by the way, is something he never used to do – and asked me if I was happy with my new job and if I thought it would work out okay to basically work in the same room with Julio."

"I think I'm confused," Hassie said and took a sip of the water.

"So were we, but after I told Jake that everything was fine with my working in the Copa Room, I never heard another word about the threat to my uncle and his so called *ban* seemed to disappear.

"Did he think your uncle was planning to give you his job or something?"

"Maybe. My uncle was quite ill around this time and died unexpectedly. As soon as Jake realized that he was in full control of the Sands, he got off my back and told the family that he owed it to my uncle to look after my aunt and that she could live here at the Sands for as long as she wanted."

"Wow," Hassie said. "A real mister nice guy."

"Yeah, I guess." Henry took another sip of water and continued. "The important thing is that my relationship with Julio survived, but neither of us are brave enough to flaunt it in Jake's face. We just really keep a low profile."

"So you and Julio are a couple. And you live together?"

"No, honey," Henry said, and laughed. "See how little you know about me? You're so busy running around after Jake, you don't even know where I live."

"I know you live in a suite in the hotel. Right?"

"I promised my uncle, on his deathbed, that I would look after my aunt, so Jake moved her into a large suite and consented to convert part of it into a studio apartment – which is where I live – and I employed one of the chambermaids with a bit of nurse's training to help look after us."

Hassie lightly shook her head and said, "Where does Julio live?"

"He shares a small house with Toots and Chad – a real bachelor pad that you want to avoid at all costs. It's not an ideal arrangement and we rarely get to spend any time together, but it's a job, honey. And a damn good one for me and for Julio – working in *the* Copa Room with Frank Sinatra and now the Rat Pack. We've made the best of it and, even though it's kind of odd at times, Jake leaves us alone."

"What if he changes his mind and one day just sends you away?"

"Now do you see why I'm not anxious to get on his bad side?" Henry said, taking hold of her hand. "Honey, how much do you know about Jake?"

She had to stop to think before saying, "Not a lot, really. He never wants to talk about himself."

"Do you know where he was born or if he has any brothers or sisters or if he's ever been married or has any children?"

She could feel her face redden as she thought about each question, and the bottom line was that she didn't know anything. She shrugged and said, "He just doesn't like to talk about himself."

"Have you ever wondered why?" He watched her squirm and then continued, "Let's talk about the real problem here. Why do you think Jake wants to keep you away from the Copa Room unless he's there?"

"He thinks I've got the hots for Frank and, Henry, you've lectured me about this before. I swear, I've made a conscious effort to keep what little contact I have with Frank very low key."

Henry breathed deeply as he said, "I know you have, but there's something else going on here as well."

"Something else about Frank?"

Henry nodded. "Just before you arrived on the scene, big Sid showed up and there was a lot of scrambling going on for days into weeks. I only know what I heard, but the bottom line was that Frank and Jake were about to tear each other's heads off about something and Frank threatened to leave and never work at the Sands again. Maybe you've learned that Frank is the reason that the Sands is the hottest spot between New York and LA, and Sid told Jake to do whatever he had to do to make Frank happy."

Hassie's mind was darting all over the place with recollection of the various comments that Jake had made about Frank.

"In the end, Frank took over the Copa Room with the Rat Pack and Sid gave Frank part ownership in the Sands."

"Seriously? Frank owns part of the Sands?"

"Yep," Henry continued. "Something like two percent of the hotel, which, by most people's standards, is not enough to think about. But it was something that Frank could lord over Jake – and anybody else who tried to tell him to do something he didn't want to do. As you can imagine, it's been a recipe for disaster, but, as you can see, Frank ain't going away."

"So does that make Frank more powerful than Jake?"

"I don't know that I'd say that, but the two of them seem to compete for everything around here, and your getting in the middle of their feud is not a wise thing to do." Henry drained the coffee from his cup, set it back in the saucer and continued, "And don't ever forget that Sid's more powerful than the two of them put together."

She suddenly felt lost in a world that she really didn't understand and said, "So what should I do, Henry? How do I get Jake to get over this Copa Room ban of his?"

Henry studied her for a few seconds before saying, "Based on my experience with Jake, he just needs to get comfortable with the arrangement or at least believe that he knows what's going on. Why don't you tell him that you're not remotely interested in anything to do with Frank and that you'll prove it to him by only spending time in the Copa Room when you know Frank's not there?"

"Why would I want to do that? The whole point is that I can't let him tell me who to talk to, where to go and when to go there."

"Okay, don't get upset."

"I'm not upset." She scooted to the edge of the bench and said, "But I think it's time to leave."

"Hassie, wait," he said, grabbing her arm. "I'm not telling you all of this to upset you or frighten you or turn you against Jake. I told you in the hopes that you would think about what you're doing with him and consider the complexities of the situation where Frank's concerned. You're very young, honey. And, with all due respect, you haven't done very much living. But Jake's done a lot, and I believe he's in for keeps. He may swing a big dick – pardon the expression – but he's a very insecure person who, believe it or not, probably lives in fear of losing you every day. So, of course, Frank Sinatra and any other man who says more than two words to you, is going to worry him and cause him grief."

"Does that give him the right to control my every move and treat me like I don't have a brain or any feelings?"

"Of course not. But if you really care about him and wanna make this work, you just have to find a way to make him feel confident enough to trust you with the rest of the world."

Henry had just hit on the root of her anxiety with Jake. "You know. You're right. I am very young and I haven't lived very much. Maybe I made a mistake in getting so involved with Jake so quickly. Maybe I need to get uninvolved just as fast." She stood up and reached her hand out to Henry.

"That's an option," he said, moving out of the booth. "But before you get too carried away, you might want to consider what you'll do without him and better yet, where you will go."

chapter thirteen

HASSIE REFILLED Jake's coffee cup and furtively observed him as he read the newspaper. She'd been thinking about Henry's accusation that she really knew nothing about Jake and focused on him as he sat in the same chair, going through the same motions as every other morning. As she studied his face, she noticed for the first time, a perfectly round mole on his left temple and wondered how many other things she'd never noticed or, better yet, how many things about him she didn't know. She walked over to the coffee table and rearranged the magazines, then emptied the ashtray and exchanged the clean one for the dirty one on the breakfast table. Jake dropped the paper on the table and looked at her. "Are you practicing to be a chambermaid or are you just bored with me this morning?"

She giggled and said, "Who, you? You're probably the most *un*-boring person in the world."

"Oh you think so?" He placed a newly lit cigarette in the ashtray and motioned for her to sit. "I think you need a new dress. Something glamorous but not too sexy."

"What for? I've got lots of nice dresses," she said and poured a glass of orange juice before sitting down beside him.

"We're going to have a very important guest in the hotel for a few days, and I'm hosting dinner in the Copa Room tonight."

"Really," she said. "Does this important guest have a name? Do I know him?" She sipped the juice and listened.

He picked up the newspaper off the table and continued, "His name is John Kennedy, but the press has dubbed him JFK."

She nodded and said, "He's a senator from Massachusetts, and some say he's headed for the White House."

"And how do you know so much about him?"

She didn't like the implication of his tone and curtly said, "Jake, I know how to read, and I've been known to listen to the news."

He laid the newspaper down and smiled. "Okay, miss *current events*, I just didn't know you were so interested in politics."

"Maybe there are other things you don't know about me," she said and then scrunched her nose before continuing, "Not that I really know so much about you either." She studied him for a minute. "You do realize that you practically know my whole life story but I know almost nothing about yours."

He moved uncomfortably in the chair and picked up the cigarette. "You'd be wise to keep it that way. The less you know the better."

"That's not fair, Jake. We've been together for quite a while now, and I'd like to know more about you."

"What is it that you think you need to know?"

"Things like where you come from and if you have any brothers or sisters – are there any more Contratas running around in the world?" She smiled at him and he relaxed.

"I grew up in southern California with a mother who was hardly a candidate for mother of the year. She was a Latino beauty and loved beautiful things but excelled at keeping men in her life who weren't able to maintain the extravagant lifestyle. So, I ended up with one father, two stepfathers and two half-brothers."

"Do you still see any of your – family?"

"Not if I can help it." He finished the coffee and stubbed out the cigarette. "I was the oldest kid, and my father ran off and joined the Navy when I was two years old. I never saw him again and got word that he died about ten years ago."

"What about your brothers?"

"A year after my father left – or as soon as my mother could get unhitched from him, she married a man that she claimed was the movie actor Gary Cooper's cousin, and my brother, Clayton, was born a few months later. Clay's father was a good man, which meant that my mother got tired of him and screwed around behind his back, or as he used to say – in front of his back. He tried to compensate for her lack of ability to be a decent mother and took good care of me and Clay until he couldn't stand it any more. When he left a year or so later, my mother moved us up to LA and we lived with my grandmother so that my mother could become a movie star."

"Really? What's her name?"

Jake laughed and said, "Oh, she never got close to making a movie and eventually turned up at my grandmother's again with husband number three, a real loser with a temper that could bring on an earthquake. He was the bad guy who loved his bourbon and thought it was cool to hit women. After he kicked my mother – by the way, her name was Teresa. After he kicked Teresa down some stairs when he found out she was pregnant, my grandmother threatened him with the police and he disappeared as well."

"Then you got another brother?"

Jake nodded and said, "Conrad – called Rad – Alvarado or Eldorado or something like that. He was born angry and, as far as I know, he's still angry."

"You don't see your brothers – or your mother – now?"

"Teresa died of cancer when I was nineteen. I left home as soon as I could get out the door – barely sixteen – but stayed in touch with my grandmother until she died. Clay Cooper stayed in LA and hooked up with some guys in the record business. It seemed to be a natural calling for him and I heard that he's working up in Reno now – doing what, I'm not exactly sure, but it's bound to be something to do with the music industry. I have no idea where Rad is. Haven't seen or heard about him in almost twenty years now."

"Where'd you go when you left LA?" She stood up to refill his coffee cup.

"A buddy and I just started driving east. We didn't know where we were going and didn't really care as long as we got away from California." He stirred a little cream in the coffee and chuckled to himself. "We had about two hundred dollars between us and thought we were the richest sons of bitches alive. But we got as far as Chicago and ran outta money, so we stayed there for a while and got menial jobs at the Lexington Hotel, which, as you may know, was home to Al Capone before he went to prison." He paused to light a cigarette and said, "Now am I boring you?"

"Not at all." She took a cup and saucer from the room service trolley and poured herself some coffee, stirring in sugar. "Is that where you began your career in the hotel business?"

He nodded and said, "You could say that. The short story is that I met some guys there that thought I had great instincts for the business and after a few months, sent me to work for their company in New York. I guess the rest is history."

Hassie rarely saw Jake without his veil of bravado and suddenly felt that the man she really didn't know very well at all was actually a good person with a lot of baggage. "Do you remember your father at all?" she asked.

He shook his head. "I have an image of him that's probably a result of seeing his photographs. He was dark –"

"And handsome, I'm sure," Hassie said, taking hold of his hand.

"Well, he was Italian." He hesitated and smiled at her. "My grandmother always said that he was a lover and not a fighter, which made him a bad match for my emotionally explosive mother who just wasn't satisfied with a normal life. I never blamed him for leaving us, but I never got over it either."

"I know what it feels like to lose touch with your family," she said softly.

"I know you do," Jake said. "Why do you think I gave you so much slack when you told me about your mother and your stepfather and your desire to get away from home? I could have taken the attitude that men are different and have the right to do whatever they please and that women should just stay home and grin and bear it."

"I believe you did think that for a while," Hassie said.

Jake moved closer to her and took her face in his hand. "You know good and damn well that, after that first night in the Regency Lounge, I was never gonna let you leave."

She leaned forward to kiss him and said, "I didn't appreciate it then, but you really did treat me like something special that night."

"You have no idea the restraint I used. And the integrity that emerged that I had no idea I possessed." He kissed her lightly and said, "You may be responsible for uncovering the nice guy buried inside Jake Contrata."

"I think you are a wonderfully nice guy," she said. She wanted to ask him if he'd ever been married but didn't want to risk the loving mood that their conversation had evoked.

"Yeah, well, don't tell anyone else and ruin my reputation."

She laughed and stood up to sit in his lap, put her arms around his neck and said, "I'm sorry you never really knew your father – I know I miss mine every day. And talking about your mother made me think about mine. She's not really a bad person, but she refused to see how much trouble Bobby caused. I mostly feel bad about walking out on my little brother, Travis. He was so young when I left, and that whole mess wasn't his fault."

He pulled her closer to him and kissed her cheek. "This may not be the right time to ask – and I'm sure you'll tell me if it's not, but what happened between you and your stepfather?"

She relaxed in his arms and was silent, wondering how to verbalize her real feelings about Bobby. She took a deep breath, stood up and walked away from the table, then turned back to him and said, "Sometimes I think it was all my fault."

"What was all your fault, Hassie? Come here and talk to me." He stood up and reached out to her before sitting in the armchair; his unruly hair and unshaven beard gave him the youthful, brooding look of a young Hollywood star, and her feelings for him at that moment were deeper than she'd ever before recognized. She walked toward him and sat on the ottoman in front of him. He sat still and held a newly lit cigarette.

Her lips formed a straight line across her face as she said, "I've never really said any of this out loud. It always sounds so strange in my head."

Jake laid the cigarette on the ashtray and leaned close enough to touch her. "Did this – Bobby. Did he molest you?"

She felt the muscles in her face contract, her brow forcing a tight frown that she knew gave away her feelings. Jake didn't move and waited for her to speak. She reached for his hand and then softly said, "He wanted to. He – um – tried." She swallowed and pressed her lips firmly together. "I swear. I didn't want him to touch me. I tried to stay away from him, but he always seemed to know when I would be at home and when my mother would be away." She closed her eyes to force the tears away and continued, "And finagled ways to drive me places so that he was alone in the car with me." Jake pulled her up from the ottoman and held her close, his head right next to hers, and for a long moment, they stood still as if time was all that was needed to erase the pain.

Without moving, he spoke softly next to her ear. "Let me finish the story for you. He hugged you a little too closely when he saw you and held onto you longer than he should have. When he kissed your cheek, it was always a little too close to your mouth – sometimes he'd quickly brush his tongue against your lips. When he was sure nobody was watching, his hands were all over your body and he took every chance he could to let you know that you excited him until the opportunity came along for him to show you. He tried to force himself on you and you fought him, which made him angry and he threatened to tell your mother that you came on to him and that would have shut the door between you and your mother forever."

She cried softly in his tight embrace. "But, honey, you did nothing wrong." He took hold of her shoulders and pushed her back from him so that he could look at her. "*You* did nothing wrong."

"Then why wouldn't my mother believe me when I tried to tell her that Bobby upset me? Why did she blame me for being the cause of his behavior?"

"I don't know." He took a handkerchief from his pocket and handed it to her. "Mothers make mistakes too."

"I'll never forgive her for taking Bobby's side. It's just unforgivable." She wiped her face and blew her nose and quietly calmed herself before sitting back down on the ottoman. Jake sat in the chair in front of her and brushed her hair from her face with his fingers, then gently smiled before saying, "The problem here is easy to see." She looked at him as if to say, "What?" He picked up her hand and kissed it, and then looked into her eyes and said, "You are sweet and you are kind and you are impossibly beautiful."

She smiled and released a deep sigh, still unsure of what she wanted to say.

Jake held onto her hand and sat still like he was giving her time to process what he'd said, then lifted her chin as he said, "Personally, I would like to thank Bobby Pervert for running you out of Texas."

Hassie laughed and said, "Maybe you'd like to send some of Sid's goons to rough him up a little."

"What do you know about Sid's goons?" he said, suddenly serious.

"Oh, you know how everybody talks around this place. Which reminds me that I haven't seen Sid for a while. Is he going to be at the dinner tonight?"

He stood up and said, "Nah. Sid's not much of a fan of the Democrats. Some boring story there, I'm sure."

Hassie stood in front of him, kissed him and said, "Thanks for helping me get that out of my system. But how did you know all about what happened? It almost sounded like you were there and witnessed everything."

He looked at her like he wasn't surprised at her comments and then smiled as he said, "I know how men think and I know that some men are missing that switch in their brain that shuts off when they're getting ready to do something stupid. Bobby's a classic example of that guy, and I've known it since that first day you talked about him." He kissed her forehead. "Whadaya say we put this behind us now? You're safe and you're loved and I'm not ever gonna do anything to hurt you." They remained still and quiet for a long moment until Jake took hold of her shoulders and said, "Now. About that new dress. Go shopping and do all the things that you gals do to make yourself beautiful." He studied her for a few seconds before saying, "Are you gonna be okay now?"

She nodded and smiled and, with a lump forming in her throat, mouthed the words, "Thank you."

Hassie dialed the number of the shop where her personal shopper, Abigail, worked, explained what she needed and thanked the woman in advance for sending over her best options. She had initially thought that she would never get used to such outlandish extravagance, but Jake's propensity to spring these occasions on her with little notice made her appreciate the ability to just pick up the phone and leave the details to someone else.

Despite Abigail's help, she still had a full day of salon appointments where she heard a lot of talk about Mr. Kennedy's arrival. She didn't know why, but something about the fuss that everyone was making made her nervous. She decided on a deep red dress that Abigail had described as understated elegance. It was simple and strapless with layers of flowing chiffon fitted from an empire waist – a perfect choice to wear with the mahogany mink stole that Jake had bought for her in New York.

When everything was finally in order, she kicked off her shoes, poured herself a drink and sat down to relax. She was ready except for putting on the dress and shoes. Between dealing with her hair, nails and makeup, she'd had very little time to eat, which she was now reminded of as she felt the rush of the vodka through her body.

The door slammed and woke her from a light sleep. When the blur cleared from her eyes, she saw Jake standing in front of her, smiling and holding a flat, black box.

"Hi," she said, sitting up in the chair. "I guess I dozed off for a minute."

"You had a busy day," he said. "Are you pleased with the results?"

"Are you?" She batted her eyes at him and pursed her lips.

"Where's the dress?"

"Shall I put it on?"

He pulled her from the chair and into his arms. "I'd rather have you naked, but we don't have time for that now." He pushed her toward the bedroom and slapped her gently on her butt. "This dress had better be stunning."

When she came back into the room, Jake was leaning on the console table, his back to her and his head bowed, cigarette smoke encircling his head.

"Jake," she called out.

He turned around to face her and leaned back on the table. She stood there for a long, tense moment, waiting for him to speak.

"Come here," he finally said.

She walked across the room, the slick soles of her new shoes sliding on the thick carpet, and stood in front of him, her arms by her sides. "Will you please say something?"

"Stay here," he said.

She didn't move while he went back to the sitting area, returning with the black box.

He opened the box, stared at the contents for a few seconds and then took them out and laid the box on the console. "Turn around." She felt the cold metal land on her skin and waited for him to fasten the clasp. "There. Go look in the mirror."

She teetered back across the carpet to the mirror at the entry, stopping short at the first sight of the necklace. She moved toward the mirror slowly; the sparkle of diamonds and rubies was breathtaking. She turned to Jake, who had followed her, and said, "It's beautiful. And perfect with the dress. Almost like you knew which –"

"Don't you know by now that I don't take chances with things that are important?"

Hassie felt disappointed that Jake had gone behind her back to find out what dress she selected – even if he did pay for it.

"What's the matter?" he said. "You don't like the necklace?"

She fingered the jewels carefully as she dealt with the reality that she couldn't do anything on her own.

"If you don't wanna wear it, don't wear it." He poured another drink and headed for the bedroom. "I'll change and we'll leave in about fifteen minutes."

She looked in the mirror again. The image of the man that she'd seen in a magazine earlier that day flashed through her mind – the handsome politician from the rich, powerful East Coast family and the beautiful socialite wife who most certainly had a dozen necklaces like the one around her neck.

Jake reappeared within a few minutes neatly dressed in a tuxedo and black bowtie.

She saw him behind her in the mirror, turned to him and said, "You look very handsome."

"Why, thank you, my dear."

Hassie walked back to the table where she'd left her drink, picked it up and took a sip. "Have you met this Mr. Kennedy?"

"Not yet. This is his first trip to Vegas, and I doubt we would ever have crossed paths back east."

"He seems like the perfect man to be the next president."

"You sound like a fan." Jake said, picked up her mink stole and walked over to her.

"I read an article in an issue of *Life* magazine in the beauty salon today. There was a whole spread on him and his family." She gestured and talked while Jake put the stole around her shoulders. "His wife is very beautiful, and he looked really taken with his little children."

"Yeah? People love that kinda crap. I'm sure he puts his pants on the same way as every other man. Now, stand still." He held the two ends of the stole and hooked them together as he said, "So do you like the necklace or not?"

She nodded and said, "It's beautiful."

He took hold of her shoulders and looked into her eyes before saying, "*You* are beautiful, and I am very proud of you."

She smiled and lowered her eyes.

"Don't ever leave me," he said softly and kissed her forehead.

There were so many people trying to get into the Copa Room, Jake took Hassie in through the service entrance and down to the center table at the foot of the stage. The band was already playing and the buzz was sensational. Hassie gave her stole to the maitre d' and observed the excitement as the tables filled with the lucky few who'd nabbed a place in the Copa Room's most successful show for years.

"I've got some business to take care of before our guest arrives," Jake said. "Will you be okay sitting here for a few minutes?"

Hassie nodded and smiled, recognizing that this was probably the first time Jake had shown consideration toward her feelings where his job was concerned. Since she was the only one at the table, she decided to take a stroll around the room and look for Henry. The room was decorated with red, white and blue streamers; the musicians were dimly lit by soft blue light. She walked along the edge of the stage and spotted Henry talking to two of the girls at the entrance to the dressing room. She moved quickly toward him, careful not to trip on the hem of her dress.

"Wow," Henry said as she approached him. "You look amazing. Nice rocks."

"Thank you," she said and looked back through the gathering crowd at their table again. There were now several people standing around it, but she still didn't see Jake. "This is all pretty exciting, isn't it?"

"Yeah, I suppose there is a bit more mania than usual," Henry said. "I see you're sitting at Sid's table."

Hassie reached over to straighten Henry's bowtie and said, "Sid always says that his is the best table in the house. You think Jake wants to look less than the best for Mr. Kennedy?"

"Of course not," he said. "Do you know who else is sitting at your table?"

"No, do you?"

"Don't know them personally, but understand, they're mostly linked to the campaign plus a few stray women who were brought along to decorate the table."

Hassie slapped Henry's arm and said, "Shame on you, Henry Berman."

"I didn't have anything to do with it. It's just what I heard. Anyway, there's Jake. You better get back before he thinks you've deserted the party."

"See you after the show," she said and rushed over to where Jake stood.

"There you are," he said, looking beyond her shoulder to see who was behind her.

"I was just talking to Henry."

He gave her a look that said, "I don't believe you," and then smiled at the man and woman standing directly beside her, an older couple from Texas who were thrilled to learn that she was from oil-rich Corsicana. They, too, were oil people, evidenced by the fact that the woman was wearing the contents of half a jewelry store. She wasn't introduced to the other two gentlemen, but caught the two other women watching her as they attempted to talk about her without moving their lips.

Jake kept his hand glued to the small of her back and steered her around as he deemed necessary to greet the guests and make sure they were comfortably seated.

"Where's Mr. Kennedy?" she finally asked.

"He'll be here soon. He travels with a protective entourage who prefer for the room to be pretty well settled before he's ushered in."

"Who's the other chair for?" she asked.

"Just someone from his party," he said, pulling out her chair. "I think we should sit down now."

Hassie hadn't had a drink since she arrived, and when she realized that Stella was their cocktail waitress, made a subtle motion to bring her some champagne. When she turned her attention back to the table, she saw a tall, dark haired man with large, white teeth standing across the table, talking to the Texan. Jake joined them and shook the man's hand, then led him over to her side of the table. As they neared her seat, Hassie caught the man's eye. He smiled and looked at her like he'd met her somewhere before.

Jake pulled her chair out as a signal to stand. "Hassie Calhoun, this is Senator John Kennedy."

"Please, call me Jack," he said and kissed her hand.

"It's a great honor to meet you, sir," Hassie said while he held her hand.

"You must be the young lady that Frank told me about."

Jake pulled a cigarette from his pocket and tucked it between two fingers. "I can't imagine why Frank would tell you anything about Hassie. Maybe he was talking about someone else."

"Maybe," Kennedy said and let go of her hand. "It was a pleasure to meet you, Miss Calhoun."

"Thank you," she said. "Enjoy the show."

Jake escorted JFK back to his seat and instructed the waiters to serve the first course. He sat back down beside Hassie, lit the cigarette and said, "Do you think you could be a little less awestruck?"

"Jake, I only said that it was an honor to meet him," she said as Stella filled her champagne glass.

"Like I said. Behave yourself and don't be so obviously desperate to sleep with him."

Hassie glared at Jake before swallowing half of the glass of champagne. From what she could see, Kennedy had no interest in anyone at that table other than the gorgeous, dark-haired woman sitting beside him.

chapter fourteen

HASSIE CHATTED with Mr. and Mrs. Moneybags, smiling and nodding politely through their conversations, occasionally catching the lilt of JFK's voice as he spoke and laughed with the brunette who strikingly resembled Elizabeth Taylor. She wore a deeply cut black dress and long white gloves, which she removed after the senator was seated next to her. He listened intently as she spoke and seemed much more interested in what this woman had to say than whatever else was going on in the room. More than once, Hassie caught herself staring at them, and if Kennedy looked her way and their eyes happened to meet, Jake would put his arm around her shoulder and gently apply pressure with his thumb and forefinger.

As the show came to a close, Sinatra poured a drink from the rolling bar and handed it to Sammy while whispering to him. Sammy stood at the front of the stage and said, "Ladies and gentlemen, I would like to introduce you to the next president of the United States, Mr. John Fitzgerald Kennedy." He pointed down to their table and raised the glass. "Mr. Kennedy, will you please stand?"

A spotlight focused on their table and JFK moved his chair back and slowly stood up like his back would allow him to move just so fast. He turned to the room, smiled and waved while the guests applauded, whistled and cheered. Before the ovation died, Jake checked his watch, then leaned over to Hassie and said, "I've gotta make a quick phone call. Stay here and I'll be back in a few minutes." He pushed back from the table and left the room as Frank made some closing comments.

The band played out the end of the show and the emotionally charged audience clustered around the room buzzing and chatting about the distinguished senator. Hassie stood at the table, absorbed in all of the excitement, humming along with the band's reprise of the closing number and one of Frank's signature songs, "Come Fly With Me." She looked around for Henry and then back at the entrance but recognized no one in particular until she turned back to the table and saw JFK walking toward her. She looked back to the place at the table where he had been sitting with the brunette; both chairs were empty and he soon stood at her side.

"Did you enjoy the evening?" he asked her, smiling gently.

"Yes, sir," she said, feeling her cheeks warming. "I always love Frank's shows."

She saw a slight reaction to her mention of Frank by name and quickly added, "The Rat Pack is probably the greatest entertainment in the country."

Kennedy nodded and looked up as the woman from the table approached them. He placed his hand on her elbow and they both looked at Hassie. Before either could speak, Frank walked up and put his arm around Kennedy, said something into his ear and then kissed the woman on her cheek, barely missing her lips. The woman gently pulled away from Frank and then accepted a cigarette from him while continuing to focus on JFK as if to make it clear that she thought he was the only other person in the room.

Frank turned to Hassie and said, "Hello, Hassie. Have you met Senator Kennedy?"

She nodded while JFK said, "Jake introduced us earlier."

Frank lit the woman's cigarette and Hassie studied JFK as he watched her take the first drag, recognizing the look as one that she had received many times from Jake before he took her in his arms or led her to bed. She couldn't help thinking of the magazine article and the photo of Kennedy's wife and children. Maybe this woman was really there with Frank and was sitting with Kennedy as a courtesy during the show, but there was no doubt which of the two men *she* preferred. She drew slowly and methodically on the cigarette, carefully blowing the smoke toward the ceiling and away from Kennedy's face.

As Frank prepared to introduce her to Hassie, Jake walked up behind her, took hold of her arm and said, "It's time to say good night."

Frank was visibly surprised and said, "The party's just getting started, Jake."

He motioned to the waiter to bring Hassie's mink stole and said, "Hassie's not been feeling too well today, and I don't want her to overdo it."

"She looks pretty good to me," Sinatra said. "Don't you think so, Jack?"

"Beautiful," he said, his eyes focused directly on her.

The woman moved closer to Kennedy and smiled as she said, "You are a lovely young woman – I didn't catch you name."

"Hassie," she said. She'd never seen a woman smoke a cigarette with such elegance.

"Hello, Hassie. I'm Judy. Your dress is stunning. Isn't it, Jack?"

Kennedy nodded and smiled, but before he could speak, Jake took the stole from the waiter and placed it around Hassie's shoulders. "You guys go on ahead to the lounge. I'll walk Hassie home and see you in a little while."

"That's too bad," Sinatra said. "Take care of yourself, doll. Maybe we'll see you tomorrow?"

Hassie barely opened her mouth before Jake said, "We'll see. Let's go." She smiled at Kennedy and looked at Judy before saying, "It was very nice to meet you."

Jake took her firmly by the arm and moved away from the table. "You're being very rude," she said, squirming from his grip. "And, anyway, I'm not ready to leave yet."

"It's time for the ladies to disappear," he said. "This party is for the boys now."

"It doesn't look like those other women are leaving."

"Why can't you just do as you're told? You've had your fun here tonight and now it's time to go home."

They continued out of the room into the corridor where they met Donnie McGinley, dressed in a dark suit instead of his police uniform. He motioned for Jake to join him privately and they spoke in low voices until Jake walked back to where Hassie stood.

"Something's come up that needs my attention. Can you make it back on your own?"

"Of course, I can, Jake."

"I mean, *all* the way back to the suite. No side trips."

By now she felt that there was absolutely no way she would win any kind of debate with him and just nodded and said, "I'm tired."

"Good. Go pour yourself a nightcap and have a nice bubble bath." He kissed her lightly on the lips, gave her a chilling look that said he was displeased with her but said, "Sweet dreams."

She turned away and moved slowly through the corridor back toward the suite. Although she hadn't had much opportunity to speak with Mr. Kennedy, she would always be able to say that she met him and that he kissed her hand. She felt that there was something quite magical about him – similar to the way she felt when she first met Sinatra. These were two very powerful men. She understood more every day why Jake was uncomfortable around them.

When Hassie awoke the next morning, Jake was not in bed nor was there any sign that he had been there. She got up, put on her robe and walked out into the living room, which was exactly the way she had left it the night before. She opened the curtain and then called down for coffee and a light breakfast. It was already past nine o'clock. Could the party still be going on? She paced the floor a bit and suddenly wished that she smoked. She waved an imaginary cigarette in the air in the same fashion that she'd seen Judy do at their table last night. Maybe she would try to smoke again the next time someone offered her a cigarette.

The morning passed without a word from Jake and Hassie started to worry. Regardless of how late he partied with the guys, he would need to at least shower and shave before going to work in the hotel. She decided that she would make a casual phone call to his office. As she reached for the receiver, the phone rang. She sighed, picked it up and said, "Where are you?"

"I'm actually in my suite and I'm not decent."

"Sorry, Frank. I thought you were Jake."

"Nah, just Frances Albert Sinatra, son of Dolly and Martin."

Hassie laughed softly and said, "How was the party?"

"The usual, I suppose. But there's no doubt that Jack enjoyed himself." She could hear him take a drag on his cigarette. "Anyway, the reason I called is to see how you're feeling today."

Hassie was silent for a few seconds; she could feel Jake's fingers digging into her shoulder. "I'm feeling much better now, thanks. I think it was just all of the excitement and maybe a little bit too much champagne."

"Well, I wish you'd made it to the party, doll. I've never been a fan of Natalie's."

Hassie felt her head go light and sat down in the desk chair. Her mouth filled with saliva and she swallowed before saying, "Natalie?"

"She looks okay, I guess, but she's nowhere near your league, kid. I really don't see what Jake sees in her."

"That was my fault," she said. "I shouldn't have left him without a date." Her voice cracked and she knew that she had to get off the phone.

"Hassie," Frank said soberly. "Honey, don't let him make a fool of you."

She felt the tears welling in her eyes and couldn't trust herself to speak without letting Frank know how upset she was.

"You deserve better than this, I don't care how many diamond necklaces he gives you." Hassie stayed quiet; Frank drew on his cigarette. "Are you okay?"

She took a deep breath and swallowed. "Yeah."

"Are you sure? Do you need some help?"

"I'm fine," she said as the doorbell rang. "My breakfast is here."

"Relax, kid. I'll speak to you later."

She hung up the phone, lowered her head into her hands and cried. The doorbell rang again but she ignored it and went into the bathroom. Nausea rose from her empty stomach and she fought the need to vomit until her body forced her to heave into the toilet bowl.

She moved restlessly as Jake covered her with the heavy quilted bedcover. "Where am I?" she said as she tried to sit up.

"I just picked you up off the bathroom floor," Jake said. "What happened? I got a call that you were looking for me and that you had some kind of problem."

Her conversation with Sinatra flashed in her head. She stared at Jake while trying to remember what had happened.

"Hassie, talk to me. Are you sick or did you just have too much to drink last night?"

"Would you please get my bathrobe?"

He stood up from the bed and looked around the room. "Where is it?"

She said nothing while he went into the bathroom to look for it. She got out of the bed and stood there until he came back with the robe and helped her put it on.

He took her hand and led her into the living room. "Do you want some coffee? Or some juice?"

She shook her head and sat down on the sofa, covering herself with a blanket that she'd left crumpled in the floor.

"Hassie, please tell me what's wrong with you."

"Where were you last night?" Her voice was hoarse and her head pounded.

"You know where I went," he said without looking at her and lit a cigarette.

"Where were you, Jake? After you banished me to my room because it was a *boy's* party."

He stood up and walked toward the window, aggressively puffing on the cigarette. "Okay, there were girls there, but I don't need to tell you what kind of girls they were. It was Frank's idea to have a party for the men, and that means hookers." He walked over to the sofa and sat down beside her. "I was the host of the party. It would have been rude for me to leave."

Without premeditation, she slapped his face so hard she thought she'd injured her hand. He jumped up and shouted, "What the hell was that for?"

"And would it have been rude for you not to fuck Natalie too?" Her hand stung and her nerves went haywire. She started to shake and thought that she might pass out again.

He stood over her, glaring; a bright red mark, the size of her hand, on his face.

"You're not even going to deny it, are you?" She screamed, "Are you?"

He slowly backed away from her and walked over to the bar, returning with a glass of vodka. He sat down in the chair across from the sofa and took a big swig. "I don't know who you get your information from – although I have a mighty good idea. But I didn't fuck Natalie," he said and ground out the cigarette. "And, by the way, that's not very nice language for a lady."

"Fuck you, Jake."

He laughed and shook his head. "I can't talk to you when you're like this so I'm gonna ask you one more time. Why did you call me? What's the matter with you?"

"I didn't call you."

"The message specifically said that you called for me and that you needed for me to come to the suite and help you with a problem."

"I didn't call you."

He stood up and walked back to the sofa. Before sitting down he raised both hands and said, "No hitting."

She stared directly out into the room. He sat down at an arm's length.

"I don't know whose game this is, but it's not funny and it's wasting my time. We will not discuss anything more about the party last night and you will get yourself together and stop being childish. Natalie is a hooker. Hookers attended the party, therefore Natalie attended the party. That doesn't give you the right to assume that I had anything to do with her and certainly doesn't mean that I slept with her."

"Then why wouldn't you let me go to the party?" she asked, looking directly into his eyes for the first time that day. "Why did you send me back to the room like a kid without ice cream?"

He took a cigarette out of his pocket and lit it before he said, "I warned you." He exhaled while she stared at him.

"Warned me about what?" she asked.

"I warned you not to flirt with Kennedy, but you just can't help yourself, can you?"

"Jake, he was obviously with that woman – Judy – sitting beside him at the table. Was she one of those women who were there to entertain the men the way they want to be entertained when they're away from their wives and children?"

"Oh, Hassie, grow up. Frank introduced that woman to Jack and it's a good thing or Jack would have been yapping at your heels all night."

Hassie stood up and walked over to the bar. "Don't be ridiculous. Mr. Kennedy was lost in everything about her and the feeling looked pretty mutual to me." She poured a little vodka in a glass and walked back over to the sofa. "That still doesn't explain why you didn't come home last night."

"The party went on until dawn. And, in case you forgot, I have a hotel to run regardless of my party schedule."

"Why didn't you come back to change?"

"I didn't want to wake you and it's just as easy for me to shower in the steam room." He moved a little closer to her and said, "Hassie, look at what I'm wearing. Is this what I wore to the party?"

She checked out his clothes, which were definitely not the tuxedo that she'd last seen him in. She knew that this was not the first time that he had showered and changed outside of their suite.

"Now, I'm sorry if you're upset that I didn't want you to go to the party, but I thought we agreed a long time ago that you didn't want to be a hooker."

She ignored his attempt at making a joke and said, "That's a poor excuse –"

"I've had enough of this foolishness. There's mass mania going on over Jack's visit and I have a job to do." He stood and straightened his tie and then put his hand to his face. "Man, you pack a mean punch. Where did you learn to hit like that?"

She looked up at him and then reached for her glass, swallowing a small sip and wincing as it hit her esophagus. "Sorry," she said without looking at him.

He reached for her; she gave him her hand and stood up. Then he tightened his hand around her throat and said, "Don't ever do that again." His tone made her skin crawl, and she was afraid to breathe; his eyes locked on hers for what felt like minutes until he released his grip and walked to the door in silence.

When the door closed behind him, she took a deep breath, walked over to the telephone and picked up the receiver. She put her hand on her throat and remembered Frank's words to her, then softly left a message for him with the operator.

Despite Jake's criticism of her inability to make a decision without first consulting Henry, Hassie knew that talking to him would calm her nerves. She sat down in a chair in front of his desk as he said, "I hate to say it, honey, but you look like shit."

"Thanks, Henry. That's an accurate description of the way I feel."

"You were gorgeous when I saw you last night." He set a cup of coffee in front of her and said, "What happened after the show?"

"Nothing really." She couldn't look him in the eye, which she knew he would interpret as permission to ask more questions.

"Okay, what did Jake do?"

"What makes you think Jake did something?"

"He's the only person I know who can make you ecstatic one minute and miserable the next. Now what happened after you left the Copa Room last night?" The phone on Henry's desk rang. "Hold on. I'll get rid of this." He answered it, and then said, "Hi, Frank. What can I do for you?"

Hassie watched his face while he listened to Frank before saying, "Yeah, she's here." He peered at her over the top of his reading glasses and said, "Okay, I'll tell her." He stared at her. "You're welcome, Frank ... good-bye."

Henry hung up the phone and interlocked his fingers, resting his hands on his desk. "Frank got your message and would like for you to meet him in his suite." Hassie sat, waiting for his next remark. "Would you like to tell me what's going on?"

She stood up and leaned on the desk. "I can't go into it now, but I promise I'll tell you later. Just don't say anything to anyone about this."

"I hope you know what you're doing," Henry said, stood up and walked around the desk.

"It's not what you think, Henry. I mean, it's nothing bad – wrong – oh, you know what I mean."

"I'm not sure I do, honey, but I can see that you're in a pretty bad way about something. Are you sure Frank's the right person to help you?"

She nodded and hesitated before she said, "I'm sure."

As she turned to leave the room, he grabbed her arm and said, "Be careful."

Halfway to Frank's suite, Hassie stopped and considered that the safer – and smarter – thing to do would be to turn around and go back to talk the whole thing through with Henry. But something about the tone of Frank's voice when she spoke to him earlier that day drew her to talk to him again, and she carried on down the corridor to meet him. When she reached his door, she could hear music coming from inside. She ran her fingers through her hair and pressed her lips together, then rang the bell and waited. When he opened the door, he was dressed in a casual, short-sleeved pale yellow shirt – something she imagined was worn in southern California – and dark slacks. He looked tired and a little hung over and seemed smaller than she'd always thought of him.

"Come in, Nia – what was that Choctaw name of yours?"

"Nia Hushi," she said and smiled.

"That's it. Come in, Nia Hushi." He bowed deeply and moved like a Chinese servant. "Welcome to Chez Frank or is it Chez Fr*ah*nk?"

His light-heartedness made her relax, and she was glad she decided to come. "I like Chez Fr*ah*nk."

"Then Fr*ah*nk it is." He clasped his hands together and said, "Now, I know it is a little early for cocktails, but may I remind you that it is five o'clock somewhere in the world and very rude to ignore the cocktail hour of our foreign friends."

She laughed again and nodded her approval.

"So what's your poison? Scotch, vodka, wine, champagne?"

"I've had enough champagne lately. How about a vodka gimlet?"

"Gimlet? Did I say this was the Oak Room Bar at the Plaza?"

Hassie was nearly giddy now and laughed as she said, "Okay, just vodka."

"Just kidding, doll. If you want a vodka gimlet, you got it."

He made the drinks and sang along with the music. She looked around the big room, suddenly aware that she was in Frank Sinatra's suite – the sensation both surreal and exhilarating.

"Here you go," he said and handed her the drink. He raised his glass to her and said, "Cheers. To Hassie. To Life. *La Chaim*!" He took a sip from his glass before saying, "Sorry, it's a habit. For my good friend, Sammy."

Hassie wasn't exactly sure what he meant, but she was comfortable and felt the drink rush to her head.

Frank walked over to the hi-fi, lowered the volume and closed the lid, then turned to her and said, "Have a seat, doll." He set his glass on the coffee table and looked at her. "I'll be back in two shakes." He walked out of the room and down a short corridor. Hassie sat quietly on the sofa, sipping her drink when it all of sudden occurred to her that he might have expected her to follow him.

chapter fifteen

THE CURTAIN fluttered with a gust of brisk autumn air, which explained the slight chill in the room. The suite seemed much larger than Jake's, with doors leading to several rooms off the big main living room. Hassie gazed down the corridor after Frank and then walked over to the open window. Why did he leave the room without explanation? Was this normal – some sort of code that she had yet to learn about?

"Sorry about that," Frank said as he reappeared buttoning a dark blue cardigan. "I forgot that this town gets a little cool this time of year, but I like the fresh air. Is it too cold for you?"

She turned to face him, then shook her head and said, "The fresh air is nice." She watched him adjust the sleeves on the cardigan and wondered if he would think to warm her in his arms. She slowly moved to the sofa and sat down as she said, "What's it like in LA right now?"

"A little warmer than here. But not a lot until you move over to Palm Springs or down to San Diego." He studied her for a few seconds and then walked over to close the window, then sat down in the chair opposite her and lit a cigarette. "Okay, doll. Are you relaxed?"

She nodded and smiled, unsure of what to do with her hands.

"You know, Jake and I have known each other for quite a long time. We go back to the old days in New York, working the clubs and – well, you don't wanna hear all about that. My point is – I know him, and he's a complicated guy. Hey, he'd probably say the same about me. But he's not always been great with women and I can kinda see history repeating itself with you." Frank stood up and went back over to the bar. "Can I freshen your drink?"

Her glass was almost empty, but considering that she already felt light-headed, she smiled and said, "No, I'm okay."

He sipped the top of his drink and silently gazed at her. "You can tell me that it's none of my business, but do you plan to marry Jake?"

"I don't know, Frank. I'm eighteen years old. I don't plan to marry anyone right now."

"Good answer." He walked over and sat down on the sofa beside her.

She didn't know if it was the vodka or the mere proximity to him that made her notice those famous blue eyes. She felt herself staring at him and finally said, "You really do have beautiful eyes."

He laughed and said, "Thank my ma and pa."

"Sorry. I didn't mean to behave like a starstruck teeny-bopper."

He smiled and touched her hair. "You are such a beautiful woman – so charming and so young." He stared at her like he was looking through her eyes into the soul of someone else, then pulled himself back into the moment and said, "Let's get back to the reason you're here. You called me, remember?"

"I was very upset, and you were so nice to me this morning."

"What were you upset about?"

"Jake came back and found me passed out in the bathroom floor. He said someone called him and told him I needed help."

"You did, didn't you?"

She nodded and fidgeted with her glass. "I confronted him about Natalie."

"What did he say?"

"That she was at the party because she's a hooker but that he didn't have anything to do with her."

"He's a liar," Frank said and sat back in the seat. "I'm sorry, but I was there and he had plenty to do with her."

Hassie felt the alcohol churn in her stomach and for a moment, she thought she'd be sick.

"I know you don't wanna hear these things, but this is the real world of adults, doll. It's not always roses and champagne. In fact, it rarely is. I said it before and I'll say it again, don't let him make a fool of you." He moved uneasily in the seat. "Jake has you where he wants you and – look, I'm not saying he doesn't love you, but he'll always do exactly what he wants." He looked directly at her. "You're too good for that. You've got so much living to do. And you could have any man in this world."

She half listened to Frank's words, still rankled by the fact that Jake had insisted that there was nothing going on between him and Natalie. Why was she unable to get him to take her seriously when she was angry with him? Why was he always able to turn the scenario around and make her look petty and foolish? Frank was right about one thing: Jake had her where he wanted her and she didn't know how to deal with him without taking a risk that she'd make things worse. She looked at Frank and said, "He scares me sometimes."

"How?"

"It's hard to explain."

"Has he ever hit you?"

"Oh, God no," she said, thinking of the big red mark on his face that she had delivered.

"But he likes to control what you do, doesn't he?"

She finished her drink and put the glass on the table.

"Come on, Hassie. You weren't sick last night. Jake didn't want you around me and Jack."

"He just kept saying that the party was for the men."

Frank was reflective for a minute before saying, "You say that Jake scares you, but are you afraid of him?"

"Sometimes," she said, staring at her hands. "Like today. He grabbed me by my throat and –"

"And what?"

"I slapped him."

"When he grabbed you?"

"No. Before. When I thought he had slept with Natalie. Later, he grabbed my throat and told me never to do it again. Never slap him again."

Frank picked up her glass and went to the bar in silence.

She stood up and walked over to him. "I think I've said too much. Given you the wrong impression."

"What did you say that wasn't true?" he said.

"Nothing." She stared at him and wondered why she was there.

This whole relationship business was new to her and she felt confused and out of control – Frank must see her as a young, stupid girl and she was unsure of what to say or even think. But she was drawn to him in a way that gave her strength. She breathed deeply and looked away from him as she said, "I don't think I love him anymore."

Frank handed her a drink. "You know, regardless of his actions, I know he really does love you."

"He has an odd way of showing it sometimes." She sipped the drink and felt a tear drop from her chin.

"If I was honest, I'd admit that I know how he feels. And if I was really his friend, I'd tell him to be careful." He took her face in his hand. "Because shit like his causes people to lose the ones they love whether they mean to or not."

They were silent for a few seconds before Frank said, "What do you really want, doll?"

"I don't know, Frank. I don't want to leave Vegas or the Sands or any of my friends."

He took the drink from her hand and set both glasses down, pulled her close to him and said, "You say that you don't know what you want. But you came here because you wanted to. Right?"

She nodded and felt safe and comfortable in his embrace as he said, "So. Does that mean you want to stay with me?"

Her impulse was to say yes and to just forget about Jake and his apparent need to turn to Natalie whenever he wanted to. Then she had a sudden thought of her conversation with Henry and his warning that she should not get caught in the middle of some sort of nasty feud between Jake and Frank. The suggestion that there had been a woman involved made her think that maybe they had once fought over Natalie and that Jake had won and now Frank wanted to get back at Jake by seducing his so-called girlfriend. She looked into Frank's eyes, wanting to question his motives but instead was caught in the moment with a burning desire for him, nodded and said, "Kiss me."

Frank held her face with both hands and kissed her tenderly on the lips and then said, "If we start this now, it's not gonna stop."

She put her arms around his neck and pulled his mouth to hers. Everything about him was strange and new – the way he held her firmly at the small of her back pulling her closer to him with the intensity of their kiss which was slowly, deeply passionate yet soft and sensually determined. His arms were strong, and he caressed her like he had no intention of letting her go. She wanted him desperately and hesitated not a second when he finally took her hand and led her into his bedroom.

The pungent aroma of sex pricked her senses as she lay loosely enclosed in Frank's arms. She'd been slightly surprised by the urgency with which he'd approached their lovemaking. To reflect on it then meant an inevitable comparison to the slow, sensuous sessions with Jake, and she couldn't help feeling a slight disappointment over the lack of satisfaction with Frank. Was it because she was inexperienced with men other than Jake – what if she'd disappointed Frank as well? Or was it that she really did love Jake and had needed to be with another man in order to truly appreciate that love. She had no idea what time it was and carefully moved away from Frank, hoping he'd remain asleep. When she attempted to slide over to the edge of the bed, he reached for her and said, "Going somewhere?"

"I didn't mean to wake you," she said.

"I was just – re-revving the engines."

She laughed softly and said, "Do you know what time it is?"

"Not exactly, but I'm sure it's past the witching hour. You got somewhere you need to be?" He reached over and switched on the bedside lamp while checking the clock.

"Don't you think Jake is wondering where I am?"

"It's one-thirty," he said. "I don't know if he'll think that's very late or very early."

Hassie kissed Frank's shoulder and with no thought about what Jake would do if he found her in Frank's bed, she looked at him and said, "I had a wonderful time."

"Oh, you can do better than that," he said and kissed her on the lips. "You must have read about my ego. I need to hear what a fantastic lover I am and how you've never had anything like it."

His expression was very serious, but she sensed that he was relaxed and wished that she could say the things he wanted to hear. The truth was, despite their recent intimacy, she felt a sort of distance coming between them, like he was thinking about something else while she was thinking about Jake. She propped herself up on her elbow and said, "You said something earlier about hurting people that you love, and losing –" She stopped and watched his face. "Were you talking about your wife?"

Frank grinned and said, "Which one? And I think you mean ex-wife."

"The beautiful, dark-haired one – Ava?"

"Ah, yes. The beautiful, dark-haired one." He sat up and pushed the pillow against the headboard. "You know, you remind me of her."

"Really?" she said. Could she really be anything like Ava Gardner – the gorgeous raven-haired movie star whom some considered to be the most beautiful woman in the world?

"She was once an innocent small-town girl. Like you." He paused and touched her face. "Of course, that was before I knew her." He laughed softly and was silent for a few seconds. "We weren't much good for each other. Some say worse than dynamite."

"But you loved her, didn't you?"

"Oh, yeah," he said quietly. "I'm sure I'll always love her and I still think about her almost every day. Especially when I see someone like you struggling with someone like Jake."

"So do you think Jake and I are bad for each other?"

"Can't really say. I know that Jake loves you, but he also wants to possess you." Frank reached over to the bedside table and pulled a cigarette from the pack. "Big fucking mistake." He lit the cigarette and exhaled toward the ceiling. "You know – men are basically animals."

"I wouldn't say that," Hassie said, then pulled away from him and sat up. "At least not *all* men."

"No, it's the truth, and we're pretty damn proud of it." He drew deeply on the cigarette and exhaled slowly before saying, "You said that you don't think you love Jake anymore. Did you mean that?"

Hassie shrugged and said, "I don't know. I mean, sometimes when we're together I can't imagine loving anyone the way I love him."

"And other times?"

She looked at Frank, her eyes filling with tears and said, "He's gonna blow a gasket, ya know."

"Tell him you fell asleep in Stella's room. She'll back your story, won't she?"

"I'm sure he's already been in touch with her, looking for me. In fact, he's probably been to her room to see for himself."

"Are you worried about dealing with him?" He put the cigarette on the astray.

She took a deep breath and laid her head on the pillow, staring at the ceiling. "I think I'm just going to tell him the truth."

"That you spent half the night in my bed and let me make love to you?" he said, and rolled over on top of her. "He'll kill me. He'll more than kill me. He'll roast my balls for breakfast. Got any other ideas?"

She put her arms around his neck and kissed him sensuously knowing that she would arouse him and delay the inevitable. He pulled back from her and rolled back on to the bed. "I could literally do this all night, but I'm worried for you – and for me – now."

"If I had someplace else to go, I'd just never go back to him and lay low while he got over it."

"He's not gonna get over this, doll. He's gonna be out for blood. And I gotta go to work in a few hours."

She got out of bed and dressed in the dim light of the bedside lamp. Frank went to the bathroom, returning in his dressing gown, tousling his hair and looking half asleep. She felt deep affection for him and a sudden urge to make love to him again, but she also sensed that he wanted her to leave.

He walked over to her and put his arms around her. "I really do have a big day coming up in a few hours. If you stay, I'll never get any sleep."

"It's fine, Frank. I have to face Jake eventually."

He pulled back from her and looked into her eyes. "I still think I'd play the Stella card if I were you."

"You might be right. But it's too late now. Putting off going back until tomorrow will only make it worse. Besides, for all I know, Jake's not even back in the suite yet." She kissed him and started toward the door. "Don't worry. I'll be fine."

She left Frank and meandered through the corridor, the sound of her heels echoing against the bare floor as she reached the lobby. There was still enough activity to blend in with a crowd. Maybe Julio or some of the band was still playing. Maybe she could hook up with them for a while before Jake found her: safety in numbers. But there was no sign of anyone she knew as she walked past the brightly lit space toward Jake's suite.

She could still taste Frank's kiss and feel remnants of his semen and sweat, and was a little disappointed that he'd seemed so anxious to get rid of her. Did he sense that, despite everything she'd said about wanting to get away from Jake, she was hopelessly linked to him and that even he – Frank Sinatra – couldn't get him out of her head?

The fact remained that she had slept with Frank and was different now, and she knew Jake would be able smell and even taste that difference. The thought not only excited her but made her feel more like a real woman and, for a moment, she felt empowered to make sure that everyone knew that she was the only woman in Jake's life and to see Natalie off once and for all. But as she approached Jake's suite, a rush of panic shot through her system when she imagined what Jake would do if he ever found out that she'd been with Frank. Would she be able to convince him that he was wrong like he'd tried to convince her that she was wrong about him and Natalie?

She opened the door to the suite; it was dark and cold. She called out to Jake and switched on the lights in the living room. It was eerily quiet as she moved into the bedroom, which was also dark. She called out his name again but there was no response or sound of any kind. She went back into the living room and poured a brandy, then went into the bathroom and started to draw a bath. She heard the door open and shut; her stomach jumped with fear. She had undressed down to her underwear and put her bathrobe on before turning off the water. When she stood up from the tub, Jake stood in the doorway. She flinched and said, "You scared me."

"I'm sorry, darling." He moved closer to her, seemingly calm and unfettered. He reached for her and held her in his arms. She subconsciously held her breath before returning his embrace.

"Isn't this an odd time to be taking a bath?"

"I couldn't sleep." She tightened the sash on the robe. "Where have you been?"

"Just – out," he said and pulled back from her to look at her face. "Out with Sid, out with Jimmy. Out with Frank."

Was he trying to cover his own tracks or testing her? She ignored him and went back to the tub and turned on the water. She felt vulnerable with her back to him but was more comfortable than when trying to avoid looking at him. When she turned back around, he had taken off his clothes and reached out to her.

"Let's make love," he said, untying the sash on her robe. "It's been a while and I've missed you." He jerked her closer to him and started to kiss her neck and face.

She pushed back from him and said, "Not now, Jake. I feel sweaty and dir –" She stopped and tried to move away.

He laughed without smiling and said, "You feel dirty? Why is that?"

She hated this tone of his and wished she had jumped in the tub when she heard him come through the door. She'd never considered that he would want to make love to her. In fact, she had assumed just the opposite and now, she didn't know what to do.

"I want you just the way you are," he said, took her by the hand and led her out of the bathroom; she caught sight of his erection.

She resisted his hold on her and said, "Seriously, I'm not –"

He pulled her toward him and then threw her on the bed. Before she could move or speak, he pushed her down and pulled off her panties, then straddled her across her thighs and pinned her arms back with his hands, the weight of his body heavy over her chest. He held her still for a few seconds and then let go of her arms and raised his body to sitting position. She knew better than to fight him. He moved his hands over her body in gentle, sensuous strokes; she winced slightly when he squeezed her breast. His hand continued down her body toward her pubic mound; she held her breath and closed her eyes.

Then, with no warning, he thrust his finger up into her vagina, pushing it deep and deeper until she called out to him. He moved his finger in and out of her a couple of times and then removed it and put it in her mouth. When he told her to suck on his finger, she started to cry; he laughed, lowered his face to where his lips touched her ear and said, "What's the matter? Don't you like the way you taste?" He removed his finger from her mouth and moved back from her. She lay still but breathed heavily and wiped her nose on the edge of the pillowcase. He took hold of her face and spoke in a voice that sent chills through her body, "Remember this the next time you accuse me of fucking Natalie."

She watched him go back into the bathroom and heard the shower go on. She silently screamed at his revolting actions and sat up in the bed. The intensity of his anger roared back at her and she felt dizzy and completely out of control. Did he really know she'd been with Frank or was he just being his usual, suspicious self, using the moment to punish her for her questioning him over Natalie? She was obviously no match for Jake's prowess where controlling relationships was concerned. She would never best him in that way and, if she really cared about what happened between them, she was walking on dangerous ground now.

Yesterday, they'd been a happy, loving couple and he'd told her never to leave him. But she had left him, and in the worst possible way. She was suddenly stricken with guilt and prayed that he would never find out the truth. But the reality of the situation swarmed her brain, and with the lingering taste of Jake's finger in her mouth, she knew that before she could face him again, she had to clear her head. She had no idea where she would go, but, before he emerged from the shower, she quickly threw on some clothes and walked out of the suite into the dim yellow light of the empty corridor.

chapter sixteen

HASSIE SPENT a couple of nights on the sofa at Dotty and Jimmy's house after she walked out on Jake and eventually heard Jimmy tell Dotty that Jake had gone to New York for a few days. Dotty was convinced that if Hassie wanted to work things out with Jake, she could never tell him about her little indiscretion with Frank and was thoroughly opposed to her going back to his suite before they had a chance to work things out. She'd wagged her finger at Hassie saying, "Jake's ego is the size of Wyoming and he won't just welcome you back with open arms."

But Hassie strongly believed that if she had a chance to just sit and talk with him – calmly and soberly – she would explain that his continual desire to return to Natalie's bed embarrassed her and hurt her and that, if he really loved her, he should care more about her feelings and then she wouldn't feel the need to talk or spend time with Frank or any other man – with the exception of Henry – and things could go back to the way they were before JFK's arrival. She would say all of these things to him when he got back from New York and went back to the suite to wait for him.

There was one consolation while Jake was gone: she could come and go as she pleased without worrying that he'd get crazy over where she'd been or who she'd been with. She popped in and out of the Copa Room, ostensibly to visit Henry or check for free time at the piano. She hoped that she would run into Frank. They hadn't spoken to each other since the night in his suite. But when she didn't see him and he didn't phone her, one morning after a particularly long couple of days on her own she decided to phone him.

She finished her breakfast and dressed in a soft woolen skirt she'd found at Bloomingdale's on her trip to New York and a short-sleeved cashmere sweater, her father's chiffon scarf around her neck. If she reached Frank, he might want her to meet him for a cup of coffee, and she didn't want to keep him waiting. She brushed her hair away from her face and held it back at the nape of her neck with a tortoiseshell and rhinestone clasp that Barbara had given her for her sixteenth birthday. As she slipped the low-heeled pumps on her feet, she thought about what Barbara's advice to her might have been on that night she walked out of Frank's suite and right back into Jake's domain. Barbara would have asked her what she really wanted and told her that she had to account for her actions no matter what she decided to do. Hassie honestly did want to work things out with Jake, but she also wanted to speak to Frank and to know that he thought about her and maybe even wanted to see her again.

She stood at the desk and stared at the telephone. A simple call could do no harm, she thought. After all, she and Frank were friends before they were lovers, and she couldn't stand the thought that this had changed. She reached for the receiver. What if things *had* changed between them and he really didn't want to talk to her? What if his easy dismissal of her that night had meant that he didn't want anything else to do with her? She felt her nerve waning at the thought and was then startled by the shrill ring of the telephone.

"Hello."

Dotty noisily cleared her throat before saying, "Curiosity got the best of me. I gotta know what happened when you saw Jake again."

Hassie was still thinking about Frank and was caught off guard at the mention of Jake's name. "Dotty, what are you talking about?"

"Don't tell me you don't know that Jake's back. He got back day before yesterday."

At first, all Hassie could feel was relief that she hadn't made the call to Frank or met him and then run into Jake and created another scene like the one in the Copa Room on her birthday. "Well, I haven't seen him. He hasn't been back to the suite."

There was a brief silence before Dotty cleared her throat and said, "Guess he's been busy. Maybe you should go look for him. Maybe it's a good time to let him know –"

"Dotty, I've gotta go. Thanks for calling." She hung up and stood still, then stared at the door as though Jake was due to walk through any second. Why didn't he tell her that he was back? And where was he staying if he wasn't coming back to his suite? She couldn't stop herself from thinking that he'd gone straight to Natalie – the one person he knew would take him any time and under any circumstances. So should she assume that he'd found out about Frank and was deciding how to deal with her? If anyone knew what was going on with Natalie – and any possible connection to Jake – it was Stella. Hassie called her and arranged to meet for coffee.

Hassie arrived at the coffee shop entrance just as Julio was leaving.

"*Hola*, chica," he said, reaching out to hug her.

"Good morning."

"Where've you been hiding? We haven't seen you in the Copa Room for days. You're not avoiding anybody, are you?"

"Of course not," she said, wondering if Frank had said anything to the musicians. "I've been in a few times, but it's been really crazy with you guys and the Rat Pack."

"Yeah, but that's getting ready to change," he said. "They wrap up the filming at the end of the week and Frank told Toots that he'll be going back to LA for a while. Something about a new recording and all the stuff you do when you're a big star."

"So Frank's leaving." She felt her face heat up and wished she'd made more of an effort to speak with him. He couldn't leave without saying good-bye to her. She wanted to sit down. "I'll be in to see you guys soon. I've missed working on my music with you."

"I'll be looking for you." He kissed her cheek and left. She entered the coffee shop and sat down in a booth near the entrance.

She hadn't decided exactly what she was going to say to Stella. The fact that she sought refuge with Dotty and Jimmy made it necessary for her to tell Dotty about her involvement with Frank. And, as difficult as it had been, she had opted to keep the details from Henry despite his inclination to question her about the meeting every chance he got. Julio's suggestion that she'd been hiding from someone made her wonder if the men gossiped as much as they accused the women of doing. The whole scenario made Hassie a little crazy, and she was relieved to see Stella walk toward the table.

"Sorry I'm late," Stella said, sliding into the booth. "You okay? You look a little pale."

She smiled a greeting to her friend before saying, “Stella, have you seen Jake in the Copa Room lately?”

“He came in last night. Why?”

“He’s not coming back to the suite.” Hassie hesitated and watched Stella’s face.

“Where’s he staying?” Stella asked.

She shrugged and said, “I thought maybe he was with Natalie. I was hoping you could tell me.”

“Hassie, what the hell are you talking about? Since when do you toss out such hogwash?”

Hassie didn’t respond and just sat there like Stella hadn’t said a word.

Stella waved the waitress away, grabbed Hassie’s arm and said, “I need something stronger than coffee if we’re gonna have this conversation.”

They left the Sands, walked down to the Desert Inn and sat at one of the bars in the casino. Stella ordered two Bloody Marys and took her cigarettes from her purse and lit one, inhaling the first drag deeply and exhaling slowly.

Hassie was physically exhausted and emotionally worn out and had consumed way too much alcohol in the previous week. She looked at the Bloody Mary and pushed it away. She really wanted to lay her head down on the bar and sleep.

“I can honestly say that I’ve hardly seen Natalie at all outside of work,” Stella said. “She never comes home at night and I don’t know when she comes in to change. So I haven’t had any conversation with her about where she is, but I never just assumed that she was with Jake. That’s insane, Hassie. You *live* in his suite.”

“But he hasn’t been there for days. He’s avoiding me, I guess.”

“This sounds bizarre,” Stella said, dragging on her cigarette. “But why do you just assume he’s shacked up with Natalie?”

Hassie pulled the drink closer and took a big sip. “He’s punishing me,” she said, softly.

“Punishing you? For what?”

“For sleeping with Frank.” She swallowed another gulp of her drink, refusing to look at Stella who had already motioned to the bartender for another one.

“Oh, my fuckin’ Christ,” Stella said. “No wonder he’s not talking to you, and it’s a miracle Frank’s not dead.”

"I don't know for sure that he knows, but he's treating me like a whore with syphilis."

"Well, can you blame him? He must be furious, not to mention humiliated. When did this happen?"

"About a week ago. When JFK was here. I didn't plan for it to happen. It just did."

"And what does Frank say? Boy, does he have balls." She smiled at the bartender as he placed a fresh drink in front of her.

"I haven't spoken with him. I've stayed away from the Copa Room and he hasn't called me."

Stella stared at her drink, puffing on the cigarette. "So, I gotta ask. What was it like? With Frank."

"It was really – nice. I know I'm not the most experienced person when it comes to this stuff, but it was – I mean, he was passionate and loving and –"

"Hassie what are you trying to say?"

"He's kinda old, Stella. I mean, like my father's age."

Stella laughed and said, "He's not old. You're just young. But are you okay?"

Hassie nodded and said, "I'm fine. In an odd sort of way, the time with Frank made me understand Jake a little better. I can't really explain it."

Stella wrinkled her brow and stubbed out the cigarette. "This is not the Jake Contrata I know. I can't believe he just didn't kick you out and banish you from the Sands or even the whole of Vegas. He's not known for his generosity when it comes to dealing with shit like this. There's gotta be something more to this, Hassie."

Hassie remained still and stared at her hands.

"So what are you gonna do?" Stella asked.

"I just saw Julio and he said that Frank is probably leaving Vegas at the end of the week. Maybe Jake will talk to me again, and if he's really finished with me, maybe we can stay friends and he'll find another place for me to live."

"Hassie, no offense, but you're living in a gigantic dream world. Jake doesn't operate like that. And if he's really involved with Natalie again, she'll be having something to say about it as well. I'm sure I don't need to tell you she wouldn't care if you fell down the Grand Canyon."

"Then I don't know, Stella. Jake's gonna have to make the first move, and if he kicks me out, I'll deal with it then." She propped her elbows on the bar and rested her head in her hands. "When I was with Frank, I felt no love for Jake."

"Are you falling for Frank?" Stella asked. "I mean, despite the fact that he's old."

"No. It was fun being with him and the thought of him excites me, but I'm not in love with him – at least not the way I've loved Jake."

"Do you want me to try to find out what's going on from Natalie's side?'

"Not really," she said at first, but then said, "Yeah, okay."

"Man, you're a real mess," Stella said and asked for the check. "And don't you want to say good-bye to Frank?"

"Sure, I do. I'll see him before he leaves."

In the late afternoon of the last day of filming, Hassie arrived to a Copa Room full of rowdy revellers and quietly snuck into Henry's office.

"Hi, honey," Henry said, waving her in the door. "Wow, you look a lot better than the last few times I've seen you. What's the occasion?"

"Nothing special," she said. "I just treated myself to the beauty salon this morning. It was way past time."

"Well, you look good." He sat down and shuffled through some papers.

"So, what's going on?" she asked. "I hear the filming finished today."

"Yeah, looks like it. The guys are gonna take a little break while Frank takes care of some business in LA. But they'll be back soon."

"What's happening in the Copa Room while they're away?" Hassie was surprisingly unnerved by the thought that Frank would be coming back. On one hand, she hated the thought that he might leave before she got to see him, but on the other, the damage between her and Jake needed to be repaired. There was no doubt that it would be easier if Frank were anywhere other than Vegas.

"For one thing, Nat King Cole is recording a live concert here next week."

"Whose idea was that?"

"I don't know. Jake would've worked it out with his people. It's gotta be easier for a colored man to work here now that Sammy's a permanent fixture."

Hassie smiled and walked over to the door. "Do you know where Jake is right now?"

"He's supposed to be out chasing the film producers for reimbursement of some costs that landed on his desk. So just relax." Henry studied her while he took a quick call, then hung up the phone and said, "What's going on in that beautiful head of yours? You look a little lost, honey."

"I don't know," she said. "I just wish Jake would talk to me. I can't stand the silent treatment any more, and it's pretty lonely in that big suite."

There was a sharp rap on the door; Hassie turned around just as Frank walked in. He looked at her, and then at Henry, then back at Hassie before saying, "Am I interrupting something?"

Henry stood up and said, "Come in, Frank. How's the filming going?"

Frank walked around to the end of Henry's desk. "I'm officially done." He pulled a cigarette out of his pocket and patted his jacket for a light.

"Here," Henry said, offering the chunky lighter that he used as a paperweight.

"Thanks," Frank said, looking over at her. "How are you, Hassie?"

"I'm fine, thanks." She wanted him to touch her.

He kept his eyes on her until Henry stood up and said, "If you'll excuse me, I need to check on tonight's reservations." He walked out of the room without looking at either of them. Frank reached out to Hassie and she took his hand.

"You look beautiful," he finally said.

"Thanks. I hear you're leaving."

"Yeah, but I'll be back. We've evidently created quite a stir with this 'Summit at the Sands' as it's come to be known, and we gotta ride the wave for as long as it's there." He propped on the edge of the desk and said, "How'd things work out with Jake?"

"Haven't you spoken with him since –"

"I've been working flat out on the set and still doing these shows. I've hardly had time to sleep and, no, I haven't spoken with him or even seen him."

"Things aren't so good," she said. "I don't see him and he doesn't talk to me."

"I'm sorry, kid. I didn't mean to cause you any trouble."

She felt that Frank was sincere and softly said, "We'll work it out."

"Well, I hope you do. Like I've told before – the guy really loves you."

Her throat ached; she just nodded her head and smiled. Henry walked back in and told Frank that someone was looking for him. Frank smiled at Hassie and touched her cheek, then nodded at Henry and left the room.

Henry busied himself around his desk for a minute or two while Hassie clicked the lighter a half dozen times, staring into the flame until it extinguished itself.

Something about her conversation with Frank made her sad – like their intimacy had been a routine part of life or maybe hadn't even happened at all. She had never felt that way where Jake was concerned. A simple thought of him would bring her emotions so close to her skin, she could rub her arms and feel him touching her and that sensation would shudder through her and she would fall in love with him all over again.

"Do you want to tell me what's going on?" Henry said, taking the lighter from her.

"I miss Jake."

"Tell him."

She had dreaded going back to the suite, fearing both that Jake would be there and that he wouldn't. Now, she was so emotionally exhausted, she looked forward to a quiet night on her own and opened the door to the deserted cavern. Once inside, she turned on the nearest table lamp and kicked off her shoes. She went over to the bar, perused the decanters and then opened the small fridge and removed a bottle of Coca-Cola. She'd barely had anything to eat but she'd had very little appetite for days now, which was starting to show in the loose fit of her clothes. She took a couple of sips of the cold drink, then stretched out on the sofa, dozing in and out of a light sleep until she heard the door close and saw Jake standing over her.

"Here," he said, dropping a piece of paper on her chest. "You owe me four dollars."

She sat up and focused her eyes on what looked like a bill from the hair salon, but before she could speak, he sat down in the chair opposite her and said, "You don't have the right to sign charges to this room."

She felt acid from the cola rising in her throat and without speaking got up from the sofa and walked over to the bar. She poured the rest of the bottle into her glass, and then asked Jake if he wanted anything.

"What are you drinking?" he asked and lit a cigarette.

"Coca-Cola," she said softly.

"I sure as hell don't want that. Bring me a scotch."

She poured the whiskey over one ice cube like she knew he liked it, walked over to him and offered the drink.

He nodded toward the table beside his chair; she set the glass down before returning to the sofa. She started to say something, but when she caught his eye, he said, "Don't speak."

Her face reddened and she was reminded of the times that her father had scolded her for doing something that had disappointed him, his brooding silence unnerving her and making her sweat. She sat there sipping her drink until she could feel him look at her before he said, "Why did you let Frank seduce you?"

"I don't know." Her fingers were cold from holding the icy glass. She set it down on the table and rubbed them together. "Why do you keep sleeping with Natalie?"

He glared at her and then rested his elbows on his knees and ran his hands through his hair. "I should have –" He stopped and stood up, walked away from her, then turned back and said, "I should have thrown you in the street after you came back into this room."

She hesitated for a few seconds and then said, "Why didn't you?"

"Because I know Frank. And I knew that he would eventually go for you." He sat back down, looked at her and said, "I just hoped you wouldn't fall for his tricks."

Hassie lowered her head, the pain in her chest as sharp and vivid as if he had stabbed her with a knife. There was so much that she wanted to say to him, but the emotion boiling inside her would surely overtake her ability to speak. She looked up at him and waited.

He walked back over to the bar and poured another drink then returned with two glasses and set one on the table in front of her. "Damn you," he said without looking at her.

"What did you say?"

"You heard me. Any other woman in this world would not have a hide right now, and she sure as hell wouldn't be sitting on that sofa drinking my booze."

He was reaching out to her, and she wanted to somehow assure him that she wanted him and needed him, but the words and thoughts were just a jumble in her head. And she dare not try to touch him. Not yet.

"Do you love him?" he finally asked.

"No, Jake." Without thinking, she said, "I love you."

The words seemed to annoy him more than appease him. She wished that she could take them back when he stood up and moved over to her, sitting on the sofa but at a distance to discourage physical contact. He somehow seemed older – the flesh under his eyes sagged; the lines on his forehead had deepened. Her pulse quickened with the sense of him and with another ounce of courage, she would leap at him and just hold on to him. Instead she looked at him and said, "Can you forgive me?"

He dragged deeply on a cigarette and pushed his hair back from his forehead. "I doubt it," he said. "But you're sitting here now."

She could wait no longer for him to touch her and reached over and took his hand. He neither responded nor recoiled, but she would not let go unless he told her to. Finally, he tightened his fingers around her hand and pulled her towards him slowly and hesitantly as if he were touching her for the first time. In a way, it was a new experience, and, as they moved through an invisible curtain between the past and the future, she couldn't help but wonder if he had come back to her or she'd come back to him. Either way, they had another chance and she lifted her face toward his, begging him to kiss her.

chapter seventeen

HASSIE LEANED on the bow of the piano as Julio played the third version of her song's introduction. He looked up from the keyboard when he heard Henry's voice, then looked at Hassie and said, "I think Henry's calling you."

She ignored him for a moment. "Julio, now that Nat's gig has finished, what are the chances of me singing with the band one night?"

Julio nodded and said, "We'll have a few nights of playing to small crowds next week – could be a good time. I'll check it out."

She waved at Henry and looked back at Julio. "Maybe we should rehearse again, just in case."

"Maybe you should go see what Henry wants before he comes down here and tells us who's boss."

She worked her way through the room back to Henry's office, more annoyed than curious as to what he wanted with her. She'd had some great sessions with the band while the Rat Pack took a break and didn't want to lose a minute of that time. She pushed his door open and stood there, saying, "What's wrong, Henry?"

He removed his reading glasses and looked at her. "I know you're probably gonna tell me that I'm a worrywart, but it just occurred to me that Jake has never told me that he's okay with your spending time in the Copa Room when he's not here."

Hassie paused at the door for a few seconds and then sat down in front of Henry's desk, smiled at him and said, "Henry, stop pretending that you're worried about my being here in the Copa Room and just ask me how things are going between me and Jake."

"It's just that the rumor mill seems to be working overtime right now and there are bets out there that, any day, Jake will regain his senses about your little – thing – with Frank and you'll be gone."

She sat back in the chair and crossed her legs. "I didn't realize that my business was common knowledge, but my little *thing* as you call it is history. Jake admits that he tried to torture me with Natalie and we have an agreement now. We will talk to each other openly and honestly, and I really think that Jake's gonna try very hard to treat my *thing* with Frank as exactly what it was."

Henry stared at her through squinting eyes. "And what is that?"

"To use Jake's words – an 'egomaniacal blowhard's' attempt to use a young, inexperienced girl to get back at him for something that happened a long time ago."

"And you have no idea what that might be," Henry said, like he was waiting for her to tell him something he already knew.

"Oh, I don't know," she said. "Something to do with a woman but nothing to do with me."

"So, just like that, he's forgiven you and everything's back to normal."

Hassie had no delusions about why there was less tension with Jake. She didn't even speculate about what would happen when Frank and the guys came back to the Copa Room. "He loves me, Henry," she said and reached across the desk for his hand. "It's just that simple. His birthday's on Saturday, and we're going to have a quiet, intimate weekend. Just the two of us."

"Well, good for you," he said, pulling his hand from her grip. "Whatever makes you happy." He leaned back in his chair and put on his glasses.

Hassie watched him for a few seconds, knowing all too well that there was something else on his mind and that she would be wise to get to the bottom of it now. She sat back in the chair, uncrossed her legs and re-crossed them, and then sighed deeply while saying, "What's really bothering you?" He looked at her over the top of his glasses but said nothing. She kept her focus on him and said, "I'm not leaving until you tell me why you really called me in here."

Henry removed his glasses and leaned back in his chair. "I tried to tell you a few months ago. I've known Jake for a long time and I've been through a lot with him and his – distinctive – way of doing things. And I don't think that you really understand how much you humiliated him."

"I told you," she said. "We talked through it and worked it out. Remember, he humiliated me as well."

"Yeah, but don't you understand? You don't really count."

Hassie stood up from the chair and put her hands on her hips. "I think it's time for me to go back down to the musicians and people who don't feel the need to treat me like I have straw for brains. Is that all you have to say?"

Henry remained in his chair and calmly said, "I've tried every way I know how to help you see Jake for what he really is."

Hassie remained still and glared at him.

"He has to control and he needs to possess. And I've seen him do it with a dozen women before you or even Natalie came along. I've never cared about any of those women the way I care about you. And regardless of what he tells you, he's never gonna get over what you did with Frank."

"Fine," she said and walked to the door. "But tell me, what do you think he's gonna do about it? Have me killed?"

"Make jokes if you like, but I know how to read him – as do quite a few others around here. And since he's been back from New York, his behavior's been a lot more reckless in the casino than usual. Rumor has it he's run up quite a big debt and when he's not there, he's in the Regency Lounge. The excess just isn't normal, and I want to go on record as having warned you."

"Your rumor mill *is* working overtime."

He stood up as she opened the door and said, "Hassie, please be careful."

In the middle of the day on Friday, Hassie called the Garden Room and asked the chef to help her with the food arrangements for Jake's birthday dinner. The bar was stocked, and she'd picked up some scented candles that she strategically placed around the suite in what she imagined was high bordello fashion. She had a standing arrangement with Jake's private steward, Carlos, to keep fresh flowers on the entry table at all times, and she double-checked that the magazines and newspapers were all current and everything was in the order that Jake liked it.

She had carefully prepared the ivory satin peignoir set that he'd bought for her in New York. She treated herself to a manicure and pedicure that morning and had returned from the hair salon with just enough time to soak in a warm bubble bath, where the relaxing scent of lavender permeated her senses, intensifying her mood for romance.

It had now been almost three months since she'd spoken with Barbara. A couple of weeks after the phone call, she received a package containing the eighteenth birthday present that Barbara had promised – a first edition of Margaret Mitchell's *Gone With the Wind* in perfect condition, like a page had never been turned. Hassie had sent her a note thanking her for the beautiful book, promising her that she hadn't lost sight of all that Barbara had tried to do for her and that she would stay in touch in the coming months. She'd desperately wanted to tell her about Jake and their trip to New York but decided that she would wait for an opportunity to talk to her again. What would Barbara think if she knew that she'd been to bed with Frank Sinatra?

She giggled to herself at the thought and then wondered if Barbara had ever had a lustful romantic interlude with an interesting, perhaps exotic, man. She was still quite an attractive woman and certainly was even more so when she was younger. One day she'd get Barbara to tell her about her life before she met Willis Crumpler. Plus, Barbara's life wasn't over yet – surely she would understand Hassie's attraction to Frank.

Hassie was also aware that her experience with Frank had brought her closer to Jake as her lover, almost as if it had shown her how special the intimacy between them was and that it shouldn't be taken for granted. But sometimes after they made love, she would feel a sort of tension overtake him. Many times he would find an excuse to get out of the room and leave her alone. She thought about Henry's suggestion that Jake's behavior in the hotel had been out of character lately, but, despite Henry's insistence to the contrary, she was certain that Jake had put their problems with Frank and Natalie behind him.

She dressed in a casual pair of slacks and soft woolen sweater. Jake insisted that she dress "like a lady" when the staff was coming in and out of the suite; the peignoir would have to wait. She dabbed the light powder from the Estee Lauder compact they'd bought at Lord & Taylor in New York across her forehead and nose, adding a light coat of dark pink lipstick before pinching her cheeks. Her hair had been styled loosely around her face the way Jake liked it. She wet her fingertips with the *Joy* perfume that he had given her, and then touched her fingers to both wrists and behind her ears. For a moment, she was back in Manhattan in the Copacabana where the men rushed to help her with her chair or her coat, or in the Oyster Bar at the Plaza Hotel where strange and mysterious men in suits had watched her as she walked through the forbidden space.

An hour passed without a word from Jake. A bottle of champagne had arrived earlier, which she decided to open around eight o'clock. As she loosened the cork from the bottle, she heard Jake put his key in the door and rushed to open it for him.

"I thought you forgot about our date," she said, putting her arms around his neck and kissing his cheek.

He kissed her tenderly and then followed her to the sofa while saying, "Nah, I just got some news that I wasn't particularly happy to hear."

As she carefully filled the first of the two delicate glasses with champagne, she asked, "Was it bad news?"

He loosened his tie, took the glass from her without comment and downed the contents in one big swallow. He wrapped his free arm around her waist and pulled her into him. His eyes were a little glassy and she could tell that he'd already had a few drinks.

"I'm all yours for the next –"

"You better say two days," she said, playfully.

"Not sure about that." He let go of her. "But at least for tonight and tomorrow morning."

Hassie started to argue with him, but she could see that he was worried about something. She wanted him to relax and picked up the bottle to refill his glass.

He took it from her and said, "If you don't mind, I'd like to have something a little stronger. You drink the champagne and get me some Jack Daniels."

"It's your birthday. You can have anything you want."

She started toward the bar; he grabbed her arm and pulled her close to him again, kissing her with the intensity that usually led straight to the bedroom. Then in a voice that she could barely hear, he said, "Please don't ever leave me."

He changed his clothes, then walked over to the dining table and pulled out her chair. They took their time with the meal that Hassie had arranged, which he seemed to enjoy a good bit less than the contents of the whiskey bottle. She continued to monitor his mood, sensing his preoccupation and trying to lighten the atmosphere.

When they finished eating, she pointed him to the sofa, implying that their dessert would be best served in a reclining position.

"I heard some interesting news today," she said, snuggling up to him.

"News or gossip?" He kissed her on the top of her head.

"Well, *I* think it's news." She hesitated, sensing that he wasn't really listening to her.

"So? What is it?" he said.

"Dotty and Jimmy are getting married," she announced like there had been some kind of royal decree.

"I thought they were already married."

"Nope. That's what everybody thought." She stood up and took her glass to the bar, refilling with the last of the champagne. "Evidently, Jimmy never wanted to get married and he just kept telling her that the time wasn't right."

"So what changed his mind?"

"Dotty," she said, returning to the sofa. "She told him that if he didn't agree to marry her by the end of last year, she'd leave him. Evidently he met the deadline by a split second with – to use Dotty words – a 'goofy, Jimmy-like proposal' and they've been making plans since the New Year."

"They can't be wanting a big wedding now?" he said and drained his glass. "At their age? God knows Dotty could never pull off the whole virginal-bride-in-a-white-dress thing."

"Don't be cruel. They deserve to have whatever kind of wedding they want."

"Sure they do. But in my opinion, people like them are what the wedding chapels are for. You know, a wedding in a box. Run in, run out. Voila! You're married."

Hassie slapped him on his shoulder and then hesitated with a sudden discomfort with talk about marriage. "Anyway, I think it's great and that they should do whatever makes them happy."

"Speaking of making someone happy," he said, pulling her close. "Why don't you go get comfortable?" He kissed her firmly on the lips and then aimed her toward the bedroom.

When she returned to the living room wearing the ivory robe and gown, it was dark except for the glow of the candles casting curious shadows and filling the air with a soft floral scent. Jake had tuned the radio to a local station that played the vocal recordings currently topping the charts. At first glance, she couldn't see him and called out his name.

"Come here," she heard him say and walked around the sofa. The candlelight made him appear mysterious, perhaps untouchable outside his own realm.

She moved closer to him before hearing him say, "Wait." He sat up and picked up a lit cigarette from the ashtray. "Let me look at you."

She stood still and waited for him to speak. After a few seconds, he sat back in the seat and said, "Take off the robe."

She removed the satiny cover and sensed the sheerness of the long gown; the soft folds that carried no weight and clung to her hips and breasts, making her feel breathless. She lifted her hair off her neck, pushing it into a soft pile on the back of her head. The simple move caused the gown to tighten around her breasts creating a more pronounced cleavage and she suddenly felt like Marilyn Monroe, exuding an inimitable sex appeal that no man could refuse.

Jake stood up and slowly moved closer but didn't touch her. He stood still and carefully drew on a cigarette. She didn't know what he really wanted her to do but felt that she shouldn't move or speak. She finally let her hair fall loose and reached her right arm out to him.

He took her hand and led her to the bar. He ground out the cigarette and without speaking, poured himself a brandy, and then lifted the bottle as an offer to join him. She nodded and smiled, then took the glass and raised it to him. "Happy birthday, Jake."

He touched her glass with his and then swallowed the contents. She walked away from the bar while he poured another drink and stood next to the sofa waiting for his next move. As he set the decanter back in its place, she heard the musical intro to one of her favorite songs and set her drink on the table. She rushed over to Jake and took hold of his hand and said, "I love this song. Come dance with me."

He reluctantly let her pull him away from the bar, her arms encircling his neck as Sinatra's voice began:

I'm a fool to want you.
I'm a fool to want you.
To want a love that can't be true
A love that's there for others too.

Hassie could feel Jake tense as she swayed in his arms; she tightened her embrace and sang along with Frank:

I'm a fool to hold you.
Such a fool to hold you
To seek a kiss not mine alone
To share a kiss that Devil has known ...

Without speaking, Jake pulled her arms from around his neck and walked over to the hi-fi and switched off the radio, then took hold of her hand and led her to the bedroom. His hand felt cool and clammy; his mouth slightly distorted as if he were trying to disguise the pain and agony of something unspeakable having happened.

She stopped beside the bed and pulled his hand close to her. "Are you okay?" she asked before reaching to touch his forehead. "You look a little –"

"I'm fine," he said and placed her arm around his neck. "I'll be even better after you make love to me."

She responded to his kisses, which became a little more aggressive than she was used to. He practically tore the delicate gown off her and then yanked his own clothes off like they were burning his body. Then, in a move that caused her to gasp with surprise, he jerked the covers off the bed and threw them in the floor, falling onto the bed and pulling her down on top of him.

Though slightly alarmed by the hostile nature of his behavior, she felt him relax and soften to her presence in his arms and lovingly kissed his chest. He pulled her up to his face and delivered such luscious kisses that she thought her chest would explode. She pushed herself up on her arms and started to move down his body with her lips and tongue.

He took hold of her arm, pulling her back up to his face and whispered, "I'm not ready yet." He kissed her harder and deeper until she collapsed on top of him, grinding her body against him in an effort to pull him into her. When she reached for his penis, she found that his body had not responded; that there was no sign that he had any intention of making love to her.

Without thinking, she moved away and looked at him in shock but said nothing.

"I told you I wasn't ready," he slurred, and then laughed softly.

"I'm – sorry," she said, hesitating to touch him. "Did I do something wrong?"

He sat up and lit a cigarette, then swung his legs off the edge of the bed and with his back to her, he said, "Yes. Yes, you did."

She jumped up from the bed and ran around to the other side to face him. "What, Jake? What did I do?" She tried to touch his face but he moved her hand away and shouted, "Shut up," then stood up and went into the bathroom. She picked the bedcovers up out of the floor and laid them on the bed, the events of the night racing through her head and clawing at her insides. What could she possibly have done that could cause such a vile reaction from the one person she had only wanted to please?

She went to the bathroom and pounded on the door. "Jake, please come out and talk to me. You're scaring me." She spotted her terry cloth bathrobe on the stool beside the dressing table and grabbed it while listening for movement in the bathroom. She slipped on the robe and called his name again, but she could hear nothing and finally leapt at the door and pounded it with her fist.

Jake opened the door, his face wet and splotchy; his lower jaw trembled. He brushed past her and tightened the sash on his robe, then turned to look at her. She walked closer to him and started to speak. He held out his hand to stop her and said, "Shut. Up."

She followed him out into the sitting room but kept her distance. He went to the bar and poured another drink, sat down in the large armchair and lit a cigarette. Her insides ached; her worry for him turned to sympathy and a desperate need to help him. "Maybe you just had too much drink," she said carefully. When he didn't respond, she continued, "I've read about how too much alcohol can make it more difficult for a man to – perform."

"Where the hell would you read something like that?"

The fury in his eyes frightened her, but she needed to understand if this could be the cause of his problem – that it was nothing to do with her. "I don't remember, but don't you think it could be true?"

He stood up and threw the glass against the wall, then leapt at her and grabbed hold of both of her arms. "You really are a stupid cowgirl." He pushed her away with such force that she fell to the floor. "You really don't know what you did wrong?" She didn't move or answer. He paced around a small area of the room, then picked her up off the floor and tightened his hand around her arm. "You fucked Frank Sinatra. You let him kiss you and touch you and – you're nothing but a two-bit whore."

He let go of her arm and fell down into the chair. His face was wet with either sweat or tears, but she was afraid to get any closer to him.

"That was a long time ago, Jake," she finally said. "It was a mistake, and you said you forgave me."

"Well, I –" he said without looking at her. "I tried, but I can't. He was inside you and he'll always be inside you. You betrayed me in the worst way, and you think I can forgive you? You think I should forgive a *whore*?"

She had no idea what to do and shivered with the thought of Henry's warning. Her heart practically beat through her chest. She had never believed that Jake would do anything to hurt her. He'd sworn how much he loved her and had begged her not to leave him. How could he be so kind and gentle to her and then, without warning, turn into such a hateful beast? His various moods of the evening quickly moved through her mind. She started to speak, and then hesitated before quietly saying, "Frank's coming back, isn't he?"

Jake never said a word or even looked at her before he jumped up from the chair and grabbed her again. She screamed and begged him to stop but his hand gripped her throat and pushed her up against the wall. She couldn't breathe and clawed at his hand, which angered him more and he tightened his grip until she swung at him with her fist, catching him on his left temple. He backed away, and his eyes looked dead, unfocused, and his face was no longer that of the man she loved. She tried to calm him – to tell him that everything would be all right. But he grabbed her again as he shouted, "You fucking whore," and then slapped her in the face with the back of his hand; his knuckles catching her right eye and sending a searing pain through her head. The back of her head hit the wall, her vision blurred and her legs gave way beneath her. She fell to the floor, calling out to him as he looked down at her and growled like an angry animal. She couldn't move but looked up at him just as he slammed his foot into the left side of her face, sending her into unconsciousness.

part two

reno 1963

chapter eighteen

THE WALK along East Fourth Street had been part of Hassie Calhoun's daily routine for the almost two and a half years since leaving Las Vegas. It was one of those days when the atmospheric pressure made the high cheekbones of her Choctaw heritage ache, and, as she entered the office building and climbed the stairs, she wondered if her face would hurt for the rest of her life, forever reminding her of that last night with Jake Contrata.

A little breathless from the steep climb, she stood in front of the office marked *M. Bachman, Attorney-at-Law*, took her keys from her purse and opened the glass-paned door to the basic but adequate space with knotty pine walls and a thin, industrial carpet in that nondescript color of brown that easily camouflaged everything from coffee spills to ink stains. Thanks to Julio's connections, Morty Bachman's office was home from nine to five, Monday to Friday. And, thanks to Morty, she'd finally gotten to meet the intensely private Clay Cooper – Jake's half brother and local talent agent who, if he was ever going to put his money where his mouth was, should get her that new job offer today and she'd kiss the entire goddamn state of Nevada good-bye.

She flipped the three switches that turned on the lights throughout the office and then quietly surveyed the room that looked exactly the way it did when she left on Friday evening. She raised the Venetian blinds over the window that faced the downtown area of Reno, revealing an impressive view of the Mapes Hotel, the tallest building in Nevada – though hardly a skyscraper by New York standards.

The morning was clear and sunny and if she squinted and used her imagination, she could see the windows of the Sky Room, the popular nightclub at the top of the hotel that frequently hosted acts from LA and Vegas. She remembered the time that Sinatra took Julio with him to the Sky Room for a one-week engagement, when Henry was all but certain that the Copa Room would fall apart.

Hassie opened the door to her boss's office and raised the blind on the small window behind his desk. The two African violets perched on the windowsill cried out for help of all sorts – mostly a new home where they could get the proper amount of sunlight and the daily attention that they craved. She pinched off a couple of dead leaves and went into the kitchenette to get the watering can and the special mix of plant food.

The faint, stale smell of Morty's cigars hung in the room, but she somehow couldn't picture the middle-aged entertainment lawyer without the fat, disgusting stogies. He promoted a reputation for being hard-assed and ultra demanding, but, as Hassie had quickly come to know, he was actually a caring, nurturing professional with a heart of gold, even if he did try, sometimes quite sternly, to warn her off the shitty men that she seemed to attract. He disapproved of her relationship with married Felix Morales and had threatened to strangle her when he learned that she'd slept with John Jacobson – a talent scout that came sniffing around Felix's hot little jazz club where she sang several nights a week.

She fed and watered the plants before settling down at her desk and removing the plastic fitted cover from the IBM Selectric typewriter, which sat crooked in its place on the black vinyl mat. Hassie was sure that the lazy old bag of a cleaning lady left it that way on purpose to try to fool her into believing she'd moved it to clean underneath. She kept looking at the telephone, massaging her left cheek with two fingers of her left hand, wondering how long Clay would make her wait for his call. He liked to make her sweat; he didn't approve of her methods of operation. He also knew that she'd slept with John Jacobson and it had quietly pissed him off. Clay had scruples and believed that success came from hard work – poor naïve bastard. If she'd counted on hard work to get her out of Reno and on to one of the big clubs in New York, she'd be singing at Felix's for the rest of her life.

In her own way, she *had* worked hard to get this far – sometimes too hard, Barbara would have said, if she'd known all the dirt about her life that Morty knew. Barbara Crumpler had three basic rules for living: Be a lady, be true to yourself and always preserve your integrity. She had lovingly lathered these rules on Hassie from the day she began dance lessons until the day she pushed her onto the stage at the talent show in Dallas. These days, Barbara would agree with Morty: Hassie spent too much time in the jazz club, drank too much, smoked too much and used scant judgment when it came to men.

Morty had a board meeting over at the university that morning, which was just as well because he would take one look at her and know about her weekend. He'd shake his head and, in his old cowboy drawl, say something like, "Don't you look like somethin' the cat dragged in," and then berate her for reneging on her sworn oath to give up smoking and say, "Good job givin' up the booze and cigarettes. You sound like you ate sandpaper for breakfast."

Okay, so he knew her pretty well. But there was still one thing that neither he nor Barbara nor anyone would ever know about her life in Reno – one thing that both haunted her and intrigued her when she thought about it. It had taken several weeks after she arrived in Reno following the incident with Jake for her face to return to its natural shape and color, but it was easy enough to hide in her efficiency apartment until she was back to normal and ready to face the world. She'd heard about this place called Felix's and thought that it might offer some clues about the opportunities for singing in Reno. On the night that she decided to visit the club, she put on the only dress she owned that didn't remind her of Jake, carefully applied her makeup to conceal the splotchy, yellowish-brown remnants of the horrific bruising, and went down about ten o'clock. That night, only half of the tables were occupied, but the band was in full swing and she'd felt most comfortable sitting on a stool at the end of the bar where she ordered a vodka gimlet and opened the first pack of cigarettes that she had ever actually purchased. When she'd struggled to get the first cigarette loose, a man in a dark suit appeared at her side and took the pack from her hand.

"Women and their fingernails," he'd said, smiling behind a thick moustache, emitting the aroma of a spice she didn't recognize. She didn't speak as she removed the cigarette he'd offered her, and then waited as he clicked open his black and gold lighter and ignited the flame.

"Thank you," she'd said, and carefully inhaled the smoke.

"It's always a pleasure to assist such a beautiful woman. Do you live here in Reno?"

She'd nodded, hesitated then said, "Do you?"

"I live everywhere and nowhere, but this is my first visit to Nevada."

"How do you like it?"

"Reno's not New York."

"I love New York. I've only been there once. I'd love to go back." She told him about her few days there, neglecting to give him details of whom she'd been with but reiterating her desire to return. Perhaps he had gotten some sort of wrong impression, she couldn't imagine what after such a brief exchange, but he stood smoothing his moustache for several seconds before lightly placing his index finger on the back of her hand.

"Yes, I see that you must visit me," he had said and slowly tapped her hand three times. "I can show you great and wonderful things, and from my penthouse, there's a good view of the city. If you like boats, there's always the harbor. Have you been to the Statue of Liberty?"

She'd shaken her head and reached for her drink, remembering the view of the harbor from Battery Park. She'd begged Jake to take her to the great national monument, but he had insisted that it was just as impressive from a distance and that boat rides to Liberty Island were for tourists. When she'd turned back to face the handsome man, he'd put his hand on her cheek and said, "I would be honored to show you *my* New York, but I'm on my way to the Far East, and I may never come back to Reno."

She'd been unaware that he was studying her until he lifted her chin, moved her face from side to side and said, "Did you have a run-in with someone's fist?"

She'd rubbed the nubby ridge of the scar just above her eyebrow, triggering an image of Jake's foot coming toward her face as if it had all happened yesterday. She'd felt her cheeks get warm and moved uncomfortably on the stool before saying, "I'm fine, but I'd like another drink."

The man laughed, caught the bartender's eye and pointed to her glass. He then picked her cigarette out of the ashtray and ground it out for her as if they had been lovers for many years. "Something tells me that Reno's not home. I hear a tiny bit of a southern accent – Texas, maybe?"

"Very good observation," she'd said as the bartender set the drink in front of her and then poured another shot of something from a bottle she didn't recognize into the man's glass. "I grew up near Dallas – not that I'd call it home anymore."

He'd picked up his glass and focused on her mouth, then stared into her eyes and said, "What brought you from Texas to Reno?"

"I came from Las Vegas to Reno," she'd said softly, then sipped her drink again. Something about the way the man looked at her made her want to spend more time with him and tell him more. After all, he was a stranger passing through town; she'd never see him again. She'd picked up the pack of cigarettes and said, "And that's a story you don't want to know."

He'd waited for her to remove a cigarette from the pack and then offered his lighter again. "You're right. I'm much more interested in your future." He'd touched her scar and then slowly moved his finger along her jaw, then reached into his jacket pocket and pulled out a money clip loaded with bills. He'd flicked through a dozen or so and pulled them from the clip – she'd assumed he was going to pay the bar tab – then held them up to her and said, "Here's what it would cost to really show you a good time in New York. Why don't you just take the money and one day you'll owe me a visit."

"I couldn't do that," she'd said. "I may never get back to New York."

"Then take the money and show me Reno." He'd pushed the bills into the palm of her hand and closed her fingers tightly around them.

His hand had been intensely warm and large enough to practically engulf her tightly clenched fist. She'd felt an intense quiver in her stomach as he moved closer to her ear and said, "You could take me to your apartment and cook me a late supper." Then he'd lifted her hand to his lips and kissed it before saying, "Or breakfast."

Her pulse had quickened as she thought of her dingy little apartment and knew that it wasn't an option. But the money in her hand could go a long way toward helping her get her life going in Reno. The temptation had been overwhelming; she'd refused to acknowledge the sense of Barbara's presence, like a parrot sitting on her shoulder, perched to squawk if she made a bad decision. She'd looked at the man, caught up in his charming, seductive manner and ignoring the warnings in her nerve endings and had said, "Are you at the Mapes Hotel?" He nodded; his eyes danced in the bar light. Fuelled by his sweet attention and a little too much vodka, she had smiled at him and said, "If I was to consider doing something so wicked, I'd want to be in the best hotel." He had laughed, looked around the bar, and said, "You are something else."

It had been just one night and now it was in the past, but with the money from that night, her job with Morty and only a little bit of her own savings, she'd been able to support herself pretty well; perhaps this was why Clay had taken her seriously.

She stood and paced across the mottled carpet, humming the melody of Cole Porter's "Love for Sale" that she had heard on the radio late the night before. She couldn't seem to get the haunting melody out of her head. Maybe she'd ask JJ to learn it with her for her show. She could use a few new songs – unless Clay came through today and she was on her way to the big time. She took a deep breath, and then went into the kitchenette to make coffee, muttering, "God damn it, Clay. When are you gonna call?"

In their initial meetings, Clay didn't pay much attention to her desire for a singing career and barely recognized her ability to write songs. A few weeks into her stint at Felix's, he started showing up in the audience at least once a week and finally admitted that she did have talent and took her on as a client. But he took an awfully long time to decide that she could handle herself in a bigger market – his disapproval of her lifestyle didn't help matters – and he eventually suggested that he seriously look for a reputable club outside of Reno for her to take her act. Although LA was closer to Reno and Clay probably had more clout there, he had contacts on the east coast as well and all Hassie was asking was for him to get her to New York. Maybe she wouldn't make it to Jilly's right away, but wherever she ended up, she'd wow them, her hair flowing freely to her shoulders and wearing the deep red dress that Clay had helped her pick out. "You were born to wear that dress," he'd said, just before he told her that she needed to grow up and take responsibility for her actions.

The shrill ring of the telephone startled her from her thoughts, causing her to drop the dented percolator on the counter. She ran back to the desk and leapt at the phone. "Good morning. Morty Bachman's office."

"Can you meet me for lunch at the Mapes at one o'clock?" Clay's voice was calm and even and disclosed nothing that would give her a hint of what he had to tell her.

"Yes, I can," she said, coolly. "But Morty's not here right now and I'm not sure when he'll be back."

"He'll be back in plenty of time. See you there."

She hung up and thought of the exact way Clay had said each word to her – was his tone positive? Was he eager to see her? She finally shrugged and opened the bottom drawer containing her standby supply of makeup and was tempted by the sight of the pint bottle of vodka that she kept in case of an emergency. "No!" she said, and closed the drawer.

Hassie arrived at the Mapes Hotel at exactly one o'clock, where she was to meet Clay in the dining room. She asked to be seated at his table in the far corner; he'd never been on time in his life. If today were like any other, she'd sit there a good fifteen minutes on her own. She dug around her purse for her cigarettes, laid them on the table and sat back to wait. Although she spoke with Clay fairly often, it had been a few weeks since she'd seen him.

In most ways, Clay and Jake looked absolutely nothing alike; Jake was dark and brooding, Clay was boyish and blonde. But they both possessed a certain quality that, although it affected each of them in different ways, created the force that drew her to them and gave them their respective opportunities to complicate her life. Clay's cobalt blue eyes had a very calming effect. Her romantic attraction to him was the first to anyone after the swelling on her face went down – excepting the man from New York, whom she'd nicknamed "Mister Satan" for encouraging her single unprincipled action but who continued to ravish her dreams. She chuckled to herself with the thought of her spoof of the Chordettes hit, "Mister Sandman," which she sang at Felix's, substituting *Satan* for *Sandman*: "Mister Satan, bring me a dream, Make him the cutest that I've ever seen..." The poor drunks in the audience were none the wiser and it always made her feel a little wicked.

When Hassie first met Clay, he kept her at arm's length with a strictly business attitude, which made her extremely attracted to him. She never admitted to herself or anyone that the fact that he was Jake's younger brother had anything to do with this attraction, and although she knew it was best to maintain the businesslike relationship, she couldn't help following a different instinct. A harmless flirtation ensued, and she believed that it was just a matter of time before she ended up in his bed.

Then she took a job singing at Felix's – starting with the late set on Thursday nights, where she developed a following that earned her top billing Wednesday through Sunday, usually to a packed house. The weekend parties carried on into the wee hours where she would end up any number of places, oftentimes the back room that Felix kept at the club when he was more interested in spending time with her than going home to his wife. Clay's reaction to the illicit affair had been one of indifference. But it had gotten back to her that he'd passed it off as her needing to "sow her oats," and he basically ignored her until the night John Jacobson came to town.

The waitress stopped by the table, deposited two menus and asked if she would like a drink while she waited.

Before Hassie could answer, Clay slid into the chair adjacent to her and said, "Just bring us some water right now," then looked back at Hassie and said, "Sorry, would you like some coffee or something else?"

Hassie knew damn well that he knew she wanted a martini, but slowly shook her head and opened the menu.

He placed his hand over hers and said, "Let's get the business out of the way and see if we have something to celebrate."

"It's fine, really," she said while studying the menu. "I don't need to go back to work loaded."

He smiled saucily and opened the menu.

The waitress delivered the water and took their orders. Clay asked Hassie about the new horn player that Felix had hired and seemed to just want to chitchat about the various band members, making obvious remarks and getting on her nerves. When she couldn't stand it any longer, she interrupted him. "So, when are you gonna tell me what I came here to find out?" She knocked a cigarette out of the pack and reached for the matches.

"Patience, my dear. And I thought you were gonna give up those things," he said as he took the matchbook from her.

She put the cigarette to her lips and motioned for him to light it, and then exhaled toward the ceiling as Clay said, "You should know that the guys in the band have a lot of regard for you. Felix says that you're the best thing that's ever happened to that place. Are you really sure you want to leave?"

"Felix is a great guy. And don't get me wrong, I love working at that club. They totally understand my style and not one guy has ever suggested a song that I should do that's anything but perfect for me."

"What about your own songs?" he asked. "Do you still work on those pieces you brought with you from Vegas?"

She smiled and flicked her cigarette in the ashtray. "Every chance I get. But JJ's not as interested in them as Julio was."

Clay watched her and listened before saying, "Julio's a rare specimen of gifted, caring musician. I've known that since the first time I saw him in a studio in LA when he was a skinny kid with too much hair and bad skin. Sounds like you miss him a little bit."

Hassie nodded and pictured Julio's dark eyes shining at her when they worked at the piano on the Copa Room stage.

Clay was silent for a long moment and then said, "If you could work in any club in this country, where would it be?"

Without hesitation, she replied, "I think you know the answer to that question. The Copacabana or Jilly's in New York. Oscar's Pub down in the Village. Why are you asking me this now?"

"What about the Tropicana?" Clay asked, leaning his forearms on the table.

"What about it?"

"Ever heard of a lounge there called La Chanson?"

"The Tropicana. The one in Vegas?"

"Is there any other? Of course the one in Vegas," he said.

Watching his face, she stubbed out the cigarette and sipped her water. "This is a joke, right?"

"Why should it be a joke?"

"Clay, you told me that you were looking for a job in LA or New York."

"That may be what you heard, but I think we agreed that I would find you another gig outside of Reno. Vegas is outside of Reno. And, frankly, that's where the best offer came from."

The waitress arrived with two plates of food, left a couple of bottles of sauces on the table, asked if they needed anything else and walked away.

Hassie glared at Clay, pushed her plate away and sat back in the chair.

Clay poured the brown sauce on the side of his plate, picked up his fork and said, "Surely you remember the talent scout that came in to see you at Felix's a few weeks ago – a Mr. Jacobson?"

She moved uncomfortably in the chair and said, "What does he have to do with this?"

"Evidently, he was very impressed with your – *performance* – and told Felix that he'd never seen crowds react so enthusiastically to one of his shows in Vegas. Of course, Felix told him that you are a star and that people come from miles around to hear you. You can imagine how much he poured it on."

Hassie lit another cigarette and inhaled deeply before saying, "What do you mean – one of *his* shows?"

"Didn't he tell you? John Jacobson is a scout for the Tropicana. They need a new act at this place – La Chanson – and he contacted me to offer you the job, which, by the way, he said he was certain you would be interested in." Clay calmly finished the sentence and tucked into his potato. "So you're not going to eat?"

Hassie rested her arms on the table, picturing the little weasel of a man, buying her expensive champagne, telling her what an amazing singer she was and how she belonged in one of the hot, jazzy clubs in New York while she locked the door in Felix's back room and gave him an hour of passion that he was likely not to forget too soon.

She drew deeply on the cigarette again and then exhaled as she leaned in closer to Clay. "You really think I want to go back to Vegas?"

"Why not? It's a job at the Tropicana. Which means you'll get paid very well, you'll get proper billing – your own poster with your picture on it – and the band is reputed to be one of the best around."

"You can wrap all this up in shiny paper and put a big bow on it but it still means going back to Vegas." She laid the cigarette in the ashtray, took a deep breath before touching the scar on her brow and saying, "I'm about as close to Vegas as I ever want to be again."

Clay took hold of her hand and said, "Is this about Jake?"

Hassie pulled her hand away and said, "Of course, it's about Jake!

Look at my broken, scarred face, Clay. I know it's not your fault, but don't ask me to go back."

"Jake's at the Sands. I'm asking you to consider going to the Tropicana, which, as you very well know, is at the other end of the strip – a world away. And, by the way, I think your broken, scarred face is still pretty damn beautiful."

She laughed and looked around for the waitress. "I need a drink."

"Hassie, I think this is a really good opportunity for you, and it's time for you to let the past be the past."

"That's easy for you to say," she said and picked up the cigarette.

He took a deep breath and looked at her, his deep blue eyes unable to hide what he was really thinking.

She was on the verge of telling him to just forget the whole thing when the waitress arrived. "Bring me a vodka martini, straight up with olives. And make it quick."

The waitress looked at Clay. He said, "Not for me," then looked at Hassie and said, "You know, your life at the Sands and in the Copa Room was something like a fairy tale. You – or someone – just kinda sprinkled fairy dust everywhere you went and things just happened. That's not the real world, and I'm sorry if I don't have a magic wand and can't get you your dream job in one of your dream joints."

He stopped to let her speak but she just looked around the room for the waitress, ground out the cigarette and said, "Where's that drink?"

"You're forgetting something here," he continued. "You're a nobody, and nobodies in this business don't always get to choose where they work. By the way, the Tropicana is no two-bit hole in the wall. I know a lot of people in this town that would jump at such an opportunity. If I were you, I'd get over bad luck in the past and look at the bright side, which is that one of the better hotels in the entertainment capital of the country has offered you a gig in their lounge starting the beginning of next month – which, in case you don't have a calendar, is only three weeks away – singing seven shows, five nights a week. That's two on Friday and Saturday, and the whole damn gig is negotiable. You'll have a contract with stipulations that, once you agree to them, will be the laws of your existence while you're there. You'll work with whoever they tell you to and you'll probably wear what they tell you to wear."

The waitress arrived with the martini and set the glass on the table in front of her. Hassie plucked the toothpick containing a single olive out of the glass, looked at the waitress and said, "Is your bartender a moron?"

The waitress lowered the tray to her side and said, "Sorry, ma'am. Is there a problem?"

"Any bartender with half a brain knows that a martini is supposed to have three olives." She waved the toothpick in the air and then dropped it back in the glass. The waitress reached to take the glass away, but Hassie grabbed it and said, "Never mind. Just leave it."

As the waitress walked away, Clay sat, waiting for Hassie to speak. She took a couple of sips, and then looked him in the eye and said, "So, say I take this godforsaken job. What happens next?"

"I'll ask Jacobson to send a contract and we'll review it with Morty."

She pulled the olive off the toothpick with her teeth and was reflective for a moment before saying, "Does Morty know about this yet?"

Clay nodded. "He doesn't think you'll do it. He thinks you have your heart set on going to New York or LA and, to be fair, we know that you were blindsided by Jacobson. He made you think that he represented a lot more than just the Tropicana."

She swallowed the rest of her drink and said, "So I'm not the only fool in the room."

"Let's get the negotiations under way. You can always change your mind if you don't like how it works out."

"I'm still not sure what to do," she said and took another cigarette from the pack and lit it.

"If you're over the trauma of having only one olive in your drink, I'll tell you." He gave her a chance to respond and then continued, "You go to Vegas and you sing at the Tropicana and see how it goes. And while you're there, let's look at doing some recording. We've made too much progress to ditch those efforts now."

"*Let's* means let *us* look at doing some recording. Does that mean you're coming to Vegas with me?" She dragged on the cigarette and smiled at him. "You want to follow your woman to Las Vegas?"

He grinned in that youthful way that accentuated the dimple in his right cheek. "I'll talk to Julio and ask him to help you with the demos. He knows everybody in Vegas and is in the best position to recommend a good studio. After all, the way I see it, he's already pretty involved with a couple of your songs."

"That's not a bad idea." She laid the cigarette in the ashtray and took a deep breath. "The thought of being close to Henry and Julio again makes me very happy. And, according to Henry, Dotty's the queen of the Tropicana now. I know she'll be there if I need her."

"So what are you worried about?"

The image of Jake standing over her with his fist in the air loomed close, she looked at him and said, "I don't think I can do it, Clay. It's just too soon. You gotta find something else."

He leaned back in the chair, folded his arms across his chest and said, "That's all I got, Hass. It's La Chanson or Felix's. Your choice."

"I thought you said that La Chanson was the *best* offer."

He shook his head and avoided looking at her. "It's the only real offer I've been able to get so far." He hesitated, but when she didn't comment, he said, "You can fire me if you like. Maybe you should ask John Jacobson to be your agent."

She stubbed out the cigarette, pushed her chair back and said, "I better get back to the office."

Clay motioned to the waitress for the check. "I'll drive you over there. Maybe Morty can talk some sense into you."

chapter nineteen

HASSIE LOVED the view from the big picture window in Clay's living room; the wet, grassy plains were a softer, more inviting alternative to the dry, dusty terrain of the Mojave Desert in Vegas. Clay had obviously done very well for himself in the ten years he'd been in Reno. His home was a monument to his success – wide and sprawling with a warm, unpretentious elegance that was the perfect setting for the meeting that was about to take place. Morty had helped Clay negotiate an excellent contract with the Tropicana and had managed to convince the hotel's representatives to travel to Reno for a ceremonial signing of the documents.

In the end, Morty was sympathetic to Hassie's concerns about going back to Vegas and talked the Tropicana into giving her a thirty-day contract to start, with an option to renew for another thirty days. Even she had to agree that the whole opportunity was worth at least one month of effort.

As Hassie waited for Clay to finish a phone call in his office and for the others to arrive, she sat down at the Steinway baby grand and turned the chunky plastic knob to adjust the height of the leather-covered bench. She loved to tease Clay about owning such an instrument, as it was obvious that he'd bought it to fill the space in the corner of the glass-encased sun porch. Whatever the reason he owned it, she loved the opportunity to play and rolled out the sequence of chords that were the underpinning of her favorite composition.

When she first arrived in Reno, she'd been afraid that she would lose touch with her music and that Julio's arrangements of her songs would eventually leave her. But the job at the jazz club gave her access to an Acrosonic upright that had seen hours of talented fingers across its keys and enabled her to keep her music fresh while she developed a comfortable relationship with JJ, the club's music director. JJ was a good guy and very talented in his own right, but no one really felt Hassie's music the way Julio did, and she was thankful for the basic training she'd gotten from Barbara, which now made it possible for her to work on her own compositions without Julio's help.

She plunked out the latest melody she'd been working on while her mind drifted back to Corsicana and the last time she'd really talked to Barbara. Rarely a day went by that Hassie didn't think of Barbara – some piece of advice or words of encouragement that she had offered her along with the strict warnings that running away to Vegas would do nothing to advance her life. What would Barbara think of her now? She had trained her so well and endlessly inspired her where her love of music was concerned. Clay and Morty had convinced her that the move to the Tropicana was a step forward in her career, but she felt sure that Barbara would see it as a step backwards – that returning to a town that she should never have gone to in the first place could do nothing but cause her more heartache.

Barbara had gone to great lengths to support and encourage her, and it pained Hassie to think of how disappointed she would be if she ever found out that she had allowed herself to be seduced by a complete stranger and that, in full consciousness, she had given herself to him for money. Hassie occasionally came across the calling card that Mr. Satan had given her that night, and every time she saw it, she experienced feelings that both tortured her with guilt and heightened her sense of finally becoming her own woman.

She'd also wondered if Mr. Satan had pegged her for a prostitute from the moment he saw her sitting at the bar. He'd certainly noticed the scar above her eye – maybe he jumped to the wrong conclusion. Through years of mulling the situation over in her mind, she'd never been sure of what actually occurred. She not only hoped that Barbara would never find out about this lapse in judgment, but also that she would never find herself in that sort of situation again.

When she was in Vegas, she'd worried too much about what everyone thought and, of course, given in to Jake's controlling demands. She'd pushed her life in Corsicana out of her consciousness, except for the occasional twinge of concern for what Barbara would think of her actions. But her mother's influence eluded her thoughts; she simply didn't care what her mother would have said. Bonita had made selfish decisions that hurt others deeply and, in doing so, had destroyed another human being and driven her daughter away from home. In Hassie's heart and mind, forgiveness was not warranted.

She hummed the melody while finding the notes on the keyboard. Clay's voice rang through the corridor, "Are you okay out there?"

"I'm fine," she called. "Where is everyone?"

She heard him enter the room and looked up at him as he said, "I love hearing you play. Don't stop."

She went back to the song that she knew best and played the arrangement she'd learned from Julio. "I thought you said that this little charade would start at three o'clock."

"Now, now," he said and walked over to the piano. "The plane from Vegas was late and Morty called a few minutes ago to say that they're on their way." He stood next to her at the piano, listened for a few seconds and then said, "How do you feel?"

"I'm fine, Clay." She stopped playing. "I just don't understand all the fuss that you guys insist on making over the signing of this contract. You'd think I was Judy Garland getting ready to sign on with MGM for a dozen movies."

Clay crossed his arms over his chest. "Just humor Morty, please. Try to acknowledge what he's doing for you."

She wrinkled her nose and said, "What's he doing?"

"He's making sure that these guys – and therefore anyone else in Vegas – understand how lucky they are to have you in their lounge."

Hassie laughed. "I thought *you* were my agent. Shouldn't you be handling this?"

"Morty's an old friend of Lou Walters, the entertainment director at the Tropicana, and thought it might be to your advantage if he were a little more involved."

She shrugged and stood up from behind the keyboard. "It doesn't matter to me who works it out. Is this Mr. Walters coming to this meeting?"

"I doubt it," Clay said and led her into the living room. "That would be like Jake Contrata showing up at the signing of an act in the Regency Lounge at the Sands. No offense."

The mention of Jake's name took her straight to the world that she'd hoped to avoid for the rest of her life and to which now she was planning to return. The thought made her wish she'd picked another week to give up smoking. Before she could comment, she heard the slam of car doors and stood beside Clay waiting for the little circus to get under way.

Clay took hold of her arm and said, "Just follow Morty's lead and smile for the camera."

"You're kiddin' me," she said as Clay laughed and Morty burst through the door, followed by a small entourage of men. Morty pointed two of the men into the dining area and then motioned for Hassie to join them at the large table in the middle of the room. He reached out to take her hand and pulled her closer to where they stood. "Randall Jergens, this is Hassie Calhoun."

The man stuck out his hand and said, "Hello, Miss Calhoun. It's a pleasure to finally meet you."

Hassie shook his hand and relaxed when she realized that John Jacobson had not made the trip. "Please, call me Hassie."

"Randall is the hotel's lawyer," Morty continued. "He represents the owners and is acting on behalf of Lou Walters."

Clay stepped up and shook the lawyer's hand and said, "I thought we'd be seeing John Jacobson since we handled the negotiations through him."

"John's taking care of some other business for Mr. Walters," Jergens said. "I can assure you everything's in good order."

During this exchange of niceties, one of the young guys that Morty had ushered into the dining room had rearranged the chairs at the table into a "their side, our side" configuration. Morty pulled out the chair in the center of their row and Hassie sat down. As soon as everyone was seated, the two men reappeared from the dining area, one with a big black camera with a large flash bulb, the other toting a steno pad with a much too serious look on his face.

Morty took charge, reviewed all the points of the document that he cared to draw attention to and suggested that they get on with the formality of signing. Hassie bit her lip to keep from giggling as he directed everyone into their respective places before sitting down beside her and offering the first pose for the camera.

When every document was signed by each party and sealed by Morty and Randall Jergens, Clay motioned to Jorge, the Mexican houseboy, to bring the tray of glasses to the table while he fetched a bucket containing an open bottle of champagne.

Morty leaned back in his chair, rested his hands on top of his stomach and said, "It sure is nice doin' business with the Tropicana. Looks like we're gonna have a little drink to cement the deal."

Clay took the bottle from the bucket and poured the champagne into the glasses while Jorge passed them around the table. Morty stood up with his glass, faced Hassie and said, "Gentlemen – and lady. This is a great day for Hassie Calhoun and the Tropicana." He peered past the table to where the man with the steno pad stood and said, "Make sure you get all this down, son." Morty gestured to include Clay and continued, "We know that this is just the first of many such great days in Hassie's future and are very honored to be here today." He lifted his glass while saying, "Here's to Hassie. May all your dreams come true, now and for many years to come."

"Hear, hear," Clay said amidst the mumble around the table as they all took a drink.

"Oh, and one more thing," Morty said as he took hold of Hassie's hand. "You better come back to Reno when this gig is done."

She smiled at him and said, "I thought you wanted all my dreams to come true."

The men laughed and pushed back from the table. Clay waited for Morty to give her some space and then walked over to her and touched her glass with his. "I'm very proud of you."

"Thanks, Clay. I know you are just as responsible for all of this as Morty is. I hope you know how much I appreciate what you've done for me."

"Just go and have a great time," he said. "And make them beg you for more."

She swallowed and looked into his eyes; he lifted her chin, studied her for a few seconds and said, "Are you sure you're okay?"

She nodded and said, "I'd like to get out of here. I want to speak to Henry."

Clay took the glass from her and set it on the table. "Morty, I'm taking Hassie home. She's got a lot to do and something tells me you and Mr. Jergens would like to celebrate with something a little stronger than champagne."

Morty waved at them and said, "You two go on ahead. I'll see you tomorrow."

Hassie turned toward Randall Jergens, but, before she could speak, he lifted her hand and said, "Mr. Jacobson sends his apologies for not being here but asked me to tell you that he looks forward to seeing you in Vegas."

She shook his hand slowly and forced a smile before saying, "Thank you," then turned to Clay with a look that begged him to get her out the door. Clay gripped her elbow and led her out into the driveway where she shoved her hand into her handbag like a raccoon scavenging a trash bin. "Ah ha!" she said and pulled the pack of cigarettes out of her bag.

Clay grabbed for the pack and knocked them to the ground, then took hold of her arm and said, "Oh, no you don't. You're a professional singer now, and you promised me and Morty that you would take care of your voice."

"I just need one to calm my nerves," she said and tried to free her arm from Clay's grip.

He pushed her towards his car and said, "You'll always find a reason to have 'just one more,' Hassie. I know you can go and buy another pack as soon as I leave you, but I hope you won't. I hope you'll use some better judgment and really give yourself a chance to quit."

"Okay, I'll try," she said and craned her neck in the direction of the lost pack.

Hassie was unsuccessful in reaching Henry that afternoon, but tried again the following day, when Morty took some clients out for lunch. The phone rang a few times before he answered, "Berman speaking."

"Berman, this is Calhoun," she said in her most mysterious voice.

"Hassie? Honey, is that you? I was just saying that I haven't heard from you for a while."

"Hi, Henry." Her nerves were calmed by the sound of his voice. "It's me. I'm calling you from Reno, but I've got some news."

"You sold one of your songs?"

"No," she said. "I got a job."

"That's great, but I thought you already had a job."

"A job in Vegas," she said; the words still sounded strange to her. "At the Tropicana. In the lounge called La Chanson. Do you know it?"

"Of course. It's a great little spot, honey. You've never been there?"

"You know how rarely I got out of the Sands when Jake –"

"Does he know you're coming back?"

"I don't think so. And don't tell him. In fact, don't tell anyone yet."

"Not even Julio?"

"Well, Julio's the exception," she said and lit a cigarette. "In fact, I want to record some demos while I'm there and I need Julio to help me. Do you think he might be able to do that?"

"I don't know. Ask him yourself."

She heard a muffle of voices before Julio spoke into the phone. "What's this I hear about recording demos?"

"Hi, Julio. It's so great to hear your voice."

"You too, Hassie. You're in Reno but coming to Vegas?"

"It looks that way," she said. "I'll let Henry fill you in, but briefly, Clay wants me to record some demos while I'm there and I need your help."

"Sounds like Clay's been really good for you," Julio said then quickly interjected, "Professionally, I mean."

She hesitated for a few seconds before saying, "Clay's been great for me. I'll see you next week."

"Wow. Okay, chica. Here's Henry."

Henry got back on the phone and said, "Okay." He took an audible breath. "Where you gonna stay?"

"I can stay at the Tropicana, but I'd kinda like to be on my own for the first four weeks until we see how it goes."

"Hold on for a minute." She could hear his hand covering the mouthpiece and another muffle of voices. She waited and drew deeply on the cigarette. Finally, Henry came back on the line and said, "Listen and don't ask any questions yet, but you can stay with me and Julio until you decide exactly what you wanna do."

"Are you serious?" she nearly shouted. "You and Julio live together?"

"Uh-huh," Henry said calmly. "So, when are you coming?"

"My contract starts August first."

"That's next week," he said.

"I know. Is that okay?"

"Of course it is." Henry hesitated.

"But?"

"Honey," he said. "Are you worried about seeing Jake again?"

She laid the cigarette in the ashtray and considered her words carefully before responding. "I'd be lying if I said I wasn't worried. I have a serious reminder of the last time I saw him, and I see it every time I look in the mirror."

"He was a brute that night," Henry said. "I bet you wished you'd listened to me when you look in that mirror."

So Henry was still not over the fact that she hadn't heeded his warning about Jake's state of mind just before he put her in the hospital. "Anyway, the Sands is his territory," she said. "I'll be at the Tropicana, and with my two favorite people in the world."

Henry was quiet again, and she knew that he had something else to tell her. "Henry, what's the matter? What are you not saying?"

"Jake's been with Natalie since you left."

She took a quick puff on the cigarette and said, "That's no surprise. You know he always had trouble keeping it in his pants where she was concerned."

She could hear him breathing and knew that he was sitting up straighter in his chair. He cleared his throat twice and finally said, "Natalie had a child."

He may as well have told her that Morty was her biological father. She ground out the cigarette and said, "When?"

"Almost two years ago. Honey –"

"Henry, it's fine." She swallowed and breathed deeply. "You want to tell me why you've never told me this before?"

"If I recall, you didn't like it when I tried to talk to you about Jake."

"Okay, you win. I fucked up. But that's all in the past and has absolutely nothing to do with his having a baby with Natalie."

"I guess," he said. "But the good news is that Jake's really changed."

"Yeah, well, so have I," she said, revealing more emotion than she intended. "I've been through a lot since I left the Sands and – well, I'm a different person now. I'm just not sure going back to Vegas is a good thing for me." She continued to wrestle with Barbara's warnings against bad choices where advancing her life and career were concerned. Would Henry understand this?

"What can't be good?" Henry said. "Your friends are here. Julio's dying to work on your songs again. And then there's the Copa Room – your favorite place on earth, right?"

"My favorite hell on earth," she said almost inaudibly.

"Aw, come on, Hassie. You know you're happiest when you're here. And in heaven when you're up on that stage. It's all still here just waiting for you."

She sighed and thought about the signed and sealed contract. "You're not listening to me. I'm going back to Vegas to work at the Tropicana. Nobody said anything about the Copa Room."

"Whatever you say," he said. "Just let us know when you'll get here and we'll meet you with bells on."

She hung up the phone and checked her watch. Morty would be on his third or fourth double-double by now. She picked up her purse and, out of habit, locked her desk drawer before going to the ladies room. She switched on the light and walked over to the sink. In the mirror's reflection she saw a dark haired, dark eyed woman with pale, washed out skin and a scar along her brow bone just above her eyebrow. She knew that she was lucky that the damage hadn't been worse, but this physical reminder was nowhere near as deep as the emotional wounds that still weighed her down.

The pain of never seeing her father again was something that she was learning to live with. The acceptance that Jake had never really loved her was taking more time. She had been warned about him – about his inability to really give of himself to anyone. But he had made her love him and in the midst of the searing passion that held them together, he had brutally dismissed her from his life.

She laid her purse on the vanity and splashed cold water on her face and neck. The nerve endings in the tips of her fingers were dead – a sensation that quickly spread throughout her body. She held onto the basin and stared up at the ceiling; the air in the room seemed to disappear.

The image of a dark haired toddler flashed through her mind and she felt that she would be sick. She splashed water on her face again and took several deep breaths but it was no use. Before she could turn away from the basin and make it into a toilet cubicle, she retched up the several cups of coffee she'd had that day.

chapter twenty

THE GREYHOUND SCENICRUSER pulled out of the depot in St. George, the last stop in Utah before it would cross back into the state of Nevada and the home stretch to Las Vegas. The big bus rolled along the deserted highway much like a train on a track, the view from the windows black as pitch except for the occasional pair of headlights. It had been less than four years since Hassie had made a similar journey from Dallas. Her recollection of that trip had faded into oblivion except for her choice of seat – the front row almost opposite the driver, where she had a clear view of the open road.

She had boarded the enormous vehicle before anyone else, claiming the seat next to the window. The middle-aged driver eyed her suspiciously when she placed her overstuffed vinyl tote bag on the seat beside her. He made her think of a deputy sheriff who'd been put in charge for the day. Her polite smile brought a puppy-like expression to his face, which prompted her to rest her head against the back of the seat, a weary sigh signaling her desire to be left alone.

Clay had tried to insist that Hassie take the short flight between Reno and Vegas, but she wasn't in that big of a hurry to get there and the long ride on the bus would give her some quiet time to think about where she was going and what she would do when she got there. Despite her bullheaded refusal to admit it to Clay, the opportunity at La Chanson was genuinely a good one. She just wasn't convinced that the distance between the Sands and the Tropicana was as great as he wanted to imply.

She'd phoned Dotty a couple of days earlier, who seemed surprised that she had opted to stay at Henry and Julio's house over the Tropicana. "Of course you should take a room in the hotel," she'd declared. "You just let me know if you change your mind and wanna spend some time on the right side of the tracks." Dotty had taken a job at the Tropicana as assistant to the food and beverage manager after Hassie edged her out of her so called job in the Copa Room and, in true Dotty fashion, thought that her opinion was the only one that mattered.

Fortunately, there was a sparse showing of passengers that night and the seat next to Hassie remained empty. Although she escaped the annoyance of idle chitchat during the eighteen-hour journey, she was unable to relax. While many of the others slept and some snored, Hassie sat engulfed in darkness except for the soft green glow of the lights in the driver's dashboard, casting a mysterious aura that distorted and hardened the features of his otherwise soft and pleasant face.

As she realized that their arrival at the Vegas strip was only a couple of hours away, she yawned and wondered why she'd been so determined to choose the bus over a short, comfortable flight. She had promised Clay that she would stop smoking and she intended to keep her promise, but eighteen hours on a strange and dark road without nicotine was nowhere near the good idea it had sounded at the time – if only she could sleep for the rest of the trip.

She felt the bus lean to the right as it slowed to round the next bend. The gentle rock of its movement lulled her to relax while focusing on the patches of light that occasionally appeared on either side of the road as they rolled past small towns or farms. The air around her remained warm and comfortable until all of a sudden and without warning, a chill – almost a shudder – passed through her body followed by the warmth of human presence beside her.

"Are you really going back to Vegas?"

The familiar voice startled her, but she continued to look straight ahead.

"Hassie," he said a bit louder. "Are you really going back?"

She looked over to the seat that had been empty and into the eyes of the person she had most feared seeing again. "Jake, what are you doing here?"

"You wanted to see me."

"I never wanted to see you. Never." She stared out of the window; her body shook as the cool air intensified around her and her pulse quickened.

"I'm still waiting for you."

The voice was different and only vaguely familiar. She jerked her head toward the empty seat, now occupied by the man from New York – Mr. Satan – his thick moustache having grown into a long, dark beard flowing from his chin. Before she could catch her breath to speak, his face erupted into a lascivious grin revealing strong, white teeth and he spoke again, "I want more of you, my beauty. And you want me."

Hassie shook her head almost violently and buried her face in her hands, speaking softly to herself, "Go away. Please, go away." The air whooshed around her, the movement of the bus upsetting her equilibrium. She leaned her head against the window and closed her eyes, then felt Jake standing over her, his hand around her neck as he whispered into her ear, "You want to see me." Mr. Satan repeated, "I'm waiting for you." She felt his hand on her breast, his tongue and penis in every crevice, his presence taking her back to the night of crazed, passionless sex and filling her senses with the smells of insatiable desire and the sounds of primal ecstasy that she'd only ever imagined coming from the throat of a whore.

"Leave me alone," she shouted out loud. "Both of you. Leave me the hell alone."

The bus suddenly decelerated when the driver took his foot off the pedal and peered over his right shoulder, moans erupting from some of the passengers.

"Are you okay, miss?" the driver called out. "Do I need to stop the bus?"

Hassie moved to the edge of her seat, her face on fire and her legs quivering from the ache in her groin. She grabbed hold of the rail and leaned toward the driver. "No sir, it's okay. Please, don't stop."

She sat back in the seat and struggled to catch her breath. Her heart raced and she dared not look at the seat beside her. What was happening to her? The image of Jake's angry face appeared again with a flash of the violent beating; her battered body lying crumpled in the floor, barely conscious and repeatedly mumbling, "I'm sorry."

She shuddered and gasped; the air in the bus seemed thin and stale, and she could feel her palms damp with perspiration. She grabbed at her bag, digging deep to locate her cigarettes, and then remembered that they were inside her suitcase, locked deep within the bowels of the bus.

The road lay flat and straight before them, but from her seat, she imagined the city coming into view. Her insides shook; she felt nauseated and dizzy. She touched the scar on her eyebrow and wondered what her friends would think or say when they saw her. The blemish had faded only slightly in the time she'd been away, but she'd learned a few tricks for covering it with stage makeup at Felix's. Felix – and Clay – had assured her many times that it was hardly noticeable and certainly not from the seats in the audience.

But the night with Mr. Satan – he'd insisted that the scar was sexy and gave her an air of intrigue and mischief – a mark of indecency against perfection. And now, as the sense of him invaded her consciousness, she wondered why she continued to think about that night and why now in the midst of her return to Vegas – the land of Jake Contrata – did he appear as a threat to her well-being. Was there a theme to this subconscious invasion? She'd loved Jake, but she hadn't loved Mr. Satan; sex was sex – the result of the power of seduction whether it be Jake's desire to own her life or Mr. Satan's desire to own her for a night.

Barbara would argue that she'd brought all of this on herself by going to Vegas and immersing herself in a world of debauchery. What did she expect – her co-workers and roommates were prostitutes, her colleague and best friend nothing more than a pimp. How had she escaped being seduced into that arena, and would she be able to escape it again? Where would a dance with the devil lead?

She stared out the window and took a slow, deep breath. For the last stretch of road, she preferred the black sky as a dark slate for her mind's eye. No thoughts, no images. Just darkness and peace.

The bus followed the occasional bends in the road until all at once she spotted a vague shimmer of light in the distance and watched intently as the light grew brighter. They would soon reach Las Vegas; her memory triggered by the halo of reddish light that hovered over the city, intensifying in her mind but gradually disappearing as the bus moved closer.

The sense of déjà vu set in as they drove down the famous strip and into the bus terminal. At first glance, everything looked exactly the same as it had when she left and, although she hadn't allowed herself to anticipate exactly how the return would make her feel, Hassie knew that what had come to her in the guise of a dream had been everything that she had shoved to the back of her consciousness. That she could not escape the past; that she had repeatedly pushed the people away who brought goodness and light into her life and taken the road to darkness and pain. How would this time be different? *Would* this time be different? It was up to her, and she would start by making sure everything was right with her friends.

It amazed her how the bus could make such a long, tedious journey and manage to arrive at its destination at the exact scheduled time – twelve forty-three. She stepped down into the parking lot, and then waited for her suitcase to be unloaded from the cargo compartment while the hot, desert wind blew sand around her feet.

She spotted what looked to be a new shiny, red Dodge Rambler pulling into the terminal, an arm flailing out of the passenger window. For a moment, it looked like her father's red Chevy pickup with their big collie, Chief; his coat blowing freely in the truck's bed while she sat in the front with her dad. Hassie saw Julio's face first. He was smiling and waving madly. She waved, picked up her suitcase and ran to meet them. Henry jumped out and left the car door open; the sight of him made her heart soar. He'd put on a little weight since she'd last seen him, but then that's what being happy can do for you.

"Man, are you a sight for sore eyes," Henry said, scooping her in his arms. "You are gorgeous."

She dropped her suitcase, held him tight and then reached out to Julio. As the emotional trauma of the past two hours threatened to overtake her, she buried her face in Henry's shoulder and cried what she hoped they would interpret as tears of joy.

"Hey," Julio said, placing his hand on her back. "This is a happy time, chica."

She looked up at the two men, a big part of her needing to get out of the bright neon light and safely behind closed doors. "I've really missed you guys," she managed to say. "Thanks so much for coming out to meet me at this hour."

"We wouldn't have missed this for anything," Henry said. "Let's continue this party at home with a nice bottle of champagne."

Hassie took Henry's handkerchief and wiped her eyes. "We'll

start with the champagne, but please tell me you have a bottle of vodka."

"Let's get you home first," Julio said, picking up her case. "You're gonna love our little house."

"The operative word being *little*," Henry said and hooked his arm through hers. "How are you, honey?"

"I'm good, Henry." She felt him look at her and knew what he was thinking. "Really. I'm good."

The big car quietly hummed as they trundled back down the strip, past the Sands, and then over a couple of streets to a tidy neighborhood with houses shaped like boxes with pitched roofs that reminded her of the plastic pieces in a monopoly game. Even in the dim light cast by the car's headlights, she could see that the front lawns were well kept and breathed contentedly when they wheeled into a driveway near the end of the street. This was home for a while, and she felt safe and comfortable.

As she walked in, she was greeted by the smells of a recently cooked spicy meal and lemon-scented furniture polish. The décor was that of a well-settled couple; each of their personalities evidenced in the choice of furniture. Knowing Henry's conservative tendencies, he would have imposed the rather dull fabric-covered sofa and armchairs while there was no doubt that stylish Julio would have insisted on the chrome dinette table with the Formica top and armless chrome chairs covered in black and white vinyl. The one thing that couldn't be disputed was the feeling of shared love and happiness, and she was pleased that she hadn't let Dotty talk her into staying at the Tropicana.

"This is lovely," Hassie said, nodding her approval.

"It's been pretty warm lately," Julio said. He and Henry had immediately switched on the fans. The big one in the living room oscillated sufficiently, but it just blew hot air around the room.

"July in the desert," Henry said. "What do you expect? Let's have a drink."

"Do you think I could take a quick shower and wash away the last day's worth of travel."

"Of course, honey," Henry said. "Come with me."

She stood under the forceful stream, regulating the temperature from cool to warm, back to cool again, feeling the water run down her back and drip off her arms at her elbows. In all the months she'd lived in Jake's suite, she'd never used the shower. It always felt like his territory and, anyway, she preferred the luxury of the deep bathtub – the ability to submerge herself into the warm fragrant water and under the froth of bubbles. She wondered if Jake still lived in that same suite, with a baby and – a wife? Henry didn't say that Natalie and Jake got married, but she couldn't believe that they would have a child without doing so. She hadn't even thought about this before – supposed she'd pushed it out of her mind. Surely Henry had the full scoop.

When Hassie reemerged, feeling fresh and relaxed, Henry and Julio were sitting at the dinette table, talking softly between themselves. She stood quietly, observing the loving connection between the two men, grateful that her persistence to rid Henry of his animosity towards her had eventually paid off. She cleared her throat before approaching the table, "Are you sure I'm not keeping you up too late? We can always catch up tomorrow."

"No way, chiquita," Julio said and pulled a chair out for her while Henry took the champagne out of the fridge. "We're all yours tonight."

Henry filled three glasses with the cold bubbly before returning the bottle to the fridge. He sat down, lifted his glass and said, "Welcome back. We've missed you."

She touched each of their glasses with hers and swallowed most of its cold, tasty contents before saying, "I'm so happy to be here – in this house with the two of you. You're living proof that love conquers all."

"Thank you, honey. We're very happy." Henry smiled at Julio, took a big drink and then was quiet for a few seconds. "What about you? How do you feel about being back in Vegas?" Julio hopped up to retrieve the champagne bottle and refilled the glasses.

"You may as well leave that bottle on the table," Hassie said. "It's not gonna be here long enough to get warm." Julio nodded and winked at her, then excused himself for a few minutes.

Henry studied her with the look that she knew so well, demonstrating patience to let her tell him what was on her mind when she was ready to talk. After a brief silence, Hassie smiled sadly at Henry before saying, "Is Natalie's baby a girl or a boy?"

"It's a girl," he said. "They named her Norma after Natalie's mother."

Hassie pressed her lips together and stared at her hands resting on the table, then looked up at Henry and said, "Did – *they* – get married?"

He ignored her momentarily, refusing eye contact and obviously thinking about what he should say. "Are you sure you want to talk about this now? Can we talk about your great new job at the Tropicana? Or your music? Or anything else?"

Hassie had pushed the cigarettes out of her mind as long as she could. She jumped up and went to retrieve the unopened pack from her suitcase. When she returned to the dining area, she looked at Henry and said, "Don't lecture me." She tore open the pack, shook a cigarette loose and then walked over to the coffee table where she'd seen an ashtray and matching lighter made out of some sort of marble or stone. The gesture mainly gave her time to think about what she needed to say and as she sat back down at the table, her eyes welled with tears; Henry took the lighter from her and lit the cigarette.

"If you don't tell me about Jake and Natalie, I'll just ask someone else," she said, slowly inhaling a lungful of smoke. "I need to know or I'll never be able to concentrate on anything else and then I'll do a lousy job at La Chanson and end up getting fired and Morty and Clay will be so disappointed in me, they'll never speak to me again." She laid the cigarette on the ashtray and breathed deeply as she took the tissue that Henry handed her and wiped her eyes, then swallowed and looked at Henry and said, "Please tell me the truth so I can put it all behind me and move on."

"You know he doesn't love her," Henry said.

"Henry, did he marry her?"

Henry poured the last drops of the bottle in Hassie's glass while he considered his words. "Yes," he said softly. "At least that's what everyone says. But I've never heard it directly from Jake."

Hassie wiped her nose with the tissue and picked up the glass. "Do they live in his suite?" she asked and took another sip.

Henry shrugged, stared at his hands and said, "He still has the suite, but I couldn't tell you who lives there."

She smiled at the thought that her friend was trying to protect her, picked up the cigarette and said, "Thanks." She drew on the cigarette and hesitated with some other thoughts that had resurfaced as she prepared to return to Vegas, and then continued, "Once you told me that there were big problems between Jake and Frank and you were pretty sure that it was something to do with a woman."

Henry looked puzzled and stayed quiet for a few seconds, then sat back in the chair and said, "Why ever would you bring that up now?"

"I'd like to know if the woman was Natalie." She wasn't about to tell him that it had bothered her for years that Frank had only invited her into his bed to get back at Jake for taking Natalie away from him.

"No, honey," he said. "To my knowledge, Frank has never had anything to do with Natalie. But then, I'd never pretend to have kept up with all the women that Frank's bedded."

Hassie felt her face flush and stubbed out the cigarette while Henry jumped up from the table and grabbed the bottle of vodka. He took two glasses from the sideboard, sat down and poured a shot in each glass. "Sorry, honey. That didn't exactly come out right."

She swallowed a sip of vodka and said, "It came out just fine, Henry. If they didn't fight over Natalie, then who was it? You made it sound pretty critical."

Henry released a big sigh and scratched his head while he said, "I don't know why this important to you now, but the word circulating the trenches was that Jake had a thing with Ava Gardner back when she was married to Frank but *estranged* from him."

Hassie felt a nervous laugh brewing and said, "No shit," and then swigged back the rest of her drink. Here she'd been concerned that Frank was getting revenge for Jake's screwing Natalie. But Ava Gardner? Hassie suddenly felt the long day closing in on her and stared at the empty glass.

"Really, honey," Henry said. "That's all history and all the more reason that you need to use this fresh opportunity to move on."

Julio had come back into the room and stood behind her with his hands on her shoulders, then leaned down close to her ear and softly sang the first line of her song that he'd helped her arrange. She reached up to touch his hand and said, "I thought you would have forgotten that song by now."

He stood up and walked around the table. "Not a chance. When can we start to work on the demos?"

"Whenever you're ready," she said while Julio sat down beside Henry at the table. "I'll know my schedule at the Tropicana after tomorrow's rehearsal." She started to pour another drink when Henry jumped up and said, "Shit. You have a rehearsal tomorrow - which is actually today. We gotta get you to bed!"

Hassie looked at the two men and said, "You're right. I'm really beat and it's almost three a.m. We'll continue this little party tomorrow."

Julio led her out of the kitchen while Henry cleared the table. "I hope that bed is okay for you. It's the best we can do in the space."

"It's perfect." She kissed his cheek and hugged him just as Henry appeared and said, "You okay now?"

She nodded and hugged him, then moved quietly into the little nook in the hallway that they had lovingly tried to turn into a guest room. The absence of a door was successfully camouflaged by strands of orange and green plastic beads that hung from ceiling to floor and made a clacking sound when they knocked together.

She removed a cool, shortie nightgown from her suitcase, promising herself to unpack and put everything in the simple two-drawer chest the next day. She slipped on the nightgown and lay down on the small bed; her body felt like she wore a lead suit. Sweat ran down her temples and between her breasts as she tossed around looking for the best chance for comfort on the old mattress.

When she finally settled down, dog-tired and ready for sleep, she reached over to turn off the small bedside lamp bringing on total darkness and conjuring up the starless journey through the desert. She closed her eyes, welcoming the silence until the air moved around her and a voice whispered close to her ear, "Hassie. Hassie Calhoun." She rolled over quickly and turned on the lamp, but she was alone in the room, her door of beads hanging perfectly still.

chapter twenty-one

HASSIE AWOKE to the noise of two dogs barking in what sounded to her like friendly conversation until one of the dog's owners caterwauled its name five or six times and peace was restored to the neighborhood amid the sound of twittering birds. She felt the warmth of the morning sun through the window while the curtain fluttered feebly in the faint summer breeze. She lay still and closed her eyes until her curiosity drew her to the window where she pulled back the curtain to a bright, blue-skied day. She spotted the dogs' owners and wondered if they were as nosy as the neighbors on her street in Corsicana – sniffing around their house when her mother came home from the hospital with her little brother, asking questions about where her father was and tsking over his misfortune at missing the arrival of his son.

She yawned as she heard the shuffle of feet in the kitchen. The smells of coffee and frying bacon wafted through the beads. She put on the lightly quilted robe that Morty's wife had given her a couple of Christmases ago. She'd thought it strange that this Jewish woman that she barely knew would find it appropriate to give her a Christmas gift, but she'd graciously accepted it as a token of seasonal cheer from her boss.

She went to the toilet before making an appearance, and then joined Henry standing alone by the stove. "Where's Julio?" she asked and looked longingly at the coffee pot on the kitchen counter.

"He's working at one of the studios." Henry reached for a coffee cup. "How do you feel today?"

"A little rough, and I'm starving."

Henry poured the coffee and pushed the cup in her direction. "I was just about to cook some eggs to go with the bacon. Or would you rather have a jelly doughnut?"

"Very funny," Hassie said, stirring sugar into the coffee. "Bacon and eggs would be great. I'll be too nervous to eat anything this afternoon before my rehearsal at the Tropicana." She took the cup and sat down at the dinette table while Henry poured the bowl of beaten eggs into the sizzling pan. "By the way," she said. "If you're not busy today, why don't you come with me? I could use the moral support."

"In case you forgot, I have a job at the Sands. Anyway, Dotty will be there. Does she know you're coming in today?"

Hassie nodded and swallowed a sip of the coffee. "I told her I'd give her a call this morning. La Chanson has really little to do with her but she's offered her support so I'm gonna take it."

"Of course, you are." Henry scraped the eggs onto a plate along with two slices of bacon and a piece of toast. "Here you go." He placed the plate on the table in front of her and bowed. "Show me that big appetite of yours."

She mouthed a kiss at him, and then looked at her plate before saying, "You got any jam or jelly for the toast?" and then took a big bite of the eggs.

Henry laughed and opened the refrigerator door. "I knew you wanted some gooey sugar."

"Yum. This is delicious," she said and ignored Henry's smirk. "Julio told me that he was the cook in the family."

"Yeah, well, that's what he likes to tell everyone. But unless you like enchiladas and beans for every meal, I'd be careful of his offer to cook for you."

She laughed and held up her cup as a signal for more. "Sit down and join me for a few minutes."

Henry brought another cup and the percolator to the table, refilled her cup and poured some for himself before sitting down. She devoured the plate of food, and after she'd taken the last bite, Henry pushed the plate away from her and watched her stir sugar in her coffee before saying, "You know, I'm not very good at keeping things to myself where you're concerned."

She had felt him looking at her scar several times; now was as good a time as any to broach the subject. "That might be an understatement," she said.

He reached over and gently touched the nubby reminder on her eyebrow. "If I'd had a gun, I would have killed Jake that night."

Hassie took the open pack of cigarettes from the pocket of her robe and laid them on the table next to the lighter. "I don't really remember much about it after he –"

Henry sat still while she lit a cigarette and took a deep drag. "I'll never forget that first sight of you in the hospital," he said softly. "We couldn't recognize your face – between the bandages and the swelling. It was like a bad dream and so scary to realize that Jake was capable of such violence."

"Although the memory is vague, I still relive parts of it in my dreams and keep thinking that it was all my fault – that I did something to set him off – but I also remember trying to apologize to him. He wouldn't listen." She laid the cigarette in the ashtray, put her hands over her mouth and rested her elbows on the table, tears filling her eyes.

Henry took hold of her hands. "You listen to me. You could never have done anything that would have warranted what he did to you. Don't tell me you forgot how long it took you to recover. And I'm just talking about the physical recovery." He touched her scar again and said, "This is nothing compared to what it must have felt like to realize that someone who claims to love you more than life itself can turn on you like a mad dog and, in one destructive moment, basically put your life at risk." He sat back in his chair and breathed deeply. "And the sickest part of this now is that I don't know if Jake is really aware of how badly he hurt you."

"What do you mean?" Hassie wiped her eyes with her napkin. "He never came to the hospital or even called to see how I was?" She picked up the cigarette and inhaled deeply.

"Are you kidding? He was in hiding for days into weeks – ran off to New York or LA or somewhere." Henry stopped and looked at her. "Are you sure you want to talk about this now? Do you want more coffee?"

"I'd like a drink, but that's a bad idea before I go to work."

He gave her a disapproving look and said, "Never mind the fact that it's only ten o'clock in the morning."

She laid the cigarette on the ashtray. "I can talk about all this now, Henry. I'd actually like to fill in some of the missing pieces that have haunted me since I left Vegas. What happened right after the – fight?"

"To be honest, I don't know how you got to the hospital. Julio was in the Copa Room and heard that you'd been hurt and that Donnie had been called to get you to a doctor. Julio found me and we called Donnie's office and learned that you'd been taken to the hospital. When we got there, you were in the emergency room and we weren't allowed to see you. Donnie was there. He said you'd be okay and that we should go home and wait for a phone call. You can imagine our response to that suggestion. We made a few calls and paced around the waiting room for a couple of hours until I was finally able to coerce a nurse into telling us what was going on." Henry finished the coffee and then took his cup and the percolator back into the kitchen.

Hassie stubbed out the cigarette and followed him. "I was unconscious all of this time?"

"I would think so," Henry said and plugged in the percolator to brew a fresh pot. "By the time we were allowed to see you, you were heavily sedated, which was a good thing because Julio and I completely fell apart." Henry cleared the emotion from his throat and put his arms around her. "I hate Jake for what he did to you. And I don't ever want to hear you say again that anything about that night was your fault." He pulled back from her and held her forearms while looking into her eyes. "There will never be a valid excuse for his brutality. And you must never forget it. Stay away from him and get on with your life and this great new opportunity."

Hassie's throat ached; she knew that everything Henry said was right. His mention of the emergency room and the bandages brought back flashes of memory of waking up under the fog of drugs and swathe of gauze; the agonized faces of people around her, calling her name and holding her hand. She leaned back against the kitchen counter and wiped the tears from her face. "I had forgotten how bad it really was."

Henry handed her a tissue and said, "Well, I'm not gonna be an 'I told you so' now, but I'm here to make sure that you remember and that you'll remember no matter what happens where Jake is concerned. In his own distorted way, he loves you. And I won't be surprised if he tries to make it up to you."

"He'll have a tough time with that because I won't be going anywhere near the Sands. Anyway, he's got enough going on with a wife and child." She studied him for a few seconds and then said, "You told me on the telephone that Jake has changed. What did you mean by that?"

Henry took a step back and checked the percolator. "After everything else I've said, this is gonna sound strange. But in a perverse way, his treatment of you turned him into a nicer guy – after you left, of course. He's more rational and patient where the rest of us are concerned. And, needless to say, he surprised the universe by his responsible handling of the situation with Natalie and the kid. That's why I'm fairly certain he'll try to make it up to you. Somehow, some way."

Hassie crossed her arms over her chest and said, "I don't care what he says or does. Jake Contrata is ancient history. And that's a promise."

"Good," Henry said. "I'm gonna hold you to that. So. Why don't we get off this dreary subject and talk about the rest of your day?"

Hassie took a cup of coffee and walked into the living room, motioning for Henry to join her. She furtively relocated the ashtray and lighter to the coffee table, her cigarettes tucked back into the pocket of her robe. They sat on opposite ends of the sofa and for a moment, everything was strangely normal. She was in the safe company of her best friend who knew her so well and always had her best interests at heart.

Henry held the coffee cup with both hands and said, "What time is your rehearsal?"

"I'm not exactly sure, but it's not until the afternoon so I think I'll go over to see Dotty around lunchtime. When are you going to the Copa Room?"

Henry looked back at the clock on the dining room wall. "Technically, I'm late. But there's nothing pressing me today so I'll go over soon. I'd offer to drive you to the Tropicana but don't think you'll be ready to go yet. Did Morty work out something for transportation in your contract?"

"Yeah, I think so," she said. "I need to sort out all those details today so maybe I can just take a taxi over."

Henry set his cup on the coffee table, walked over to the telephone on the sideboard and located a small pad of paper. He jotted something on the top sheet, then tore it off and came back to the sofa. "Here's the number for Casino Cabs. Call them with a fifteen-minute warning and they'll pick you up and take you anywhere you want to go. And that's our address."

"Thanks, Henry. I'm so glad I decided to stay here with you guys." She sat on the edge of the seat and pulled her hair off her neck. Her skin oozed sweat, and she wanted another shower. "I think I'll make a couple of calls and then organize my room. *My* room," she said, smiling at him.

"It's not much but it's yours for as long as you need it," Henry said and cleared the cups from the coffee table. "Something tells me Dotty will be on a campaign to coral you into the Tropicana. Do whatever you want to do, honey. You know you're always welcome here."

The taxi dropped her at the front entrance to the Tropicana. It had been quite a long time since she'd been inside the imposing building. The abrupt termination of her last stay in Vegas had prevented her from seeing most of her friends outside of her hospital room before she left for Reno. Dotty had called her once a week for a couple of months after she got there, which meant a lot to her and made her wish she'd stayed in closer touch with Barbara. It was also a painful reminder of the lost relationship with her mother.

As she pushed through the heavy brass and glass door, she half expected to be greeted by Jimmy; a flash of her arrival at the Sands brought the image of Jake to mind. "Get outta my head, Jake!" Then she saw Dotty coming toward her from across the casino lobby. She waved and rushed forward to greet her in the smoke-filled space.

"Hassie," Dotty said as they embraced. "Honey, you look just great." Dotty pulled back from her, and Hassie could tell that she was trying not to look at her scar.

"It's wonderful to see you, Dotty," she said. "I can't believe I'm really here."

"And to work in this great lounge!" She took hold of Hassie's arm and started back through the casino. "I'm so proud, I could pop."

Hassie laughed and followed Dotty's lead. "Do you know the musicians in La Chanson?"

"Do I know 'em?" She suddenly lengthened her stride. "Make a note, honey. Dotty knows *everybody* at the Tropicana."

"So, you know a man named John Jacobson?" Hassie asked, practically running to stay in step with Dotty.

"'Course, I know John. I believe he's the reason you're here." Dotty veered around another corner as she said, "Now, hurry up. I just ran into the music director and he says they'll all be waitin' for you."

"But I thought I would have a little time to talk to you first." Hassie had half convinced herself that she would never see John Jacobson again – that his role in getting her to Vegas had been accomplished and he'd have moved on to some other unsuspecting target. Now, it sounded like she was destined to see him.

"We'll talk later," Dotty said and pulled open the door to a small, dimly lit space. "Go on in. I'm right behind ya."

The room was something of a cross between Felix's and the Copa Room with an ornately decorated ceiling and crystal chandeliers meant to conjure up the feeling of something French. The stage was small, with barely enough room for the baby grand piano, drum set and two stools; the double bass lay in the floor beside one of them. A lone microphone stood far downstage, which had been extended at two strategic points to hold the sound monitors.

"Go on, Hassie," Dotty urged her from behind. "I see the boss over there." She pointed to the tables closest to the stage entry.

Hassie spotted several men clumped around two of the small tables and immediately recognized John Jacobson. She picked up her pace a little as Dotty called out, "Wake up, guys. Miss Calhoun's here."

Hassie reached the tables just as the men turned around to face her. They stood up; Jacobson walked over to greet her, stuck out his hand and said, "Welcome." She shook his hand as he said, "Can we call you Hassie?"

"Of course," she said and smiled. "It's nice to see you again, John." The man standing to his right was short and slight with thick, black hair that was graying at the temples and wore round, black-rimmed glasses that made him a dead ringer for Poindexter from the Felix the Cat cartoons. Jacobson put his hand on the man's shoulder and said, "This is Daniel Forrester, your keyboardist, arranger and generally the glue that holds this wild bunch together." The man seemed unimpressed by it all but shook her hand and nodded politely.

"Yep. Dan's the man – our fearless leader," one of the other men said. "My name's Tony. I'm the drummer. And that there's Art. He's our horn blower."

The man he'd referenced hit him on his arm with his fist while the others laughed and cajoled, then turned to Hassie, offering his hand, and said, "It's nice to meet you, Hassie. We've heard a lot about you."

Daniel crossed his arms over his chest and studied her before addressing Jacobson, "Are you sure someone who looks like her can sing?"

"Oh, for Chrissake, Danny." Dotty had worked her way into the middle of the group. "Give the poor girl a break. She just got here. Where's your fiddler?"

Jacobson took hold of Hassie's arm and led her away from the guys while they mouthed off at Dotty and chatted about the missing player. With a half-serious expression, he looked at her and said, "I know you've worked with lots of lounge musicians so I'm sure you can hold your own. But you might like to know that the act preceding you was a hairy Latino bongo-playing songster who smelled like rum and thought he was Desi Arnaz. So you can imagine how the appearance of a beautiful, young woman would make the guys act like half-witted apes."

She laughed and tried to relax before saying, "I'm sure we'll be fine. I'm eager to go to work."

He smiled uncomfortably and angled his body to ensure none of the others could see his face, then focused closely on her and said, "I'm glad you're here, Hassie. I'm a thousand percent sincere when I tell you that signing you on for this show was a real coup for the Tropicana."

She fiddled nervously with her hands and said, "But it's not exactly New York, is it?"

The color in his naturally pink cheeks intensified as he laced his fingers together and rested them on the mound of his stomach and said, "No, it's not New York, and this is not Reno."

She remained still and hoped her slightly addled nerves didn't show.

He dropped his hands down to his sides and carefully said, "Can I just say that that night with you in Reno is something that I will always remember and, regardless of what you might think, it had nothing to do with your being here now."

She suddenly noticed that a couple of the guys were looking at them and smiled sweetly as she said, "I think the natives are getting restless, so maybe you should just say what you really want to say." She inhaled and then held her breath, awaiting his response.

He looked over his shoulder and then back into her eyes. "I live in Vegas and have a family here and, as odd as it may sound, I love my wife."

Hassie exhaled and then offered her handshake before saying, "New York or not, your job offer got me out of a dead end life in Reno. I'm grateful for the opportunity and I promise I'll do a good job."

"Of that I have no doubt," he said and shook her hand. "There are a few details of your contract that we need to review, and you'll want to have a good orientation of the facilities. I can see that Dotty has appointed herself as your minder, so unless you object, I'll let her be."

Hassie nodded her head and smiled. "Dotty's the best. I'm happy to have her by my side."

"Good." He led her back down to the stage where it was evident that the guys were ready to begin. "Go have your first session and I'll see you later."

Daniel stood behind the keyboard and fumbled with some papers and a few pieces of music. She walked up on the stage and stood next to the piano at its bow, waiting for his direction as to where they would start. A tall, wiry black man had joined the stage and was plucking on the double bass and twisting the knobs at the top in an effort to bring it in tune. She smiled at him and offered a little wave, which he accepted with the nod of his head and hint of a smile while Daniel played the introduction to "My Funny Valentine." Hassie looked back at him. He hesitated at the cue for the vocals, and then looked up as if to say, "Ready?"

She nodded and launched into the first verse of the song; the other musicians joined in on the second line. Daniel's arrangement was simple and elegant, and she felt that the piano actually breathed with her as she sang. They made it all the way through without stopping; the ending took a beautifully harmonic turn that sent goose bumps down her arms.

"Not bad," Daniel said as the other players whistled and tapped their instruments.

"That's a beautiful arrangement," Hassie said, then smiled and beguilingly continued, "Is this a sample of what I'm in for?"

Daniel nodded and said, "Your agent forwarded this list of the songs you like to sing. No surprises really. Torch song, torch song, torch song, ballad. Whose version of "I'm a Fool to Want You" do you do? Holiday or Sinatra?"

Hassie froze at the mention of the song that had somehow been the unraveling of her relationship with Jake, and then quietly said, "I don't really do that song, but if I did, I'd do *my* version."

He looked at her, shrugged and said, "It's on your list, but so are a lot of numbers that I'd like to change. You're heavy on gut-wrenching Porter and Ellington. We need some upbeat stuff – some Gershwin and maybe a little current Broadway. I think the audience is going to like you, Hassie, but frisky drunks need to be jostled every now and then." He studied her for a moment. "You've seen Sinatra in the Copa Room, haven't you?"

"Of course."

"Frank's a great crooner and gets to the heart of a song better than anyone, but he also has a lot of fun with the audience. It's a mandatory part of working the lounges in Vegas."

"I get it, Mister – Daniel –" she said and felt her face flush as the guys chuckled.

Daniel stood up and walked over to her. "Call me Dan." His demeanor had softened a bit, and she relaxed as he turned to the other musicians and said, "Let's take a break. Be back in ten and we're gonna sort out this program before the sun goes down."

She started to walk off the stage when Dan called out to her, "Hassie, can I ask you something else about this song list?"

"Sure," she said and joined him at the keyboard.

"I see a couple of pieces here that I don't recognize – maybe some original stuff?"

Hassie nodded and said, "Yeah, I've written it – me and Julio Villanueva. Do you know him? From the Copa Room?"

"Of course, I know him," Dan said. "Julio and I worked as studio musicians in LA before being lured to sin city. I used to play the guitar while he pounded out the beat on the Latin percussion instruments. We also sub for each other on the keyboard from time to time. He's a good guy."

"And one of my best friends," she said, her loyalty to Julio implicit in her tone. "In fact, I'm bunking in at his house for a few weeks."

"I heard that you're pretty tight with Henry Berman. Give them my best," he said and sat down on the piano bench. She smiled and walked away, but before she reached the stage steps, Dan called out to her, "And, Hassie? You might wanna think about laying off the cigarettes for a while."

His expression was hard to read but she took a chance and said, "How am I supposed to end up a fragile, gravel-voiced old woman if I don't live a tragic life full of cigarettes and booze?"

"You mean cigarettes, booze and men. If that's your goal in life, so be it." He stood up and laid her song list aside. "Just bear in mind that I don't kiss girls who smoke."

She smiled, looked directly at him and said, "One out of three's not bad."

chapter twenty-two

THE FIRST REHEARSAL lasted until two a.m., but Hassie had been so artistically stimulated, the guys had to practically push her out the door. Taking nothing away from Julio, she believed that Dan Forrester was the most gifted musical arranger alive. His sense of what worked best amazed her, with surprising turns in the harmonic structure or unexpected changes in key or time signature. He had an uncanny ability to turn a standard medley of songs into one long melodious creation. Her favorite was Cole Porter, which started with "Delovely," danced though "Night and Day" into a bold rendition of "Just One of Those Things" and ended with the beloved "From This Moment On." Her dull and gloomy song list turned into the envy of any serious singer, and the musicians were so generous with their support she felt that she had known and worked with them for years. They each contributed something to the arrangements, and by the end of the long day the repertoire for the first week of shows was set.

During one of the breaks, Dan called her over to the piano. "How do you think it's going?" he asked while placing a sheet of music on the stand.

She watched him for a few seconds and said, "How do *you* think it's going?"

He looked at her, then at the sheet of music, and then played Julio's introduction to her favorite composition. Before she could speak, he looked up and said, "Sing."

She sang through the song once, recognizing some subtle changes in some of the harmonies, and was mesmerized by the depth of emotion that emanated from his keyboard arrangement. For a moment, she didn't know what to say and felt her cheeks get warm as she realized that she was staring at him, then cleared her throat and said, "Where'd you get the song?"

He tinkered through an alternative ending and, without looking at her, said, "I've always been leery of people who claim to be songwriters, and eight times out of ten, I'm right."

She stood still, watching him and waiting for the answer to her question. His hands were small but strong and knew their way across that keyboard like a man knows his lover's body. His face was soft and, despite the mere smattering of gray hair at his temples, she could see the dominance of gray in his beard's stubble. He wasn't a handsome man, but something about him was extremely desirable and she blushed again as she found the nerve to say, "So where did you get my song and –" She stopped and reconsidered if she really wanted to know what he thought, then took a shallow breath and continued, "What do you think of it?"

"I like it." He stopped playing, looked directly at her and said, "Who really wrote it, you or Julio?"

The suggestion that she might not have written the song that she was so close to made her so mad that without thinking, she reached over and jerked the page of music off the piano stand. Her intention was to turn and walk away, but instead, she looked at him squarely, hesitated for a second and then said, "You don't know me." She tapped her finger on her chest and continued, "You don't know what's going on in here. And you sure as hell don't know how hard I've worked to convey my feelings through my music."

Dan's serious expression turned to more of a smirk than a smile as he said, "Just relax. I wasn't accusing you of anything. I just happen to know that Julio's not a great songwriter. He's a great guy and a fantastic musician, but I didn't believe that he could have come up with a song like this and I wanted to hear you tell me that you wrote it."

His comments left her speechless for a few seconds, then she leaned into the bow of the piano and said, "I wrote the lyrics and the melody. Julio helped me with the bridge and developed the harmonics. The arrangement on that paper is his."

"At the risk of sounding like a pompous ass, I knew that." He hesitated and then continued, "It's a good song. I like it, and I'd like to put it in the show."

"Your arrangement or Julio's?" she asked, consciously lightening her tone.

He took the music out of her hand and propped it on the piano, then sat down at the keyboard as he said, "What do you think?"

She smiled and said, "You do sound like a pompous ass, but you're right. Your arrangement is better. When do we put it in the show?"

"I'll let you know," he said. His expression was blank but, behind his black-rimmed glasses, his eyes were alive and smiling. She watched him for a moment and then turned away just as a smile spread across her face. She was going to enjoy working with this man.

When the rehearsal finally finished, Hassie left a message for Dotty saying that she would call her in the morning and they could arrange a time to meet. One of the hotel's cars took her back to Julio and Henry's quiet, dark neighborhood, their little house marked by a dimly lit porch. She tiptoed inside the squeaky screened door and locked it behind her, and in so doing was reminded of the hot, sticky nights in Corsicana when they'd leave all of the windows and doors open to allow in every wisp of summer breeze. At least Las Vegas was dry, desert heat, but she was soaked with perspiration nonetheless.

She kicked off her shoes and unbuttoned the top of her blouse, then lifted her hair off her neck as she eyed the row of liquor bottles on the sideboard. She should go to bed and get a good night's sleep, but Dan's pleasingly dissonant arrangement of "Can't Help Lovin' Dat Man" kept her brain working overtime. She poured some vodka in a cut-glass tumbler sitting next to the decanters and sat down on the comfortable sofa. As she softly hummed the melody, she could hear Art's muted trumpet playing "Blue Moon" as a counterpoint to her singing. The two songs worked beautifully together, but the idea to intermingle them would never have occurred to her.

The vodka slowed her adrenaline and the air around her became heavy as she continued to unwind. In only a few minutes she gave in to exhaustion and crawled into her little bed without even washing her face.

The next morning, she walked into the kitchen hoping to find Henry standing by the stove and waiting to cook her breakfast. But the room was empty, and when she glanced at the clock it was already a quarter past eleven. She'd thought that Henry and Julio's morning routine would wake her and she'd get up and tell them all about her first rehearsal. She guessed she'd been more tired than she'd thought and propped against the stove for a good look around the room.

While deciding what to do next, she noticed that the set of four canisters on the counter was exactly like the one in her mother's kitchen – the smallest shaped like an egg, the next size a baby chick, then a hen and the largest was a big ceramic rooster. She'd always thought it an odd choice of things to display prominently on the kitchen counter and even more so in this otherwise tastefully decorated house until she spotted the cream pitcher shaped like a cow with its mouth for a spout sitting beside a mug resembling Porky Pig.

A note from Henry under the cow's right hoof told her to help herself to whatever she wanted and to call him when she knew about her day. He said to plug in the percolator for coffee and asked if she could join them for dinner. The word *dinner* made her stomach rumble and, not in the mood to sort through the fridge, she decided that lunch at the Tropicana with Dotty would be a good start to the day. She'd need a shower before she went anywhere and headed to the bathroom, still singing "Can't Help Lovin' Dat Man."

Although it had been over two years since she'd lived and worked at the Sands, it felt strange to walk into the Tropicana instead and know that it would be her point of existence in Vegas. She liked the feel of the hotel, which was much less formal than the Sands, though still impressive in its own way. She also liked knowing that she didn't have to worry about running into Jake, that he was safely harbored in the Sands at the other end of the strip. Dotty was here at the Tropicana, Henry and Julio were her housemates and, after just one day of working with the guys in La Chanson, she had a strong, contented feeling that she had already made some new friends. Dan Forrester was foremost in her thoughts. She'd thought about Stella several times but had neglected to ask about her. Maybe Dotty was still in touch with her and could arrange for them to get together away from the Sands.

She walked along the corridor, wondering what Barbara would think about her decision to return to the place that had caused her so much pain and sorrow. Would she be upset – or disappointed? Or would she agree that this was a positive step in Hassie's life and that her decision to stay away from Jake showed that she'd learned her lesson and was focused solely on her career as a singer. This was a good thing. Right? But below the staged determination to stay away from Jake, the warnings from Henry, the psychic messages from Barbara, the desire for other men and the souvenir scar, was a strong, carnal desire to be resting in Jake's arms. She could smell his dangerous passion, making her short of breath, and she had to stop for a second, thinking, "Man, what's this about?"

Through stretches of ceiling-to-floor glass, Hassie carried on through the corridors overlooking gardens and meticulously manicured lawns with trees and flowering bushes of every size, shape and color. She strolled along the wide paths, following the signs to the all day dining room that Dotty had suggested. She'd been back in Vegas for less than forty-eight hours and a lot of positive things had already happened. So why did she have a feeling that if someone walked up to her and offered her a ticket back to Reno, she'd take it and be out of there like a shot.

She finally spotted Dotty standing at the restaurant's entrance. She wore a dark brown dress with big, white polka dots; the fitted skirt was cinched at her waist by a wide, white belt. Her yellow hair looked like she might have just left the beauty salon. Dotty's own brand of goodness and light lifted her spirits and Hassie rushed toward her just as she directed the maitre d' to seat them at the table next to the window with the most perfect view of the tropical gardens.

"So what do you think of your new home?" Dotty asked and gestured manically at one of the waitresses. "I tell ya, these girls have peas for brains. If they can't even do a decent job for the boss, what the hell do they do the rest of the time?"

Hassie waited for Dotty to settle down and then said, "So you're the boss here?"

"Technically, I'm the assistant to the boss, but he pretty much put me in charge of this dining room."

Hassie stifled a smile and said, "Kinda like when you were in charge of the Copa Room?"

"Exactly," Dotty said. "I've taken the liberty of orderin' the daily special for us. The chef is the best in town."

"Sounds great," Hassie said and placed the white linen napkin in her lap.

"Now, missy. I gather you caused quite a stir in La Chanson yesterday."

"Really?" Dotty's pronunciation of the lounge's French name for "song" was atrocious, but Hassie knew that it was senseless to bring this to her attention.

"Word is that the guys are in love with you and Daniel Forrester thinks you're gonna be a big hit."

Hassie took a pack of cigarettes out of her purse. "Dan thinks that? How could he know that already?"

"They know these things, honey. They've been through lots of performers in the last few years and they know their audience." Dotty stopped and watched Hassie remove a cigarette from the pack. "And what do you think you're doin'?"

Hassie took the matches out of the ashtray and said, "I know. I swear I tried to quit, but I'm just too nervous right now." She offered the pack to Dotty. "Want one?"

Dotty said nothing but took a cigarette from the pack, then waited while Hassie lit hers and offered Dotty the match. "You better not screw this job up," Dotty said. "I'm gonna be watchin' out for you and helpin' you with your makeup and dresses. Which reminds me. What do you have for a wardrobe?"

"I was told that the hotel might want to get some things for me, but I brought a couple of dresses that I've worn at the club in Reno."

"What do they look like?" Dotty asked.

"They look good enough," Hassie said eyeing the waitress as she walked by with two highballs on a tray. "Clay helped me pick them out. He's got great taste."

Dotty laid her cigarette on the ashtray and said, "Who the hell's Clay?"

"Clay Cooper. He's a talent agent in Reno and one of the reasons I'm sitting here right now." She drew on her cigarette and pretended that she didn't know that Dotty was watching her, then looked at her and said, "I think we should celebrate my new job and our being together at the Tropicana. Let's have a drink."

"What took you so long?" Dotty said and picked up her cigarette. "I thought that would be the first thing outta your mouth." She motioned to the waitress and ordered vodka gimlets for the two of them.

"How's Jimmy doing?" Hassie asked. "I'm assuming he still works at the Sands."

"Yeah, he's still Jake and Sid's slave and loves every minute of it. But I wanna know more about this Clay person."

The waitress delivered the drinks, and Hassie ground out her cigarette. "There's not a lot to know. I met him when I got to Reno. And now, he's my agent."

"Is he a friend of Julio's?" Dotty asked. "How did you meet him?"

Hassie took a sip of her drink and quietly said, "Jake told me about him a couple of months before I – left Vegas."

"So he's a friend of Jake's?"

Hassie sat back in her chair and said, "He's Jake half-brother. There. Are you satisfied?"

Dotty picked up her drink and held it up to Hassie while saying, "Congratulations. You are the stupidest woman alive."

Hassie laughed and said, "See why I didn't want to tell you. I knew you would judge me. And Clay. But will you believe me when I say that Clay is nothing like Jake? They couldn't be more different if they'd been born in different centuries."

The waitress arrived with plates of roast chicken and vegetables that smelled delicious and reminded Hassie that she hadn't eaten much of anything since Henry's bacon and eggs the day before. Dotty asked for ketchup, which made Hassie smile. She really cared about this woman and wanted her to understand that Clay was a positive thing in her life. She asked for another drink and cut into her chicken while waiting for Dotty's next comment.

"So are you involved with him?" Dotty finally said.

"You mean romantically?"

"I mean, are you sleeping with him? Are you in love with him? Does he float your boat?"

Hassie laughed and took the last sip of her drink. "Like I said, he's my agent. Don't make a romance out of a business relationship."

Dotty dumped the ketchup next to the chicken, and then segregated the vegetables into two areas on her plate. She looked up at Hassie and said, "I never have liked carrots since I was a kid and my mother cooked them with the Sunday roast and made me eat them come hell or high water." She wrinkled her nose, sipped her drink and then smiled. "So is there a man in your life now?"

"Nope. Oh, there've been a few guys but nothing special." The waitress arrived with her second drink, asked if they needed anything else and walked away. "It took me a long time to feel attractive to men again. Which reminds me, you haven't said anything about my gift from Jake. I hope you're thinking about how you're gonna cover it up with makeup."

"We can deal with that little scar, honey. I'm more concerned about the scars that I can't see."

Hassie swallowed another bite of chicken and pushed her plate away. "That's very sweet, but I've had a lot of time to deal with that pain and I'm actually okay now." She sipped her drink before asking, "Have you seen Natalie's child? What's her name – Norma?"

Dotty nodded and motioned to the waitress for another drink. "Yeah. She's very sweet, and Jake seems to have mellowed a bit since she was born. Mind you, the shit hit the fan in a major way when Natalie announced she was pregnant. Jake accused her of whoring around and swore he'd never accept the child as his. It was dreadful, and I felt really sorry for her because, after you left, Natalie went real straight – gave up bein' a hooker and dedicated her life to Jake, which, as you know, is all she ever wanted to do. Your disappearance was the best thing that could have happened for her and she was determined to have Jake for herself. Do I need to spell out the rest?"

"You mean you think she got pregnant on purpose?"

Dotty nodded and took another cigarette from the pack. "I'd bet on it."

"The Jake Contrata I know detests anything to do with manipulation." Hassie lit Dotty's cigarette and one for herself and continued, "Never mind that he's a master manipulator himself."

Dotty exhaled the smoke as the waitress delivered her drink. "Jake and Natalie are each other's problems right now, and I want to hear you say that you will have nothin' to do with him, no matter what."

"You don't have to worry, Dotty. As I told Henry yesterday, Jake is history. I've moved on and I'd like for everyone to do the same."

Dotty flicked the cigarette in the ashtray a couple of times and studied Hassie. "I think there's somethin' you're not tellin' me about your love life in Reno."

Hassie laughed and said, "Do you want details?"

"You gotta remember that I've known you since you arrived in Vegas from Podunk, Texas, a young, simple girl who was too beautiful for her own good. I've watched you grow up fast, tangle with one of the most immature, selfish men in the world, sleep with one of the most famous men in the world and exit the scene as fragile as a lemon soufflé." She drew deeply on the cigarette before continuing, "But you're different now – somethin' that I can't really put my finger on. You even look a little different, and I'm not just talkin' about your eye. What happened to you that you're not tellin' me about?"

Hassie listened to Dotty but almost heard Barbara's voice – as if Barbara had sent Dotty to try to keep her focused on the things that she had instilled in her and guide her through those iffy times where tough decisions challenged her integrity. The night in Reno with Mr. Satan had been one of those times, and Hassie knew that her decision to take the man's money in return for sex was way out of the boundaries that Barbara had set for her. But she had sworn to herself that she would never tell anyone about that night and, therefore, the lack of admittance that it had happened would somehow make it invalid – a mistake that she would take to her grave.

She slowly exhaled and looked directly into Dotty's eyes. "I probably am different, Dotty. I've made some pretty stupid mistakes, and in some ways, I'm lucky that I somehow managed to land on my feet. I was so frightened at the thought of coming back that I almost turned down this opportunity. But Clay and Morty – he's my boss at my day job – and Felix, the owner of the club I worked in, pushed me out the door." She ground out the cigarette and sat back in her chair. "I still sometimes wonder what I'm doing here, but the one thing I do know is that Jake Contrata will never hurt me again."

Dotty grinned and said, "Clay, Morty, Felix. As usual, there's a gaggle of men huddled around you and you still can't seem to settle down with a man who's good for you."

"I'm not interested in settling down any time soon, which reminds me that I've got a rehearsal in about an hour. The big decision is whether to have another drink or a cup of coffee."

Dotty motioned for the waitress and looked at Hassie. "You order another drink and I'll break your arm. Your first show is Friday, right?"

"Uh-huh. Actually, there are two shows that night so it's gonna be doubly nerve-racking. But I'm kind of excited as well. Dan's introduced me to some great songs, and his arrangements are really wonderful."

Dotty ordered coffee for both of them, then tucked the pack of cigarettes in her purse. "No more booze and no more smokes. And I wanna see these dresses you mentioned in case we need to do some shoppin' before Friday."

"I wanna wear the red dress that Clay bought for me," Hassie said. "It's really beautiful and connects me to him, which will boost my nerve and give me a lot of comfort."

"I see," Dotty replied. "And he's the guy who's just your *business associate.*"

Hassie ignored Dotty's tone and thought about the impending rehearsal, then looked at Dotty and said, "How well do you know Dan Forrester?"

"I know he has a great reputation and people love his shows."

"Is he married?"

Dotty leaned back in her chair, scowled at Hassie and said, "Good Lord, woman. Don't tell me you've already gone sweet on the guy."

Hassie was slightly embarrassed at the thought but knew that it would be easier to get this kind of information from Dotty than Henry or Julio. "I think he's kinda sexy. I mean, his talent is kinda sexy."

Dotty slowly shook her head from side to side and lowered her chin to her chest while she studied Hassie, then looked up and said, "I don't think he's married. I do think he likes women, and I can't see the two of you together in a month of Sundays."

Hassie laughed and said, "Why? Okay, he might be a little shorter than me but I find that kinda –"

"Sexy?" Dotty said then laughed and pushed her chair back from the table. "The main thing I can say about Dan Forrester is that he's *not* Jake Contrata. Go for it, honey. Jimmy's no big prize in the looks department, but I wouldn't trade him for Rock Hudson."

chapter twenty-three

ON THE MORNING of the first show, Hassie slept as late as her nerves would allow, then dressed in slacks and a cotton blouse for the last run-through of the program. She'd imagined many times how she would feel when she performed on the Copa Room stage. La Chanson was as close as she would get – at least, for now – and her excitement had turned to sheer terror. Dan and the guys in the band were wonderful to work with and assured her that the show would be a raving success. But she missed Julio's charming ability to keep her calm in moments of stress, and hoped that Dotty would somehow have the same effect on her.

She had taken the red dress that Clay bought for her in for Dotty's approval a couple of days earlier, giving in to Dotty's skeptical reaction by agreeing to wear the dress for the run-through. When she arrived at the dressing room, Dotty was impatiently puffing on a cigarette and snapped her fingers while saying, "Let's go!"

Hassie undressed down to her strapless bra and panties, wriggled the body-hugging satin gown up from her toes and then motioned for Dotty to zip it up. The zipper went up much more easily than the last time she'd worn it, which was testimony to her lack of proper food in favor of coffee, cigarettes and vodka.

"Okay, stand still," Dotty said and drew on her cigarette as she took a couple of steps back to get the full-length picture. "Hmm," she finally said. "You're tellin' me that a man picked this out for you?"

Hassie nodded and said, "Yeah, Clay. The guy who –"

"Yeah, I know. Mr. Wonderful who's your best friend or somethin'."

The beautifully designed strapless gown fit snugly against the curves of her body before flaring out at the bend of her knees into what was called a "fishtail." Attached to the left side at the waist, a drape of the luscious satin had been tied into an elegant sash and added an extra bit of glamour that made her feel like Susan Hayward in *With a Song in My Heart*. The saleslady had called it "garnet red," but Hassie thought it was more the color of the rich red fruit on Barbara's pomegranate trees.

She looked at Dotty in the mirror and said, "Well?"

"Pull your hair up off your neck," Dotty said and moved closer in.

Hassie pulled the shoulder-length tresses up and twisted them loosely against the back of her head. Her bare neck made her think of the diamond and ruby necklace that Jake had given her to wear on the night that she met JFK. It was the first time she'd thought about the necklace – or any of the other things he'd given her – since he left her crumpled on the floor of his suite. Was Natalie now the proud owner of her jewels and mink stole?

She let her hair fall back around her neck and said, "I think my hair looks better down."

"Well, I like it up," Dotty said. "It's more sophisticated and, if you're worried about the bare neckline, I've got a dandy little paste necklace that will look great."

Hassie studied her image in the mirror again, recalling the times that she had spent hours having her hair done in stylish twists and piles on her head only to get back to the suite and have Jake remove the pins and push the soft curls around her face and shoulders. "Your hair fits your face like an expensive frame around a priceless painting," he would say in the days that he could be a hopeless romantic. She brushed it back in place with her fingers and said, "I like it better down."

The run-through went smoothly, with just enough flaws to ward off the superstition that a perfect rehearsal on the day of opening night was a sign that the performance was doomed. Hassie was allowed to reserve one table during the second show for friends, and chose one close to the stage for Henry and Julio. Stella would join them if she could find a replacement in the Copa Room. The first show started at eight o'clock. Hassie took a break after the run-through but returned to the dressing room at six so she would have plenty of time to get ready and still relax before she was called on stage.

"Dotty, I'd like a little drink, please," Hassie said like she was asking for a glass of milk.

Dotty shook her head and said, "No way, missy. We cannot have you out there tipsy."

"All the others singers are sloshed for the majority of their shows."

"You're not all the other singers, and everyone's gonna be watchin' you like a hawk – lookin' for anything to criticize you for. Believe me. I know what I'm talkin' about."

Hassie squirmed in her chair and said, "Dan won't let me smoke. You won't let me drink. I'd like to see how you'd handle all this nerve-racking tension."

Dotty dabbled with Hassie's makeup and said, "Aw, stop your bellyachin' and sit still."

Hassie studied her face in the mirror, tilting her head to study her eyes in the light. "You're pretty good at this," she said to Dotty. "If I didn't know that pesky scar was there, I'd never see it."

Dotty looked into the mirror and smiled. "You're gonna be great out there tonight. And, no doubt break a few hearts. Don't forget that you've got two shows, so don't shoot your wad on the first one."

Hassie stood up and turned to face her friend. "Thank you for everything. I couldn't do this without you."

Dotty hugged her and then pointed her to the rack where her dress hung. "Just remember me when you get rich and famous. I've given up on Jimmy gettin' me to the big time."

There was a knock on the door. Dotty called out, "What do you want?"

"It's Dan," a voice said. "I'd like to speak to Hassie."

Hassie stood still while Dotty zipped up her dress and then stepped into her shoes while Dotty opened the door. "Hello, Daniel," Dotty said. "Come in."

He remained just outside the door with a look that said he wanted to speak to Hassie alone. Dotty checked her watch, then looked at Hassie and said, "I'll go put a couple of glasses of water backstage."

Hassie motioned for Dan to come in and closed the door. "So, this is it, huh?" she said.

He smiled, looked at her and said, "I just came to tell you to have a great time out there tonight. You're ready for this, the audience is ready for you and it's going to be good."

She felt that she should touch his arm or hug him around his shoulders but opted to stand still, her arms at her sides as she smiled and said, "Thanks. You give me a lot of confidence, and I'll do my best not to disappoint."

He looked at her like he wished she could read his mind, then took hold of her hand and said, "Break a leg. And have fun." Before she could say anything else, he turned and walked out the door. She felt light and almost giddy, like a schoolgirl with a crush on one of her teachers. Then, as she heard the click of Dotty's heels nearing the dressing room, she checked her appearance in the mirror and finished the last drink of vodka in the glass hidden inside the dressing table drawer.

The audience for the first show was mostly comprised of male conventioneers. She knew this customer very well from her days at the Copa Room. The band clipped through number after number exactly as rehearsed to enthusiastic applause that gave Hassie a rush of satisfaction she'd never quite felt in Reno. Was it Dan's sexy repertoire of songs that elevated her performance or was she actually performing for him? At any rate, the first show felt more like a warm-up for the later one. The hour break between them rushed by like a quick breath of air and she ignored Dotty's tightly drawn expression when she poured a shot of vodka.

The second show was much more electric and she was energized by the adrenalin that pumped through her system from song to song. The program had been designed to give her a break from singing while the band played their instrumental favorites. It gave her a chance to leave the stage where Dotty stood armed with a powder puff and a glass of water. Hassie sipped the water and waited while they played a medley of jazzy Gershwin, then reappeared behind the microphone during the applause in a spotlight of soft amber. She closed her eyes while listening to Dan's introduction of Cole Porter's "Love for Sale," which she'd recently heard in Reno and added to her song list. It had been one of the songs that Dan wanted to remove and replace, but after she convinced him to let her sing it at a rehearsal, he'd finally agreed to keep it in the show and she seamlessly joined him on the first line.

She relaxed with her hands loosely holding the microphone stand and swayed to Art's sultry saxophone interlude. This was her chance to survey the house, where despite the bright light focused on her, she could get a sense of the audience's mood. Earlier, she'd had a glimpse of Henry, Julio and Stella sitting to her left. Now, as she lingered over the tables on the right side of the room, she spotted a man sitting on his own, his elbows propped on the table, a cigarette in his hand as the smoke encircled his head of dark hair. She stared in his direction; her stomach clenched involuntarily as he leaned back in his chair. She couldn't distinctly see his features, but she would recognize Jake in the dark. Her cue to sing the reprise brought her back to her performance.

Love for sale
Appetizing young love for sale

She felt lightheaded and slightly out of control and glanced over to the piano where Dan's calm commitment to perfection steadied her nerves.

If you want to buy my wares
Follow me and climb the stairs

Her pulse was strong and fast, but she wouldn't give in to the bitter tug at her gut. She stared straight ahead and sang the last line directly into the spotlight.

During the applause, she looked at Dan, whose expressionless face was soft and content and helped her relax. She managed to avoid looking at the spot where Jake sat for the rest of the show, but, as they neared the end, she grew anxious with thoughts of how she could escape the room without being seen. She closed the show with Dan's jazzy arrangement of "I'll be Seeing You," and then waited impatiently for the applause to die before leaving the stage.

Dotty stood at her point of exit, holding a lowball glass of vodka on ice. Hassie grabbed the drink out of Dotty's hand and downed the entire contents. "They want you back on stage," Dotty cried as Hassie pushed past her and headed toward the dressing room.

"I'm not going back out," she called over her shoulder. Once inside the room, she kicked off her shoes and sat down at her dressing table, then stared into the mirror and waited for Dotty to appear.

"What's the matter with you?" Dotty said. "You were great. They loved you."

Hassie held up the glass, silently asking for more. "I'm glad, but I'm tired and I wanna go home." She soon changed back into her slacks and blouse and walked out.

She caught the guys as they were leaving the stage and thanked them for such a great night. They gushed over her performance but seemed to sense that she wanted to be alone and wished her well until the next night. She stood in the right wing and glanced out at the tables, now mostly empty except for a few stragglers nursing nightcaps. She focused on the table where she'd seen Jake, and then suddenly remembered that she had asked Henry to wait for her and turned to exit the stage. Jake stood a few feet away, his eyes softly reflecting the dim light. Her stomach clenched again and she heard herself gasp, but she didn't speak or move.

He took a few steps toward her and said, "Hello, Hassie."

"Hello."

"You were sensational." He crossed his arms over his chest. "And you look incredible."

She felt her hands shaking and clasped them together at her waist. "Thank you. That's very nice of you to say."

"Why didn't I know you could sing like that?"

When she looked at him, she saw the man that she had met on her first night at the Sands – handsome, charming and kind. She smiled and tried to relax. "I don't know. How did you know I was here?"

Jake dropped his hands to his sides and smiled. "I knew you were coming here before you did."

She didn't doubt it and wanted to get away from him, but her legs were locked at the knees and she wished that Henry or someone would come backstage looking for her. She brushed her hair away from her eye; her hand touched the scar at her eyebrow. "Thank you for coming," she said and took a step toward the exit. "I shouldn't keep my friends waiting." She gathered the courage to walk away but, when she tried to walk past him, he grabbed hold of her arm, stopping her in mid-stride.

"Have a drink with me," he said softly. "Just one drink."

"No, Jake. I can't."

"Of course, you can," he said and pulled her in closer to him. "And I think you want to."

The dream on the bus flashed in her mind; she stood frozen and calm and allowed him to look into her eyes. His smile faded to a look of concern. He dropped her arm and reached for her face, touching her scar and gently stroking her eyebrow. "Did I do this?" he said.

She swallowed the emotion in her throat and nodded.

He grabbed her with both arms, his spicy scent forcing her to another time when she would have practically melted when he held her like this. He relaxed his hold on her and looked into her face. "I'm so sorry. I'd give anything – how could I do something so vicious – I'm so sorry."

She remained silent, her promise to her friends to stay away from him a vivid reminder to be strong. She backed away from his embrace and said, "I really must go now."

He kept hold of her wrist and said, "I hope that one day you will be able to forgive me." He lifted her hand to his lips and kissed it. "I will always love you."

Hassie pulled her hand from his grip and rushed away, damned if she would let him know how seeing him affected her. When she reached the backstage entrance, she saw Dan standing in the shadows. Had he been waiting for her and did he witness the scene with Jake? It was more than she could deal with at that moment and she kept going until she was outside the doors of the lounge where she spotted Henry talking to Stella. She breathed deeply as she approached them, painfully aware of Henry's ability to read her like a book.

"There's the star!" Henry reached out and grabbed her by the hand while Stella hugged her.

"Oh, Hassie," Stella said. "You were just great. I had a lump in my throat the whole time you sang."

Hassie hugged Henry and then said to Stella, "Thanks. I'm so glad you came."

Dotty walked up to join them, and from her expression, Hassie had the feeling that she'd seen Jake. She steered Hassie back toward the main lobby and said, "Let's go get a drink."

They found a table in the lobby lounge and ordered a round of drinks. Hassie took the cigarettes from her purse and offered them around the table. Her hands were still shaking and she suddenly felt very cold. She looked at Henry and said, "Where's Julio?"

"He had to rush back to play the late set in the lobby lounge, but he said to tell you that you were fabulous and he'll see you at home." Henry lit the ladies' cigarettes and, for once, didn't frown his disapproval. "He's really sick that the Tropicana hired you before the Sands did. He hasn't said anything, but I'll bet he's gonna campaign to get you over there after your contract here expires."

Dotty blew smoke up in the air and said, "Well, the Sands is just too late."

"What do you mean?" Hassie said.

"Word is that John Jacobson's gonna offer you an extension on your contract before anyone has a chance to take you away."

"And when do they plan to do this?" Hassie said calmly.

"Guess you'll just have to wait and see."

The waitress set a martini in front of Hassie. She was distracted by the thought of Jake; the smell of him lingered, and she could feel the sorrow that he expressed when his fingers touched her eyebrow. She sipped the drink and tried to put him out of her mind.

Henry put his hand on hers and said, "Honey, are you okay?"

"Yeah, you look a little pale," Stella added.

"I'm fine. Just exhausted." She flicked the cigarette in the ashtray. "This is so different from singing in a little jazz club in Reno where everything was slow and easy and the booze flowed freely." She looked over at Dotty and smiled before saying, "Thanks for letting me calm my nerves with Dr. Vodka."

"I'm still not sure why you think you need it, but as long as you keep performin' like you did tonight, what can I say?" Dotty was trying to be stern, which made everyone smile.

Hassie took a deep breath and swallowed the rest of the drink. "I think I should get some rest. I've gotta do this all over again tomorrow night. At this rate, I'll be dead in a week."

Dotty looked at Henry and said, "You guys go ahead. I'll take care of the check."

Hassie stood up and took hold of Dotty's hand. "Thank you again for being my rock."

"Just go and rest and come back tomorrow night fresh and ready to go."

Hassie could feel Dotty's eyes on her as she walked away. There was no doubt that Dotty had seen Jake, and little doubt that Hassie would hear more on the subject the next day. But the look she'd seen backstage on Dan's face made her feel sad, and she wished she'd put her arms around him when she'd had the chance.

chapter twenty-four

THE REACTION from the men in the audience at La Chanson was reminiscent of the long, sultry nights at Felix's and the party scene that often ensued. But her response to the subtle advances of some of the men at La Chanson was, surprisingly, almost that of a shy, inexperienced girl who was being watched or guarded to ensure she didn't make a foolish mistake – to make certain that she didn't fall under the spell of another Mr. Satan and end up in one of the hotel rooms with money clenched in her fist.

From the moment she walked away from Jake during his backstage visit, she would relive the incident over and over again – his face, his voice, his touch, his projection of love. The effort to be strong and to keep her promise to stay away from him sapped her energy, despite the fact that Barbara and Dotty were like bookends around her dilemma; heeding their advice would keep her safely out of his reach and allow her to exist in a world of normality, where people who were good for her could have a fair chance to make her happy.

But she'd never really tried normal. She preferred what she'd had with Jake or Felix or even Mr. Satan. Did this make her a bad person? Was Barbara so right in her belief that moral integrity came in only one form? Wasn't she entitled to live her life for herself and to take her own emotional risks?

Her life had only been interesting when she allowed herself to abandon the puritanical beliefs that had been part of her upbringing. Maybe this was the reason that she couldn't bring herself to contact Barbara after she left Corsicana. To be judged by the one person who had encouraged her to distinguish right from wrong and to live a better life than the one her mother had chosen.

Jake understood this about her. Maybe it was because his own mother was not so different from hers. Both women were selfish and had deeply hurt the men they claimed to love. Jake had recognized Hassie's desire to free herself from her mother's grip and had helped her make a safe, comfortable transition in an otherwise wicked and dangerous world. Jake had tried to be there for her, and she knew that in his own way, he loved her.

Not like Clay, who, despite having shared Jake's mother, didn't seem to suffer the ills of having grown up in a home with a mother who drove two men away from their children. She had also learned from Jake that Clay's father had been a big influence on both their lives as young boys and that losing him was especially devastating to Jake, having already lost his own father, certain that his mother was to blame. If Clay was similarly affected, he didn't seem to show it, except that Hassie never felt that he trusted her emotionally, was never willing to take the risk that he suspected was part of being involved with a woman like Hassie.

Loving Jake was the ultimate emotional risk and, as he had demonstrated, a physical risk as well. She remembered his face when he discovered her scar – the painful recognition that he had really hurt her. Surely, he would never do such a horrible thing again. But should she take that chance? And, if she did, would her friends support her again if she needed them?

Hassie shuffled into the kitchen late on the Wednesday morning following her first week on the job. She'd been awake for an hour or so, but lay quietly in bed, rationalizing her inclination to say to hell with it and just give in to her desire to see Jake again. Julio sat at the kitchen table reading the newspaper.

"Good morning, sleepyhead," he said. "I hope this means you got some extra sleep."

Hassie went to the cabinet and picked out the pig's head mug, then poured the dregs from the coffee pot and stirred in some sugar. "I wish," she said and joined him at the table. "I can't seem to sleep more than a couple of hours without waking up – sometimes from bad dreams. And then, when and if I do go back to sleep, it's time to get up."

Julio took his cup and went back into the kitchen. "Maybe you should get some sleeping pills. If you're gonna keep the pace you've had this past week, you need more rest, chica."

"I know," she said as she watched Julio putter about the kitchen. He wore plaid cotton shorts and a T-shirt that stretched tightly across his muscular torso and revealed a waist that she thought might be the same size as hers. He was a very good-looking man, which she had never really thought about before seeing him half naked. "But with my luck, I'd get addicted to them and end up like Marilyn Monroe."

Julio looked at her and said, "A little drastic, don't you think?"

"You know what I mean. I just need to get my head clear, Julio."

He brought a plate of white powdered doughnuts over to the table and sat down across from her. "Here, you need some sugar. Eat one of these and then I'll make you something else."

Hassie took a doughnut from the plate and dunked a piece of it in her coffee. "Why don't we have a good old family style dinner here tonight? Just me, you and Henry."

"That's an excellent idea," he said. "I can make my famous enchiladas – my mamacita's recipe and the house specialty."

Hassie remembered Henry's warning about Julio's cooking but didn't dare dampen his spirits. "That sounds wonderful as long as we have tequila to go with them."

"Margaritas, of course! But I'll need to do some shopping. Why don't you get dressed and come with me to the supermarket?"

"Okay," she said, swallowing the last of the doughnut. "Let me have a little more coffee." She grabbed a second doughnut and said, "And another one of these and I'll throw on some clothes."

They drove through the quaint desert neighborhood past the local high school – a banner spelling out "Go Tigers" in bright red and gold letters strung across the entrance. Julio followed the back streets to the local supermarket, which was actually only a few blocks away. When they entered the store, he grabbed one of the carts and took off like he was in danger of missing the last bag of corn meal while Hassie strolled past a display of chocolates packaged to look like a stack of casino chips. As she turned to look for Julio, she saw a dark-haired toddler sitting in the wire seat of a cart, a woman squatting down to reach something on the bottom shelf. When the child kicked it's feet against the cart and shouted, "Mama!" the woman stood up and said, "I'm right here, Norma," Hassie's knees locked and she stared at the floor. She turned back to the chocolate display and waited for the squeaky-wheeled cart to disappear down another aisle. She spotted Julio going into the produce aisle and quickly joined him as he tossed a bag of onions in the cart.

"There you are, chica," Julio said. "How good are you at selecting tomatoes? They're the key to a great salsa."

She thought the question odd but wanted to get out of the store before they ran into Natalie and her love child. "Aren't you in luck? Texas is a great tomato state." She handled a couple of the ripe red fruits like she was selecting a winner at the county fair, stuffed them in a brown paper sack and laid them in the cart as she said, "Got everything you need?"

The next few minutes turned into the scene that Hassie had dreaded since the minute Henry told her about Jake and Natalie's baby. Julio wheeled toward the front of the store past shelves full of loaves of bread. Hassie happily followed along beside him until they turned a corner and almost collided with Natalie's cart, the toddler chewing on a soft plastic doll.

Hassie stopped and took hold of Julio's arm while he said, "Hello, Natalie."

The color drained from Natalie's face as she feebly nodded at Julio before focusing on Hassie. "I didn't know you were back in Vegas."

"I thought Jake would have told you," Hassie said coolly. "You always said that he tells you everything."

Julio turned to get a closer look at the little girl and said, "Is this little Norma?"

Natalie smiled as she took hold of her hand and said, "Yeah. Doesn't she look just like Jake?"

Hassie stared at the back of the little girl's head; curly locks of hair the color of Jake's. She felt a thud in the pit of her stomach, looked up at Natalie and said, "If you're interested, I'm singing in one of the lounges at the Tropicana. And if you're wondering if I'm any good, ask Jake. He's seen the show."

Julio took hold of Hassie's arm and said, "Nice to see you, Natalie. We're in a bit of a hurry." He tugged on Hassie to follow him while Natalie just stood still. When they reached the checkout register, Julio frowned at her and said, "Did you have to be such a bitch to her?"

"She's never been anything but a bitch to me," Hassie said. "And what did I say that wasn't true?"

They stood silent in the line until he finally looked at her and said, "You know, no one likes the way you behave when Jake is involved."

"What the hell does that mean, Julio? Jake is nothing to do with me now."

"Come on, chica. He's under your skin and he'll always be under your skin. You can deny it if you like, but nobody buys it."

Hassie looked over her shoulder to see if she could get another look at the child, then turned back to Julio and quietly said, "Whether you like it or not, it upsets me to know that Natalie has that piece of Jake."

"Well, get over it because Jake and Natalie are married now," Julio said as he emptied the contents of the cart onto the conveyer belt. "That means, hands off, or you'll really be asking for trouble."

Hassie's face reddened. "I don't have any intention of putting my hands on Jake so, give it a rest."

Julio picked up the bags of groceries and nudged Hassie toward the door. When they were inside the car, he turned his body toward her, took hold of her hand and said, "I know you still love him. It's obvious and painful to watch, but please stay away from him. You know how hard Henry and I worked to get you out of Vegas and away from Jake and on to a better life. I know coming back was a career move that you couldn't turn down, but please don't get involved with him again. Nothing good can come from it."

The evening with Henry and Julio was a great break from her routine at the Tropicana, and, despite Henry's warning to the contrary, she loved Julio's meal of enchiladas, beans and rice. Julio wisely opted not to mention the meeting with Natalie to Henry – at least not in front of Hassie. She smoked too much and had too much tequila and awoke the next morning, after a very restless night, feeling fuzzy and dehydrated.

Hassie entered the empty kitchen and plugged in the percolator. Henry had finally stopped leaving her notes telling her to help herself and to call him if she needed anything. At that moment, the only thing she needed was to sleep for a day and wake up with a head clear of booze. She found the last sugar doughnut in the breadbox and ate the whole thing while waiting for the coffee to brew. She'd kept an image of Natalie's child in her mind. Only now, Hassie pictured Jake holding Norma on his knee, bouncing her around while she touched his face with her small, chubby hand – the little doll-like creature that looked so much like Jake she couldn't bear to think about it – the child that she and Jake had never had cause to discuss.

The aroma from the percolator brought her back to the empty kitchen, and as soon as the coffee was ready, she poured a cup full, stirred in sugar and took it into the living room where she spotted her cigarettes on the table beside the ashtray and lighter. She switched on the big oscillator and started over to the sofa when the doorbell rang. She set the mug on the coffee table, tightened the sash on her robe and opened the door, where the only thing between her and Jake was the flimsy screened door.

"Jake," she said. "What are you doing here?" She glanced down to see that the door was unlatched.

"If you tell me to go away, I'll understand. But I really hope that you don't."

"What do you want?" She pulled the collar of the robe tighter around her neck, suddenly aware that the only thing underneath it was her skimpy cotton nightie. Her entire system reacted to the sight of him and she felt her cheeks get warm.

"I only want to talk to you. Can I come in for just for a minute?" His eyes and voice made her ache with desire, his tone was serious and sorrowful and, for a moment, she considered letting him in.

"Not here, Jake. Not in Henry and Julio's house. If you want to talk to me in a public place – well, maybe I'll consider it, but not here."

Jake put his hands on the door and stood still. "Then let me say what I came to say and I promise I'll leave you alone."

She remained as still as the desert air and said nothing to either encourage him or send him away. As long as the door was between them, she'd give him a chance to speak.

"It almost destroyed me to see you the other night," he began, then stopped and looked down at the porch. "And I'm not talking about how beautiful you looked or how wonderful you were." He looked directly at her; goose bumps crawled down her arms. "Your eye – the thought that I was responsible for hurting you. I behaved very badly over that business with Frank. I should not have taken my anger out on you and I should never have hit you. I should've hit Frank, but I shouldn't have hit you. I'm so sorry, and I'm asking you to forgive me."

The image of Natalie and the child in the supermarket took over her thoughts; her eyes quickly filled with tears. She looked down at the floor and took a step back, knowing that if she looked at him again, she'd risk going against everything she'd promised her friends and herself. Without looking up, and with a heartbeat so strong she was sure Jake could hear it, she closed the door and rested her head against it.

She'd sent him away, and, despite his admission of guilt and his efforts to apologize, she still fought to keep him out of her life. She walked over to the sofa and sat down, then took a cigarette from the pack and tried to light it. Her hands shook and she started to cry. She dropped the cigarette and ran to the telephone. It was as if she were some sort of addict and needed someone to save her from herself, to keep the poison out of her reach and to prevent her from making a fatal mistake.

She dialed the number for the Sands and asked to speak to Henry, but after the eighth ring and no answer, she hung up and just stood in the middle of the kitchen. From the large window over the sink, she could see the neighbors' backyards; one with an elaborate cactus garden and several fragile looking birds perched on a molded cement birdbath in the other. Simple, normal life was happening all around her – everything that Barbara had wanted for her; everything she'd wanted as a child but struggled to maintain after her father died. She was learning to love her life at the Tropicana and, God knows, she loved her friends. But she momentarily blocked them from her thoughts and, for the first time in a long time, considered what she – Hassie Calhoun – really wanted and needed. Jake had taught her how to love and how to be loved, and she'd never come close to finding that depth of passion with any other man. He had never left her heart and he'd never left her dreams – she'd lived that night at La Chanson a dozen times and felt him touch her face a hundred times. How could she turn away from the person who was really responsible for her return to Las Vegas?

The slow walk along the hotel corridor was tentative at times; memories were like ghosts hovering in the corners, lurking around a bend. But Hassie fought the urge to turn around and go back to the safety of Henry's house and steadily put one foot in front of the other until she stood in front of the door to Jake's suite. She breathed deeply and pushed her hair from her face, then knocked with three sharp raps and waited. Dotty had told her that Natalie and the child lived in a house about a half-mile from the Sands. "Please be here – alone," she said to herself and the door slowly opened.

She stood there until he reached for her, and she walked straight into his arms where she remained still and silent until he looked at her and said, "I'm glad you –"

She leapt at him, threw her arms around his neck and kissed his face, nervously missing his lips. He steadied her face with his hands and kissed her until they were gasping for air. Hassie tightened her embrace and leaned forward to his ear. "Please don't ever let me go." He nuzzled his face against her neck, planting deep kisses that might leave a mark, her body involuntarily grinding against him as she pulled his shirt out of his trousers and started to unbutton it. He took hold of her hands and helped her finish the task, then removed it while she kissed his chest and reached down to unfasten his belt buckle. When he tried to speak, she covered his lips with hers, urging his tongue into her mouth and forcing his trousers to drop to the floor.

She slipped the straps of her dress off her shoulders, then stood before Jake while he looked at her, her nipples taut inside the thin white bra, causing her to blush as she stood still and said, "Jake, what am I doing?"

He pulled her close and said, "Isn't this what you came back for?" He held her tight, his penis like a rope against her stomach. "Don't ask me to stop."

She kissed him and said, "I don't want you to stop. Christ, don't you get how much I love you?" She practically ripped off her bra and panties and tugged at his underwear. He removed them as he said,

"Let's go into the bedroom." Hassie shook her head, then pushed him down on the sofa and sat astride him, locking her legs on either side of his thighs, her breasts against his bare chest. She moved her hips against him, lifting herself and guiding him inside her until they were completely interlocked. She controlled the movement of her pelvis, pulling him along to the edge of ecstasy and then back ever so gently, back and forth, back and forth. He dug his fingers into her back and pulled her close. But as his excitement started to overtake him, Hassie lessened the movement of her hips and kissed him gently before saying, "Not yet."

She eventually allowed him to carry her to the bed that had once been theirs and managed to push the thought of another woman having taken her place out of her mind. She craved the intensity of the pleasure she had with him and felt no guilt at being there with him now. Would this be the last time that she would make love to him? She somehow doubted it.

They lay together in Jake's bed and were quiet except for the occasional sigh, each waiting for the other to be first to speak. Hassie finally pushed back from him and sat up cross-legged in the bed beside him. She desperately needed a cigarette and leaned down to kiss his chest before saying, "What are you doing at home at this time of day?"

"Why did you come if you didn't think I'd be here?" He eased himself up and sat back against the headboard, then pulled her close to him and stroked her hair.

She rested comfortably against him and said, "I knew you'd be here. Don't ask me why."

"I needed a break from the hotel after I came back from seeing you." His voice sounded strained and uneasy; not the contented, husky whisper that she remembered after one of their long, passionate sessions. She stayed still in his embrace and said, "Are you okay?"

"I'm supposed to be asking you that question," he said and pushed her back to her sitting position.

"You just seem kinda quiet and maybe – not too happy."

He swung his legs around to the edge of the bed, then stood up and turned to face her. "I guess I'm a little bit in shock."

He walked into the bathroom as she said, "Do you want me to leave?"

He returned wearing his bathrobe. "Of course I don't want you to leave, but I don't have a robe that I think you want to wear."

She scooted off the bed and followed him into the living room, picked up his shirt and draped it around her naked body, then grabbed an empty pack of cigarettes off the table and crumpled it in her hand. "Got any more of these?"

Jake walked over to the bar, then looked at her and said, "When did you start smoking?"

She sat down on the sofa. "There's not much to do in Reno."

"Well, I wouldn't think that smoking would be good for your singing."

"You'll have to get in line with a lot of other people to preach that sermon. Besides, I've cut down a lot. I just feel like having one now. With my drink."

He looked over and smiled at her and, for the first time since she'd arrived in his suite, she felt him relax. "Still drinking vodka or shall I call down for some champagne?"

"Vodka'll do."

Jake brought the drinks over to the table and then went back into the bedroom. When he returned with a fresh pack of cigarettes, she patted the seat beside her and said, "Sit."

He sat down, opened the cigarettes and offered her one, which she pulled from the pack and waited for him to light. She inhaled deeply, and then exhaled as she said, "I saw your little girl yesterday."

He sat back in the seat and took a big swig of his drink. "I know. I heard."

"And I know that you and Natalie are married."

They sat in silence, puffing on the cigarettes for a few seconds, then Jake leaned his elbows on his knees and said, "I couldn't leave her alone with a child."

"I'm not suggesting that you should have." Hassie took a deep drag on the cigarette and chewed over her words for a few seconds, then turned to Jake and said, "So, Natalie finally got what she wanted – you – and a baby as a bonus."

He stood and walked back to the bar. "It's not like that, Hassie."

"It's not?" she said. She studied him closely. "So, what's it like, Jake? What's it like to be trapped by a woman that you claim not to have ever loved and live with her in holy matrimony?"

Jake poured the whiskey in his glass and stood at the bar for a long moment before turning to her and saying, "You've really changed. You're not the sweet, innocent girl you were when I met you."

Hassie stood up and walked over to the bar. "Don't you think you might have had something to do with that?" She set the glass on the bar and wiped a tear from under her eye. Jake took her in his arms and held her while she cried, then lifted her face and said, "I told you last week as I've told you a hundred times. I will always love you. I don't love Natalie. I never have and I never will. We have an arrangement, and as long as I take care of her and Norma, she won't interfere in the rest of my life."

Hassie took a sip of her drink and said, "What does that mean?"

"It means that as long as I give Natalie everything she needs and make reasonably regular visits to see the kid, she doesn't ask any questions about what I'm doing when I'm not there. As you can see, I live in this suite – with no signs of a two-year-old – and I don't have to answer to Natalie for anything."

Hassie thought about Natalie's reaction to her in the supermarket, almost as if her appearance had frightened Natalie. "That sounds a little unbelievable to me, after how hard she fought for you."

Jake took her elbow and led her back to the sofa. "Like you said. She finally won the prize. She may not have all of me but she's got something more powerful in a child that's part of me. The bottom line is, I've fucked up pretty badly over the past few years and now I'm paying the price. But I still want you as much as I always did." He took her in his arms and held her close. "Will you give me another chance?"

Every nerve in her body, every cell in her brain warned her: "Don't do it! Walk away now!" She pulled back from him and sat back in the seat. "Do you really think I can forget what you did to me? Just forgive and forget like nothing ever happened?"

Jake sipped his drink and hesitated before saying, "You may never speak to me again after I say this, but did you ever consider that I hit you because you betrayed me with Frank? That for that unfortunate, weak moment, I believed that your physical suffering was equal to what you did to me emotionally? That you deserved to be punished and I had to punish you?"

Hassie let his words sink in for a few seconds, and then looked at him and said, "No, I never considered your feelings at all. Men are not supposed to hit women. At least, not where I come from."

"Look, darling. Don't get me wrong. I'm not saying that what I did was right or justified. I'm just asking you to understand why I might have lost control – to see that it had nothing to do with how much I love you and want you and –" He stood up and took a few steps away from her then turned and said, "Another man *touched* you. No. Another man was inside you! You gave him part of what was sacred between you and me. Do you know how much that hurt me? How – okay, *crazy* – it made me?"

Hassie stood up and nodded slowly as she said, "I know now." She walked over to the window and gazed through the pale sheer curtain, her view softened and skewed much like her memory of the events that led to that terrible night and the unraveling of her life in Vegas. But Jake wasn't wrong. She had betrayed him for her own selfish reasons and ultimately driven him exactly where she didn't want him to go.

She turned to face him and said, "I'm sorry I hurt you." She walked into his arms and stood still in his embrace. "But you hurt me so much, and I don't know if I can –"

"Look," he said, taking hold of her shoulders. "We both made mistakes and we both have something to forgive. But I swear to you, I will never, ever hit you or hurt you again."

She looked at him for a moment and kissed him tenderly before saying, "Then I forgive you, and I love you." He pulled her close as she whispered, "Let's try this again."

chapter twenty-five

THE SCREENED DOOR slammed behind Hassie as she exited the house, Henry right behind her, sounding like a broken record, "Do you enjoy being abused, Hassie? Does it give you some sort of thrill?"

"Stop it, Henry," she yelled back at him. "I can't talk to you anymore." She stood at the curb, waiting for the taxi to take her to the Sands.

Henry walked up to her and took hold of her arm. "We're just worried about you." He waited for her to respond. "We don't want to see you make another mistake."

She pulled her arm from his grip and took a step away from him. "If I make a mistake, it's my business, Henry. Why can't you just leave it alone?" She wanted to hit him and glared at him like he was a monster.

He crossed his arms over his chest and calmly said, "Please, come back inside. I don't think the neighbors need to hear all of this."

She stared straight ahead until Henry pulled her by her wrist and they went back into the house. She could hear Julio in the shower and sat down on the sofa to light a cigarette.

"Do you want some more coffee?" Henry called out from the kitchen.

"No."

He came back into the living room and sat in the chair beside the sofa. She was determined not to speak to him until he apologized for shouting at her. He finally took a deep breath and propped his left foot on his right knee. She exhaled smoke toward the ceiling and waited for him to speak.

"You know that I love you dearly and that I only care about what is best for you."

"You're not my father," she said without looking at him.

"No, I'm not," he said and put both feet on the floor. "But I am your friend. I am the friend who has sat across the desk from you umpteen times and listened when you were ready to strangle one Jake Contrata. I'm the friend who has scraped you up off the floor when he smeared Natalie in your face or dismissed your feelings as totally unimportant. And I am the friend who sat beside your hospital bed when this man beat you so badly that you couldn't open your eyes or swallow or speak for days. That's who I am."

She heard his voice crack and looked into his face. "Why is it so impossible for you to believe that Jake really loves me and that he is truly sorry for his behavior in the past? And that being back with him doesn't automatically mean that a fresh beating is just around the corner! Why does it have to be so black and white where he is concerned?"

Henry cleared his throat and said, "People like Jake don't change. He's abused you before and he'll do it again. And for Christ sake, Hassie, he's *married* now. If there's no other fucking reason to stay away from him, that's it. Why can't you see how wrong you are? You want him to take some responsibility here but he's not going to. He's going to let you wreck your life because – hey, he loves you!"

Hassie heard the taxi's horn and ground out the cigarette, then crammed the pack in her purse and stood up to leave. "I'm sorry you feel this way, and I think it is a mistake for me to try to stay here with you and Julio in this house if this is how you're going to treat me."

"Suit yourself, honey. There's just not one bone in my body that can support this decision of yours. And I'm gonna speak for Julio as well. We love you, and we'll miss you."

One of Morty's favorite phrases, "juggling chainsaws," came to mind as Hassie got into the taxi. Henry's unwillingness to accept that she was back with Jake made her both sad and angry. And she was right in thinking that her effort to keep peace with Henry and Julio by spending time with them at home was useless.

She rolled the window down enough to let in some air. Henry's tone echoed in her head and her heart ached. She took a tissue from her purse and wiped her eyes, still arguing with him in her mind, still adamant to make him understand that Jake really had changed and that he truly was sorry for his actions. Why didn't they deserve another chance at real happiness together?

Okay, there was the issue of his wife and a child – this is where she'd also lost Dotty, who hardly spoke to her for the first couple of weeks after her reunion with Jake and basically just hissed and humphed when responding to her attempts at conversation before or during her show. But she was determined to soften Dotty's opinion where Jake was concerned, which, so far, had resulted in the occasional cutting remark about how she looked "worn out" and malnourished.

Stella was the only one who seemed to understand that treating her like a social outcast was not going to alter the situation. But then, Stella had always understood the complexity of a relationship with someone like Jake. When Hassie recalled the early conversations that she'd had with Stella when they were roommates, she smiled and thought that Stella must have believed her to be the most ignorant kid to ever fall off a hay wagon. More than once, she had gingerly explained the evil workings of the Copa Room and had patiently listened to Hassie's shocking recollections of how the men pawed at her and what it had been like to make love to Jake that first time and how it felt to fall in love with him – things that she could never have discussed with Henry.

But Stella was also Natalie's friend and saw things from her perspective, too. Because of that, she had learned to consider *Would I want Natalie to know this?* before she spoke too openly about anything to do with Jake. If Stella knew Natalie's side of the story, she chose to keep it to herself. And Hassie chose not to ask too many questions.

It was also intriguing to Hassie that the time she spent with Jake was sexually charged in a way that she didn't remember before she went to Reno. Was it the fact that he was married and technically off limits to her – something that she had learned about during her illicit dabblings with Felix? Or had their physical need for each other reached a different level – one that they had only been able to discover after that extended time apart?

She was on her way to Jake's suite and their first dinner together that week. Between her job at La Chanson and her effort to live at Henry and Julio's house, their time together had been limited, and Jake had seemed determined to make every minute count. As the taxi drove along the strip, the Sands beckoning from the distance, Hassie pictured Jake's face when he'd opened the door and pulled her into the dark suite, practically tearing her clothes off her body before throwing her down on the sofa and taking her from behind. She couldn't see his face until afterwards when she'd picked his shirt off the floor and wrapped it around her body. She shivered as she remembered her inner reaction to his aggression as one of thrill and ultra-excitement – a byproduct of her sybaritic lifestyle in Reno? But her actual response had been one of shock bordering on coyness when she'd breathlessly said, "My God, Jake. You scared me."

Jake had laughed softly to himself and pulled on his trousers. "You loved it and you know it." Then he sat down and took a cigarette from the pack, lit it and gave it to her. "Relax. Have a smoke and I'll get you a drink."

The scene felt like some sort of dream now. She'd dragged slowly on the cigarette and watched him as he walked over to the hi-fi and turned up the volume of the lively Latin beat. He'd danced a few steps of what looked like a rumba and then pulled her from the sofa and forced her to follow his lead.

"I feel good," he'd said above the music. "Don't you feel good?"

She'd smiled and nodded as he whirled her around and then held her close while he kissed her – the luscious, sensuous kiss that turned her into putty and sent that tingling sensation into her groin. She'd kissed his cheek and then winced as he tightened his grip on her waist and started to kiss her neck, down to her clavicle where he bit her and sent a pain through her shoulder. "Ow, Jake!" she'd shouted. "That hurts. You're being too rough."

He'd continued to kiss her neck until his mouth was next to her ear, where he kissed her earlobe before saying, "You don't fool me, baby. You can behave like a little prude if you like." He'd put his hand inside the shirt and lightly squeezed her breast. "But I know what you want. I know what all whores want." He'd kissed her with such force that she had to grab his neck to keep her balance. "And you are *my* whore," he'd whispered and pulled the shirt from her body. "Aren't you?"

The taxi stopped at the Sands entrance; she paid the driver, then climbed out of the cab and smiled at Jimmy. "Good evening," he said as he opened the lobby door. "There's somebody looking for you. Said he'd be waiting in the Regency Lounge."

"Thanks, Jimmy," she said, wondering why Jake didn't want her to go straight to his suite. She entered the dimly lit room and headed for his table in the corner. As she walked past the first two booths, she heard a voice say, "Hello, sweetheart." She'd know that voice anywhere and stopped in front of the table. "Hi, Frank. I didn't know you were back." She'd often wondered if she'd ever see him again and, if she did, would he even remember her name.

"Have a seat," he said.

She glanced at the table in the corner and said, "I'm supposed to be meeting Jake."

"No you're not. I asked Jimmy to send you in here."

She slid into the booth, fully aware of the dangerous line she crossed. Frank offered her a cigarette, which she took from the pack and waited for him to light while covertly surveying the room for signs of anyone close enough to Jake to report her meeting with Frank as something more than it was.

"You look amazing," he said and motioned for the waitress. "Where the hell have you been?"

"Reno," she said and inhaled the smoke deep into her lungs, then asked Sheila, the big-bosomed cocktail waitress, for a vodka martini. "How'd you know I was here?"

"A little bird told me." He smiled and just looked at her. "What the hell were you doing in Reno?"

"Working."

"You should have told me. If I'd known you were there, I could have found my way into the Sky Room at the Mapes. Have you been there?"

She nodded, wishing that she sat on the side of Frank that gave her a view of the door. She had no reason to trust that Jimmy wouldn't tell Jake where she was and imagined him striding in at any minute. "Frank, I don't think I should be here with you right now."

"Why not?" He smiled like he knew exactly what she meant. "We're just two old friends who haven't seen each other for a while."

He put his hand on top of hers and said, "Did I tell you how great you look?"

"I don't think Jake would like to find me having a drink with you." Sheila set the drink on the table; Hassie practically downed it in one gulp. Frank watched her, took his last swallow and motioned for another round.

"So you're back in the saddle with him? Are you back in Vegas for good?"

Hassie took a deep drag on the cigarette and hesitated before speaking. "Didn't that little bird tell you that I'm singing over at the Tropicana?"

"No kiddin'," he said, a hint of amusement in his eyes. "You've got your own show in the Theater Restaurant?"

"No, nothing like that – just the little lounge called La Chanson. Do you know it? It's pretty small and usually full of horny businessmen, but the music director – this guy called Dan Forrester – is so great and –"

He put his forefinger on her lips and then pulled her face close to his. "Stop talking," he said and kissed her like she belonged to him.

Hassie sat back in the seat and waited while Sheila delivered another drink, but before she could speak again, Frank looked at her and said, "You didn't answer my question. Are you back with Jake?"

Her hands were a little shaky and she couldn't look him in the eye. "We spend time together."

Frank put his elbows on the table and dragged on his cigarette. "I see." He reached over to touch her eyebrow and said, "I'd like to have seen the black eye that went with this."

Hassie pulled away from him and stubbed out her cigarette. "I really do need to go now. It was great to see you. Are you back to work the Copa Room?"

He took a deep breath, studied her a few seconds and said, "We're actually gonna record a live performance. In a couple of weeks. Will you be there?"

She shook her head and said, "I doubt it. It's not a good idea for me and you to be in the same room when Jake is around." She moved to the end of the banquette seat; Frank stood up to help her. He took hold of her hand and said, "Can I see you again?" He kissed her hand. "Please."

She looked at him, his expression soft and inviting, and said, "Like I said. Not a good idea."

Frank dropped her hand and took hold of her chin. "I'll tell you what's not a good idea – getting involved with a married man. No matter what he tells you. No matter how much you think he loves you. You deserve better than that."

Hassie kissed him on the cheek and said, "Thanks, Frank. Good luck with the recording." She took a few steps away from him before he said, "Tell Dan that I said to take good care of you."

chapter twenty-six

HASSIE WAS slightly disappointed to meet Carlos, the room service steward, coming out of Jake's suite, having just delivered their dinner. The recollection of her last visit, when Jake had surprised her at the door and loved her hard, had her thighs trembling with anticipation, and, despite the brief, unnerving interlude with Frank, she was ready for a replay. She smiled and started to speak to Carlos as Jake grabbed her hand to pull her inside. He pushed her up against the closed door and kissed her with the electrifying urgency that she'd become accustomed to when she hadn't seen him for a few days. As he ran his hands across her breasts and then up her back, she tightened her embrace around his neck and welcomed his deep, sensuous kiss until he pulled back from her and said, "Who've you been drinking with?"

She eased back from him and said, "Stella. I met her downstairs this afternoon."

Jake stepped away from her and wiped his mouth with the back of his hand and then, wordlessly, turned toward the bar.

She watched him, knowing that she should also mention that she had run into Frank. She knew damn well that Jimmy or Sheila or any one of a number of people that had seen her go in and out of the Regency Lounge could tell him, or worse, had already told him. It wasn't too late to back track on her lie, but instead, she carefully moved toward the sofa and said, "What have you been doing today?"

Jake stayed still for a few seconds, then looked at her and said, "What do you want to drink?"

"A martini, please." Her body's anticipation of their sexual romp had been shaken by his reaction to their kiss, and she was suddenly nervous at the thought of her conversation with Frank.

Jake poured the martini into a glass, then splashed some Jack Daniels over ice and joined her on the sofa.

She took the drinks from him and set them on the coffee table, then grabbed his hand and pulled him down next to her. "I've missed you and have been looking forward to this all day." She held his face in her hands and kissed him softly and gently until she felt him release the tension in his arms. He pulled her so close to his chest, she could feel his shallow breathing and the quick beat of his heart.

He held her in his arms and said, "I've been waiting for you."

"I'm not late, am I?"

"It's just interesting that you've been in the hotel for a while and found it more important to have a drink with Stella than to come up and spend time with me."

Hassie sat back from him and carefully took a sip of her drink before saying, "Jake, you are never finished with your day so early." She sipped her drink again. "I haven't seen Stella since the first week of my show." Her pulse quickened as she picked her words. "And remember, I told you," she continued, "Henry, Julio and Dotty have basically dismissed me from their lives because I'm here with you. Stella's practically the only friend I have left."

"If it's such a problem for you to be here, why don't you just leave?" His tone was very uneven, and she couldn't look at him as she said, "I don't want to leave." She stood up, took hold of his hand and pulled him off the sofa. "Let's eat before the meal gets cold, and then we can get down to serious business."

A delicious looking shrimp cocktail had been placed at each of their places on the table, and she expected that the chef had prepared something special for the main course. "This looks great," she said. "I'm starving."

As they sat down, Jake said, "Did you eat lunch with Stella?" He picked up the cocktail fork, speared one of the shrimp and then laid it on the plate.

She breathed deeply with the chance to get away from her lie and said, "No. I had one of Julio's big breakfasts. He loves to cook for me –"

"I'm not interested in your life with the queers."

"Jake, that's not very nice." She had intended to use her fallout with Henry that morning to address moving in with Jake – something that he had wanted her to do since the night of their reunion. But now, she must tread carefully and pick exactly the right moment to focus on her future with him. "I don't know what I would have done without those *queers* since I came back from Reno."

"For Chrissake, Hassie. You're a grown woman. Why don't you just move back in here with me? Or would that cramp your style too much?"

It was the perfect opportunity to open the conversation without having to tell him anything about her problems with Henry. It would leave him believing that he was in control – that it was his idea for her to move in with him and she could ease right past the false scenario that she had created when she arrived. She could get what she needed and appease Jake's concerns. But, instead, she thought about Frank and his invitation to see her again; his kindness and his concern for her relationship with a married man. Instead, she stood up to retrieve her drink from the coffee table and said, "We've been through this a hundred times."

Jake looked up at her. "Yeah. And I don't get it. You don't want to move in with me, but *you'll* decide when you want to sleep here and fuck my brains out – Miss I'm-a-star-at-the-Tropicana, maybe-you-can-have-a-piece-of-me Calhoun."

He pushed back from the table and walked over to the bar. Hassie was so shaken by the harshness of his tone, she was afraid to move and sat back down at the table. Her pulse raced as she recognized the abrupt change in his demeanor and she couldn't think what she should do. She had spotted a bottle of wine in the ice bucket earlier; the cork was loosely lodged in the top. She stood up slowly, walked over to the bar and softly asked, "Could I have some wine?" Jake removed the cork from the bottle and hesitated for a few seconds; she held her breath, imagining him losing control and hitting her again. He poured wine into a clean glass and returned the bottle to the bucket. She wanted to say something but decided against it, took the wine and went back to the table. When Jake returned to the table, she served the hot food, which he took one look at and pushed the plate away.

Without looking up, she said, "You didn't even taste the food."

"I'm not hungry," he said and pulled a cigarette from the pack.

She put down her fork and picked up her wine glass. "Can you at least *try* to understand why I am hesitant to live with you in this suite like we're an old married couple?" He puffed on the cigarette and didn't look at her. "Don't you even care that I don't really have a future as long as I'm with you and that my friends really hate this for me and just don't want me to get in so deep that I'll wake up one day and you'll be with your family and I'll be all alone?"

"That's the biggest pile of crap I've ever heard," he said and took a big swig from his glass. "You've got two fruits and an old hag telling you how to live your life and you're letting them." He set the glass on the table, looked directly at her and said, "What do you really want, Hassie? What's really important to *you*?"

She felt her throat tighten and for a moment she was afraid to try to speak. Henry's words ran through her mind: *"You want him to take some responsibility here, but he's not going to."* And Frank's *"... no matter how much you think he loves you."* She swallowed and gently said, "It kills me to think that you are – that you will never really be mine. That you belong to another woman and that you have a child who needs a father. Can't you see that I feel that I can never *really* be the woman in your life? "

Jake started to laugh and then looked at her and said, "Get out."

She could feel her face get hot and stared at him before saying, "What did you say?"

"I said get out." He stood up and picked up her purse, opened the door and threw it in the corridor. "You are a lying, conniving little cunt and I want you to get the fuck out of my life." Hassie stood up and moved toward the door as he shouted again, "Get out. Now!" Her legs shook and she thought she might collapse; the nubby scar over her eye throbbed and sent a shock through her nervous system. She made it outside the door and heard it slam behind her. She picked up her purse; the contents had scattered all over the corridor. Her head pounded as she gathered her belongings. She didn't want things to end this way, and, despite the fear of his deadly behavior, she realized that he had kept to his promise to never hit her again – that he had controlled himself and she wanted to calm him and assure him that she loved him and wanted him in her life.

She stood in front of his door and put her hand against the cold surface, then lightly knocked twice as she said, "Jake?" She knocked again, louder. "Jake? Please open the door and talk to me." She stood quietly, listening for his voice or some sign that he could hear her and was willing to let her back in. But, as she prepared to call out to him again, she was stopped cold by the unmistakable sound of dishes and glasses breaking as the room service trolley fell hard against the floor.

Without thinking, she pounded her fist on the door and shouted, "Jake, let me in. I'm not going away until you talk to me." She waited for what felt like several minutes for another sound or for the door to open and the opportunity to make everything right, but the door remained closed and the silence soon became his message: Go away and leave me alone. I'm finished with you.

Hassie stood next to the wall, gathering strength to make her way back toward the lobby. She moved slowly, her thoughts jumbled in her head and for a moment, the emotional pain of Jake's dismissal hurt much worse than the physical pain of his beating. How could he really have ever loved her as much as he claimed and be able to throw her out of his life so easily? He'd done it once before and, as her friends so loved to remind her, he'd intended to hurt her deeply. So what if he thought she deserved it? She'd been a fool to think that things could have ever been the same between them and, despite the sadness weighing on her heart, she'd never let him hurt her again.

She walked through the lobby toward the casino with no thought as to where she was actually going. It was moments like these that she felt the hateful impact of how she'd ruined things with her friends, and, despite everything Jake had told her about his flawed, dysfunctional relationship with Natalie, Hassie suddenly envied Natalie's imperfect life and could think of only one person who might be happy to see her.

It was the time between the close of the day's events and the beginning of the evening festivities when a mass of people went for a little action in the casino. Hassie kept her head down as she walked through and held her breath when she heard Eddie the pit boss's voice. She picked up her pace and moved through to the next building, past ten or twelve rooms, until she stood in front of a room marked "Triple Crown Suite." Her pulse raced, and she was slightly disgusted that she could so easily turn to Frank for consolation. She stood there, considered what she was doing, and then lightly knocked on the door.

When Frank opened the door, she walked in without looking at him. He touched her arm and said, "You're shaking. Are you okay?"

"He's a real bastard, Frank." She moved into his arms; he leaned back, looked into her face and said, "Did he hurt you again?"

She shook her head; he took her hand and led her to the sofa. Without asking, he gave her some vodka, then sat down in the armchair and lit a cigarette. He welcomed her into his life while everyone else pushed her away.

"Did I get you into trouble?" His eyes were sad and sincere.

She thought about Jake's reaction to the alcohol on her breath. "Maybe. He was fine when I first got to the suite, but then –" She stopped and thought about the point where things changed. "It was like someone flipped a switch and he turned into an evil – monster. Then he told me to get out."

He handed the cigarette to her. "What do you think happened? And why did you come to me?"

She thought of her lie about their drink together, then looked into his eyes and said, "I don't know." She took a deep drag on the cigarette and continued, "I just don't seem to be able to handle things well with him. And he doesn't really see the problem where Natalie is concerned. Like he's truly just written her out of his life, like she's dead or something. And he only has to think about her when he has to do something for the child."

Frank went over to the bar. Hassie watched him while he poured himself a drink, then joined her on the sofa and lit a cigarette.

"I'm gonna tell you a little something about men and their women." He laid the cigarette on the ashtray and then took a swig from the drink. "Not that I'm an expert or anything, but – well, I've done my time in relationship purgatory." He smiled, and she tried to relax, despite the fact that her friends being so right about Jake niggled her.

Frank paused like he was waiting for her to clear her thoughts, and then slowly exhaled as he said, "There's no doubt in my mind that Jake loved you. When you arrived at the Sands all sweet and innocent – not to mention sexy and gorgeous – he fell hard for you and you became the perfect woman for him. All the other women that had ever been part of his life, including Natalie, were nothing to him anymore. Unless they threw themselves at him at a weak moment when he was either pissed off at you about something or just felt like banging his fists on his big ape chest." He stopped and dragged on the cigarette. "Remember what I told you? Men are basically animals." He sipped the drink and continued, "Anyway, you were still the only woman Jake really wanted. Hell, I think he would have eventually married you, and he wasn't the marrying kind. Then, enter Frank Sinatra. And you weren't his sweet, innocent girl any more. Hey, don't get me wrong. It's not just because it was me. It could have been any man. And, after that, he could never see you or treat you the same way again. All of sudden, you were no better than any one of those other women who lined up for a piece of him."

"A *whore*," she said, almost inaudibly and felt like there was lead weight on her chest.

Frank stubbed out his cigarette and said, "And then you left him. You went off into another world with all kinds of other influences – other men and other experiences."

She wondered what Jake would actually do if he knew about her night with Mr. Satan.

"The sad part of all of this is that he really does love you and probably more than he ever thought he was capable of loving anyone. So, he's tortured by all that you represent now, and I'm sorry, doll, but you can't go back to the life that you remember when things were good between you and you believed that he was the only man in the world for you. That man doesn't exist anymore. You just can't go back."

Hassie's face streamed with tears and she ached from the inside out. "So why didn't he just tell me to stay the hell out of his life? Why did he beg me to come back to him? So that he could abuse me?"

Frank looked at her, his expression soft and sad, and said, "Like I've said before, you deserve better than this. And I'm truly sorry if I did anything to provoke him." He hugged her close to him. "I'd never forgive myself if he hurt you to get back at me. It's no secret that there's no love lost between me and him, but that's our problem."

She sat up and swallowed the last of her drink. "Can I ask you something?"

"Sure."

"Did Jake ever have a relationship with Ava?"

"Maybe," Frank said, his face revealing nothing. "I gave up trying to keep up with all of Ava's men – if I'm honest, I didn't have the stomach for it." He swigged back his drink and said, "Let's put it this way. If he did, I've tried to forget about it or else it would make me a pretty small person, wouldn't it? I'd never want to be accused of – what do they call it – tit for tat?" He laughed and went back to the bar, then returned with two fresh drinks.

Hassie suddenly felt like she was somewhere outside reality. If Henry's information was correct, she'd been a pawn in a childish game between Frank and Jake and, at that moment, she didn't know how she felt about either one them. She looked at Frank and said, "So you're saying that it's not true that you – pursued me – to get back at Jake for something that happened between him and Ava?"

"Who told you that?" Frank asked as he handed her the drink and sat down.

"It doesn't matter," she said and stared at him. "Is it true?"

"Regardless of what you've been told, and regardless of how I feel about Contrata, I would never do anything like that to you. And I'm sorry that you could think that I would."

She sipped the drink, unsure of what to think and then looked at him and said, "He knows I had a drink with you when I arrived tonight."

"So? You know he has a wife and kid. What's the big deal? You've got an – arrangement, as they say." He swirled the drink around his glass. "By the way, where are you staying while you're in town? I mean, I'm assuming you're not staying with Jake. At least, not now."

She pictured Jake's pained expression when he told her to leave; a reflection of the agony she'd caused by lying about her little rendezvous with Frank. But that still didn't give him the right to treat her like she'd committed an unpardonable sin and toss her aside like she'd never meant anything to him. Frank was reaching out to her, and with the thought that she had walked out on Henry that morning, she looked at him and said, "I seem to be doing a great job of alienating myself from everyone these days."

"What do you mean?"

"I've been staying with Henry and Julio, but they – like all my friends – have been opposed to my reunion with Jake." She stood up and walked away from the sofa. "And, hey, aren't they all the clever ones! Look at me. Jake threw me out of his life. Henry threw me out of his house, and now what?"

Frank walked over, touched her arm and said, "I won't throw you out." He swallowed the rest of his drink, and then said, "The gentleman in me wants to offer you one of the guest rooms, but the man in me who knows what it's like to be close to you wants to offer you my bed. With me in it, of course."

She smiled, dismissed thoughts of Jake, then looked at Frank and said, "You're right."

"About what?"

"I deserve better than Jake's treatment." She kissed him solidly on the lips.

"Then do you want to stay here tonight?"

She slowly nodded. "And I want the man. Not the gentleman."

chapter twenty-seven

CHASSIE WRAPPED HERSELF in Frank's thick terrycloth robe, then walked into the bedroom and surveyed the wreckage across the room – evidence of a passionate concurrence between two people in need of something out of the ordinary. So Frank had a couple of drinks too many. Maybe she shouldn't have brought up the issue of Jake and Ava, but then none of this was a real picnic for her either. Anyway, he wasn't bothered by it enough to let it interfere with making love to her last night. Or that morning, before he kissed her good-bye and left her for some kind of breakfast meeting.

She stood at the window and looked out into the desert morning. The weather was still warm enough to sunbathe and swim but a little too early in the day for a dip in Frank's private swimming pool. She was due back at La Chanson the next evening, so she had a little over twenty-four hours to decide what to do about her living arrangements. There was no doubt that she could take up residency at the Tropicana with a simple phone call to John Jacobson. But the thought of going back to an empty hotel room in the Tropicana at the end of every long day made her wish she'd been less brutal at Henry's attempt to talk sense into her, especially now, as she had to face the fact that living with Jake was no longer an option and that Henry and Julio – and Dotty – had been right to be concerned about her.

Why was she so determined to be right? Even now, as she stood in the empty living room of Frank Sinatra's suite, she couldn't bring herself to admit that she'd been wrong. She couldn't grovel and ask Henry to forgive her and let her stay on in their house. Stella lived in a small house outside the Sands now. Maybe she had some extra room. But should she first tell Stella that she'd involved her in her lie to Jake – just in case Jake decided that he did give a damn about her and checked out her story?

Hassie turned away from the window and looked around the spacious room. The suite was certainly big enough for two people to live quite comfortably and without getting in each other's way. Through her experience living with Jake, she knew that the housekeeping staff was quite sufficient for these spacious suites. But Frank obviously needed someone to follow along behind his path of destruction – dirty towels, dirty clothes, lots of used glasses and empty bottles. Maybe that's what he was used to, but she didn't recall ever seeing Jake's suite in such a state.

Regardless of the space and the need for a full-time housekeeper, would Frank feel threatened by her presence if she stayed for a while, or at least until she figured out what she wanted to do? She decided to think about it some more and picked up the telephone to order coffee, and then dressed in the clothes that she'd arrived in the night before. She had some extra clothes and makeup in her dressing room at the Tropicana, but, eventually, she would have to collect her things from Henry and Julio's house – unless she decided to swallow her pride and ask Henry to let her move back in.

She paced the floor, chewing her fingernails, and soon realized that she had no idea when Frank might return and decided that a rehearsal session with Julio and the band would help pass the time.

Hassie stood inside the entry door to the Copa Room, allowing her eyes to adjust to the low light, then glanced at Henry's office where the door was shut and there was no evidence that he was there. She heard voices from the greenroom behind the stage and moved closer through the maze of tables and chairs. Just as she started to call out for someone's attention, she heard a whoosh of movement behind her as Julio appeared by her side.

"Hey, chica" he said; his dark eyes sparkled. "I've been looking for you. We have work to do today."

She followed him onto the stage. "Really? What work?"

Julio sat down behind the piano. "Come on, Hassie. You know Clay's expecting you to do some recording while you're here. He called me about the progress yesterday and, frankly, I've run out of excuses for the delay."

"So, tell him I don't wanna do it," she said and dragged a chair over from the center of the stage.

"No. You tell him." Julio rolled some chords up and down the keyboard and avoided looking at her.

"Sounds like you've already decided that we're doing this today."

Julio nodded and said, "I think we should record 'I Just Can't Figure it Out.' You've been working on that one for so long, and everyone who's heard it thinks it's very good."

"Does that mean that the studio is booked and the musicians are waiting?"

He smiled his gorgeous smile and said, "Pretty much." He stopped playing and just looked at her.

Despite all the encouragement from her colleagues – including Clay – the music didn't seem to mean as much to her as it once did. Maybe spending time with Frank would inspire her to concentrate more on her performance and strive to make a name for herself with her own songs. But what if Frank didn't want to spend more time with her? And what if he did and she became "his girl"? Would she lose Jake for good? She looked at Julio and said, "I'm a bit of a wreck right now. I'm just not sure I'm up to working today."

"Okay, tell me what's going on. I know Henry gave you a hard time yesterday, but you know Henry. He's just worried about you."

"It's not just that," she said, took a cigarette from her purse and placed it between two fingers. "I've made such a mess of things, Julio. I can't go back to your house now."

"Don't be ridiculous," he said. "Do you need a light?"

She waved the cigarette in the air and said, "No. I really want to give up this nasty habit. Holding it makes me feel a little less nervous, I guess."

Julio smiled and continued, " Anyway, our house is your house. Things just need to cool off between you and Henry. I'm telling you, he was miserable last night. He walked around talking to himself like he's *loco en la cabeza.*" He made a funny face as he tapped his finger on his temple, then stood up and reached for her hand.

"I'm serious," Hassie said, suppressing a smile as she stood up. "I need some space right now, and I'm not sure what I want to do.

Maybe I'll ask Sid to let me have a room here in the Sands – at least until my contract at La Chanson finishes and I decide what to do next."

Julio put his arm around her and walked her down from the stage. "That sounds a little dangerous to me, and I don't even need to suggest what Henry would say." He stopped and took hold of her shoulders. "Personally, I liked having you at home. And I know Henry misses you. But do what you think is best for you. And do it quick so we can get on with the recording. I'll drive you over to the studio."

She let him hug her and then said, "I'll meet you in the lobby in about an hour."

Julio left her outside the Copa Room where she considered again what she'd been thinking and slowly made her way to the hotel lobby. Part of her didn't want to be alone at all, and Frank's company was always good for her. But the thought of never being with Jake again made her ache from deep within her core and her mind filled with the image of him taking hold of her when she arrived in his suite – grabbing her and clinging to her with that urgency that she craved. She tingled at the thought of his hands touching her all over and possessing her and making it impossible to get him out of her head. He'd thrown her out of his suite at the mere suspicion that she'd had a drink with Frank. If she moved in with Frank, Jake would never forgive her, and she couldn't risk losing another chance at their relationship – even if it took some time.

So the answer became clear: she would ask Sid about taking a room in the Sands for a couple of weeks. Even if she had to pay for it, it would be worth it to have her own space and to be free to deal with her own life. No doubt she could do the same at the Tropicana, in fact it would be free, but she couldn't help herself, it had to be the Sands. And Henry was so important to her – she knew he meant well – but she'd had enough of his nagging and felt that their relationship had a better chance of repairing itself if there was some distance between them for a while.

She felt lighter with having made this decision and picked up her pace as she headed for Sid's office. The lobby was full of people clustering to check out and get on their way. She dodged the bellmen and their trolleys of luggage and impatiently waited behind a group of people who insisted on exchanging syrupy good-byes in the middle of the floor. She released an exhausted sigh and started to excuse herself when she heard Jake's laugh and looked up just in time to see him standing inside the door, his hand resting on the shoulder of a large man wearing a black Stetson hat.

Hassie stood frozen, waiting to see which way Jake would move through the lobby, hoping to remain camouflaged in the middle of the heavy crowd. But the Texan moved aside like a sliding cupboard door, slowly revealing a woman whose arm hooked through Jake's. Hassie heard Natalie's voice before she saw her face – a much younger and more attractive appearance than she remembered. Natalie listened attentively as Jake finished his good-byes to the gentleman, then gazed at him lovingly while he steered her through the crowd, his hand resting firmly on her back.

Hassie turned her head away; the reality of what she had just witnessed a deep, debilitating ache that numbed the lower half of her body, and she couldn't move. Her blouse was soaked at her armpits and her cheeks burned. The crowd continued to buzz around her and she felt unbalanced or possibly caught in the slow circular current of water spiraling down a drain. A bellman asked if he could help her and she realized that she hadn't moved for several minutes. She smiled weakly and walked towards Sid's office, feeling numb and utterly lost in her actions. The image of Jake's face as he escorted Natalie through the lobby drove her inexplicably to seek a foothold in the Sands, whatever the cost.

Hassie said very little to Julio on the way over to the studio, which she hoped he interpreted as a slight case of nerves. When they arrived, Toots and Chad had joined the regular studio musicians and they were all seated and primed to run through Dan's arrangement. After they rehearsed the instrumental intro for a few minutes, she walked into the sound booth and sang through the song a couple of times. But she couldn't seem to focus on the music; she missed an entrance and forgot several of the lyrics. She purposely didn't look at Julio but could feel his eyes boring through her. Finally, he stood up from behind the keyboard and walked out of the room, and she was faced with the thought that she had screwed everything up. That Julio couldn't be bothered with an amateur and that he'd gone in to tell the sound crew to close up and go home.

Julio motioned for her to join him, spoke to the technicians in a low voice and then took her into the small canteen. "Can I get something for you – coffee, water, soda?"

She shook her head and said, "What's wrong, Julio?" then lit a cigarette and sat in a worn leather chair with a rickety metal base.

"I was going to ask you the same thing. Where's your head?"

She dragged on the cigarette and felt Jake kissing her neck, then closed her eyes and saw him walking away from her with Natalie.

"You love this song, don't you?" Julio said.

She nodded and swallowed. "I do."

"So what's the problem?" He walked over to the counter and poured coffee into a Styrofoam cup, sipped it and then threw it in the sink. "Disgusting," he said under his breath and filled a paper cup with water from the cooler. "Want some?"

She shook her head and dragged on the cigarette, still avoiding a direct answer to his question.

He wadded the cup in his hand and tossed it into the trash bin, then propped against the counter, crossed his arms over his chest and stared at her. "Performance on this level is a waste of time and money."

"Then let's not do it," she said. She heard the dry, lifeless tone of her voice, but it was the best she could do to disguise what she really felt.

Julio sat down in the chair in front of her. "I don't know what's going on here. You're better than this, Hassie. You've become such a pro. When you sing and your heart's really in it, you own that stage and you own the audience and now, you've gotta own this song. It's yours. You wrote it. It's your heart and soul. You can't just go through the motions and believe that people will just get it."

She pressed her lips together and stared at the ceiling. "I'm a fool, Julio. I'm drawn in the most reckless and harmful way to everything that's bad for me."

"I can't say that I agree with that statement, but I know what you mean." He stood up and walked back to the water cooler. "But, Hassie, you're giving us none of that reckless emotion out there."

"You don't know how I feel, Julio. You have no idea how much pain I'm in."

He handed her a cup of water. "All the more reason you should deliver the most gut-wrenching, chest-splayed-open performance of a lifetime. Right now? It's dead. Give me some of that emotion raging inside of you. Make me bleed with you. Make me wish it was me that you loved so much."

She dropped her chin to her chest and fought the lump in her throat. "He threw me out of his life."

Julio took hold of both of her hands, stayed silent for a long moment, then said, "I'm sorry, chica." He gazed at her, his brow tight and low. "That's *his* loss. But explain to me, how can you *not* feel that anger and pain with every note and every word you sing? You must use it, honey. You must rise above the disappointment and channel those emotions into a performance that's gonna make everyone understand what a good writer and performer you are. This is a huge opportunity. Don't screw it up with pride and self-pity."

They went back into the recording booth. As she put the headphones on, she knew that Julio was right. She was hurt that Jake had so easily turned to Natalie and she was angry that things hadn't gone the way she wanted. But, ultimately, she had the power to do exactly what Julio had advised. Barbara would be so pleased to know that this little musical exercise had turned into a song worthy of some of the best musicians in the country and now had a chance to be heard by people outside her own following at Felix's and La Chanson. She'd had tremendous support from so many people: Julio and all the guys in the Copa Room, including Frank; her friends – even Henry – Dan and the guys at La Chanson and, of course, Clay. He and Morty had seen her through the worst time in her life and Clay had stayed right beside her when she was irresponsible and impossible and had eventually landed her right where she needed to be.

The only person missing from this list of supporters was Jake. He'd never taken her musical aspirations very seriously – even after he heard her at La Chanson and saw the reaction from the audience. So why was he the single person to occupy her heart at this moment? Why, at the thought of him, did she have trouble breathing deep enough to saturate her lungs and supply the power that she needed to get through this session? She stood still for a moment longer, then took a deep breath and motioned to Julio that she was ready. He cued the musicians and then joined them at the keyboard for the intro. Her chest ached and she struggled to keep her emotions intact, but when Julio cued her for the vocals, she focused on the big microphone in front of her and began the song again.

Once you said you loved me, no matter what I'd say
Your arms held me close and tight
The time we spent together, enmeshed in every day,
Enraptured every night
For days and nights have passed, I fear
There isn't any doubt.
You left me brokenhearted, dear.
I just can't figure it out.

She took a breath for the next passage and felt the musicians stop playing just as Julio leapt in front of her. "I don't believe you!" He looked at her for a few seconds and then said, "You're brokenhearted? Really?"

She stared at him and bit her lip.

"Then I feel sorry you. Cuz if that's you brokenhearted, you've never really known what it means to lose someone you love. You've never really loved someone enough to have them break your heart."

She shook her head, then removed the earphones and started to walk away.

Julio grabbed her arm and said, "If you walk away now, you'll never do this again." He took a handkerchief from his pocket and handed it to her. "Come on, Hassie. You're giving me more right this minute than you have all afternoon. Okay, you're singing the notes beautifully, but make me believe what you're saying. Let me feel what you're *really* feeling."

She released a big sigh, laden with emotion and the urge to scream at everyone in the room.

"Come on. Do it!" Julio took a few step backwards and then cued the musicians while saying, "From the top."

Hassie wiped her face and blew her nose, then closed her eyes while the musicians played the intro. The saxophone melody was the doleful voice of pain. It consumed her; she ached and longed for the emotional release that she so desperately needed. The music swirled around her and the song took over; her voice delivering the message that was the essence of everything she felt.

Once you said you loved me, no matter what I'd say
Your arms held me close and tight
The time we spent together, enmeshed in every day,
Enraptured every night
For days and nights have passed, I fear
There isn't any doubt.
You left me broken-hearted, dear.
I just can't figure it out.

Then I knew I loved you, no matter what you said
Your eyes gave me reason to live
I only wish you'd told me before I lost my head
Your heart wasn't yours to give
And now I sometimes shed a tear for us,
There is no doubt
You left me brokenhearted, dear
I just can't figure it out.

Late at night I dream of you, my heart so deep in strife
When darkness takes the shape of truth, I see my empty life.

Why'd you make me love you, no matter what I said?
Why did you steal my heart?
You said you'd never hurt me; those words now lost or dead
Now we're forever apart.
For once our love was strong and clear
Of that there is no doubt
You left me brokenhearted, dear
I just can't figure it out.

When the light went off to say that they were off tape, she stood motionless. The musicians whistled and Chad lightly beat his hand on his double bass. Julio walked out from behind the keyboard and grabbed his chest. She stood in the same spot with both hands over her mouth and then let out a cry that sounded strange to her. But Julio knew exactly what she meant and took her in his arms while she let go of the pain, sobbing and clinging to him for support to stay upright. He remained still and quiet, and she knew that he would never let go if she didn't want him to. The love in this moment was something that she would never forget.

Julio sent someone to get water for her and sat her down while he went into the control room. She sipped the water and waited for her breathing and heartbeat to return to normal. She heard Julio's voice through the speakers followed by the playback of the lush musical intro then the sound of her voice full of pain and sorrow. The playback provided her with the catharsis that she needed; her tears were ones of joy and thanks for the wonderful musicians that helped bring her song to life. She smiled at Toots and said, "The song wouldn't be the same without you."

"Hey, baby doll, you wrote it," Toots said. "And Dan's arrangement is perfection."

Julio busied himself with the sound guys for a while longer. Hassie stuck her head in the control room and said, "Are we gonna do it again?" She'd been so busy with her own emotions, she'd failed to notice the dark-haired man sitting in the corner of the sound booth. When she looked over and caught his eye, he stood up and shoved his hands in his pockets.

"Dan," she said softly. "I didn't know you were here."

"You were great, Hassie," he said. "How come you never sang that song like that when I played for you?"

She walked over to him and put her hand on his arm. "Your arrangement is so brilliant, but I don't think I've ever really understood that song until today."

Dan laughed softly. "That's funny. You wrote the damn thing," he said and she sensed that he knew that someone else was her emotional inspiration.

Julio clapped his hands together and said, "Okay. We've got some mixing to do and may need a couple of the musicians again, but the vocals were great. You can all go for now.

Hassie walked out with Dan and promised a repeat performance of the song in her show later that week. She watched as the technicians locked up their equipment and said good night. The musicians disappeared one by one until Hassie and Julio were alone in the canteen.

She poured a shot of Jim Beam into two Dixie cups and handed one to Julio as he flopped in the rickety leather chair.

She relaxed on the sofa next to him and said, "Thank you, Julio."

"As we say where I come from – *de nada*. I knew you could do it, and now we've gotta get that same level of performance into one or two more of your other songs and Clay should be beyond thrilled."

She sat pensively for a moment before saying, "I owe him a lot."

"Who? Clay?"

She nodded and lit a cigarette. "If it wasn't for him, I wouldn't be here right now. I wouldn't be working in La Chanson and I wouldn't be recording my song."

"And if it wasn't for Dan's arrangement, that song wouldn't be as good as it is now."

She felt her cheeks warm and didn't want to look at him. "I never meant to imply that Dan's arrangement was better than yours."

Julio chuckled and said, "But, chica, it is better. And you made the right, professional choice when you opted to work with his. Even if I did think that you liked his arrangement better because you had a little thing for him at one time."

"Was it that obvious to you guys?"

He nodded and smiled. "So, what happened? Why did you end up hurting him?"

Her expression turned serious as she thought about what had happened. "I never meant to hurt him. The timing was off, I suppose."

"When has the timing ever been right where Jake was concerned?"

She dragged on the cigarette before saying, "Don't start. It's Henry's job to nag me about Jake."

Julio jumped up. "Speaking of Henry, I'd better give him a call." He walked over to the telephone, picked up the receiver and then looked back at her and said, "Why don't you call Clay and tell him about the recording?"

She smiled and nodded and then ducked out to the toilet. When she came back, Julio had closed up the other rooms and shut off the lights. When he saw her, he grabbed her arm and said, "Come on. You're going home with me."

She resisted his grasp and said, "I don't think I'm up for another confrontation with Henry."

"You two are gonna patch things up." He closed the door behind them and steered her to his car.

They arrived back at the house; the gravel in the driveway

crunched beneath the tires. A large maroon sedan sat next to the curb in front of the house.

"Looks like you have company," Hassie said as Henry stuck his head out the door and manically waved for them to come inside.

"I don't know what else he thinks we're gonna do," Julio said. "Let's sit here for a few minutes and drive him mad."

Hassie laughed and stepped out of the car. Henry held the door open as they entered, then took hold of Hassie's arm, pulling her close to hug her. She looked at him and smiled, but when she started to speak, Henry pointed her to the sofa, where John Jacobson stood up and reached out to greet her.

"Hello, John," Hassie said. "What are you doing here?" She looked back at Julio, who shrugged his shoulders and then led her over to the sofa.

Henry handed Hassie a martini with three olives skewered on a toothpick.

She took the drink and sat down, then looked expectantly at John, who sat down beside her and said, "Hassie, I know that we've already had a preliminary discussion about your contract and our intention to honor the thirty-day renewal clause." He hesitated and she nodded. "It is with great pleasure that I am here tonight to offer you a completely new contract which picks up that thirty-day renewal and extends the total contract for six months."

Hassie sipped her drink, then smiled at John and said, "That's great."

"That's great?" Henry said. "That's all you have to say?"

"Let it sink in for a minute," Julio said, then turned to Hassie and said, "You do know what this means, chica? You'll be working in Vegas for six more months!"

Hassie looked at John and stuck out her hand. "Thank you very much, but I need to think about this and speak to my agent."

"Of course," John said, shaking her hand. "We've sent the new contract to Clay's office. He should have received it today."

"Hassie was just saying that she needs to speak with Clay," Julio said and winked at her.

John finished his drink, set the glass on the table and said, "Well, I've delivered the message and will leave you to get back to us." He took hold of her hand again. "I would just like to offer a personal note. You have brought a level of talent and sophistication to La

Chanson that we've never known and, believe it or not, you have a lot of fans."

Hassie smiled and said, "Thanks, John. You'll have an answer before the end of the week."

John stood up and Julio showed him to the door; Henry took their glasses to the kitchen. Hassie reflected on the conversation for a few minutes until Julio sat down in the chair beside her and said, "It's time to make that call."

She stood up and said, "It's past office hours."

Julio gave her a sideways glance and said, "Come on, chica. You don't have a home number for Clay?"

"Okay, okay," she said, and picked up the contract and walked over to the phone sitting on the sideboard. Clay answered on the third ring and she was immediately comforted by the sound of his voice. "Hi, it's me."

"I thought I might be hearing from you tonight." She could hear no emotion in his tone.

"So you know about the new contract?"

He hesitated for a few seconds and then continued, "Yep. I've already sent a copy over to Morty."

She knew that there was something more that he wasn't saying. "And what do you think?" she asked.

"I think you should do what you want to do. They're offering to pay you like you're a superstar. My guess is that they want to make sure you won't be tempted to go over to any of the competition."

"Really?" she said and thumbed through the document. "What's the catch?"

He took a deep breath before saying, "The terms are murder. You belong to them for six months and, short of dying, you can't get out of the contract."

"Isn't that a little unusual?"

"In the real world, maybe. But in Vegas, where there are lots of outside influences with most everything that happens, it's probably normal."

She'd been in Vegas long enough to know what he meant but couldn't believe that she was important enough to anyone to – Her pulse quickened and she pulled the phone over to the dinette table and sat down. "Clay, does this have anything to do with Jake?"

Henry reappeared at the mention of Jake's name.

"I can honestly say that this has nothing to do with Jake." Clay said.

"Then who's the *outside influence*?" She held her glass up to Henry for a refill.

Clay was silent for a few seconds, and then she heard him sigh before he said, "Isn't it enough for you to know that you are successful?"

"I don't like the thought that I *belong* to anyone," she said evenly.

Clay laughed softly and said, "Welcome to the big time. You'll never be your own person again. And, by the way, we miss you around here so if you're not sure about this, you can always come back to Reno."

For a brief moment, Clay's voice took her back to Reno and to life in a different world where most things made sense and someone was either protecting her or seducing her, but no one tried to own her. "Thanks, Clay. I miss you guys, too. But I think I'm gonna stick it out here for a while longer."

"Does that mean you want to sign the new contract?"

She hesitated for a few seconds before saying, "I don't see any other offers on the table. Do you?"

"You can always go back to Felix's," he said; she could feel him smiling.

"You know, I recorded one of my songs today, and Julio thinks you'll be pleased." Henry delivered another drink to her, then blew her a kiss and left the room.

"That's great. Can't wait to hear it."

"Hey, I have a good idea," she said. "Why don't you and Morty come here for the contract renewal. Spend a couple of days and meet all the guys."

"I think I already know all the guys," he said.

"Then come see my show. I'll wear the red dress you bought for me."

"I'll think about it and discuss it with Morty." He hesitated then took a deep breath. "Are you sure you want to sign this contract?"

"Pretty sure," she said. "Talk to Morty and call me tomorrow."

chapter twenty-eight

DESPITE NOT headlining on a main stage, the new contract would help make Hassie Calhoun a household name in Vegas. Morty had been unable to get away from Reno and handled the contract negotiations by telephone, promising that he would bring the missus down to see Hassie's show at the first available date. Clay spoke to her every day for a week or so until everything was resolved, but never really offered a reason as to why he couldn't make the trip. She decided not to push him further, other than saying that she would always love to see him.

It had been a long time now since Barbara had convinced her that her simple melody could be the basis of a song for the heartfelt poem that she had written for her father, which ultimately spoke so directly about love and loss. For the first time in a while, she needed to speak with Barbara and attempted on several occasions to reach her by phone. She couldn't believe that Barbara would ever leave her home in Angus. But when there was no answer for a couple of weeks, Hassie considered the fact that Barbara might have moved or, worse, that something had happened to her and Hassie might have to contact her mother to get an answer.

Dan included her song in every show, and the response from the audience had left her feeling like the star that she had always dreamed of becoming. Now it was happening and John Jacobson was right – she had real fans and they liked her.

No drink or drug, she felt sure, could leave her feeling as high as her reception at La Chanson that night. Frank had quietly snuck into her first show and then surprised her in her dressing room with a beautiful bouquet of flowers. He had showered her with compliments and sat with her during the break between shows, admitting that he would much rather stay and listen to her again than go back to his own show in the Copa Room.

She'd actually made the right decision when she chose living on her own over pursuing such an arrangement with Frank, and their relationship had continued casually as she gradually let go of Jake and let herself enjoy the time with Frank. He had sought her out on her nights off, inviting her to join him for a late supper or drinks after his show. When they met people who were mere acquaintances of his, he would introduce her as a star attraction at the Tropicana and treat her like she was just as big a name as Peggy Lee or Rosemary Clooney. But when they were alone or in the company of Dean or Sammy or any of the other musicians, he would refer to her as his lady, and she sometimes felt that he could be falling for her. Frank Sinatra, who was once married to Ava Gardner, and the man whom just about any woman in the country would pay gold to be so close to. Could he really ever love Hassie Calhoun from Corsicana, Texas? She had a sudden urge to see him, and left the Tropicana for the Sands, hoping to catch the end of his late show.

The doorman held her flowers while she climbed into a taxi, then handed them to her and said, "Looks like you've got quite an admirer there."

She smiled and looked at the bouquet of deep red roses interspersed with sprigs of white baby's breath and green leaves, the stems bound together with a wide, red satin ribbon. The beautiful flowers made her think of the time before her father went to Korea, when he would bring a box of long-stemmed red roses to her mother on Valentine's Day. While Bonita placed the flowers in a vase, Jackson would take Hassie aside and give her a beautiful doll mounted on a heart-shaped box full of chocolates. She breathed in the luscious aroma of the bouquet in her lap and wondered if Frank had meant for the red roses to send a message of love.

Frank had suggested she attend his show after she finished at La Chanson, and mentioned that Sid would be expecting her to sit at his table. When she opened the door to the Copa Room, Frank was singing "Fly Me to the Moon." A sharp tingle coursed through her body. The room was full and she could feel that special something in the air that she had come to recognize when the audience was particularly responsive. Frank must be used to that feeling after all these years, but she wondered if one could ever tire of adoring audiences, cheering and begging for more.

Hassie stood next to the bar; there was a sense of life breathing from within the shadows. At the end of Frank's number, she asked the bartender to put her flowers in some water and look after them until the show was over. She looked around for Henry and, out of habit, glanced at Jake's table and immediately recognized his profile and the dim reflection of Natalie's shiny, auburn hair. It had been weeks since she'd seen either of them anywhere in the Sands.

She spotted the empty seat at Sid's table. In any other circumstances, she would have remained at the bar before sitting down with Sid. Ever since the afternoon that she'd asked him to help her with interim living arrangements, he'd behaved a little differently toward her, especially after it became obvious that she was no longer involved with Jake and was possibly fair game for other men. Hassie had sensed this in their initial conversation and quickly interjected that she expected to pay for the room. As she glared at the back of his large balding head, she recalled the scene that all but haunted her now where he pulled her close to him and said, "Don't worry about it, doll. Let's just say that you owe me. And one day, I'll collect."

She had accepted his comments as harmless and coyly replied, "Only if I let you, big Sid." But deep down, she knew that he was much too powerful for her to tell him that she would call the shots. She also knew that Sid and his wife had divorced while she was in Reno, and that for a reason she couldn't fathom, he considered himself to be a "whale of a catch for some beautiful doll."

Hassie shuddered at the thought, breathed deeply and walked down to Sid's table. He motioned for her to sit and signalled for the cocktail waitress, then studied her before leaning over to speak to the man sitting to his left. Hassie focused on the stage as Frank removed his bow tie and took a swig of his drink. She took a cigarette from her purse and put it between her lips. Before she could reach for her lighter, a hand came out of nowhere and lit it for her; she never saw the gentleman's face. The band played the next intro while Frank settled in on his stool. The lights dimmed and he explained that his next song was his latest recording and launched into a powerful rendition of Sammy Cahn's "Please Be Kind."

This is my first affair – please be kind
Handle my heart with care – please be kind

She felt the lyrics like a knife in her chest; her proximity to Jake was more than she could bear and her eyes filled with tears by the end of the song. She dug around her purse for something to blot her makeup with and then heard Frank say her name. She looked up and into his eyes as he said, "I just realized that we have a very special person in the house tonight, sitting right here at the boss's table. George, bring up the lights." He walked to the edge of the stage and pointed down to their table. "Hassie, please stand up. This audience needs to get a good look at you."

Hassie felt hundreds of eyes on her and slowly stood, offering a tentative wave to the people within her sight line, thankful that the light blurred her vision as she looked directly at Jake's table.

"Ladies and gentlemen, I'd like to introduce you to Miss Hassie Calhoun, the next great singer in Las Vegas." A mild applause erupted and Frank continued, "Actually, she's probably too good for Vegas." He laughed and she waved to him as she sat down. "But if you wanna have a great night of music in the presence of one of the most beautiful women in the world, catch Hassie's show over at La Chanson in the Tropicana." He chuckled and said, "I'm not her agent so I don't have her schedule, but take my word here. It's damn well worth your effort."

Hassie took a big sip of her drink, revelling in the moment while Frank motioned for the lights to be lowered and the band started playing his closing number. He crooned through "All the Way," said his very appreciative goodnights and left the stage while the band played him out.

Hassie stood up to look for Henry, well aware that the focus of the room was now on her, and hoped that Jake and Natalie would have left as soon as the show ended. Sid walked over to her and grinned before saying, "I didn't know we were in the presence of royalty tonight."

"Right, Sid," she said. "Just call me Princess Grace." She spotted Henry walking across the back of the room and waved him over to the table.

"I think Frank's got a thing for you," Sid said. He puffed on his cigar and glanced over at the bar.

"We're just friends," she replied. "And what can it hurt for him to endorse my show?"

Henry arrived at the table and nodded at Sid before saying to Hassie, "Julio is finishing up now. I think we're gonna call it a night."

"What's the big rush, Berman?" Sid said. "Miss Hassie needs another drink, don't ya, doll?"

Before she said anything to either man, she saw Dotty and Jimmy coming toward her. She was relieved that Dotty was speaking to her again and hugged her while she asked Jimmy if he was ever going to get around to seeing her show, then she heard Frank's voice and turned to see him standing at the next table. He looked at her and winked; she turned back to Henry and said, "I'm gonna have a drink with Frank. Why don't you guys stay and join us?"

Before Henry responded, Frank walked up behind Hassie and put his arm around her waist. "How is everyone tonight?" he said to no one in particular. "Did you enjoy the show?"

The small crowd nodded. Henry said, "Of course, we did," and then waved at Julio to join them. Sid grinned at Frank, winked at Hassie and left the room.

Hassie moved slowly toward the bar while speaking to Frank, "That was a very nice thing you said."

"I didn't say anything that wasn't true. You were dynamite in that lounge tonight, and you are a fantastic singer-songwriter."

"Thanks, Frank. You don't know how much that means to me."

They joined the others at the bar. Frank leaned closer to her, kissed her neck and then said, "Talk is cheap. Why don't you show me?"

Hassie smiled, but before she had time to respond, the crash of glass breaking at the end of the bar preceded Jake's appearance from out of the shadows. Jimmy rushed toward him, but when he started to speak, Jake pushed Jimmy out of his way and glared at him like he was a dead man if he said a word. Jake stood in front of Hassie and Frank for a few seconds, tense with anger and breathing heavily, obviously struggling to contain himself.

Frank looked at him and grinned, "What's going on here, Contrata? We were just gonna to have a drink." Frank gestured toward

Hassie, but before he said anything more, Jake stepped closer to him and punched him square in the left side of his face.

As Frank fell backwards, two men showed up to help him regain his balance, but Frank struggled from their grip and leapt at Jake. Jimmy grabbed Frank's arm before he could swing at Jake; the two men took hold of him and ushered him away from the room while Jimmy turned back toward Jake, who had already caught Hassie around her throat. Henry shouted to Julio for help and then took hold of Hassie's arm and tried to pull Jake's hand off her throat. Jimmy grabbed Jake's shoulders from behind and shouted, "What the hell's wrong with you, man? You're hurting her! Stop!"

Jimmy tugged at Jake until he finally let go of Hassie and took a swing at Henry, knocking him into a table and chairs. Jake lost his balance and stumbled into Hassie, who screamed and pushed him away; she couldn't recognize this madman whom she thought she had loved. Henry stood up and glared at Jake, but when Jake leapt at him again, Julio interceded and pushed Jake back just hard enough to throw him off balance, then grabbed him and pulled him to his feet, swinging his fist at Jake's head.

"Get outta my way, you goddamn wetback," Jake screamed and pushed Julio away. When Julio came at him again, Jake regained his footing and, from his solid stance, punched him with such force that his feet appeared to leave the ground, his head crashing against the nearest tabletop before he landed on the floor.

Hassie, Henry and Dotty ran to help Julio, who lay crumpled and crooked like a broken doll. Jimmy was finally able to get hold of Jake and pulled him away while Henry leaned over Julio.

Henry slapped Julio's face and shouted, " Wake up, Julio. Wake up! Somebody help!"

"He needs a doctor," Hassie shouted. "Julio's really hurt. Please. Call an ambulance." She looked in the direction that Jimmy had taken Jake and saw Jimmy pushing him out the door, then looked around for Frank, who'd been rescued by his men. Damn Jake Contrata! Only minutes before, it had been such a great night. Now she just felt numb as people stood by, shaking their heads, men shielding the women as they buried their faces in the men's shoulders or covered their mouths in disbelief.

Dotty got Jimmy's coat, folded it a couple of times and placed it under Julio's head. Hassie knelt down beside Henry and saw tears rolling down his face. She put her arm around him and said, "It's gonna be okay, Henry. The ambulance will be here soon and he'll be fine."

"He doesn't look fine," Henry said; Hassie knew he was right.

Hassie jumped up as Donnie and one of his patrolmen entered the room. She ran to meet him and said, "Donnie, where's the ambulance? Julio needs to go to the hospital."

Donnie said something to the other policeman and then rushed over to where Julio lay. He knelt down and felt his pulse, then looked at Henry and said, "He's out cold but he's gonna be okay. An ambulance just arrived. There's the stretcher so just keep calm."

Hassie asked Dotty to stay close to Henry while she went to get water. As she walked back toward the bar, she became aware of how many people had been involved in the destruction that Jake had caused with no apparent concern for who he hurt or how much he hurt them, except for Natalie, whom he'd evidently sent away before he'd gone completely mad and punched Frank in the face.

She wished that Frank would walk back through the door and that Julio would get up from the floor and chastise Henry for fussing over him, and they would all laugh and have a drink and forget that they ever knew Jake Contrata. But an ambulance took Julio away and Frank was nowhere to be seen and all that remained was the evidence of a melee that she could never have imagined – broken glass, damaged furniture, spatters of blood and a bouquet of flowers that had been torn to shreds.

chapter twenty-nine

For eighteen days, Julio lay unconscious within the gray-green walls of his room in Sunrise Hospital. On this day, Hassie arrived to find Henry sitting by Julio's side, amid his daily routine of relating the news from the neighbors or telling him about the arrival of the new Sears catalog or the zany details from a recent episode of the *Dick Van Dyke Show*. Henry would also fill him in on what was happening in the Copa Room, relaying everyone's best regards and assuring him that he could never be replaced.

Julio lay in a mummy-like trance; the image accentuated by the layers of white gauze encircling his head. Hassie ached at the sight of Henry in so much pain, but nothing she said or did could get him out of that room during visiting hours. In her mind, she was the family that Henry didn't seem to have, and he needed her support just as much as Julio needed his. Nothing in her life was more important than being there for both of them.

Dotty came by to visit most days, loaded with sandwiches, slices of cake and thermoses of coffee, which, to Hassie, felt a little too much like her own hospital stay – the handiwork of the same man, whom no one had seen again since that night in the Copa Room. Hassie had tried to get information from Donnie when he visited Julio just after the incident, but he told her that he wasn't free to discuss the details of the investigation and that, basically, she should just stay out of it.

She had maintained regular communication with Clay Cooper after Julio's first couple of days in the hospital and the reality of his condition sunk in. She tried to get Clay to find out what had happened to Jake but he refused, saying that it was none of his business and that, once and for all, she should forget about Jake, get her emotions in order and go back to work as soon as possible. But she knew that Clay was genuinely concerned about Julio as well when a nice dish of leafy green plants was delivered with a get-well message in Clay's own words.

Stepping into the room, Hassie coughed and said, "Knock, knock."

Henry took hold of her hand and said, "Hi, honey. I think he looks better today, don't you?"

Hassie looked at Julio's pale, sunken face and fought back the urge to cry, then sniffed and nodded and said, "Yeah, he does."

She pulled a chair over to the bed and sat beside Henry. "You know, I was thinking last night about Julio's birthday."

"What about it?" Henry said like he knew what she was going to say. "It's not for a few more weeks."

"I know. But I was thinking that it might be good if we have a little party for him soon – a festive atmosphere would be great for everyone, including Julio, don't you think?"

Henry took hold of Julio's hand before looking at Hassie, "Do you think it will cheer him up to know that we're celebrating his birthday early? Like, in case he *dies* before the actual day?"

Hassie stood up and put her arm around Henry's shoulder, her eyes filling with tears as she said, "I don't mean to upset you, Henry."

He removed her arm from his shoulder and said, "Then why would you suggest such a thing? You know, he shouldn't even be laying in this godforsaken place."

This was not the first time that Henry had made such a remark – one that she couldn't help but take personally. She swallowed and continued, "The doctor says that head injuries like his are very difficult to survive."

Henry stood up from the bed and walked over to the window. Hassie followed him and stood beside him as he said, "So you think we should all just give up?"

"That's not what I'm saying," she said softly. "Let's just have a party to celebrate his life."

Henry turned to face her, tears streaming from his eyes, and said, "What if he doesn't make it?"

"Don't give up, Henry," she said and held him close. "Don't let go."

Hassie discussed the idea of the party with Dotty, who immediately took charge, and within a few days, the entire hospital had been convinced to cooperate with their plans. Julio's room was transformed into a balloon and crepe paper fiesta with a huge banner across the wall behind his bed spelling out "Happy Birthday, Julio" in bright blue and orange letters.

"Dotty, this looks wonderful," Hassie said as she peered into the box containing a large cake with chocolate icing and big yellow flowers with bright green leaves in the upper left-hand corner. White icing simply spelled out, "We love you."

"Thank you for handling all these details," Hassie said. "I know this was my big idea but I don't know how I would have done it all while trying to be here with Henry as much as I could. You know, if the hospital would let him, Henry would never leave Julio's side. He doesn't want him to wake up and be in the room all alone."

Dotty took hold of Hassie and pulled her over to two chairs near the window. "Sit down for a minute." Hassie fumbled with her skirt pocket like she was looking for cigarettes, then focused on Dotty as she said, "What are you doing with yourself when you're not here holding Henry's hand?"

"What are you asking me, Dotty?"

"It's just that I know what visitin' hours in the hospital are and, well, you're not livin' with Henry right now so I hope you're doin' what's best for you too."

Hassie leaned forward and lowered her voice to say, "If you're going to lecture me about La Chanson, don't. I told John and Dan that I would be back as soon as Julio is out of the woods. He's gotta get better soon, right?"

Dotty nodded slowly and said, "What did Jacobson say?"

"Not a lot. At first, he was very concerned about Julio and said that they had a list of substitute acts to call on. I haven't spoken with him again so everything must be under control."

"You need to talk to him, Hassie. You're not Jake Contrata's girlfriend at the Sands where you're untouchable and you can do anything you like. This is your career, and I think you're makin' a big mistake if you say to hell with your contract."

Hassie stood up and spoke close to Dotty's face, "I am not leaving Henry to deal with this on his own. A job is a job. Henry and Julio are my family."

"What are you two so serious about over there?" Henry said as he moved closer.

Dotty reached for Henry's hand and said, "Miss Hassie, here, has been shirkin' her responsibility to La Chanson for the past few weeks. Maybe you can talk some sense into her."

Hassie wouldn't look at Henry and glared at Dotty as Henry moved close enough to speak to her out of Julio's earshot. "What does she mean?"

Hassie stood up and moved away from him toward the window. Henry followed close behind and said, "You haven't been going to work? Are you crazy? And how do you think that would make Julio feel, after everything he's done for you?"

Dotty walked over to them and, in a loud whisper, said, "You two take this out in the hallway. There's enough negative energy in this room to start a war."

Hassie followed Henry out into the corridor, grabbed his arm and said, "I've been too upset to work, Henry. I hate seeing Julio like this and I don't like leaving you alone."

"That's all well and good, but we all have to keep going. You can't let this affect your life and your career. I don't understand you."

She let go of his arm. "You think that it's my fault that Julio's laying in that bed."

Henry stood still, taking short, shallow breaths.

"Admit it, Henry." She waited and glared at him. "Admit that you think that it's my fault that Julio's laying in that bed. You've said it more than once and I know you believe it. How do you think I feel? How am I supposed to stand on that stage every night and sing about love and starry nights and flowers? The thought of being there in front of all those drunk, happy people while Julio hangs on here for his life makes me want to vomit. How do you think I can sing?"

"Maybe it's the vodka that's making you sick. Did you ever think about that?"

She wanted to leap at him; her knees started to shake. "How dare you! Who do you think would sit here with Julio while you take care of the rest of your life?"

"That's my point," he said calmly. "I *am* taking care of the rest of my life, and so should you. Don't you ever use Julio's illness as an excuse to deal – or should I say, *not* deal with your own problems." He turned away from her and spotted Jimmy coming toward them with Toots and Chad.

"I ran into these two characters on my way up so now the party can begin," Jimmy said.

Hassie wiped her eyes and forced a smile as she hugged Toots. "It's so good that you guys are here," she said and took hold of Chad's hand.

Toots put his arm around Hassie and said, "Is Frank here yet? He said he'd try to make it by."

Hassie smiled and shook her head, "Haven't seen him yet. Let's go get this party started."

They stood at the foot of Julio's bed. "Leave it to Julio to find the most unusual place for a party," Toots said and released his basso laugh, then looked at Henry and said, "How ya holdin' up?"

"Pretty good," Henry said and smiled the first real smile Hassie had seen in days. "Anyway, he'll kick my ass if he wakes up and finds me acting like an old girl."

"Careful, now," Dotty said as she passed around the cups of punch. "This *old* girl is puttin' on this party."

Jimmy put his arm around Dotty and said, "Hell, woman. You're not old." He nudged his head against hers. "I plan on havin' you around for a long time."

Dotty pushed him away and said, "Stop droolin' on me."

Hassie stood by Julio's side and witnessed the gathering of friends, laughing and joking like it was just another day. She leaned down to where her lips were right next to his ear and whispered, "My darling Julio, I hope you can feel how much we all love you. Please come back to us. You mean so much to me." She kissed his forehead and squeezed his hand, then looked across the room into Henry's face and felt what she could only imagine was her heart breaking; pain and emptiness accompanied by excruciating sadness.

As Julio continued to hold on to his fragile existence, Hassie convinced Henry that he should encourage Julio's family to come for a visit. She knew that Henry had avoided the issue because he'd always been weak when it came to dealing publicly with his and Julio's relationship. But they both knew how Julio felt about his family, and Hassie believed that surrounding him with all the people who loved him would strengthen his will to survive.

Julio's mother and brother arrived a week after the birthday party and Hassie assumed the role of best friend; Henry was a colleague. But Mrs. Villanueva was a wise old woman, and Hassie sensed from the moment the two of them arrived that his mother didn't buy the charade. She watched Henry as they carefully communicated in broken English laced with Spanish, sharing stories of Julio's life as a boy through to his determination to be a musical sensation in America. Mrs. Villanueva said very little and appeared as the strong support for Julio's brother, Enrique, as he grew increasingly distraught with the prospect that he might never see his older brother again. The next day, as they said their good-byes, Mrs. Villanueva hugged Henry and said, "Thank you for loving my Julio."

The following morning, Hassie arrived just as the doctor left the room; Henry sat beside the bed, holding Julio's hand and speaking softly to him. She stood on the opposite side of the bed and stared into Julio's face as she took hold of his other hand, which was colder than she remembered, like life was slipping away through his fingertips. When she looked at him, she saw the gorgeous, caring man that had given her so much and that she had grown to love like her own flesh and blood.

"What did the doctor say?" she asked.

Henry shrugged and said nothing. Hassie felt an emotional breakdown brewing and walked over to the window. She could see the strip of hotels, and imagined where the Sands was set among them. Jake was out there somewhere like a fugitive, an exile. What would she do if he were to walk into the room and tell Julio that he was sorry – admit that he was a beast and that he never meant to hurt him? Her nerves rattled at the thought and she wanted a drink to calm herself and to clear Jake out of her head.

"What's happening to him?" Henry asked. "Why's he shivering like that?"

Hassie rushed back from the window and looked into Julio's face. "His eyes are opening," she said.

Henry moved in close to her, their hurtful exchange of words momentarily forgotten. He grabbed Julio's hand and said, "Wake up, Julio. It's Henry. And Hassie. We're here. Can you hear me?"

Julio's eyes opened slightly, his body continued to shake and a faint gurgling sound came from the back of his throat.

A shock ran through Hassie's body. "I'm getting a nurse," she said and ran into the corridor, then returned with the kind, old sister who'd been looking after Julio since the day he arrived.

"What's going on here, Julio?" the sister said and pushed Henry away. She leaned in closer to him and said, "He's having a seizure. We need the doctor. Don't touch him."

She left the room, and Hassie and Henry stood quietly beside the bed, their fingers interlocked; Hassie felt an occasional squeeze. The doctor came back in, carefully attended to Julio for a minute or so, then placed his stethoscope around his neck and said, "I'm sorry."

Hassie stood still, shaking her head and silently repeated over and over, "I'm so sorry, I'm so sorry, I'm so . . ." She felt that hollow, dark place in her chest that she had first experienced when her father died. The moment when she imagined winding back the clock and living the terrible incident all over again but, this time, with a different ending – one where she was able to save him. She looked at Henry and quietly said, "This was all my fault."

There was never any question that the Copa Room would be the site for a memorial tribute to Julio's life. Friends and loyal supporters filed in, one by one. Some gathered around the bar, some around the stage where there was an open invitation to join the jam session being led by Toots. The piano seat remained vacant; Henry's favorite photograph of Julio rested on the piano's closed lid.

Hassie was thankful that Sid took charge of the event; she'd never have found the strength. But she was one of the first to arrive and, armed with vodka, kept to herself as much as possible. She wondered if Jake knew of Julio's death. Maybe Jake hadn't meant to hurt him and certainly not to kill him, but would he have the nerve to show up for his memorial? Despite the thought that Jake didn't belong in that room, she found herself watching the door. Maybe he would stop by to pay his respects – with Natalie, of course. Maybe he would tell her how sorry he was for her loss. She knew he possessed the ability to express such sorrow. Maybe she needed the opportunity to forgive him. On the other hand, maybe he'd been taken into custody by the police and would finally have to answer for the disaster he'd caused.

Hassie swallowed the last of her drink, turned to revisit the bar and saw Sid walking toward her. Sid was the last person she wanted to chat with that day, but he'd already seen her and also appeared to be bringing her another drink.

"How we doing, doll?" he said and took the empty glass from her as he handed her a fresh one.

"I'm okay, Sid." She gestured around the room and said, "Thanks for pulling all of this together."

He set the empty glass on a table and steered her deeper into the room. "I know how much Julio meant to you." He put his arm around her waist and pulled her closer to him. "But tell me, how do you manage to look so good, even at a time like this?"

She moved out of Sid's grip when Donnie walked by, distracting him. He motioned for Donnie to join them and looked at Hassie like she might want to find somewhere else to be. Hassie saw it as an opportunity to ask about the so-called investigation that she'd heard about after Julio died.

"Are you on or off duty?" Sid asked as Donnie approached them.

"I'm always on duty, Sid." He looked at Hassie and said, "How you doing?"

Hassie sipped her drink, then looked at him and said, "Have you determined yet that a crime was committed?"

"Of course a crime was committed," Sid said with the gruff impatience that some people considered part of his charm. "A man died, for chrissake."

"I know a man died," she said. "Jake killed him."

Donnie seemed uncomfortable with the conversation and gave Sid a look that said he wasn't sure what to say. Sid basically ignored him and led her away. "Don't worry about this, Hassie. Donnie is doing his job and Jake will be dealt with properly. Now, tell me, how are you enjoying your little room over in the Churchill Downs?"

She spotted Henry coming through the door. "There's Henry." She worked her way out of Sid's grip and said, "It's fine, Sid. Is there a problem?'"

"No, no. Just making sure that you're comfortable." He smiled the menacing smile that she had seen off and on for years.

"Yes, I'm very comfortable. I must get over to Henry now." She could feel his eyes on her as she walked away, a feeling she'd become accustomed to since the day she asked Sid for a favor. He'd since made it clear – more than once – that he would one day come around to collect. She'd felt quite alone since Julio's accident. Despite Jake's madness in the bar that night, it bothered her to think that he was truly finished with her, and not one person in her life was interested to be the shoulder she cried on. Oh, there was always Sid and probably Frank. But did either of these men really care about her or did they just want a piece of her? Was it simply that there was a bit of Mr. Satan in every man and it was her decision as to how she dealt with it?

Henry stood next to the table where he usually shared a drink with Julio before or after a show. Hassie carefully approached him; when he noticed her, she said, "Can I get you a drink?"

He shook his head and sat down at the table. She joined him and, after a brief silence, said, "This is a great turnout, huh?"

Henry nodded, and then said, "Just about everybody who's anybody's here. And thank Christ Jake has the good sense to stay away. I don't know what I would do if he walked through that door."

"Well, don't worry. I just heard from Donnie and Sid that Jake will be dealt with. He's not going to get away scot-free this time."

Henry was quiet for a moment, then looked at Hassie and said, "I'm taking his body back to Ensenada."

"Is that really what you want to do?" She'd heard him say that he would never let Julio leave Vegas.

"It's the right thing to do. He belongs with this family. I've got my memories."

She nodded her head slowly and said, "And we've all got to get back to work."

chapter thirty

HASSIE QUICKLY puffed through a cigarette while she waited for John Jacobson in the coffee lounge of the Tropicana. She'd telephoned him after Julio's tribute about her upcoming schedule, and was not surprised by his lukewarm reception of her call and his suggestion that they meet. When she spotted him at the door, she stubbed out the cigarette and stood up to greet him as he approached her table.

"Please, sit down," he said. "I'm glad we finally have a chance to talk face-to-face."

Hassie smiled and waited for him to sit before saying, "I'm sure you know that Julio Villanueva passed away last week."

"Yes, I heard."

"I'd like to thank you for allowing me –"

"Hassie, I need to stop you right there." His eyes were cold and she knew that she was in for the battle that she'd been warned about. "You need to understand that we did not *allow* you to do anything relative to Mr. Villanueva's unfortunate accident – and untimely passing. You have a contract with the Tropicana and the terms are very clear."

She took a deep breath before she spoke. "But you said that you had plenty of substitute acts –"

"We were willing to give you a few days, but not the better part of a month."

"Julio was hurt very badly and I was partly to blame."

"I understand that, and I'm sorry. But you had a responsibility to your job, and Hassie, you didn't even call me to tell me what was going on. You didn't return my phone calls. You seemed to have just disappeared."

"Dotty knew where I was," she said with a belligerence that she regretted as soon as she'd spoken.

"Surely you know that this is not Dotty's responsibility."

Hassie took a cigarette from her purse and waited for John to light it. When he just stared at her, she picked the matchbook out of the ashtray and lit it herself before saying, "Then you need to tell me what I should do next, because I cannot and would not change anything about the last several weeks."

John sat still for a long moment before he said, "Are you telling me that you don't understand what I'm saying to you? That you believe that you should just be allowed to waltz back into La Chanson and take up where you left off?"

She drew slowly on the cigarette and tossed her head back while considering what to say next. "Julio was not only one of my dearest friends, he was part of my family. Would you have such an unfeeling attitude about someone in your family?"

John leaned back in the seat and rested his left leg on his right knee. "Hassie, this is going to sound like a lecture but, to be honest, I think you need lecturing. We all have issues to deal with in our personal lives – family members die, some do extraordinary things that need special attention, and guess what? Life goes one. I know that sounds clichéd and harsh, but it's the truth. One of the things I've never cottoned to in this town is that there are those of you who somehow believe you exist in your own world where you can make up the rules as you go. Just once, I'd like to hear one of you say that you made a mistake and that you have something to answer for."

He stopped and gave her a chance to speak, but she suddenly felt a heavy weight in the pit of her stomach and just looked at him while he watched her. After a few more seconds of silence, he put both feet on the floor and sat up in the seat before speaking, "Well, then. I'll make this short and sweet. Your contract has been terminated, effective – oh, I'd say a couple of weeks ago – and I would suggest that you no longer have a career in Las Vegas."

Hassie slowly drew on the cigarette and then looked at him squarely and sternly before saying, "Maybe we should go back to Felix's back room and start the negotiations all over again."

He glared at her and said, "Don't be a fool."

She glared back at him but said nothing.

"I think you should take your advice from Clay and Morty."

"I don't need their advice." She stubbed out the cigarette and stood up from the table. "Do whatever you will. I'm better off without an association with such callous, uncaring people." She picked up her purse and started to walk away, then stopped while he stood up to face her. "Just one more thing. I think you probably owe me some money for my last couple of weeks here."

"I'll check into that for you, but I would suggest that you shouldn't count on it. My boss would argue that you owe *us* money, and again, you're gonna learn a lesson about what it means when you sign a contract and what the consequences are when you don't honor it."

She tucked her purse under her arm as he touched her elbow and said, "For what it's worth, I'm sorry about Julio's death."

She looked at him and said, "Thanks, but that's not worth a lot right now. Have a nice life." She walked away and steadied herself as she aimed for the hotel entrance. There was no limousine waiting for her this time; the doorman simply tipped his hat and whistled for a taxi.

She stepped out of the taxi at the entrance to the Sands and im mediately made her way to the Copa Room. About a dozen people scurried around with last-minute instructions for what she'd been told was Frank's last show. The stage buzzed with musicians, and her shoulders sagged with the thought that not only had she never quite had her chance on that stage but now she had to face the reality that she would probably never work anywhere in Vegas again. She heard Sid's voice behind her and turned around to see him finish speaking with Frank and then casually meander through the tables in the back and down toward the stage. The whole room seemed oblivious to her presence until she felt a hand on her shoulder and heard Frank say, "I'm really sorry about what happened to Julio."

She reacted to his touch by turning to embrace him, but his arms hung limply by his side and she stopped herself and said, "Yeah, it's really sad, isn't it?"

"I'm also sorry that I never made it over to visit him in the hospital. You know, I went down to Palm Springs for a while after the –

incident. It was crazy around here when I got back to work. These guys don't work so good without a leader like Julio."

She smiled and nodded. "I saw you at the memorial. You were with Sammy and stood back from the crowd so I didn't want to intrude." She swallowed hard and looked down at her hands. "Actually, I really had trouble talking to anyone that day. It was one of the hardest days of my life."

He touched her arm and then pointed her to a chair at the table in front of them. "How are you doing now?"

"Not so good." She pressed her lips together and wished she'd taken a little more time with her makeup.

"This can be a hateful town." He draped his jacket around the back of his chair before he sat down, then offered her a cigarette, took one from the pack himself and lit them both.

She took a long draw and then exhaled slowly. "I never got a chance to ask. Are you okay since Jake – punched you?"

"It was nothin' really. And if I'm honest – I probably deserved to be punched. I knew he'd go off the deep end when he found out you stayed with me again. But I didn't care. He's an asshole and I still say you deserve better than that." He looked around the room before saying, "Would you like a drink? I'm sure we can scare one up."

""No thanks." she said. "Well, I would really but – no thanks."

He touched her face and studied her, and for a minute she thought that he would ask her to leave Las Vegas and travel with him wherever he went. But when she looked into his eyes, he carefully recoiled like he'd just remembered that she had a contagious disease.

"So what are you doing after your show tonight?" she asked.

"A new film," he said and dragged on his cigarette. "First call is Chicago. I'll be pushing out in a couple of days."

"That's nice," she said and felt her stomach tighten. "Are you coming back?"

"I always find my way back to Vegas – and the Sands."

His eyes were full of pity and she became uncomfortable.

"You gonna stay around now?" he asked, more like an afterthought than genuine interest.

"You mean, now that I don't have a job?" She flicked her cigarette in the ashtray and then let it rest on the side when Frank took hold of her hand.

"You are a very talented lady. You can do whatever you want, wherever you want to do it."

"Yeah, well tell that to John Jacobson and the Tropicana." The thought that Frank might whisk her away from Vegas and everything that now caused her so much pain started to fade as she watched him slowly pulling away from her. Her mind raced with thoughts of how she could convince him that she belonged in his world – that he shouldn't think of leaving her behind.

"You'll be fine, doll. Take my word for it." He stubbed out his cigarette and pushed his chair back from the table. "Just one more thing I'd like to know."

She sat very still and looked into those blue eyes that had offered her comfort so many times.

"Are you gonna run back into Contrata's arms the next time he tells you he's sorry and swears how much he loves you and can't live without you?"

The tone of his voice was unfeeling and almost cruel. She felt her face flush and looked down at her hands.

Frank leaned over to take hold of her chin, lifted her face and said, "He's like some sort of drug for you – a poison that lures you into his hell and you forget who you are. Get away from Vegas, Hassie. Find some place else to sing and make a decent life for yourself."

"Where, Frank? Nobody's really begging me to work for them."

He let go of her face and was silent for a few seconds before saying, "You don't know what you have. Oh, I think you know you look good and audiences have adored your music, but I don't think you know how special you are. I knew it from the moment I met you. And there were some moments between us that took me to another place in my life – when I was really happy. I care about you, doll, but you've gotta get a grip and figure out what you really want."

She didn't trust herself to speak and just looked at him and nodded.

He stood up and took his jacket off the chair, then leaned over and kissed her gently but firmly on the lips. "And if you do figure it out, maybe I'll be around to see it. Meanwhile, I'll miss that beautiful face and those divine lips. Take good care of yourself, kid."

The sweet smell of his cologne lingered as she watched him walk away, the memory of his loving touch as fresh as that last kiss.

chapter thirty-one

HASSIE MOVED carefully as she stood up from the edge of the bed and reached for her bathrobe. Sid rolled over to face her and said, "Where the hell do you think you're going?"

"It's time to get up." She pulled the robe over her arms. "I have things to do and I'm pretty sure you do too."

The bed creaked as Sid hauled his bulk into a sitting position, and then yawned as he said, "What are you so busy about? It's not like you have a job to get to." He stood up and went into the bathroom. Hassie walked to the window and looked at the flat, gray roofs of the buildings that sat parallel to the Churchill Downs – Sid's choice of buildings for her to live in. She'd wondered if, in his perverted way, he'd known that this was the place Jake had left her on that first night at the Sands and had later thought, "Ha! I nailed her here and you didn't!"

"You're losing it, Hassie," she said to herself as she walked away from the window and back to olive green sofa. She tightened the sash on her robe and slouched down in the seat, the weight of Sid's body imprinted onto hers, the smell of his cigar-breath embedded in her senses, causing her to silently wretch when she thought about the vile odor when he stuck his tongue down her throat. He kept a bottle of *Eau Sauvage* cologne in her bathroom and lathered it across his face and neck before getting into bed. She'd wondered how such a large, boorish man could enjoy wearing such a flowery fragrance, especially since it created quite a putrid smell when mixed with the cigar stench and his body's natural odors.

With thought of his large, fat fingers kneading her body like it was a lump of dough, she accepted that she'd adjusted to his crude style of making love. There were times when she enjoyed it; the loss of girlish inhibition that she'd achieved with Jake served her well.

Sid emerged from the bathroom, gathering his clothes from their various posts around the small room, which was nothing like the elegant suites that she had once inhabited. But she would never see the inside of his grand living quarters until she agreed to marry him – the simple terms for becoming a headliner on the Copa Room stage as well. Until then, she would remain in the small, average guest room, dependent on Sid and playing the part of his mistress. The only positive note in all of this was that he made sure her make-shift bar was fully stocked with good booze and her own cut glass decanter of vodka.

"So?" Sid grunted. "What *are* you doing today?"

She spotted a half-empty pack of cigarettes on the desk and did her best to ignore them; her head started to spin slowly and she felt a wave of melancholy take over. She turned back toward Sid and lied, "I've got a meeting and a few people to see."

Sid put on his jacket and pulled a piece of paper out of the left breast pocket. "Well, don't bother going over to the Tropicana," he said and threw the paper on the coffee table. "Looks like your job's been filled." He motioned her over to him and took hold of her shoulders. "Think about what I've offered you, sugar. It's not such a bad deal, is it?"

She kissed his cheek and smiled, then shut the door behind him. She went over to the vodka decanter, poured a large shot and downed it in one gulp. With the second glass of vodka in hand, she sat on the sofa and picked up the paper – a slick flyer advertising the new singer at La Chanson, with a photo of a young, blonde woman, her head slightly cocked and wearing a toothy smile in that starstruck way that Hassie had once been taught to affect – the next young *nobody* with visions of stardom and probably a better sense to hang on to the job. The photo made her cringe with the memory of her own, now embarrassing, poster and her dismissal by John Jacobson.

She swigged vodka as she thought about La Chanson and the stage that had been such an important part of her life. In fact, she had *owned* that stage. Dan and the musicians had told her that more than once and, as she let an image of the beautiful French-styled room fill her mind, she felt lonely and empty with the thought that she might never go back. How could the Tropicana give her job to someone else? The clientele loved her; no one had ever packed them in the way she had. With another swallow of vodka, she decided that something must be done to get her job back and picked up the telephone to speak to her greatest ally.

After a few rings, she asked the receptionist to put her through to Morty. "Is that you, Hassie?"

"Hi, Morty," she said, speaking carefully to avoid slurring her speech.

"Is everything okay? You okay?"

Hassie sighed heavily and said, "You know damn well everything's not okay, Morty. Those assholes at the Tropicana hired a new singer. They didn't even give me a chance."

Morty cleared his throat; she could tell that he was moving his ample weight around his swiveling desk chair. "You wanna tell me why you're surprised about this? I mean, it sounds to me like Jacobson was pretty clear about letting you go after you decided to be your own boss. Did you think they would just close the damn place down after you left?"

He hesitated, and she refused to answer, swallowing vodka instead.

"Hassie, are you drinkin' somethin' besides coffee? Ya know, it's not even lunchtime."

She ignored him and then cleared her throat before saying, "Morty, what am I going to do? Is there any way that you can get my job back?"

"Not only can we not get it back," he said. "I'm working hard to keep us all outta court."

She shifted her weight and momentarily sobered up. "What do you mean?"

"Three little words. Breach. Of. Contract. I think Jacobson might have mentioned this to you."

"But –"

"Ain't no buts. To put it crudely, your bad judgment got your pretty little ass in a crack and we're working to get it free. Or should I say, Clay is knocking himself out to convince those boys that you made an innocent mistake and that they should cut us all some slack. That man would walk over hot coals for you."

Hassie could picture Morty shaking his head, and sat down in the desk chair while saying, "What's Clay doing?"

"He's there in Vegas now – talkin' to Jacobson and that lawyer of theirs. You haven't heard from him?"

She felt weak and nauseated and softly said, "No. When did he get here?"

"A day or so ago. He's got a bit of other business to deal with as well – I imagine you'll be hearin' all about it."

Hassie needed some air and slid to the edge of the seat. "I've gotta go now, Morty." She nervously fussed with her hair. "I'm sorry for all the trouble I've caused. I don't seem to be able to do much right these days."

"Look, doll, just take care of yourself and when you finally come to your senses and recognize that you belong here in Reno, we'll all be waitin' for you. The wife asks about you all the time. I'm tellin' you, you've got your own Jewish mother whether you want one or not."

She smiled with affection for her old boss but wanted to find out what Clay was up to and why he hadn't been in touch with her. "Tell Ruth I said hello and that I'm fine. Bye, Morty." She hung up and leaned on the desk, confused as to whether or not she was sober. She went back to the sofa, slowly lowering herself to the seat before finishing the contents of her glass in one swallow.

Morty was right. John Jacobson had left no gray area as to her position relative to her job. She blew it, pure and simple. She made a conscious decision to put her guilt over Julio's accident and her grief over his death above her responsibility to the Tropicana, but she couldn't be convinced that anyone in her position would not have done the same thing, especially given the level of success she'd achieved. Had everyone forgotten that fact? Maybe she should phone Morty back and remind him of this. She stood up and walked toward the telephone, then realized her glass was empty and detoured over to the vodka decanter.

Jake had talked many times about the power of the players in this world of gambling and entertainment where the stakes were sometimes much higher that they might appear. She'd never really understood this before. But the picture was getting clearer, and, evidently, no one really gave a rat's ass about her or her career. Except Sid, who was trying to use her weak position to his own advantage?

She sat down on the sofa and took a sip of the drink, remembering the afternoon she sat across from Jacobson at the Tropicana and wondering what might have happened if she had asked for his understanding and forgiveness instead of insisting that she'd done nothing wrong. Of course, she'd been wrong. Dotty warned her, Morty warned her and Henry wanted to wring her neck over her actions. What made her think that she was so right? There was no denying that she had been the creator of her own downfall, and the thought that she was now stuck without a job, and reliant on Sid in a devil's bargain, terrified her.

Drinking vodka in the morning was about as good an idea as sending a child out to play in the traffic. She cracked the window open just enough to let in fresh air, then turned on the radio to liven up the room. Sinatra was singing "High Hopes." She wondered where Frank was at that moment and then poured a glass of water and sat down. Bastard. His last words to her still stung, and now she pictured him again – walking away from her. Leaving her to do whatever it was that she was going to do, with words of encouragement regarding her career but with a warning where Jake was concerned. Had she blown it with Frank as well? Hell, yes – she'd had him wrapped around her little finger at one point. What had she *not* blown in the wake of her breakup with Jake?

As Frank's song finished, Hassie remembered that Clay was in town and wondered why she hadn't heard from him. She knew exactly what he would be thinking while arguing her case with the Tropicana. And she knew exactly what he would want to say to her when he finally faced her – how he would make a vague attempt to hide his disappointment in her.

Since Clay had never been to Vegas when she was there, she didn't know where he would stay. Should she try to track him down? She could phone the operator at the Sands or the Tropicana and check if he was registered. Based on what Morty had told her, she shouldn't be so eager to know what was going on. But then, this was her career that they were talking about. Why shouldn't she be just as involved as everyone else?

The more she thought about the whole scenario that Morty had described – together with the fact that Clay was in Vegas – the more irritated she became with the entire bunch of them. She paced around the room for a few minutes, glancing periodically at the glass of vodka and grabbing the pack of cigarettes instead. About the moment she decided to go for it and call John Jacobson, her phone rang. She pulled a cigarette from the pack, then shoved in back in as she grabbed the phone on its third ring.

"Hello, Hassie. It's Clay."

Her first instinct was to lay some sarcastic or cutting remark on him before he could get the first word in, but the sound of his voice had an opposite effect on her and she sighed and simply said, "I wondered when I'd hear from you."

"You spoke to Morty?" he said.

"Yeah. But I think you already know that."

"Hassie, I'd like to come over to see you."

Whatever he had to tell her was not good news. "Things aren't going so well at the Tropicana."

"It's not just that," he said quietly. "Can I come over in about half an hour?"

She looked at herself in the mirror above the console table across from the desk, unsure if thirty minutes was enough time to make herself presentable.

"Please," he continued. "It's important."

"I'm in room 742."

Hassie ordered coffee and dressed in a comfortable pair of slacks and a soft wool sweater. She did her best to disguise the fact that she was suffering from half a day of vodka and, looking often in the mirror at a woman she barely recognized, pulled her hair back from her face with a stretchy white band. Clay arrived just as the coffee was being delivered, his face drawn and looking an awful lot like the way she felt. After the steward left, she invited him in.

"How are you, Hass?" he said and gestured for her to give him a hug.

She moved slowly into his arms and knew before another word was spoken that something terrible had happened. He pulled back from her and looked into her face. "You look good."

"You're a lousy liar," she said. "You want to sit down?"

He nodded and led her to the sofa. Hassie studied him, and when he finally looked at her, she said, "What's wrong, Clay?"

With no show of emotion, he said, "Hassie, Jake's dead."

She looked at him. Her eyes involuntarily blinked back tears as she frowned and said, "Jake's dead?"

He nodded. "Some kids found his body in the desert a couple of days ago."

She stood up slowly and started to walk toward the door. Clay called out to her and then went after her and reached for her arm. She turned around and slapped him and said, "You're a liar," then put her hands over her mouth and silently screamed while Clay took hold of her and held her close. Her body shook. She had that feeling again – the one where she turned back the clock and started over and the story had a different ending. The body they found belonged to someone else. But she couldn't keep away the image of Jake's body lying lifeless and twisted in the sand. She saw Sid and then Sinatra's men and then Henry and all sorts of faceless strangers dumping him in the desert and laughing and patting each other on the back as they left him and disappeared.

She pulled away from Clay and looked at him for a long, empty moment, then started to laugh and said, "This is like the fucking movies. The evil bastard gets his comeuppance. Gets dragged out to the desert and tortured for his sins and then is left to the wolves."

"Hassie, that's not what I said happened. Please, come sit back down."

She pulled away from him in a near violent move and shouted into his face, "Then what the hell happened to him, Clay? Where is he and – and, what the hell happened?"

He stood still and just looked at her. She couldn't move and felt Clay take hold of her arm and pull her back down to the sofa. "I've heard a couple of versions of how he was found, but I only know what I've been told."

"And what is that?"

He wouldn't look her in the eye and sat still with his head in his hands.

She stood up. "What were you told, Clay?" she said, then walked away from the sofa and kept her back to him. Except for the quiet thump of her own heartbeat, she heard nothing. When she turned around to speak to Clay again, her face now covered in tears, she quickly moved back to the sofa and grabbed his arm. "What happened to Jake?" she shouted. "And where is he *now*?"

Clay pulled his arm from her grip, shook his head and said, "It's over, Hassie. I dealt with his remains yesterday, which is why I'm just now getting to you."

Hassie stood in front of him with her arms folded across her chest, practically choked on her tears then calmly said, "You *dealt* with his remains? What the hell does that mean?"

He moved closer to her and took her arm, forcing her to walk away from the table. "Maybe you should have a chat with Donald McGinley. He has all the facts and will give you the full story."

"Donnie?" She stopped and glared at Clay. "Of course. Donnie knows everything." She looked down at the floor. She kept thinking of her father – the day that she came home from school as an ambulance was taking him away. Her mother had tried to tell her that he was going to be fine – that he was just sick and would be better soon. She could tell by the faces of everyone else there that he was not coming back. The room felt out of balance; she tried to focus on Clay, his grim, somber expression confirming her fear that Jake would not be back. Her head throbbed and her cheeks burned as she said, "I can't believe it. I can't believe he's really dead."

He pulled her close to him while she cried softly into his shoulder. When she was quiet and still, he continued to hold her and spoke close to her ear, "Do you want to talk to Donnie?"

She pulled back from him and said, "I guess so. But, don't leave."

"I have a room here in the hotel," he said. "But I'm not going anywhere right now." He walked over to the phone, pulled a card from his pocket and dialed.

Hassie waited for confirmation that Donnie was on his way, then excused herself to the bathroom. How many times had she stood in front of a mirror, mourning the loss of some part of her relationship with Jake? How many times had she wished him dead and then euphorically welcomed him back into her life – determined that their love could overcome the apparent obstacles and that the knowledge that they would somehow survive it all had kept her alive and burning with desire for him – and had probably ruined her ability to truly love another man. She sobbed and felt that her heart would explode. Jake was gone, and she didn't know how she would be able to live without this man who had taught her how to love – who had both cherished her and ravaged her and had now left her in the worst possible way.

She reentered the bedroom as Clay opened the door to let Donnie in. He looked like he hadn't slept for days, but his demeanor assured her that whatever he said would be official. She shook his hand and said, "Thanks for coming over. Please sit down. Coffee?"

Donnie removed his hat and said, "No thanks." He and Clay sat in the chairs on either side of the coffee table while Hassie sat on the edge of the sofa between them. She gazed at Donnie expectantly before saying, "Clay told me that Jake's body was found in the desert?"

"That's correct," Donnie said. "A couple of college kids were camping out in the desert near Route 157 and came across the body in a rocky patch about a quarter of a mile off the road."

"How did they – I mean, how did you find out that it was Jake?"

Donnie and Clay exchanged looks; Donnie breathed deeply and replied, "The young men came to the station a couple of hours later and two of our men went out to the scene with them. In a routine check, they found Jake's wallet in his pocket and a set of keys that were later identified as his as well. And, of course, he was properly identified by next of kin."

She looked at Clay and said, "That's you?"

Clay nodded and Donnie fidgeted with his hat before saying, "That's right."

"What about his wife?" Hassie quietly asked.

Donnie shook his head and said, "If you mean Natalie, they weren't officially married, but she's been informed. We thought she had a right to know – with the baby and all."

Hassie felt like Donnie had slapped her in the face and that the room was slowly spinning around her. Jake had lied: he never married Natalie.

"... one of the saddest scenes I've ever witnessed," Donnie continued. "We ended up bringin' in the doc and he sedated her. She's in pretty bad shape. Little Norma's with a friend for a few days.

Hassie looked at Clay and said, "Did you know that Jake and Natalie weren't married?"

Clay walked over to the sofa and sat down beside her. "The sum total of what I know about Jake wouldn't fill a tea cup."

She felt disoriented and the room seemed unfamiliar. "Clay, when did you get here?"

"I got the call on Tuesday night. I probably should have jumped on a plane and made it easy on myself," Clay said. "But I assumed there might be some personal effects to deal with and decided to just get in my car and make the drive down."

Hassie gripped the tissue tightly and said, "So you got here yesterday and you, um – saw Jake?"

Clay nodded. His face looked pale.

Hassie looked at Donnie and said, "I want to see him."

Donnie sat on the edge of his chair and leaned his elbows on his knees. "Miss Calhoun, that's not such a good idea."

"What's with the *Miss Calhoun*? You've always called me Hassie."

"Okay, Hassie. It's not a good idea for you to see Jake's – remains."

"That's what my mother said when my father died," she said. "But I needed to see him to be sure that he was really gone. I *need* to see Jake."

Clay walked over to the sofa and sat down beside Hassie, then looked at Donnie.

"Something terrible must have happened to Jake before he died," Donnie said.

"Something terrible – like what?" she asked.

"I really don't think you want to know this, Hassie." Clay said, taking hold of her hand.

"Just tell me. Please."

Donny sat back in his chair and took a moment before saying, "Jake's body – his head had been – removed."

Hassie tensed as Clay put his arm around her shoulder, then released the scream that until that moment had only been in her head. She burrowed into Clay's chest and wept until her throat ached and her eyes were swollen shut. When she was finally calm enough to move, she stood up from the sofa and walked into the bathroom, suddenly realizing that she couldn't feel the floor beneath her feet. She fought the feeling of nausea that welled in her gut and placed a cold, wet cloth over her face. When she returned to the bedroom, Donnie was gone and Clay stood at the window.

"Donnie left?" she said.

"One of his men came to get him. He was needed back at the station. He said to tell you that you should let him know if he can do anything for you. And that he's really sorry about what happened."

Hassie nodded and bowed her head, and then said, "What do you think happened to Jake?"

"I don't know," Clay said softly. "He had his share of enemies – I guess we can create all kinds of scenarios, but I don't really see the sense in all that. Do you?"

"What *do* you see the sense in, Clay? Huh? Does it make it better that Jake was a *bad boy* – that maybe he deserved what he got? Is that what you're trying to say?" She stood in the middle of the room. "Just because you didn't care anything about him doesn't mean that no one did. Maybe he wasn't perfect, but he didn't deserve to be killed."

When Clay said sharply, "And neither did Julio," she started to shake.

Clay grabbed her and pulled her close to him. "I'm sorry, Hass. I didn't mean to imply that Jake deserved what happened." He took hold of both her arms and said, "And don't think I didn't care about him. Maybe our relationship was a little – unconventional, but we shared a difficult time in both our lives growing up. Once upon a time we even had some fun. Maybe that's why I can't really think about what happened. We don't know what happened, and it's unlikely we'll ever know. This town chews people up. It's why I live in Reno."

She walked over to the dresser and picked up some tissues and blew her nose and wiped her eyes before turning to Clay. She felt helpless and reached out to him as she said, "I don't know what to do."

"I know," he said and took hold of her hand. "Come here and sit down for a minute."

She felt him tense a bit and realized that he hadn't told her everything yet. "I need a drink," she said and reached for two glasses and the decanter. She joined him on the sofa and poured two shots of vodka, then sat quietly staring into her lap, still uncertain of what she had just learned about Jake. When she looked up at Clay, he swallowed a big sip of the drink and then set the glass on the table.

"Morty told you about our little problem with the Tropicana and your breach of contract?"

Hassie nodded and sipped her drink.

"The good news is that I think we reached a settlement today. In fact, that's where I was when I called you earlier."

She nodded again and waited.

"The bad news is that I don't know how you're going to feel about the settlement."

"What do you mean?"

Clay emptied his glass and stood up. He took a few steps away from her, ran his fingers through his hair, then turned to her and said, "You know Dan Forrester always thought you had a great talent. Both as a singer and as a songwriter."

"That's hard to believe considering how they threw me out of the lounge."

"Anyway, Dan thinks that your final version of 'I Just Can't Figure it Out' – which, by the way, they call 'Hassie's Song' – is worth some money."

Hassie stood up at the mention of her song and walked over to Clay. "What do you mean, it's worth *some* money?"

Clay took hold of both of her arms and said, "Listen to me for a minute. These guys are real pros, and the bottom line is that they didn't appreciate the way you left them in the lurch over that business with Julio. They had every intention of prosecuting you – and me – over the breach of contract and, believe me, I know they had perfect grounds to ruin our lives. I've been talking to them for weeks, Morty's tried every tactic he knows, and today I was forced to make a deal or we would finish the negotiations in front of a judge."

"Clay, what does this have to do with my song?"

"I settled *your* debt by agreeing to trade them the rights to 'Hassie's Song.'"

"You did what?" Once again, she pulled away from him. "How could you do such a thing?"

"Hassie, believe me, I had no choice. If we ended up in court – well, I don't even want to think about it. We would have lost everything."

She wanted to slap him or punch him or somehow hurt him in the same way that she ached throughout her gut. Instead, she backed away and said, "I've got news for you, Mr. Cooper. I don't have anything else to lose. I've lost everything that I've ever given a tiny crap about, and now you've given away the one thing that I didn't think anyone could take from me. No one could kill it and it couldn't walk away. But you managed to take it away." She raced to the door and pulled it open. "Go to hell and get the hell out of my life."

He stood still with a pained look that she chose to ignore, glaring at him to leave her alone. With nothing else to say, she stared at the floor while he left, then slammed the door behind him and fell headfirst onto her bed. How could one man deliver so much crippling, heartbreaking news in one day? She hated Clay and wished that he would get out of her life forever. And of one thing she was sure – she truly had nothing else to lose.

She lay quietly for a few minutes, a deadness having set in, partially from the vodka but mostly from the desire to pretend that the last several hours had not really happened and that any minute she would awaken from a bad dream. When the numbness started to wear off and she felt that she would completely lose control, she got up from the bed and poured another drink, thinking that she needed to see and talk to Henry. Now, more than ever, she needed to mend all the broken pieces of their relationship, and she would do it if she had to glue herself to his side.

She'd emptied the decanter and the spare bottle was gone; she called down for another bottle to be sent up and that the steward should make it snappy. She stood next to the window as the sun began to disappear behind the mountains; darkness would be the perfect punctuation to the perfect day in hell. She drained the last of the vodka from her glass and glared at the door. "Where's that bottle?" she said out loud in a moment of déjà vu, recalling the night she'd lost her job at La Chanson.

After her meeting with John Jacobson, she had gone back to her room and ordered a bottle of vodka. At the knock on the door, she had thrown it open, ready to leap on the young, unsuspecting steward only to find herself face-to-face with Sid.

"Sid!" she'd gasped and then stumbled into his arms.

"Well, well," he'd responded and hooked his arm around her waist. "It's nice to see you too."

"Where's the vodka?" she'd said before teetering back into the room.

Sid had steadied her while she walked over to the sofa, but before she sat down, she'd shouted at him, "Where's the fucking vodka? What's wrong with this dreadful hotel? I asked for vodka hours ago."

He'd pushed her down onto the sofa. "Sit still and be quiet." He'd picked up the phone and said something in a low voice and when he turned back around, she had settled into the sofa and released a series of sobs. Sid sat down beside her and said, "What's the matter, doll?"

"I lost my job," she'd said through a mess of tears. "They fired me." She had taken refuge in his arms like a small, scared child.

"It's just a job, doll," he'd said. "Not the end of the world."

He'd held her close for a few minutes until she was calm and able to speak. He stood up just as the doorbell rang. He'd taken the vodka from the steward and set it on the side table, then returned to the sofa and wiped a streak of mascara from her cheek with the handkerchief from his pocket.

"Sorry I'm such a wreck," she'd said. "Thanks for coming by to console me.

He'd sat back from her and studied her. "I can't let you think I'm such a nice guy."

"Why's that?"

"I didn't come here to console you. In fact, my timing is gonna sound pretty shitty."

She'd adjusted her body in the seat and looked around for her cigarettes. "So why did you come?"

He'd taken hold of her face with his paw of a hand, pulled her mouth close to his and said, "I came to collect that debt you owe me."

He'd tightened his grip as she tried to pull away from him and said, "But I don't have a job now. How do you expect me to pay you?"

He'd roared his hideous laugh and unbuckled his belt as he said, "Let's start with you on your knees."

She shivered at the thought of all that had happened since that night and how Sid, who must have known that Jake was dead, came into her room the night before and carried on like everything was perfectly normal. What kind of person was he? And how could she consider any part of what he offered her? Her skin itched at the thought that he would be back for another piece of her.

Now, the last awful thing would be for Henry to tell her to go to hell, which was right on par with the current plot. She sat in the chair and heard Barbara saying, "My dear Hassie, look where you've ended up."

chapter thirty-two

It was after eleven o'clock in the morning when Hassie called to order coffee. She splashed cold water on her face and brushed her teeth before entering the living room where a brown bag containing a crisp new pack of Lucky Strikes lay on the desk. She shook them out of the bag and stared at them just as the doorbell rang. "Coming," she shouted and opened the door to the young Mexican steward. She ushered him in, signed the ticket and dropped a few coins in his hand; his bright, toothy smile and head of curly black hair made her think of Julio.

She closed the door behind him and switched on the television, expecting to see the daily installment of a popular soap opera. Instead, Walter Cronkite appeared on the screen, reporting what sounded like the morning news in his serious, deadpan fashion. She walked over to pour the coffee, stirring in a spoonful of sugar, then went back to the sofa with the cup and sat down to watch to the news. The reporter's face was solemn and tearful as he said, "... apparently official. President Kennedy died at one p.m. Central Standard Time, two o'clock Eastern Standard Time, some thirty-eight minutes ago."

Hassie ran over to the television to turn up the volume. She banged her fist on the screen and shouted, "What happened?" She stood in front of the television as Mr. Cronkite struggled to deliver the dreadful report, and then moved over to the chair that was closest to the set. The phone rang but she ignored it, preferring to piece together memories from the night she met JFK in the Copa Room, before he became president: his big smile as he kissed her hand;

the softness of his lips; the clean, soapy smell of his cologne; Jake's fingers digging into her shoulder when Kennedy smiled at her from across the table. She had talked to the woman who looked like Elizabeth Taylor, whom he couldn't take his eyes off of, wondering where his wife was and thinking how complicated life was with those you love and those who say they love you. His election had taken place while she was in the hospital, not that she was paying attention to politics, being so caught up in her own selfish motives – hurting the people she loved and making one fuck-up after another. She heard Henry telling her not to be so hard on herself, and saw Barbara, who was still missing in action, frowning at her lack of judgment where Sid was concerned.

"Oh, to hell with coffee," she shouted and stood up to get a glass. She poured a tall shot of vodka and swallowed half of it in one gulp. "What's wrong with this fucking world? Why do people kill each other?" She could only imagine what Kennedy's wife was going through as she dealt with the loss of her husband and the father of her children – and the children; what words does one use to tell children that their father is gone – dead and never coming back? "He's gone to a better place," she'd heard more than once. What place could be better than at home with his family, helping them grow and learn and providing a loving, nurturing existence, even if their mother was a selfish, lying, conniving – careful, Hassie. Her thoughts described the behavior of a whore. She wondered if Sid had heard the news about JFK, and if he even cared. Jake would have cared, or at least she could believe that he would have, and she would have cried in his arms and he would have let her and she would have told him how sorry she was for her selfish, lying, conniving behavior and that she had realized that life is short and that good people die and bad people carry on being bad and that sometimes you get a second chance, sometimes you don't, and sometimes sorrow overwhelms you.

She swallowed the last of the drink and fell down on the bed, drained. Her bones ached, and her eyelids felt like heavy curtains, slowly falling at the end of a tragic scene. She saw a headless corpse sprawled in the desert; a black hearse rolled through Corsicana carrying her father's casket; Frank and Jake held her down while Sid raped her, and Natalie cut into her neck with a razor.

A man's voice called her name, and she gradually came to realize that fists were pummeling her door. She stood up and steadied herself to walk across the room, then took small, careful steps until she reached the door. When she turned the knob, someone pushed from the other side, and before she could speak, Clay stood in front of her. He grabbed her shoulders and said, "I've been calling and calling. Why didn't you answer your phone?"

Hassie stood still and listened to him speak then glanced back at the television and stared at the screen.

"Come, sit down," Clay said. He led her to the sofa, and then looked at the television. "Hassie?"

She looked over at him but didn't really see his face.

He took hold of her hands. "You've seen the news about President Kennedy?"

She nodded, tears blurring her vision, but when Clay tried to hold her in his arms, she yanked herself away. "No!" she said once, then several more times. "No, no. I can't. Leave me alone – for your own good."

Clay sat with her for a few more minutes and then walked over to switch off the television on his way to the coffeepot. "Do you want some coffee?"

She shook her head and looked over at the decanter on the console table. "Vodka," she said softly. "Vodka."

Clay went back to the sofa and sat beside her. "I'm worried about you," he said and peered into her eyes.

She remained still and gazed at the television screen, now blank with a soft green tinge in the gloom that enshrouded the room. President Kennedy was dead, and she was tired. The images flooded her mind again and she tried to shut them out, recalling her mother's words after her father died: "It's best if you don't think about it." Sadness engulfed her; an unpleasant slumber slowly carried her away. Don't think, don't dream – just be; sleep now, sleep.

The telephone woke her. Hassie moved slowly beneath the bedcovers as Clay reached for the phone, his voice deep and muted by a thick haze in her head. She felt him sit down on the bed beside her and turned to face him. "Who's calling?" she muttered.

"Do you want some water?" Clay asked.

"Where am I?"

"You're in your room at the Sands. You've been asleep for a couple of hours. Are you feeling better?"

She pushed herself up on her elbows. Everything looked exactly as she remembered it, but something had changed. What?

Clay opened the heavy drapery to a sunny afternoon behind the sheer beige curtain, then walked over to the bed and said, "You must be hungry. Can I get you something from room service?"

She felt queasy and shook her head. "Just water." When he went to get the water, she pulled her legs out from under the covers and perched on the edge of the bed. Clay handed her the glass and stood beside her until she became aware that she sat there in her underwear.

"Did you undress me?"

He nodded, then smiled at her and said, "Don't worry, I didn't look."

She sipped the water and offered a weak smile, her tongue thick and slightly numb as she said, "I'm not looking my best these days." A wave of nausea swept through her.

Clay went back into the bathroom and returned with her robe. "Here, put this on and then, if you feel strong enough, come sit with me. I'd like to talk to you about something."

She finished the water and slipped her arms through the robe, then carefully stood up. Images tried to crowd in on her but she shoved them into a dark void within her. Clay led her to the sofa. "You look about a million times better than you did before your nap."

"What happened?" she asked as she sat down.

"You were very tired. I don't think this city's good for you anymore."

She studied him for a few seconds, casting her mind back to the last thing she could remember, and then thought about the phone call that had brought her out of a deep sleep. "Who was that on the phone?"

"Henry," Clay said.

"Henry? What did he want?"

"Just checking on you. I told him to come over."

She wrinkled her nose and said, "He won't. He hates me."

"He doesn't hate you. He'll be over soon."

She looked around the room, her eyes resting on the blank television screen, and then looked back at Clay before saying, "I want to go home."

"I think that's a good idea," Clay said, then hesitated for a moment before continuing, "Where do you call home?"

She looked down at her hands and studied her fingers. She hadn't had reason to consider that question for many months. Corsicana had ceased being home when she left four years earlier. Reno had only ever been a stopover point; going back to Vegas had been inevitable. But she couldn't possibly think of Vegas as home now. A deep sense of loss riddled her gut and she felt hollow and alone.

Clay let his hand rest on top of hers and waited for a few seconds before saying, "I can't leave you here, Hass."

"You mean here in this room?"

"I mean in Las Vegas. I know you're angry with me for giving away the rights to your song but –"

She shook her head and said, "I was wrong. I put you and Morty in a terrible position and I know that now. Yes, I'm upset about the song, but I know you did what you had to. I pretty much screwed up my life here on my own, and I really don't believe anyone can save me now." She hesitated for a moment, and then softly said, "I'm not sure I want to be saved – or deserve to be saved."

Clay moved to the edge of his seat. "I don't want to hear that kind of talk. Come back to Reno with me. You had a pretty good life in Reno once, and people still care about you there."

She picked up the pack of cigarettes off the table and shook one loose. "Some people say that you can never go back."

Clay took the cigarette from her and said, "You came back to Vegas. And you were gonna give up these damn things when you started singing full time."

"I was gonna do a lot of things, wasn't I?" She folded her arms across her chest and sighed. "I was never going to see Jake Contrata again. I was going to work so hard that this town would beg me to stay – the Tropicana and the Sands would fight over me and I wouldn't have time for all the goddamn cigarettes and booze."

She walked over to the window, kept her back to Clay and laughed bitterly as she said, "You shoulda seen me the night I arrived in Vegas – Jake took me to the Regency Lounge – where I must've looked like a silly lunatic waving cigarettes around, taking the occasional puff that made me light-headed and then, of course, I drank way too much champagne and threw up all over Natalie's fancy dress and had to hide the hangover from hell from Jake the next day."

Clay carefully approached her and turned her to face him. "You were young and, okay, a little stupid – that's par for the course in Vegas. But you should have learned better by now – hell, I can hear the effects of this incessant smoking in your speaking voice, never mind what it must be doing to your singing."

She scowled at him and said, "Not that I've been doing so much singing lately, but you should be pleased to know that I've really been trying to quit. And believe me, it's been damn hard considering everything that's happened." She took hold of Clay's arm and continued, "I've not said this out loud yet, but I really don't like Vegas right now. It's dull and lifeless and I can't see its meaning anymore."

He pulled back from her embrace and said, "Look, Hassie. I'm not trying to say that your life in Reno was perfect, but it seemed to be a little saner, and you surrounded yourself with people that were good for you and wanted good things for you. I can't say the same about your life in Vegas."

A brief recollection of her night with Mr. Satan intensified the skepticism that she felt about returning to Reno, but she followed Clay back to the sofa and sat down beside him.

He took hold of her hand and said, "I'm not a psychologist and I'm not pretending to know how to solve all your problems, but I think you know what I'm trying to say and I think you know that I'm right."

Of course she knew that Clay was right, and her decision to go back to Reno with him would exhibit her understanding that she had made mistakes in Vegas but that she had every intention of correcting them – changing her life for the good and leaving the negative forces behind once and for all. But walking away from Sid Casper would be one of the more difficult things that she'd ever been faced with – the image of Sid lying on top of her, grunting and sweating as he used her body left her cold, except for the fact that this "close" connection to him had allowed her not only to live – with no job or money in the bank – at the Sands but also to hold on to her dream of performing on the Copa Room stage. She owed him a lot, and leaving the Sands without speaking to him was not an option. But how could she begin to broach that subject with Clay? She looked at him and said, "When are you going back?"

"I had planned to leave today."

"Wow. Today. That's awfully quick." Through a groggy sense that things were moving in slow motion, and with all that she still had to resolve before she could leave, it was difficult to imagine that she could get herself together in such a short time. "If I go back to Reno with you now, where will I go? I gave up my apartment and, in case you haven't been paying attention, I haven't had a job in quite a long time now. I don't think I can afford to buy a carton of milk."

Clay watched her in a way that she knew meant that he didn't want to push her and she loved him for that. He moved closer to her and that little wisp of blonde hair fell close to his eyebrow. "You can stay at my house for as long as you need. I have plenty of room – you can have the bedroom of your choice, and Jorge would love to pamper you."

She loved the thought of spending time at Clay's ranchero spread. "That's very generous, but I don't know if it's such a good idea."

"Give me a good reason why not. I've already told you that I want you to come back to Reno. And I believe you know that you'll be welcomed back by people who love and appreciate you. Reno will demand far less from you than Vegas."

"I'd be leaving Henry." She inhaled and held her breath as she considered what to say, then exhaled slowly. "And I've got to deal with the T-Rex."

"The T-Rex?"

"Yeah. Sid."

"What's he got to do with this?"

"He wants me to marry him – says he'll make me a star in the Copa Room."

Clay stared at her and wrinkled his brow. "Is that what you want?"

"No," she said. "Not really. But he's pretty forceful. Hell, he makes Jake look like Mickey Mouse."

"He doesn't own you. He can't stop you leaving. And he certainly can't make you marry him."

"He can have me killed and tossed in the desert."

Clay rolled his eyes and said, "Talk to him, Hassie. That big ogre, T-Rex persona is part of his job description as much as anything else. He also has a reputation for being fair and rational as long as you're fair with him. We need to get you outta here. He probably knows that."

"You don't know him," she said. "He's a brute. A very powerful brute."

"Just try him. Talk to him. Be straight and give him a chance."

She took a deep breath and said, "That doesn't help where Henry's concerned."

"I told you. Henry will come to see you this afternoon. Assuming he does, can we leave today?"

She released a deep sigh and said, "I need more time to think about this, Clay."

He picked up his jacket before saying, "Okay. I'll go and finish my own business and come back in a little while. If you need me for anything and I'm not in my room, let Jimmy know and he'll find me."

Hassie struggled, through a somber haze, to put her thoughts in order. If Clay was right and Henry did come to see her, there was a real possibility that their farewell conversation – if she was really able to go through with leaving – would not be the one that she needed. Henry blamed her for Julio's death and nowhere near enough time had passed for that to change.

She took a shower and washed her hair, and then dressed in a pair of chocolate brown wool slacks and an olive green sweater. As she combed out the tangles in her wet hair, she studied her face in the mirror. The last couple of months had had a more dramatic effect on her than she'd realized. Her eyes seemed smaller and the soft lilac bags underneath them made her look exhausted. The scar above her eyebrow had only slightly diminished and would forever connect her with Las Vegas, but she still had hopes that someday it would disappear for good. She smoothed a light foundation of makeup over her clean face and brushed a layer of mascara onto her eyelashes. A touch of pink lipstick brought life to her otherwise pale and drawn face. She took a deep breath and considered packing her toiletries into the small cosmetics case, then dismissed the idea with thought of what she wanted to say to Henry. And she still had to talk to Sid.

Barbara's large suitcase lay open on the bed. Clay must have placed it there before he left the room, hoping that she would eventually decide to do what he was certain was best for her. She stared at the bare, satin-lined compartments, and then looked at the telephone. If she called Sid's office and he wasn't there, she could leave a message and he would at least know that she had tried to speak to him. If he was there, would she be able to tell him that she was considering the move to Reno?

As she slowly moved toward the desk, she debated what she actually owed him. Yes, she'd asked him to let her stay at the Sands when everything else failed, but she'd offered to pay; her intentions had been honorable. He'd always promised to collect. In her mind, he'd collected quite enough. Hopefully, Clay's belief that Sid was fair-minded was an accurate one. She took a deep breath and dialed the number to Sid's office. After two short rings, he answered.

"Casper."

"Hello, Sid. It's Hassie."

"This is the first time *you've* ever called *me*," he said. "Is your room on fire?"

She sighed. "Everything's on fire."

There was a long pause before he breathed deeply into the receiver and said, "What's going on, doll?"

"I'm thinking about going back to Reno."

"Really?" She could hear him breathing and imagined his suspicious mind conjuring up his own sordid story. "Did you lose something there you need to go back for?"

She swallowed hard and continued, "There's nothing left for me in Vegas now."

"I'll try not to take that personally." There was no hint that he might be joking.

"Oh, it's nothing to do with you," she said. "I mean, I'm not trying to get away from you or anything." She cringed at the thought that she was digging a deeper hole for herself. "I mean, I think it will be easier for me to get a job there. I already owe you so much, Sid. I need to start taking responsibility for myself."

"I think we've discussed this, haven't we?"

"What do you mean?"

"Who runs the show at the Sands?"

"You do." She knew exactly where he was going with the conversation.

"Who in Reno can offer you the opportunity that I've offered you here in the Copa Room?"

There was a long silence until Sid finally said, "So you're tellin' me that you don't like the terms I've laid out?"

"It's not just that." She knew that marrying Sid was not something she could go through with, but she didn't want to close the door between her and the Copa Room forever. "I need to take care of myself for a while and earn my place on that stage. Your influence has helped me see many things more clearly – you've help me so much."

"You have no idea how much I've really helped you." He breathed deeply into the phone and continued, "Who do you think was behind your contract extension at the Tropicana?"

Hassie had never even considered that Sid had anything to do with her working at La Chanson. "I guess you're gonna tell me that you were behind it." She'd always believed that Jake had had something to do with it.

"Contrata blackballed you at the Sands." There was silence. "Did you know that?"

"No, Sid. I didn't know that."

"You don't understand the depth of this thing between Jake and Frank, and Jake would have seen you in hell before he'd let you on the Copa Room stage. In fact, after that last stunt you pulled with Frank, he was determined to see you run out of Vegas."

She listened and breathed deeply at the realization of what he was saying, and then carefully picked her words: "You were Jake's boss, Sid. You could have run *him* out of Vegas."

"And I can just as easily give you that job that you've lusted after for years. Bottom line is, you owe me." There was finality to his words and to the tone of his voice. "And you owe me more than the lousy rent for that room."

There was a sharp rap on the door that she hoped was Henry. "Sorry, Sid. Someone's at my door. Can I get back to you?"

"Sure. But don't expect me to just slap you on the ass and wave good-bye."

Hassie opened the door to Henry who stood back from the doorway and waited for her to motion him in.

"It's good to see you, Henry," she said and gestured for him to sit down.

"Clay asked me to come by. He said you had a pretty rough morning."

She sat down on the sofa, hesitated for a moment and then said, "Can you believe that President Kennedy is dead?"

Henry shook his head slowly and said, "I've never seen so many grown people cry – women *and* men."

"I know," she said and blinked back tears. "I picked a really rotten time to stop smoking. I mean, between Jake's – and now – I mean, who would do such a horrible thing?" She pulled a hankie from her pants pocket and lightly blew her nose.

Henry watched her for a moment, then offered the hint of a smile as he said, "Did you really stop smoking?" She nodded and he continued, "That's great. I'm really glad to hear it."

She smiled and gathered courage to say, "Henry, I have something to tell you."

"Does it have anything to do with Sid?"

"What makes you ask that?"

He sat still like he expected her to spill her guts to him, which made her wish that she felt stronger and more in control of her emotions. She looked over at the console table for the vodka decanter, then looked at Henry and said, "Would you like a drink?"

"No, thanks. It's a little early for me, but you go ahead."

She shook her head and said, "I'm fine. Really, I'm fine."

"So what do you want to tell me?"

"I'm thinking about going back to Reno."

"Whose idea is that? Clay's?"

She nodded tentatively and said, "He thinks I'll have an easier time getting back on my feet there."

"I agree," Henry said and relaxed in his chair.

"You do? You think I should leave Vegas?" Part of her felt a little hurt and betrayed. She had hoped that he would be devastated at the thought that, after his loss of Julio, he would lose her too.

"I think you should get away from the Sands and Sid Casper. He's not good for you and, in my opinion, you're headed for more trouble if you stay here."

She remembered her conversation with Sid and realized that she had to finish it. "I know how you feel about this, Henry. And you're probably right. But I might be giving up a big chance in Vegas."

Henry looked at her, his expression a mix of disdain and disgust. "You gave up a big chance when you fucked up at the Tropicana. It amazes me how you are able to tune out the facts when it suits you."

"I know I've made a mess of things, and there's no reason to hash through all that again. Sid's been very good to me at a time when I really needed help."

"You've needed help since the day you set foot in this place. I don't know another soul on this earth who has had more help than you've had. But the fact remains that if you stay and take that job in the Copa Room, you're selling out. You're taking the easy road and doing something that I know you'll regret. And I think you know it too."

Part of her was delighted that Henry cared this much about what happened to her. But it was ultimately her decision, and Sid's message was loud and clear. She looked into Henry's eyes and smiled softly as she said, "If I had a dollar for every time someone has reminded me that I'm a *nobody* and *nobodies* don't work on main stages in Vegas – I'd never have to work another day in my life. Sid's offering me – the *star* nobody – a chance to work in the Copa Room. What kind of fool would I be to just walk away?"

Henry studied her for a moment, and then said, "Have you fallen in love with Sid, or something?"

"Heavens, no. This is nothing to do with love or – feelings."

Henry moved to the edge of his seat, took a deep breath and said, "Look. I know how stubborn you are, and if you've made up your mind that you're gonna stay here and lay in Sid's sack of shame, then there's probably nothing I can say to change your mind. I would just like to go on record as saying that I think it's a big mistake and that, if I were you, I'd ride out of town with Jack the Ripper if that's what it took to move on. You're better than this. I know it and you know it."

"Can I be very honest with you?" She asked. Henry nodded and she considered her words before saying, "I really don't want to leave Vegas with you feeling the way you do about me."

Henry laughed and lightly shook his head, and she knew that he was thinking something that he shouldn't say.

"I know that you still blame me for Julio's death and that you don't – love me the way you used to."

He stood up and ran his fingers through his hair, saying, "Ah, come on, Hassie. This is getting old. If I want to blame you for Julio's death, I will. If I want to blame you for Jake's death, I will. Hell, maybe I should blame you for Kennedy's death. You're like – Typhoid Mary of the heart!"

She sat still and watched him pace across the room. When she sensed he was calm, she quietly said, "So you do hate me."

"I don't hate you." He sat down and propped his elbows on his knees.

"Then why won't you forgive me?"

He looked up at her, hesitated for a moment and said, "Does it really mean that much to you?"

Hassie got up from the sofa and walked over to where he sat. "It means everything to me, Henry. I don't want to leave town with you feeling this way."

He stood up and slipped his hands into his pockets. "If it means that much to you – and you promise you'll go to Reno and get on with your life, I'll work very hard to get over these feelings. After all, Julio wouldn't want me to feel this way." He looked at her with a pinched smile and said, "I know you loved him too."

She reached out to touch his arm just as there was another knock at the door. "Sorry," she said. "This is probably Clay, and he's waiting for my decision."

When she opened the door, Clay bounded in and started to speak to her, then saw Henry and reached out to shake his hand. She watched the two of them; behind Henry's smile was pain that was as fresh as the day they'd said good-bye to Julio.

"Everything okay between you two?" Clay said.

Hassie looked at Henry who nodded and said, "Yeah. We're fine. But I think you need your head examined before you walk outta here with this one." He moved toward the door and then turned back to say, "She's a handful."

"Typhoid Mary," said Hassie.

They smiled and she waved at Henry. When the door closed behind him, Clay looked at her and said, "So does that mean you've decided to leave with me?"

She looked around the room and said, "I haven't even packed yet."

Clay smiled and put his arm around her. "I'll help you," he said.

She nodded. "You can put all my toiletries in the cosmetics case." While placing her clothes in the open suitcase, she thought about the task she must finish. Clay closed the latch on her cosmetics case and joined her in the bedroom. She asked him to get her shoes from the closet and stuffed the remainder of her clothes in the suitcase.

While Clay forced the overflowing case to close, Hassie contemplated calling Sid. It would be easier to finish their conversation by phone than in person. She looked at the phone; someone knocked on the door. She tensed with the thought that Sid had come to see her and took hold of Clay's arm as he sheepishly said, "I took the liberty of assuming that you'd need the bellman."

Hassie relaxed her shoulders and said, "Go ahead with the bags. I've got one more thing to do and I'll be right down."

Clay put his hand on top of hers and said, "You know you're doing the right thing, right?" She nodded and waited for him to leave, then stood next to the phone, rehearsing what she would say to Sid: "If you care for me at all, you'll let me go. This place is not good for me anymore. I don't want to be the whore that you already think I am. I love you for everything you've done for me and – you deserve better from me. I need to go." She walked away from the phone saying, "Who am I kidding here? He's never gonna think like that."

She pulled the door closed and walked through the corridor – the exact reverse of the path that she had walked with Jake that first night. Despite Sid's insistence that Jake had intended to ruin her life in Vegas, the piece of her heart that Jake still owned ached within her chest.

As she approached the lobby, she could hear Sid's voice and slowed her pace. "Please don't make a scene," she thought to herself. "Just say good-bye gracefully."

When she reached the great, glass entrance, Sid stood next to Jimmy, his arms folded across his chest, his face tight. Clay walked forward to meet her; she tensed as he put his hand on her back, steering her to the exit. She focused on Jimmy, then stood in front of him and said, "Good-bye, Jimmy. Take good care of Dotty."

"Do you think I have a choice?" he said and smiled as he motioned to the bellman to put their belongings in the trunk of Clay's car.

Hassie held her breath and looked at Sid whose expression was impossible to read and made her wish she could dissolve. He dropped his arms to his side, looked directly into her face and said, "Checkin' out?"

She nodded and waited for someone to tell her what to do next. Sid took hold of her arm and said, "I took the liberty of preparing your final bill." He pulled her away from the other men. "Let's go settle up."

Hassie walked along in silence and fought the urge to look back at Clay. Sid led her past the reception desk and into his office, pointed her to a chair in front of his desk and said, "Sit down."

Her hands shook but she obeyed. Sid walked around behind his desk but just stood beside his chair. "So you're really gonna leave me?"

She meant to nod her head but she wasn't sure if it was moving. "Sid –"

"Don't talk," he said as he sat down. "I've seen you do some pretty dumb things since you arrived back in this town. But somewhere along the way, you got under my skin and I decided I wanted you. I always get what I want and you made it real easy for me. But I haven't made it easy for you, have I?"

She didn't know what he expected her to say and her rattled nerves made it impossible for her to think for herself.

He studied her, then placed both hands on the desk and leaned toward her. "I heard what you said. You need to leave. And I'm gonna let you go."

She exhaled slowly and relaxed her shoulders.

"I'm letting you go for lots of reasons. For one, I like you. Hell, I probably love you. Which is another reason you gotta go, because however dead he is you're never gonna get that asshole Contrata outta your head, and a man can't stand that. Goddamn, I'd like to double kill the sonofabitch for getting himself all tattooed inside you."

She nodded as he spoke, amazed that he could verbalize the feelings that she'd fought since before Jake died.

"But do me a favor. Don't ever forget that nothing comes without a price. You will always have to pay that price – one way or another."

She stood up and took a breath, anxious to get back to Clay. "I'll always be appreciative of your willingness to give me a chance on the Copa Room stage. And I do understand that there was a price to pay for such a chance, which is why I can't do it."

Sid leaned back in his chair and smiled a smile that made her uncomfortable. "That's entirely your decision, but you may never get the chance again." He stared at her for a moment and then said, "There's a lotta great talent out there, Hassie, and somebody else might not see yours the same way I do. Don't make the mistake of thinking that you're something special."

She glared at him, unsure of what to say. Was he trying to hurt her for leaving him or was he offering honest advice?

He stood up and walked around the desk. "Your *special* talent has nothing to do with singing." He reached for her and she was quickly caught in his ponderous, bearlike embrace as he said, "You're a charming, beautiful babe and men are always gonna love you, but you need to take care of yourself. Go get yourself happy and reclaim that sparkle in your eye and that bounce in your step."

She looked up and felt her face tense as she tried to smile. She said, "I'd say that I'll stay in touch, but we both know that's not likely to happen."

"Oh, I'll keep tabs on how you're doin'." He kissed her firmly on the lips. "You'll never really be rid of me."

Her lips slightly quivered as she pulled away from his embrace. "I better go now. Clay's waiting."

"Good-bye, Hassie Calhoun."

"Good-bye, Sid. And thanks." Walking away, she could scarcely breathe with the thought that Sid would change his mind and reach out to pull her back. She thought about the last time she left – how devastated she'd been and how much it had felt like an escape. This time someone had let her go.

Hassie walked out to Clay's car where he stood with Jimmy. Clay reached out to her as Jimmy said, "It's sure a sad day for us all, isn't it?"

Clay nodded and shook his hand. "One of the saddest." He ducked in behind the wheel and Jimmy made sure Hassie was safe inside the car before peering in through the passenger window.

"You two drive carefully now," he said and looked up at the darkening sky. "I hear there's gonna be a special tribute to President Kennedy any minute now – Vegas style."

"Thanks for everything," Clay said and started the engine, then looked over at Hassie and said, "Is everything okay?"

She nodded and said, "Uh, huh."

"I know this isn't easy, but you should feel very good about yourself."

She looked at him and wondered if he really understood the decision she'd made, then took hold of his hand and said, "You're a good friend, Clay Cooper."

As they pulled away from the Sands, Hassie waved at Jimmy and took one last look at the place that had been her home. The rectangular sign displayed the names of Peggy Lee and Nat King Cole, the great "Sands" icon strong and bright. She'd come very close to seeing her own name up on that sign. But at that moment, and with Clay by her side, it didn't seem so important.

She let go of Clay's hand and settled back into the seat, taking in the sights along the strip as they headed out of town. With the Sands behind them and the Tropicana in the distance before them, she looked straight ahead and witnessed the phenomenon that was prompted by the death of a president.

And the lights went out in Vegas.

acknowledgements

With great respect and deep appreciation:

To the generous readers whose time and energy spent with early and final drafts was endlessly helpful. Special thanks to Bryan Kennedy, Alun Hood, Yvette Digby, Minda Dowling, Mary Canon and Lorraine Miller for sticking with me through numerous attempts to make it better.

To Dzidra Reimanis, Stanley Colbert, the late Fran Shafter and the late Mary Nell Saunders for all they have contributed to my life as a musician, singer and lover of music. And to my mother, Carolyn McMahon, for the endless hours of shuttling me to and from music and dance lessons.

To Margaret James at the London School of Journalism, who helped me give birth to Hassie Calhoun and for urging me to get her off the bus!

To Kathy Sipe, whose infinite knowledge of songwriting brought great depth and breadth to "Hassie's Song." Our collaboration was one of the best things to come out of this experience.

To Frank Sinatra, whose inimitable voice, style and music have touched the lives of so many people, including Hassie's. May she continue to benefit from having known him.

To Ian Graham Leask, my teacher, mentor, editor and friend, without whom this book simply would not exist. I am forever indebted to his intelligent, patient commitment to my sometimes clueless efforts, for believing that Hassie Calhoun's life story is worth telling and for encouraging me to follow my bliss.

And to my husband, Steven Miller – my greatest supporter and biggest fan.

questions for readers

1. How badly do you want to slap Hassie? She is of course very young, but the reader expects a lot of her at the beginning of the book. She has some guidance in her life coming from Barbara back in her hometown, but she largely ignores this. How do you explain the destructive behavior of a girl who is fundamentally good-natured?

2. Because of the era depicted in the book, we tend to think of the characters as older, but they are in fact quite young, and often immature. Are they any different from people of the same age today?

3. How did Henry influence Hassie's behavior from the night she arrived at the Sands? And how does Jake's attitude toward Henry affect Hassie? Is she influenced more by men, or they by her? Who is most in control?

4. Would Hassie's relationship with her mother have been any better if Bobby had not come into the picture? How does the death of her father play into her ambitions and actions?

5. What really attracted Hassie to Frank – his fame, her "starstruck" immaturity or an underlying desire to get back at Jake for cheating on her with Natalie?

6. Do you think that Hassie really believed that Jake forgave her for her indiscretion with Frank? Are there differences in the way men and women judge this love triangle?

7. Hassie didn't smoke at all in Part One. Why did she decide to start smoking when she went to Reno, and why did she smoke and drink so much?

8. Do you think that Hassie changed significantly after she went to Reno? Was her evening with Mr. Satan responsible for her rather loose behavior from that point on?

9. Is it possible that Henry and Julio's relationship was the only "true love" relationship that Hassie has ever known?

10. Who do you think had the greater influence on Hassie's life as a child – her father or Barbara? Who do you think has the greater influence on her life as an adult – Henry, Jake or Barbara?

11. How does Clay really feel about Hassie? How does she really feel about him? Does he have ulterior motives in taking her back to Reno or does he genuinely want to help her?

12. Do you think that Hassie is talented? Do you think that she will eventually become a successful singer/songwriter?

13. Hassie made a lot of bad decisions in the four years of her life in Nevada. What was her biggest mistake and how could a different decision have affected the outcome of her life by the end of the book?

14. What do you think is the greatest message in the story? Do you recognize any universal themes or subtexts operating in the book?